the d D0260131

the
d a n c e r

CHRISTINE DWYER HICKEY

NEW
ISLAND

the dancer
published 2005
by New Island
2 Brookside
Dundrum Road
Dublin 14
www.newisland.ie

Original edition published 1995 by Marino Books

ISBN 1 904301 69 X

British Library Cataloguing in Publication Data. A CIP catalogue record for this book is
available from the British Library.

Typeset by New Island
Cover design by Fidelma Slattery @ New Island
Printed in the UK by CPD, Ebbw Vale, Wales

New Island received financial assistance from
The Arts Council (An Chomhairle Ealaíon), Dublin, Ireland.

10 9 8 7 6 5 4 3 2 1

CONTENTS

PROLOGUE

All he had ever wanted to do was to sprinkle salt on a stage and listen to his feet shuffle through it. Or more precisely listen to his shoes shuffle through it. Oh he liked the steps well enough, liked the way they were activated somewhere up there in the hips and without being in the least bit careless dropped down loosely through thigh, knee and calf, unhinging ankle and landing down soft, soft, softer and soft.

That was the sweetness really – the movement so soft and yet the sound so audible, sound that was grateful to the salt.

Then the rest of him would follow: elbows, hands, shoulders. A little something from everything – except the head. That must stay absolutely still. Although the bits on the front of it could twinkle and purse, if he wished (though as a rule he didn't go in for that sort of thing), the actual container must stay put.

If it took a mind to wagging independently – well the whole look was gone. The mechanics would no longer be in tune.

Sometimes he untuned himself on purpose just to prove the theory to himself. Everything working beautifully there in the mirror, his short legs taking on a grace they had no natural business with, his body growing longer with each semi-stride, his hands in a gentle glide, touching the air here, stroking it there. And the music, un-demanding, coming from beneath the soles of his shoes.

Yes everything clockwork careful, clockwork perfect. *Now* – lose control of the head and see what happens. Gone is the dancer – on comes the puppet. Now, he would scold himself as if he didn't know better. Now see what happens? Now see?

He had three turns in the Empire Theatre so far. Three genuine turns, not counting the many times he had replaced a last-minute missing act. Three pre-arranged turns with his name there on the programme still giving him a little shock. As if he'd done something wrong, broken some law or something. And reassuring himself in a way that, even if he had done, it couldn't have been very grave, his name was so small. There were others up over him who had names so large that their crimes must be very big indeed.

Yes there were others who had more guilt in one letter than he had in his entire little name.

In truth, he would have preferred it if his name could stay off the programme altogether. If he could just walk on, tap his cane twice towards the orchestra and dance anonymously. Stay off the easel too that was placed at the front corner of the stage, holding up the names of the various acts in turn as they came on. Like a blackboard in a school room.

In further truth he would have preferred it if there was no orchestra at all. For what did he need with it really? He had his own music, the salt always supplying the exact amount of sound for the rhythm being produced. No extravagance.

And as for an audience – well what about it? He had his own limbs supplying the exact amount of appreciation. His own spirit too.

And if he needed criticism – why he could always look in the mirror and move his head.

Oh but he needed the theatre. The depth of it, the richness. He needed the space above his head. For once he needed to be small.

And to know that out there was enough room for the balcony boxes to thrust out their ornate bosoms and climb one over the other, right up to the top of the house. And to know that each floor could have its own separate identity, hold a separate passenger list if need be. So that you could be under the same roof as people you might never see. As if the theatre was just that – an ocean across which ships sailed; some east, some west. But all looking out onto the one horizon.

You could believe it too on a good night, when Old Masterson got them going and they all joined in. Bob-bobbing this way, bob-bobbing that.

Yes you could see it then all right.

Above all, he needed the print of moonlight at his feet following them no matter where they might choose, no matter which corner of the stage, so dark behind him, so vast before.

A flawless existence really. Solitary rehearsals during the day, waiting in the wings by night, just him and his cane. While Matilda Telford's arms, rolled full and firm as new cigars and pressed between the peacock feathers on her shoulder and the soft satin creases of her long pink gloves, glide. Backwards and forwards, swinging glimpses into his occasional view.

And later, walking back to his lodgings along streets mostly silent. And the gaslight kissing the black from his best hard hat as he passed beneath its glow. Up Dame Street. With that sweet restraint to be exercised all the way home. Not to dance. That sweet resolve. Not to start up at the slightest whisper, the slightest sound. A stray whistle, perhaps, that might come up behind him, from smug lips homeward bound. Or the surreptitious swish of gown hem skimming its way into a narrower street. Or the echo of a distant carriage clattering quayards home. These were the soft tones to keep safe, to cherish. Snatches to nurse until he could close his own door behind him. Only then could it be released – the restraint. Only then could it be dropped. Slowly, the way he imagines a woman's shift must fall to her feet.

That was of course before he had met that Limey in Bray. Who had started to tell him about the latest techniques he had picked up on his last tour of America. Ragtime, he had said.

'What time?'

'Ragtime.'

'Ragtime?'

And who there and then instead of using words to describe it had used his feet. Right there on Bray promenade, hoofing it up, with evening strollers stopping for a gawk.

A little out of control he had thought, at the time, a little braggish. That bashing of heels against the downdrop of the promenade steps, a little vulgar; that kicking of risers on the way back up, too much. And something a little impatient in the demands made on the feet themselves, no respect for the mechanics, forcing them somehow. Not because of the alacrity – heavens no, he could manage that all right. It was the sound: the bang bang abang rather than the soft, soft, softer and soft.

Not for him, he had decided there and then. Not his cup of tea and yet. He found himself, later, cautiously testing it when Mrs Gunne had gone out for the evening. And slightly ashamed of it too, of its brashness. Feeling almost unfaithful, he had to stop himself from being ridiculous and putting the salt into another room.

Before he knew where he was he found himself responding to new sounds, now harsher. Sounds he'd scarcely noticed up to now. Each time he went out onto the streets the dangers seemed to increase. He made a list of the top offenders:

1 Rain lashing into kerb-caught puddles
2 Rain spiking anything made of tin – roof, dustbin lid, etc.
3 Children irritating lampposts with a stick
4 Cobbles spanked and rolled by hooves and wheels

5 The cough from the snout of a passing motor car
6 Rain

These were no whispers to be saved for a later hour. No gentle calls that could remain unanswered. These were real temptations, discontent to be kept waiting.

There were nights when he barely got through his bedroom door before his feet took over. And dancing this time from the feet up rather than from the head down.

And although so far, so good, he still managed to contain himself until he was actually behind his own door, there was sometimes the slightest doubt nudging through that he might not always win. Might not always make it.

It was a struggle, yes, tight-reined and constant.

And he held it like Carabini held his dove. Between cupped hands and keeping it there, just a beating heart and a recoiled spring, until the hands decided otherwise. Until the moment had been chosen.

I

EASTER 1918

ONE

'There was a boy back home in Wicklow. A little slow, rather taller than he should be, rather thinner too. When he stood alone by the yard wall, you would think: there is an adolescent boy, looking (as they tend to do) a little incomplete. But an ordinary boy just the same. Soon old enough to angle his chin under the swipe of a razor blade. Soon old enough to kit out in a soldier's uniform. Not too much longer now before he has outgrown himself and passed into the way of manhood.

'Of course when he was inside his classroom, in amongst the other children, it was another matter. Then you would know he was different. In other words you wouldn't know he wasn't normal until you saw what normal was. As long as he remained alone he had a reasonable chance of remaining undiscovered. There was, however, another risk involved. The risk of happiness. It was then, you see, that he really gave himself away. His happiness betrayed him. And although it seldom came to him, when it did it was in no half-hearted manner.

'It would jolt through him like a fork of lightning. Into his hands first, lifting them mid-air; quivering through his arms next, so that they seemed to grow longer and longer. Next came his jaw, stretching outwards this way and that. And all the time he would spring himself gently from the balls of his feet up through his long knotted legs. From standing still he had become one personified shudder.

'It was then you would look at him and know: poor fellow, he's not all there. He's not all there at all.

'And that's how we see things, really. Isn't it? We see a boy alone in a field dancing to himself and we say, 'Poor fellow …' We cannot look at him and say: yes there he goes, so much life inside him, he has to expel some of it. In case he just bursts. In one shuddering shivering stretch of his beautiful long limbs. How fine he is. Like a colt. So full of his own life. So free. Bravo!

'No we couldn't possibly allow that thought to enter our well-ordered heads.'

Kate looked out at the sea to ascertain how it had taken that last little speech. Having refrained from flinging itself overboard to shut her up and seeming interested enough, quite sprightly today in fact – she felt sure she could detect it raise here and there a quizzical eyebrow, white and bushy – she decided to continue, pausing to ask, 'Have my lips been moving? No? Oh good. I thought perhaps I'd gotten carried away.'

Kate always spoke to the sea (in her mind of course) on her trips to and from London. She liked to have something at which to direct her thoughts. But it had to be something distant, vast, capricious. 'When I was small,' she told the bloat and buckle of it, 'it was to the fields that I told my stories. It's not that I'm batty. Not that way, I'm not. But I have always found thoughts easier to control if you give them some direction. Get them into line, so to speak. I always wanted to be a teacher. Did I tell you?'

She lifted her elbows up onto the railing and brought her weight to rest there. Looking down she continued, 'And there's another thing. I never have to worry about being a bore; because if I have mentioned anything last time out – well it won't have been exactly to you. Yes. You down there, squaring up to lash out at the stern. And whoosh – that's you gone. See what I mean?'

She flicked her face away from the last-minute kiss of her departing confidante, then once more pressed her hankie in a mop against her face and closed her eyes against the sting of oceanic light. 'What was I saying? Ah yes my childhood. Always chatting. Out loud then so long ago. Of course it was to smaller things: a doll, a cow once. A mother another time. Well, one by one off they all disappeared. So. I decided to broaden my audience a little. It could, after all, take days to find a new friend. A new pair of ears. Which is why I turned to things that have always been. That always will be. Like you.

'But before you, it was the back meadow. Across which Papa came one day and standing behind me listened to my chat. And then looking so embarrassed when he finally stepped forward to admit himself as if he'd caught me out in some sly and secret shame. His embarrassment irked me. It implied that there should be shame. But I knew he was there, of course I did. Did he think I hadn't seen his shadow darken the poppy-clots that had been so brightly enthralled with my story?

'"Kate," he said, in that funny accent of his, "You must come away from there now. You're too old."

'"Too old for what?" I asked.

'"To talk like that. Out loud."

'Poor Papa, his face competing with the flowers for redness. "Oh?" I said. "Well, what if I stay quiet? Stop talking out loud. May I stay?"

'He stopped a while and then said: "Yes, all right then. That's fine." And then turning to go back to his new motorbus (we kept them, you know, in our back barn, instead of cows) he offered, "Of course, you may sing if you wish." Who ever heard of it? As if I was going to put into song my whole day's adventure? Did he think I was mad?

'"Oh but I don't sing," I said. "Thank you all the same." Poor Papa. Forgive me, I must stop now. Take a little rest. Go back to my deck chair, where I can cover my lap with the rug. Like a good little convalescent.

'At least this time, I am sick on the outside too, my face like a cow's udder, waiting to be milked – that full. I knew I'd catch a cold on the way over; the wind was sharper then, displeased. But I couldn't bear to sit with him. Couldn't stand his hands, his mouth, his self.

'And that's why I came out here and stayed too long. Your breeze wrapping itself around my neck, pretending to be a concerned mother. And all the time weaving its mischief around me. You wicked thing. And even now vying for attention. How you glint today. Is it to aggravate my poor raw eyes? Have I been neglecting you – is that it? Is that jealousy I see green beneath your top skirt?

'It's because of Greta? Am I right?'

Kate walked back towards her chair, sat herself down and stretched her legs towards and then up onto the footstool. She watched the plaids wilt into folds. A book by her side was cracked open and placed on the bridge between either thigh. The breeze fluffed its pages.

'I'm not reading it, not really. You don't have to worry. It's just in case, well, you-know-who comes along. And it is almost time for his step to take him down deck. What did I tell you? Here he is. Eyes down.'

The hem of his greatcoat, the shine of his shoes, the columns of best navy serge beneath. And slow the step but coming always. In now to her corner vision, her crumpled hankie dabs again and blots it out just for a second. How cold and wet in her hand. How horribly damp. Yet to get a fresh one would be to move, to go back inside. He will be past soon, ostensible duty done. One foot past chair, two foot past now. Soon gone. But he stops then. Suddenly. And she almost looks up in surprise. Why stop? Why stop now? Stepping forwards and lowering his head towards her. And what? What is he saying?

'My dear …?'

My dear! How dare he? How dare he put his face to hers and speak those or any other words. And then she realises. Yes that's it. Up there on the upper deck. Yes of course. Mrs Sinclair looks down and smiles. On such a good kind husband. Before turning and walking away so as not to intrude upon their marital intimacy. And he turns too, walking silently on and leaving his 'My dear …?' to linger like a smell.

'You know what he'll do now? Of course you do. He'll go back inside and have a dram of Clarke's Blood Mixture. Like the old Granny Grey that he is. Afraid his health will be affected because one or two acquaintances on board force him to be seen to do his duty. *My dear.*

'And then a shot of whiskey, holding its gold in the cup of his hand so tightly, as if to deplete its light.

'And what does he think about then? Distant eyes, expressionless always. What does he think about sitting so still for hours on end? Scarcely moving, except for when a lady passes by and he must lift himself from his seat. Does he resent it, having to lift his (oh how I would love to say 'arse' out loud, just once) backside? I wonder is that why they withdraw after dinner, away from the women, to give themselves a break from all that bobbing.

'Is he thinking over what the Consultant said? He seems remarkably unvexed. Not the slightest put out. I was sure he would be raging. Certainly there is nothing like the degree of malice I would have expected. He seems so preoccupied. It's hardly the publicans' strike? Which in any case could well be settled by now. And nobody hopes it more than me. Him always at home. His presence in the house confining me to my room. Or out of doors. Like it or not. Thank God for the fine weather. And Greta and I like to have tea in the drawing room, and chat of this and that. And sometimes have an at-home with a guest or two. Maude or her friend Lottie, the mad suffragette (the one Greta thinks so modern). Making us laugh so heartily at her endless possibilities. I had to send a last-minute message on Tuesday to cancel on account of him stopping in. And do you think we could get him to commit himself either way? The times poor Maura had to discreetly ask: "Would sir be going out this evening? Only I thought I could give the study a good going-over."

'"I haven't made up my mind yet," was all he would give her. Until at the twilight hour, "Yes, go ahead on the study." So that our hearts flew up and rang with joy. But then he had to add: "I'll go into the drawing room." And back down they flopped into our boots.

'And the very day I promised Maude that we could hold a sort of meeting to be addressed by Lottie. And six or seven expected, and Maura baking scones since after breakfast. And it's not as if he wouldn't find a public house somewhere that would let him in the back door. And him a manager of the bottlery. And his boss, my own sister's husband, a publican. He wouldn't like to let them know how desperate he is. But he hates Pat Cleary and that's the truth. He hates the hand that feeds him.

'So why has he said nothing? Nothing at all. I had expected something, something like: "They don't know everything you know, these doctors." Or: "Surely you realise – people like you never really recover."

'Oh what does it matter what he says or doesn't say? "Splendid, splendid," was what the doctor said and that's what counts. And at first I didn't understand him, didn't know he was referring to me until he said, "Well done" and tapped my arm. Then I realised he meant me and my progress and I laughed a little with him.

'"Yes, she's doing well," he said of me while looking at my husband. The way doctors once looked at my father when I was a child. A different matter then of course; my deformity was on the outside, entirely visible. A different time.

'"No recurrence, for what now?" he asks him.

'But I answer anyway, jumping in with, "A year."

'"Ten months," my husband flatly contradicts me.

'"Well, well," said the doctor. "Let's call it a year. As good as. And I have every confidence. Remarkable recovery. Couldn't be happier." And he looks as if he wants to know and so I tell him. "I have a friend now. Greta. She comes everywhere with me."

'And again my husband steps in to correct: "A lady's maid. On contract. From an agency."

'"Splendid. Splendid. Keep away from the cities. A holiday in the country for another while yet. You could bring your, your …?"

'"Greta."

'"Yes Greta. For company. And be careful of that cold. You should really be in bed. Splendid."

'Outside I had to walk a little ahead to stop him seeing my smile. I had to stuff my handkerchief into my mouth to stop myself laughing out loud. A holiday. In the country. In Wicklow. Home! With dear, dear Greta. And how could he refuse now? How could he possibly. It came from the doctor's mouth. The doctor recommended by Pat Cleary. My own sister's husband. His own boss. If he refused me, if he tried to prevent it, surely he would be found out?

'The drive back towards Knightsbridge was under a different light. I hardly noticed then the soldiers. Moving in wads or all alone. Was it just one hour before their amount had shocked me so? At home we have them, yes. But not so many. No, not so many by far. And here all the talk is talk of war. By comparison at home? Oh yes the *Weekly Times* will print portraits of those killed. And for a moment, between the butter in a lump and the butter now spread, one will say: "How shocking! Poor Mrs (what's-her-name) of South Circular Road, to have lost a son. How *shocking*." But only a recognised face will spoil a Saturday breakfast and before the page is turned all tends to be forgotten. Though my circle is small, I will admit. I believe Maude has known more than a few. I seem to remember her mentioning, here and there ... But of course, what can I be thinking of? We too have lost boys. Wicklow boys. Such boys that swam in the river and ran across the tennis lawn. Such names that filled dance cards, gone forever now. And who knows how many more before the whole sorry business is done? Who knows how big a gap, how silent Wicklow summers will finally become. Hubert was the last one I knew of, almost two years ago it must be. How Maude sobbed when he went. Had to be taken out of the chapel, that distressed. I don't think she ever speaks of him now. I don't think she ever speaks of the war now either. And she used to be so well informed. Captain Maude, we used to tease her.

'Do we ever speak of it? Greta and I? On those long hikes or bicycle rides? A little I suppose. But more in the "Do you think that uniform suits or not the figure of that young man over there?" fashion. And I rib her. "Soldier mad. You're one of those soldier-mad girls that are spoken of so disapprovingly in respectable circles." But I take a good look for myself all the same. Or at dinner tables? Have I heard war-talk so much? Certainly nothing like last night. I thought they would never stop, just on and on. And so rude about the Irish too, saying anything they liked. I suppose my husband being English made them assume I was too. But you'd think that not a soul had left our shores, not an Irishman enlisted of his own free will. Thousands, Greta says, thousands and thousands. She says there's not a decent man left in the country, in fact.

'One old hen said the "Micks" should all be made to be soldiers or shot. Another said they were cowards and ought to be locked up with the conchies. She in turn was contradicted by another who said they could fight all right, but only amongst themselves. And yes that one too kept referring to Paddies and Paddyland and how that was the place to be where food was plenty and the nights were long. Oh how I longed to slap the fat off her face and round to the back of her neck. Lord save us from the drawing rooms of those pompous British Ladies. They'd make you want to join the Shinners and no mistake.

'Of course it looks as though they might well have their way, with conscription now the topic of every other conversation in Dublin. Will they be happy then I wonder, when our boys join the way their boys do, with no choice and even less free will?'

'There was a boy back home – now why did I think of him? What in particular took him into my mind? Ah yes. The colt's dance. That's what I was trying to tell you. Such a present as I have for Greta. Such a totally, marvellously modern present. Like none she's ever had before. And now here I am almost afraid I'll betray my happiness by skitting about, wild eyed, hands hopping. Just like him – that boy, that colt.

'I've let him carry too – my loving husband (I don't think!) – the box that holds it. I daren't risk carrying it myself. It's as though it were alive. My first gift to Greta. Her face when first she sees it. When first she tries it on. A hat with four corners. Who could ever imagine? Such a thing.

'And then there's my news from my doctor. My splendid liberator. My darling man who has banished me to Wicklow. Thank you, thank you, oh thank you.

'Yes there would be a definite risk of my becoming one wild undulating wave from heel right up to head.

'From on boat to off boat, from train to motor car, I will supervise its transport. This supervision I must keep covered. Never letting him see my concern. (How like him it would be to "accidentally" misplace anything that he believed brought happiness to me.) And so I keep my face impassive as a brick wall, my limbs as steady as the night.

'And yes, night light blows across you now. Skimming your waves and seeping down through your shivering skin. Coming as it has always done at just this time, in just this season. Tomorrow it is Good Friday and all over the city knees will crush themselves against stone floors and beg for a share in the pain. But not mine. Not Greta's. For us tomorrow merely means another day gone before we meet again, the last before we are together. Easter Saturday and that endless week is past.

'Hottest March in living memory, they say. For three weeks now the summer has been pushing for a premature arrival. Awakening growth. Already sleeves are rolling up in preparation for the coming crop. Heaviest in years, it promises. A confused March, that has lost its place. Yet still the day does not extend itself against its will and still the night falls as it always has at this hour, this moment, in every March. And lifts again and falls. Like now, again. Sending me indoors before he feels obliged to come and get me.'

*

Opposite, feathers breathing on top of a stranger's hat. Kate came to know their shape, each one, each delicate strand. He had, as usual, placed her on the inside, and having racked their possessions sat himself down, the precious hat box an island between them. Up against the window, she wandered with her eyes, trying to find a place where they could rest, at ease. The window itself was out of the question, being lined on the outside with a thick stretch of nightfall, so that when she turned her profile nothing of the passing world was apparent. Nothing out there, except the profile itself.

On the other side of her was his elbow intruding itself on the side of the box, his fingers tapping off its lid slowly and over and over again, annoying the life out of her. She imagined pushing his elbow off and saying, 'Do you mind?' Seeing how unlikely it was that she would ever dare to utter anything at all to him in the first place, she thought she might as well go the whole hog and shove the heel of her hand into his arm, saying, 'Here you – do you mind? You stupid, arrogant *arse.*'

Kate turned her head and stayed with the feathers. Beneath them she knew there was a face. A face she was busy trying to avoid, and which in turn was also desperately trying to avoid hers (but dying to have a good look all the same). Kate obliged by pressing her gaze against the far corner of the compartment and then slowly closing her eyes. It was as though she had gone away and left her mask for public exhibition. Over the years Kate had found it was the best tactic to adopt, this pretence at sleep, allowing, as it did, her opponent to relax sufficiently to satisfy all curiosity regarding Kate's features (or rather the lack of them). Except of course for the eyes, which she had been told and – yes, which common sense had also confirmed – were, while not entirely compensatory, really quite lovely, and surely must come as a nice surprise after all that disappointment. In any case, it wasn't unusual to open them to a smile and a friendly remark. She wondered which this evening's would be. The weather, the war or, as was the case nine times out of ten, the tiresomeness of the journey.

Kate was a little surprised to find that this time, once behind her shuttered lids, she really was rather tired after all and, despite misgivings about abandoning the precious hat-box, found herself slipping away with nothing on her mind but the cameo of her face printed on the window pane.

When you see it first, you love it. You think you're a brown bear. Yes that's what you thought, first time. Looking back up at yourself trembling down there in a water-filled trough. The startled eyes, the curly brown top, the stitched and puckerless lip. All that.

Then there was the looking-glass. Mama's one, up in the room that was later to become Maude's. There was a long centre piece through which you stare at yourself staring back out. And at either side, smaller glasses on hinges that could be made to play light clashes with each other. You could turn yourself any which way at all and see your dear little brown-bear face. And when you got a baby doll for Christmas and Maude got a bear you asked her to swap, just so that you could look into the glass together, big bear and little one. Your face as flat as a moon, rising above Mama's possessions. Like a town lying below, made of bottles carved or smooth and boxes of sweet-smelling dust.

When do you know it's a shame? When you go to school? Yes. But before that. Before that surely. Is it when the new baby comes? That strange little thing. Mama nursing him day and night and he as small, as breakable as anything in the toy chest. Her little Baba Lamb. Stroking his fluffy crown while, keenly as an abandoned lamb, he sucked on her half-hidden breast. 'He'll grow quickly,' Mama had said to Papa. 'See how he can suck.'

'Aye,' he said, 'not like poor Kateykins when she was wee.' But Kateykins can suck. Can so. Her tongue pulls at her soft warm thumb and pushes it up against the lump that runs crossways on the roof of her mouth. But that's now. Now that she's a big girl. What about before? When she was Baba in the house? When she was Baba Lamb. Did she? Suck like that? No. No her milk was trickled downwards. Drop by tiny drop. From that funny little bottle with the bulbous lid. In the back of the pantry for years. How long did it take to give a feed? Forever? Was it a terrible nuisance?

You find bits of your story all over the house, being passed like tea cakes over your head. You find other bits, too, inside yourself.

Something wobbling when you leave the doctor's house, that time in Dublin, when looking up to see Mama's eyes respond to your best smile by looking the other way. Is it pain or pity inside them? Is it shame? And homewards knowing not to speak, to let rather the clarity of the carriage wheels and the chatter of harness outside provide what your dwarfed words could only embarrass. How old then? Six or maybe seven. And always the prettier dress, always the brighter bow. Did Maude mind? She never seemed to. Always holding her prettiness back for my sake. She's been a good sister. Right from the start. Doing so much for me. And I never even took her a present home. What if she finds out about Greta's hat? Would she mind? Be jealous? No probably not. What have I ever done for her? Poor Maude. Even when she tries to get close to me I step back. Why? I can't seem to help it. I turn my face away. Just like Mama did, all that time ago, all those steps ago, outside a door with a big brass medal pinned to its chest.

Was that before or after the slap? Giving sunburn to your small fat arm while it snowed outdoors?

Ah yes. You're climbing up on a stool and your boots have buttons up. Your hands take a grip and pull you after them. And over the side, there he is. His royal tinyness. Small as a doll. And yes he's lovely and you're glad he came too soon. Hiding there inside Mama's tummy for such a long time. Making the house so quiet, so empty. No visitors to look at for too many days. And you're a good big girl now. Everybody says so. And you know you musn't lift him. Not without Mama being there, to lift you first right into the back corner of the highest chair. And moulding your eager arms into a cradle then will place him softly there. And how hard his head is. How hard and heavy. But you never complain because Mama trusts you and because you love him anyway, hard head with the fluff spread on.

And you're smiling down over him saying, 'There, there, there,' and patting the linen around his head. And all you do really is touch his nose. Not because you want to hurt it. But because its different, pointing away from the face, as if it has been plucked into position. Like Big Sister Maude's, yes it is. Like Mama's, like Papa's too.

And you know then, your brown-bear face is all wrong. You know, because this isn't a family of bears. This is a family of people. With full top lips on and noses that lead the way. Gently you prod the bone of his nose, and stroke your finger, scooplike over his nostrils, feeling saddened almost for your poor lonely face.

But Mama comes in then, brisk as a bee. 'Oh Mama why does the baby –?' And before you can ask her whatever it was you wanted to ask her, her big hand comes down and there – that's the slap. That's the sting that she gives. There. 'Wicked,' she says. 'Wicked. What are you trying to do – make him? Make him?' Make him what? Mama, make him what? You never did finish.

Kate jolted herself awake.

TWO

Maude put the two hats side by side and studied them. She stepped away from, then towards them again. Touching then spreading the tulle scarf of one, she unravelled it from its crown and left it to meander over the ebony sideboard, like a pale chocolate river. She turned the crown of the other a little to the light. Then stepped back again.

And wanting to like the four-cornered one the best; after all Kate had been good enough to bring it back from London with her. Where, by all accounts, such things were quite the rage. And it would be so nice to do something a little daring, just for once. However, her eye kept returning to the brown tulle. At least she knew it suited her, was sure of its shape, colour, the way its scarf framed her face. But all the same to arrive at the races in something so different! Why it could very well get a mention in the newspapers. (Yes but what sort of a mention?)

She picked it up in her hands and turned it all ways before deciding on the correct angle for the approach to her head.

Finally she bent down to meet it, butting it gently until it accepted her offering of hair and grips packed to capacity.

'There,' she said. 'Now. Now let's have a look.'

Just then her husband walked in through the door and had the hat not been so low down over her eyes she might well have noticed a smirk pass across his face before being checked into submission.

'New hat?' he asked closing the door behind him.

'Yes, Kate brought it home with her. Bought it herself. Can you believe it? Actually went into a shop and bought – for me. Look, over there – the hat box that it came in. The receipt too. Wasn't it sweet of her to remember me?' She turned to him. 'What do you think?'

He thought it like a washer on top of a screw. But then again, these days, since this whole business of motor lorries instead of carts had come under discussion he thought everything was like something to do with motor cars, inside or out.

'Think? I think it's lovely. Perfectly lovely.'

Besides he had been married long enough to realise that there was absolutely no point in saying otherwise to a wife fifteen minutes before an outing was due to commence.

She walked towards the mirror to see for herself.

'Good heavens,' she told the reflection crossly. And then – 'That can't be right,' consolingly, and finally – 'Unless …?'

She took the hat off again and replaced it upside down.

'What do you think now?' she asked her husband.

'What do I think, what?' he asked back, biding for time.

'Do you think it should be worn this way?'

'Oh no, darling, I hardly think so.'

'Well why not for heaven's sake?'

'Because of the dip. The dip. Look there.'

He patted the crown of his own head, to help her understand.

'*So?*'

'So if it rains? You'll have every sparrow in the country lining up for a drink.'

'Oh really.'

He came up behind her and they looked at the image of themselves, husband and wife, like a live portrait there, above the mantelpiece. She looked at him, and something gave inside her.

Oh you, she thought, my black, my dark, my beauty. Why can I not have just one part of you to grow inside me? You who can make a guinea grow out of one farthing, why not make a profit out of me?

He looked at her and he thought. Yes, a fleet of lorries. That's what I'll do. The biggest fleet of motor lorries that Dublin's ever seen. We'll start with two and see how it goes; we can then increase bit by bit. And then we'll go away the two of us. And then we'll … Yes. Lorries with our name on the side of them. C-l-e-a …

'I think I'll leave Kate's one for another day,' she said.

'It doesn't matter which one you choose,' he smiled. 'You'll be the best turned out chestnut there today.'

Filly, he used to say filly. He used to say, 'You'll be the best turned out filly there today.' But now I'm too old to call filly. And I've done nothing to earn the title 'mare'. So it's just chestnut. Oh he got himself out of that one all right.

'You do realise,' he said, 'we won't be taking the motor car all the way?'

'Why not?'

'They're forbidden today. Easter Saturday. No motor cars on the grounds.'

'How are we supposed to get there for heaven's sake?'

'Don't worry. You're not expected to walk, you know. Sam will leave us most of the way.'

'Sam? But he always takes Saturday off.'

'Yes, I've asked him to take us. There's something I need to talk over with him.'

'Oh and I wonder what that could be.'

She lifted the four-cornered hat away from her head as though her elbows were springs. Her husband's finger came up through the mirror to retrieve a strand or two. He found a gap in the smooth bump and crevice and poked the wayward piece down into the inner mantle. He then brought the remaining fingers of that hand to join the 'poker' and patted the slightest caress onto the entire arrangement. 'Upholstery,' he whispered, 'finest upholstery.'

'Upholstery?' she asked. 'Well that's a first, I must say. And anyway why can't we take a carriage? Like the old days? I hate those motor cars. Such a hullaballoo to get from here to there. I know lately by the time I get anywhere my nerves are too much gone to enjoy myself –'

'But look how much faster it is darling.'

'Faster? Oh so what. One can always leave earlier. What's the big rush? And anyway I'd rather be a little late than have to listen to all that noise and banging or to put up with all those horrible smells.'

'Oh now come on. It's hardly that bad.'

'Maybe not now. But supposing everybody started to drive a motor car. Supposing all the smells and bangs and fumes gather together. Life wouldn't be worth living. It wouldn't be safe to go out of doors. We should all die of nerve strain.'

She turned to face her husband and he looked back at her quite sensibly for a moment before throwing back his head and laughing out loud.

'Oh yes,' he said. 'And supposing women stop exaggerating, we should all die of boredom.'

'I'm glad you're so amused,' she pouted.

'Oh my, my. Who's a contrary girl today, eh –?'

She ignored him and, moving over to the sideboard, whipped up her hat, sucking up the chocolate river before draping it shoulder-wise under a haughty chin.

'I must tell you about the internal combustion engine some time,' he laughed.

'I don't care about your ridiculous combustion engine.'

'But you above all people should be able to relate very well to it indeed.'

And he followed her then out into the hallway, quite prepared to tease her for another ten minutes or so while awaiting the arrival of Sam.

THREE

Kate jerked the curtains shut and remained standing at the window. It was as if that last scissored movement was the most strenuous ever to be carried out by her and now, exhausted, she could do no more than limply stand and stare into the spears of velvet.

'I said no thank you, Maura,' she raised her voice a little. 'I'm not hungry.'

'Just the tea then maybe?'

'Nor am I thirsty,' she raised her voice again, exerting herself even further.

Going back down the stairs, Maura, through the landing window, caught sight of a passer-by glancing upwards at the darkened room. And what must he be thinking, she wondered, sunshine shut out on such a bright Easter Saturday afternoon as this? Somebody ill, somebody dead – that's what he'll be thinking.

She paused to rest the rejected tray on the window-sill. And there was another one looking up. But that was suburban life for you; the least little thing out of line with a house and everyone notices, straight away. This time it was a local resident, that nice Mrs Hardiman from two doors down. 'Poor Mrs Pakenham,' she'll probably whisper, 'Nerves, no doubt, again.' A third party approached from the opposite side of the street, causing Maura's jaw to clench before she turned her head sideways to peer down at the gate next door. And look at her there! So busy gawking up she nearly drops the messages, hardly able to contain herself in the rush to tell her mistress. Oh a skivvy, a skivvy in her heart if ever there was one.

Maura recalled a day last spring when coming from Mass the same one nabbed her. 'Is it true what they say about your Mrs P?' Of course she had made out not to know what it was that 'they said'. 'Ah go on you can tell me,' the little rip nudges, 'aren't we the same, you and me.'

'I hardly think so,' Maura had said. 'I'm a housekeeper. You're a skivvy.' It was a retort that still gave her pleasure.

She listened to the whine of the gate next door as it opened then closed and the quickening step towards the front door. Yes that's right, hurry yourself up now, why don't you? Roll your eyes and tell your tale: 'That Mrs Pakenham's gone off it again.'

Maura positioned her hands on either side of the tray. 'And it's that exact sentiment,' she muttered to herself, 'that Mr Pakenham himself would be most likely to own.' She stopped: and well well but here he is now. About to push the gate open when he stops and looks up to the drawn room above. And there he goes now, his stick tipping the flagstones. Here he is.

Maura put the tray back down. Best wait and see first if he'll use his key or not. No point in going down to the kitchen if she'd be running straight back up again to answer the door.

Upstairs Kate hears the bell call and knows it is to frighten her. She used to think it was to fool her; make her think it was somebody else. Somebody not in possession of a key. But now she knows he wants to announce himself. Now she knows he wants her to anticipate each in the series of his movements.

He will wait downstairs speaking too loudly to Maura as he layers her arms with his heavy street clothes. He will open a door and then shut it, smartly as if he has entered a room he intends to stay in.

This momentary pause before continuing onto another door is to facilitate the surge of relief and then subsequent disappointment in the upstairs room. When he has finished all this, he will take the first few stairs noisily and then suddenly stop about a third of the way up as though he has forgotten something (she can imagine him clicking his fingers to indicate same). The next attempt may see him managing the full flight but he will not be ready for her yet. Not yet. There are other doors to open and close on the landing above; there is a bathroom to be visited. Eventually his step will be on this landing. Where he will stand silently for a minute or two before finally opening her door.

She hears the bell calling to her and tries to listen to its warning. But she is so tired now. Too tired to move away from the window. Yes, there's his voice now. Soon the slamming will start. Yes there it is.

She touches the folds of velvet on the drapes and then her hand finds one particularly fat one with which to play, holding it between middle finger and thumb. With her index finger she repeatedly and softly presses down, feeling the velvet yield each time.

Her other hand brings the other thumb up to a hole in her face and sticks it inside where firm and wet a grip takes hold. She can feel her bottom lip pout to it and says yes that is my thumb, this is my mouth. An idle finger finds a length of hair, spooling it until there is no question of either finger or hair losing each other.

And she thinks yes – these are my hands all busy, none spare. No work for the devil here. No, not even the dribble, leaking now from under my thumb down over the corner of my mouth, will tempt these hands to move.

He makes his first false start on the stairway and she slides herself downwards gently on the floor, never allowing her hands to lift but rather to shift downwards with her, so that they can maintain their occupation at a lower position.

Her eyelids have become too heavy now, blinks deepening, lengthening, until they close altogether.

When he comes in he will find her folded down into herself, sleeping peacefully, perfectly still. This unexpected sight will not please him.

FOUR

Mrs Gunne called Greta into the front parlour and, for the first time since she arrived, looked her straight in the face. 'Sit down,' she said, 'I'd like a few words.'

These few words would be the first ever to be addressed to Greta directly by Mrs Gunne. Up to now the daily had acted as go-between delivering an oral list of 'the-Missus-says' instructions. Mrs Gunne's only participation was to silently inspect the finished tasks, usually by way of her index finger. And a most industrious index finger it was too. Capable of poking, prodding, flicking and generally getting itself into the most awkward of spots. Sometimes it would simply drag itself lightly along the area in question while Greta looked on in the background and awaited its verdict (thanking the Lord as she did so that cleaning the lavatory bowl was not on her list of duties). Should the finger produce cause for complaint, Mrs Gunne would keep it safe for the daily. The daily would reissue same with a childish horror that Greta found almost delightful.

From tomorrow it would be a week since Greta had made the choice between the police station and Mrs Gunne's residence. A week since she had sat waiting outside in the taxi while Mr Pakenham saw to the arrangements. And while Kate, at home and completely and blissfully unaware, had finished packing for London. Meanwhile, not more than two miles away, Greta had sat waiting in a taxi, for her future to be decided on the willingness or not of a stranger.

It had all happened so quickly that she still couldn't quite grasp the thing. So unexpected it had been that each night since in a strange narrow bed at the top of the house she lay running over the movements of last Sunday afternoon. Again and again.

First, Kate kisses her goodbye on the top of the stairs. 'Next Saturday so,' she says, 'not even a full week. It will fly – you'll see. And I'll bring you a present. Something really nice. Something really nice for Easter.'

And then coming down the stairs, turning to look back up when Kate calls out, 'Give my best to your family.' And then begins to playfully shoo her, 'Go on then. You'll miss your train. The taxi is waiting. And no talking to strangers mind, especially those in uniform!' All very jolly.

Until he appears. Out of nowhere. While she is still smiling and now also suddenly alarmed that he may have overheard Kate's little joke. He stands at the front door lowering his hand to take the travel bag. Just being a gentleman, she had thought at the time.

She climbs into the taxi and he slides the case towards her. 'Thank you so much. How kind. Well enjoy your trip to London and –'

But that's not all. He's not yet finished it seems. The case comes first but he comes after it! Edging over onto the seat beside her. Her mouth must have been as wide open as a field. (She is sure she can remember him glancing down into it.)

'I think we should have a little chat,' he says, tapping the seat in front for the driver to move along down the road.

'I'm in rather a hurry,' comes whimpering out.

And then, 'Yes,' he says, 'yes no doubt. But you see I think I should tell you. I know everything. I know it all. I know the whole sorry, lock stock and barrel of it.'

An hour later he was beckoning from Mrs Gunne's doorway. (No time wasted on gentlemanly gestures now. Now she carries her own bag.) He points upstairs. 'Straight up to the top of the house, there's a room you can have. You'll receive your instructions in the morning.'

He holds out his hand. 'You've copied out the letter?' he asks. She hands it to him. Hardly able to recall its contents, she cannot at the moment realise its significance.

He flicks it open and reads it through. He flicks it shut again. 'Very good,' he pats her on the back. 'Not one single mistake.' He holds his hand out again. 'The original please.' She gives him back the letter he had given her moments ago in the taxi with the instruction to copy it out. Word for word. 'Thank you,' he says, 'good day to you.'

'But –' she remembers saying to his impassive face. And nothing moves except an over-polite eyebrow for a second, expectant, raised, as if she is going to ask him the time or some such thing of the least importance. He holds her look for a second or so before his eyebrow resumes its normal position and then he is gone.

Standing there, she watches him leave before the curious look of a passerby brings her to her senses and she closes the door. She looks up towards her destination at the top of the flights above. There is no one to greet her, no one to tell her why or what for. Although she since has remembered being distracted by a reflection in the hall mirror. A condensed image, trapped, of a door, a gap in that door and a woman dressed in hideous blue, flicking her fingers through a sheaf of some sort of papers.

And now a week has gone, or almost. And here she sits, this time on the other side of the reflection, watching those same fingers move again. In a canter beat now on the side of a whatnot – in Greta's opinion a particularly ugly piece of furniture, all the more so for its being spanking new.

Mrs Gunne gestured for her to be seated and Greta had only just positioned herself to do so when the doorbell rang. Mrs Gunne hesitated and something in the way she looked towards the window made Greta realise that had it not been for her presence Mrs Gunne's index finger would at this moment have been curling the lace curtain to her fist so as to make a perch upon which her nose could rest. This also made Greta realise that her position was not quite the same as that of the daily's (no matter how darkened her circumstances), in that Mrs Gunne was anxious to at least appear to be a lady in her presence. Of course, Greta knew that this was due to her former employer rather than to herself. But nonetheless, it did give her some hope. Some small weakness to work upon.

'Sit, sit,' Mrs Gunne chirped, keeping one anxious ear towards the hall outside. Greta sat. Slow and long came knocks on the front parlour door. Mrs Gunne frowned and shouted.

'Come in, Frances. For the love of –'

The door came slowly away from the wall and Frances stayed standing in the gap it had made.

'A message for yer man,' she said holding an envelope up in the air.

'Yer man? Yer man? And who would you mind telling me is yer man?'

'The young gentleman, Mrs. You know the young gentleman upstairs?'

'Yes, Frances, I know him. I believe I may have seen him around.'

'Will I take it up Missus?'

'What? Certainly not. He's still sleeping. Give it here.'

She stretched out her hand and Frances tottered over, placing the envelope carefully across it.

'It was that messenger lad from the theatre, Missus.'

Mrs Gunne looked horrified.

'That is no concern of either yours or mine, Frances.'

'Oh. No, Missus. Sorry, Missus.'

'Which theatre?'

'The Empire, Missus.'

Frances tottered back out again, closing the door carefully behind her.

'That girl!' Mrs Gunne began only to be interrupted by another loud knock on the parlour door.

'Come in, Frances. What is it now?'

'Excuse me, Missus. But I just remembered. Well he said – he said I should give it to him now.'

'Who said?'

'The messenger. He said, "Give that to your lodger now," says he.'

'Lodger? Lodger? I trust you put him right?'

'How do you mean like?'

'I mean I trust you said our *guest* and not our lodger.'

Frances made no reply.

'The cheek …' Mrs Gunne looked about her as though appealing for sympathy from an audience.

'Well?' asked Frances.

'Well what, Frances?'

'Will I bring it up to him?'

'No, Frances. You will not. I'll take it up myself in a while.'

'Are you sure? I don't mind.'

'Frances really. You have no decorum. Now get outside and finish them brasses.'

'Yes, Missus. Sorry, Missus.' And she was gone again.

Mrs Gunne looked at Greta as though she had forgotten who she was.

She took a deep breath while collecting her thoughts and commenced speaking.

Greta sat opposite keeping her back straight and her hands

where they should be, trying to appear dignified (yet not so much as to cause offence), trying to be humble (yet not so much as to look hypocritical), trying to appear grateful (yet not so much as to invite complete disdain). So preoccupied she was with this contrariety of appearance, she paid little attention to the actual words Mrs Gunne was now reciting, word perfect, like an overgrown child.

Mrs Gunne walked up and down and appeared at either end of the dining table at intervals, where she would pause to ask, 'Do you understand me now? Am I making myself quite clear? I hope we'll have no dispute on that?'

'Yes, Ma'am, No, Ma'am,' Greta responded each time to another turn of Mrs Gunne's busy skirts.

'There has never been anything of this sort under this roof before. And I want you to know that only Mrs Pakenham's sister, Maude Cleary, has been a friend to me and mine, I should have nothing whatsoever to do with a scandal like this.'

'Yes, Ma'am.'

'And that only their brother has been entrusted to me as my guest and we have grown so fond of him. We are terribly fond of him you know.'

'Oh yes, Ma'am. I have no doubt. I know both ladies are extremely appreciative of your kindness to their younger brother. If you'll excuse my saying so, Ma'am.'

'Yes. Well now. Really?'

Greta nodded slowly. 'Oh indeed, Ma'am.'

Mrs Gunne bowed her head graciously before continuing:

'It's all down to losing your place in the rank, if you ask me. Mrs Pakenham made too free by far. Too free by far. You arrived as a lady's maid and a lady's maid is what you should have stayed. German lessons indeed – And the – the, eh, gentleman in question? I understand that he is now in custody. Hmm?'

'I believe so, Ma'am.'

'And that he is Jewish?'

'Yes, Ma'am, that is so.'

'And that you were hiding him? In Mrs Pakenham's *attic*?'

'I didn't hide him, Ma'am, he wouldn't get out.'

'Wouldn't get out? Oh please my girl. And how did he get in there in the first place, hmm?'

Greta looked down and made no reply. Mrs Gunne continued: 'Well I never heard the like. Mr Pakenham could have you put away for that you know; oh yes indeed. You do realise that, I suppose?'

'Oh yes, Ma'am.'

'A Jewish jailbird. I never heard the – Really Mrs Pakenham ought to know better. Encouraging such frightful carry on, under her own roof.'

'I feel I must point out, that is, respectfully point out Ma'am, that Mrs Pakenham wasn't aware of the full circumstances. She engaged the gentleman as my tutor in German –'

'And what if I may make so bold as to inquire were you wanting with a tutor in German anyway?'

Greta lowered her eyes. 'It was to better myself, Ma'am.'

'Better yourself? Well you did a nice job of that, I must say!'

'What I mean is, I was going to sit for an examination next month for a clerical position. An abstractor. I needed German as part of the … But you must believe me, Ma'am. Mrs Pakenham had no idea that – '

'That what? That you were learning a few other things while you were at it? I should think not too. But all the same she cannot be completely exonerated, you know. She did lie to her husband and spend his money to further that lie. No good could possibly come of such … such low behaviour.'

Mrs Gunne shuddered at the thought of it and walked towards the mirror. She began fussing at her collar. 'Though I understand Mrs Pakenham doesn't always be well?'

At first Greta was inclined to release another 'Yes, Ma'am' from her endless supply, but she saw a tiny glint through the looking glass from Mrs Gunne's eyes that made her hesitate.

'Mmmm?' Mrs Gunne's voice ran casually up the scale.

'Eh. No, Ma'am, though it has been quite some time since –'

'Since?' Mrs Gunne walked over to the window and started to plump out the draperies as though they'd only been freshly hung.

'Since her last little turn. Her last attack like.'

'Attack? Do you mean she has some sort of *fits*?'

'Oh no, Ma'am. Nothing like that. She can appear quite normal. She often doesn't remember a thing –'

Mrs Gunne walked back to the mantelpiece and rearranged the china in a most conscientious manner. A touch of pink across the spread of her cheeks peeped out from the side of the mirror.

'Are you telling me she … she drinks?'

'Oh no, Ma'am. It's much worse than that.'

Mrs Gunne spun on her heels and pulled a chair out from under the table. She sidled on to it, spread her arms out in front of her and gasped over at Greta.

'Worse than the drink!? Well go on then. Spit it out girl. I'm waiting.'

FIVE

Maude dragged her fingers over the bumps of upholstery button-punched onto the rear seat of the motor car. 'No, really,' she said, 'I mean it. Very nice. Very nice indeed.'

She waited for Samuel to do his thing, holding her elbow to help her through – 'Careful how you go, Ma'am. That's it, that's the ticket. Hup now, hup, we're in' – and sounding nervous enough to be guiding her along a cliff edge. By the time he had taken his arm out she was seated and just in time to acknowledge his doffed hat with a smile.

Already in the front seat, her husband was prepared. Back straight and head erect, fingers curled under the rim of the steering wheel, nothing to do but wait for Sam to take his place.

Maude looked around at the red lining and thought to herself, 'Some day I shall be in such surroundings and I won't be sitting upright either. And where will I be heading then, I wonder?' It amused her though to see the two men trying to contain themselves. It seemed to her that this great effort had succeeded in making them somewhat ceremonious – all gracious gestures, formal nods and slow over-careful movements (how long does it take to close a door, for goodness sake?). They had even managed to acquire the intermittent throat clearing that one associates with more churchlike rituals. Of course, any fool could see that what they really wanted to do was to whoop out loud and laugh with delight.

Samuel turned his head to face her, giving his hat the customary tip at the brim before speaking. 'Are you ready, Ma'am?'

She couldn't resist it. 'Ready, Samuel?' she gasped. 'Why? You're not expecting *me* to drive are you?'

Samuel looked confused and the expected small red dots on the upper apples of his cheeks duly obliged. Then, like fireworks that had been let off from a height rather than towards one, they burst downwards into a more extravagant flush.

'Now Sam, don't let her tease you. Do you hear me?' Pat removed his hat and without being asked Samuel's hand went out to take it.

'No, Sir.'

'I wouldn't tease you Samuel. Now would I?'

'Eh, no, Ma'am. No indeed, Ma'am.' And once again his fingers went up to his hat, before his face spun away, back to the safety of the front seat.

'All right, Sir. If you'd just like to take her away. Now easy does it.' Pat's shoulders moved and Maude felt the engine come to life somewhere beneath her skirts.

'Now Sir, that's it. Left and right, lovely. Off she goes, hup my lady. Hup.'

The motor car, startled at first, steadied itself up and began to roll slowly away from the house.

They often laughed at poor old Samuel, herself and Pat. He had caught them at it once too, when he came back into the drawing room to have something signed. She sitting up on Pat's knee, wearing his hat and tipping its brim, shouting her head off, with, 'Yes, Ma'am, no, Ma'am' and 'Hup, m'lady, hup.' She nearly took a faint when she saw him standing there and tried to jump up, to escape. Only for that Pat Cleary, holding her down onto his lap while poor old Samuel had to walk over and hand him the piece of paper. And wait too, for Pat to sign it sideways on the arm-chair. She could have died, she really could. The door closed softly in the drawing room and just as she was about to let Pat have it, his lips came down on hers and, well, that was the end of that.

Samuel knew that day they were laughing at him and yet he still went on tipping his hat before and after each time he addressed her, still continued to say, 'Hup, my lady, hup.' He was such an odd little man. Where did Pat say he got him again? Ah yes. The Automobile Show, wasn't it? The very first one. When was that? I must ask him later. About ten years ago was it? Let's see … how long are we? Five years? Six this June. *Six*. And I knew Pat how long? Two years and Papa met him before that at the show. That was the first time. He introduced Pat to Samuel. Or was it Samuel introduced Pat to Papa? Yes, about ten years ago. Or eleven maybe. Married six years. Who would believe it?

Yes: the first Automobile Show. Pat said he came away from it with his first motor car, complete with a funny little man who knew as much about its insides as a surgeon would about mine. He said. And who had decided, just like that, not to go back to London but to rather stay here, with Pat and the motor. A Wolsley, wasn't it? He had asked Pat if he knew how to drive, when Pat had said no, as a matter of fact he didn't know the first thing about automobiles, Samuel then said, 'Well in that case, Sir, if you don't mind, I'd like to stay with the motor.'

He didn't ask Pat, he told him. And that's how come Samuel lives in the old coach house at the bottom of the garden. All alone too, poor fellow; one has to force any luxury on him. Such a time it took to get him to hang drapes. All he seems to want to do is to stay on his own, the entrails of motor cars bleeding out all over his table.

Looking now at the back of his neck where the flush was only just beginning to subside, she felt guilty for being the cause of such discomfort and would have vowed to cause no more but for the fact that it was inevitable – to engage Samuel in any conversation that wasn't solely concerned with automobiles was to subject the poor fellow to the most excruciating embarrassment.

'Ah yes it's much quieter.' She leaned forward. 'I say it's much quieter, Samuel. Well done.'

'Yes indeed, Ma'am.'

'And smoother –'

'And smoother is the word. Indeed Ma'am.'

'Yes –'

She leaned back again, spreading her skirt over her legs and flicking off dust flecks that were not always there. She looked down at her new shoes; black glace kid with a cuban heel. Well pleased, she flexed their shiny caps and tipped off their ribbon laces ever so lightly. Yes, they weren't too bad at all and comfortable into the bargain.

When she looked up again, she noticed Pat's concentration ritual had begun. His shoulders were shifting needlessly, his head above them held tightly. She leaned forward again, resting her arm across the back of his seat, and she could feel it then, burn out from him.

'You could –' Samuel's voice was polite.

'Yes, of course,' Pat answered and his left hand came reluctantly away from the steering wheel to touch the engine into another sound. The motor car swayed a little to the right before his hand found its way back to the steering wheel.

'Woops. Steady you go.'

'She wants to go home,' Maude laughed. 'Back to her stable.'

Her head had fallen forward onto her arm crook and lifting it up again she caught the smell of him in her mouth and swallowed it down. It was strong: as though he were naked. Must be the excitement, she thought.

'What does she do?' Pat's head tilted towards Samuel and came closer to her mouth. If they were alone she would … she might …

'Forty-five tops with this body. A little less in winter.'

'Why less?' she asked, as if she didn't know.

'This is a touring body, darling, remember I told you? A winter body would be heavier to pull.'

'Oh yes, of course.'

Pat twisted his head back towards her, his hair, brushing his collar, only inches from her fingertips.

How she loved it. His hair. Structured as a crow's back, thick and shineless black. And your fingers could catch in it, that thick, your fingers could curl and pull. And he never minded. It never seemed to hurt him.

And again another question, more to justify sitting up so close behind them than to satisfy any real curiosity on her behalf: 'Has it got one of those electrical … electric …?'

'Ma'am?' Samuel asked.

'Starters,' Pat explained. 'She means electric starters.'

And then turning towards her. 'Yes, Maude,' he explained so seriously.

And how she loved him being serious like that while his hands made things move, lifting away from the wheel again now to activate another sound − now a slightly higher song.

'It has an electric starter,' he confirmed.

'Has it?' she asked softly.

'Oh yes, Ma'am.' Samuel was speaking to her. 'You may have noticed there were no need to haul her up to start her. Cranking up's a thing of the past, I'm glad to say.'

'Of course, how silly −' she whispered, closing her eyes.

Leftways down they lurched, as she brought herself back again to nestle into the corner of the seat. She unpinned her hat and carefully turned it away from her head and down onto the seat beside her. Against the window her face was gently wobbled by a nervous window pane.

It will look as though I have been wearing rouge. And on one side only. I really should sit up straight.

But she snuggled herself down even further.

Up front the voices continued to move. Questions first, then answers, then more of the same. And with this exchange of vital information came a parade of familiarly foreign names: mileages and cylinders, horsepowers and radiators. Samuel did most of the talking, his voice a little nasal. A lovely tenor though, she knew from eavesdropping via an open window. While he polished some bit from a former beloved, behind the fullness of the cherry blossoms whose pink extravagant curls, robust with a passing bloom, hid him, but not his voice, from the world outside.

'I thought, Sir, instead of taking a left on the Chapelizod Road we might go up right, along the length of the Park wall and turn in at the main entrance.'

'And –?'

'And keeping on up to Mountjoy Cross, right as far as Ashtown, where I can drop you off.'

'Oh I see. Yes, all right. Bit of a long-cut, Sam?'

'Give you a feel for her, and yourself a chance to adjust. I'd rather you stayed on the straight first time out. Eh, you could ...' he gestured vaguely.

'Oh yes, sorry, keep forgetting. Sorry.'

'No need to apologise to me, Sir. I'm not the motor.'

They moved loosely downwards towards Islandbridge. In the distance, at the bottom of the hill, the old grey wall faced them, shielding the Park. From this angle at the brow of the hill it looked to her as though it were chomping to escape. You could see green bits and black bits, bushy ones and clipped ones, all waiting for an opportunity to jump the wall, to lose control.

And to her there was something almost shocking in this spectacle. Something savage. Obscene even. Had she been confined too long to vitreous shopping streets and lacy drawing rooms – the backdrop to her daily life? Surely to find a lewdness in this display of confined nature was, to say the least, a little unreasonable?

'By God, man, you're right,' she could hear Pat's voice break out. 'She's a bloody flyer.' At last he allowed himself to laugh like a child.

The motor car took the descent of the hill like a toboggan on ice, throwing her forward again so that she was leaning on the rest of the front seat. She could see the two men, Pat grinning while Samuel's smile was smaller, almost modest, as if somehow it was himself that was being praised. When he was finished being bashful he straightened up his face and said, 'You could slow her up a bit now, Sir, we've got this hump coming up.' He pointed his finger forward.

'Oh yes. Right you are so.' And they slowed up slightly then, all adult again, bumping over the hill. She sat back again.

'Are you all right back there?' he asked her after a while. His voice, raised to her, was still panting slightly. They turned away from the Chapelizod Road where she could see the river sprinting past them, back towards the city.

'Yes,' she said, 'I'm fine.'

'You're very quiet.'

'Oh, just enjoying the jaunt.'

'Oh good. That's good.'

Oh but there was nothing nasal about *his* voice, oh no. Thick and yet fluid; the Victoria Falls. He was one of those men whose voices seemed to come from beneath their adam's apple, while Samuel's? Well Samuel's definitely came from above his.

'I was just wondering what had you so preoccupied. Maybe she's picking out a few winners for today. Eh, Sam? Or is she imagining herself as mistress of this fine automobile?'

'Could be, Sir. And neither no harm.'

He was always at that when she was a bride. Checking on her every thought, every minute they were together. Actually even when they were apart, rare times those, he would check in retrospect.

She used to make up answers with which to delight him. Even when her mind was just a canvas on which there was nothing more than a few bouncing speckles, a zig-zag or two and perhaps a sweet-cake under consideration for tea.

Was that why he married me? she half wondered then – believing I had a trove of thoughts and ideas stored compactly in my head so that he would never grow bored.

And supposing he were to ask me now on this day, the opening of the flat season, Easter Saturday, 30 March 1918. What would I tell him? That on this journey from Kilmainham to Ashtown I am thinking of another journey. One which will certainly never be the subject of a lecture at the National Geographical, nor discussed in the coffee room of the Travellers Club?

'And what journey is that?' he might well ask. And I, what should I say then? The journey that your hair makes from your forelock downwards until it stops in tiny tufts smattered across your various toes. And would he say then, 'You mad little thing,' as lightly as he can before turning his head to another subject, less demanding?

Or would he take my hand and say, 'Show me. Show me this journey with these fingers and that mouth?'

Down cliffside jaw it runs, curl-free and coarse to where it lodges thirstily around one red mouth. It waits at this oasis. Above, the strongest ones slope down over the lip most-moistened. And caressed too, parted by his fingertips slow, the point of his tongue in moments of contemplation. Now on his neck a few will fall sparse, and trickle for a while before suddenly spreading and multiplying themselves over his chest and breast. Like wings in a span, they have a centrepiece, a spine of hair, strong and dark. It runs now in a lick from the centre of this breast down the way to his belly. Then spreads, finer, more delicately. Until further down again, soft for a while, before rolling under and into each other, denser then, travelling beneath him, clinging like a vine clings, to protect its secret fruits, to keep them warm and heavy, to keep them ripe.

Would this be my answer? Would this be my truth? Or would I rather say, 'Oh it was nothing really. I was thinking of nothing. Just a speckle that bounced, a zig-zag or two. And a sweet-cake I may have for tea.'

'So tell me, Sam? Crawfords of Hatch Street, did you say?'

'That's right, Sir.'

'And how much are they asking?'

'You could show a bit of caution on this left swing, Sir, she's not as nifty as the Swift you know.'

And even with the caution the swing was wide and Pat, red-faced, pulled her straight saying: 'Yes, I see what you mean,' as casually as he could.

'We didn't quite settle.'

'Sorry, Sam –?'

'You were asking – Crawfords – how much?'

'Oh yes, Crawfords.'

'I should think you'll get her for two eighty. Thereabouts.'

'And it's 1914?'

'Yes, Sir. In my opinion the best you'll get this side of the war. Crumps wouldn't turn his nose up at this – if it had legs instead of wheels that is. A proper thoroughbred if you know what I mean.'

Maude looked up. They were on Chesterfield Avenue, running in a slice through the Park, stretching forever as far as the Castleknock Gate, beech lime and horse chestnut taking its elbows along the way.

To the left-hand side of them a bench sat snug in a bracket of railings, made just for its convenience. Four children pressed side to side sat swinging their legs and trying to appear as though they were listening to the scolding being delivered to them by the woman standing in front of them. One hand on the bar of a perambulator, the other wagging a finger of warning. Who was she? Nanny? Mother? Aunt? And what had they done? Dangled themselves from the railings like monkeys, or had they maybe interfered with the baby evergreens planted there behind them? Yes that would have been serious, all right. Their predecessors fallen in the great storm, they should be left to grow in peace, one to replace every single vacant spot. So that in a hundred years who will know that there ever was such a storm. Ever such a night. That this space had lain bald for a while.

And when I am gone, who will replace the spot that once was mine?

In front Pat was silent. He had withdrawn himself from the conversation. Samuel on the other hand had revved up his voice. He must really want Pat to buy this motor car.

But Pat wasn't listening. She could tell. He could do that. Not listen. No matter how loudly you spoke.

They passed the Wellington Monument, rising foot after foot of Wicklow granite, and still he did not speak. (He usually had some story about the man who designed it. Somebody Smirke, wasn't it? She couldn't remember the inside of the story now, but it ended with: 'Well he's not smirking now and that's for sure.') He will seem to listen. No doubt Samuel thinks every word is being heeded. But it isn't. Not really.

I tried to talk to him. I tried. That day he found me crying to myself and for once I didn't say something had made me sad. Or I had a sick headache. For once I told the truth. Telling him I had a loneliness deep inside me, a loneliness I couldn't fill. And in between all the, 'There, hush my little one, don't cry. You need never be lonely again, I'm here now I am. Maybe you're missing your poor old Papa. That could be it. That's all,' I stopped, just for a moment. And looking up at him through the tears my hand went down onto my stomach. And he knew then. That it was not him that I was lonely for. Nor was it Papa. It was neither of them: I was lonely for someone who didn't even exist.

And now he has fallen silent in that way too. Outwardly just as ever, teasing, admiring, including me in his every breath of every day. But at night another story. Withdrawing from me time and time again. Three long months since we have been that way, three long months since I have felt his long back rising and falling above me, three long months since he has licked sin into a mouth well pleased to receive it. Three chances missed. Three chances gone. Three baby evergreens.

His nights are spent at a study desk now, looking at plans of plans. While I lie waiting, hoping, my legs burning with that incurable ache.

Was it that long ago that we sat there, side by side? Before that very bandstand, listening to music that grew louder with each note behind the flapping elbows of an eager leader. And touching off each other for a moment our eyes met, and I swooned, down there. In the depth of me.

And he asked me then, as he usually did, 'Tea? Would you like some?'

And I could almost feel his heart beating against mine although there were inches between us and I did not answer him. And, 'Tea?' he asked again, his face colouring. And still I was silent.

The kiosk was only a few steps away, but I knew my legs had lost their power. I knew I'd never make it. Not for *tea*.

And although my outward self wanted to agree, to rise, to go, to move towards a table and take my place, to watch buttered scones float towards me on a plate and the stream of tea, golden brown, push out through a spout and down into my outstretched cup. To pass each other bowls and jugs and to play this game, with my head and my eyes and my laugh, going this way that, through the necessary moves. And to watch the delight buff up his eyes to an unbearable shine.

Although I knew that's what I was supposed to do, that's what I should want to do, I still stayed silent, flame-cheeked, never answering him with a word, just an upward glance, before hanging my head down again. Until he touched my arm and my one last glance saw him mouth slowly, 'Home?' And I nodded then just as slowly and rose, my legs as useless as a foal's, and followed him as best I could. Thinking all the time, if he touches me I shall die. If he does not, I shall kill myself.

We moved then, through the Sunday people. Crossing over there beside that cricket ground and leaving his motor car behind us, not commenting on it as we passed it. Both knowing by then it would never be speedy enough. And the bats and balls behind us nudging each other and flighty applause broke out in intervals and the grass grew longer beneath my feet.

One grove then another one, a smaller copse cupped within it. And his hands calmly flattened out his greatcoat and then came back for me. And over they went, across me up and down, until I grew a second heart. There between my legs and palpitating achingly. Hurting me almost; it just would not stop. I felt his fingers then ruck my skirts in folds upwards and both his hands on my thighs downwards and to think of it now makes me weak again with shame and desire and stroking me then till I was no longer myself, but a creature. Emitting noises as such creatures do. The penetration itself hurt me then. But I did not care. Sweet, sweet pain. We had taken each other as far as we could. Man and woman. If I died that second, I did not care. He wrapped his coat around me then, kissing my face, my hair, my chin. And telling me how sorry he was, and so sorry he was too, that at first I thought he meant he could no longer marry me. But no, that was not what it was at all. He had taken advantage of me, that was it. He had failed to control his passion. And now he felt ashamed. He vowed there and then we should move our wedding date nearer, just in case his actions had rendered me 'compromised'.

Poor Pat. Wrong on two counts. I am still waiting to be 'compromised'. And besides, it was I who had taken advantage of him.

The motor rounded the Phoenix monument, the sudden turn causing her hat to slither away from the seat. Her hand snapped out to retrieve it.

Does he think of it ever? Is he thinking of it now? When homeward bound his eyes, his hands, could not leave me. Hauling up the engine or steering the wheel, such distractions stealing the concentration, he only wished for me.

'That's it, Sir,' she could hear Samuel say. 'See how you've got the hang of it?'

'Yes. Yes, once you get used to it. It's really quite –'

'As I was saying, Sir, it would be very easy to manage. If you know what I mean Sir.'

'Yes indeed,' he agreed quietly and then, 'Here, Sam, you don't mean you think that Mrs –?

Maude moved forward.

'Mrs what? Did I just catch your eyebrows shifting in this direction?'

'Ma'am –?'

'I hope you don't think for one minute you're going to make an *automobiliste* out of me.'

Pat laughed. 'Well, I will be needing Sam a lot more to organise the maintenance of these new motor lorries. He can't be at your beck and call forever you know. And supposing we go over to America? Sam will have to stay here to help Pakenham out. He can't come with us you know, just so he can drive you about the place.'

'Well you'll just have to do it.'

'Me? Oh no, my dear, I'll be tied up most of the time in business meetings. Besides all the women in America drive, isn't that right Sam?' Pat winked encouragingly at him.

'Well I couldn't rightly –' Sam began.

'I bet they don't,' Maude cried. 'And if they do, I shall ask one of them for a lift.'

Pat laughed. 'And anyway,' he persisted, 'what's wrong with a woman driving? Your friend Lottie – she does.'

'Lottie is different, as you very well know.'

'Well, why can't you be different too?'

'Pat Cleary, you can get it straight out of your head now. Do you hear me? The idea of it. Are you trying to disgrace me? Driving myself around as if I hadn't a soul in the world to care for me. Why you're nothing but a suffragette.'

They turned at Mountjoy Cross and slowed up to join the rest of the traffic delivering turf-goers to their afternoon destiny. Pedestrians drifted in across grass from every angle, homing in towards Bessborough Barracks and the Ashtown Gate.

'I think we could nearly leave you off here, Sir. We'll only be sat here an hour waiting on an inch.'

They pulled in beside a granite marker which Maude fixed her eyes on as though mesmerised by the figure 2 carved into its stone. Pat was still laughing.

'Look at her, Samuel. Go on, look. Tell me, is her face on fire?'

'Well, I –'

'And her bottom lip. Is it poking out? Like … like this?'

'Well now that you mention it, Sir –'

'Arms folded?'

'As a matter of fact, yes.'

'Now, Samuel, I want you to do something for me. I want you to explain to Mrs Cleary all about the internal combustion engine.'

He ducked as her fist came down small and hard on his shoulder.

Pat walked around by the front of the motor car, calling out to Samuel as he moved, 'I'll help Mrs Cleary out, Sam, you sit yourself into the driver's seat.'

'Very well, Sir.'

Samuel had been standing holding the open door which up to now had remained largely ignored.

Maude looked up to see Pat's hand reach out to her. She looked away. Pat's hand tapped against the upholstery.

'Come on now, Missy. No nonsense. We'll miss the first race.'

He started to climb in. 'All right so. I'll lift you out and carry you all the way in.'

Her head flew around to face him. 'Oh you would not.'

'Do you want to try me?'

'You wouldn't *dare*.'

'You think not –?'

He came a little nearer to her. 'We'll just see if I don't.'

She felt his hand slide under her thighs. He drew her towards him.

'No. No. It's all right; I'll go myself. Don't lift me. Pat, don't, please don't.'

'Do you promise to be a good girl?'

'Yes. Yes, I promise.'

He stepped back outside and put forward his hand once again. Maude took it and glanced crossly at him. When she alighted he kept hold of her hand and drew her around to the front of the car where she could see Samuel positioned and ready to go.

'Well?' Pat asked.

'Well what?'

He gestured toward the fender on the front bonnet of the car and she looked.

'Oh my!' she cried. 'I don't believe it.' She covered her mouth with her hand.

There enscribed across the fender in long letters, styled enough to have been handwritten, was the name of the automobile: 'Hupmobile'.

'I'm just showing Mrs Cleary the front of the motor, Sam,' Pat shouted through to Samuel.

He in turn nodded agreeably and doffed his hat at Maude.

'Hup, my lady, hup,' Pat muttered. 'Let's go.' He waved at Samuel; the wave was returned. Just as they were about to walk away (a movement Maude longed for so that she could laugh in peace), Samuel poked his head over the door and called out.

'If Mrs Cleary is interested in the combustion engine, might I suggest that she consults her brother –?'

'Her brother?' Pat asked.

'Oh yes, Sir, he knows a lot more about it than I would.'

'Thank you, Samuel, she will. I'm sure.'

Hat being tipped, horn being honked, the car was ready to resume and it took Samuel slowly away with it, back the road they had come.

'My brother?' Maude reached out to take her husband's arm. 'I didn't know they even knew each other.'

'Oh yes, he's a regular visitor to Sammie's den, you know. Sam thinks there's nothing like him. He reckons he's an expert on – well almost everything.'

'How could he possibly think that?'

'Well you've always said he's more than just a pair of dancing feet.'

'Yes. But for Samuel to know that, he'd have to get him to talk. I haven't heard him say more than a few words at a time since he was a boy. Why I have to practically force a 'Good-day' out of him at the best of times.'

She rolled her index finger around the cuff of her kid leather glove and patted it neatly into the curve of her wrist. 'All the same you'd think he'd walk up the garden path to visit his sister, now and then.'

Boys with bunches of racecards appeared and reappeared at different points. Pat stopped one of them. While she waited, she fiddled with her hat and thought of the long narrow path that ran without distraction from Samuel's den to her house at the other end of the garden. How long had these visits been going on? Six months? A year? Longer? And how often? Once a week? A fortnight? Every other day probably. You'd think he'd pop up to say hello, even once a month. Really. Only for her he might be still in Wicklow. After all it was she who talked Papa into letting him pursue this dancing business in the first place. Such ingratitude. Just wait till she told Kate. She would go and see her tomorrow after lunch and tell all. Internal combustion engine indeed. The pup.

She looked around. What a shame Kate was ill though. Such a lovely day too. Everyone dressed up in their new spring clothes; how she would enjoy this. Still no doubt Greta would coddle her for the day. And it did prevent one from having to wear a hat with four corners …

Pat came back and handed her a race card. 'Now. Let's see what you can do with that, my beauty.'

A familiar couple walked passed them, hooked together in much the same manner as they themselves. Smiles and nods were exchanged.

They turned onto the diagonal and crossed towards the railings.

'I tell you, there's some crowd here today.' Pat waved his rolled-up card in recognition of a business acquaintance.

'Yes. But so many soldiers. Are we expecting an attack?' Maude smiled at an acquaintance of her own.

'It's free entrance for them today.' Pat bowed at the proprietor of a rival public house.

'Ahh …' Maude bowed to his wife.

Arm in arm again they moved, through walking sticks and parasols, weaving their way across the grass where skirts swayed and hats stayed in position despite being constantly nagged by over-anxious fingers.

'Pat?' she asked, nudging him softly. 'Isn't that – over there in the Irish Guards uniform – ?'

'Where?'

'There. Look. No don't look. All right now. Well, isn't it?'

'Yes, by God, it certainly is.'

'Since when did he enlist?'

'Since this morning when I paid him his wages and he asked for the rest of the day off.'

'What? Are you serious?'

'But I'll tell you something. His brother's enlisted a long time since.'

'You don't mean –?'

'Ah but that's exactly what I mean.'

'Just to get in for nothing? Well really. The nerve. Quick, look the other way; he's passing. Let's not spoil his day. All the same, you'd think he'd find something that fitted him properly while he was at it. He looks a show.'

Through Ashtown Gate then their step improved, taking them with the others past the vendors' cries and over towards the second set of gates on the opposite side of the road. This view in particular was hers, the racecourse entrance slanting at its peculiar angle, a pert little phoenix, one on either pillar, rising out over solid flames. Full-gaped, it had opened itself to the crowd, sucking them into the thick of it by the common purpose of the day.

Feet agitating gravel now and the turnstiles whacking punters through, one by one. Pat was fumbling for their membership badges: almost in.

'Hupmobile! Who would believe it? Felt sure it was a joke. Poor old Sam. Fancy anything in the first? Number five's got an interesting form, good for a lady's bet, beaten last time out by – Lady's bet? You've got a cheek. Oh look, that's a pretty name there.'

Such last words they threw to the air as they moved deeper in, through the crowds and the tantrum of a brass band playing from within.

Six

'The tarpaulin reeled like a great flabby beast getting ready to attack. It pounced up and out, strutting and blowing until it had shaped into itself and a broken murmur ran round its base, confirming its completion. I looked down onto the lawn where a scurry of workmen tapped pegs and twanged ropes like an orchestra tuning up. They began to disappear then, back towards the front barn and the next phase in the preparations. The abandoned marquee was perfectly still now except for one ripple which passed loosely through it; a shudder up its canvas spine.

'The dawn was making itself known by now and after a while I saw them return through the greyness, tottering like rocking horses; a string of benches with a man posted at either end. Then Paud began unloading baskets of flowers from two carts at the paddock gate and I remember thinking, 'Papa is really giving me all this time.' I worried a little about the cost but there was a smell of money in the air that summer. It was just after Papa had sold the motorbuses, you know. I had heard or rather overheard that the sum was more than considerable. And besides it was my day. My wedding feast. And so I didn't worry too long.

'Scratches of light began to appear through the trees, drawing my eye towards them. There was about them a sullenness which seemed to distort them from their dependable beauty into the sinister.

'It was then the outline of a figure came to me – I only saw it because it happened to move. For a second I thought it was just another of those distortions, but then I saw ... No – a man. Bareheaded and shirtsleeved, just standing there, watching the movements creep backwards and forwards from the house to the marquee.

'I pulled myself away from the window, bad luck and all that. Yes, it was him. My groom-to-be. And do you know, at the time I didn't even wonder about it? Him standing there bareheaded and shirtsleeved, not even a jacket. Him of all people! And looking in from the outside. A spy at his own wedding.

'I moved back to my bed then, where my wedding dress lay, and sat down beside it careful not to crease it. And my fingers played again and again with its guipure trim, terrified that the least indiscretion would stain or make a tear. Yet I could not leave it alone.

'When I came back to the window each blob of darkness had been cleaned and daylight had spread. Below the bustle increased, bright moving colours, voices brighter too. And the trees over to my right had reformed into the dependable and the beautiful. Although no man stood amongst them now. Now they were quite alone.'

Kate nuzzled her head further down into the pillows and closed her eyes. She stayed like that long enough for Maude to think she had finally fallen asleep. And contemplating a sneaky retreat from the bedroom, her foot just about to tip down on the floor when Kate opened her eyes.

'Are you leaving?'

'I thought you were sleeping.'

'I was just visualising the next part of my story. I'm not used to speaking aloud so long. Well, not to you anyway.'

'But to Greta?'

Kate lifted her arm and stretching her finger pressed it against her sister's lips. 'No,' she whispered, 'not that name. Not in my house.'

'But you must tell me sometime, surely? We are going to speak of it?'

'Not now.'

Kate's eyes closed again. This time Maude waited.

'You came into me then,' Kate started again, keeping her eyes shut.

'Did I dear? When?'

'Then. On my wedding day.'

'Oh yes. Of course.'

'To help me dress.'

'Yes.'

'And you dressed me like a doll. Every stitch.'

'You were so nervous.'

'I wasn't, you know.' Kate opened her eyes.

'No?'

'You must have some little trace of fear to be nervous. Even the fear of happiness will do. I wasn't afraid. Not in the least.'

'I see.' Maude sounded disappointed.

'I can still see my foot pointing into the ball of wrinkled silk.'

'Ah yes, the Italian stockings we scoured London for – so beautiful.'

'And then you unrolling the wrinkles over my calf and my knee, till it was so smooth. It was as if my leg had been lacquered.'

'And the garter. Don't forget the garter.'

'You gave me your wedding garter for luck.'

'Yes, for luck.'

Kate went quiet again. Maude nudged her back. 'Shall I tell you a little secret about that garter?' she began.

'If you like.'

'I had Pat's initials written under one of its petals.'

'You what?'

'Yes. Silly isn't it? I did it the night before my wedding day. I don't know why.'

Maude's face was full with embarrassment. Her eyes glittered.

'You …' Kate was smiling, 'you mean to tell me that I walked around my wedding with Pat Cleary's initials stuck to my leg. Well that's a fine one, I must say.'

The two sisters laughed together and then Maude began to cry.

'Oh Maude, stop it. For God's sake just –'

'I'm sorry, I'll stop now in a minute, I will. I promise.'

There was only the whispering shift of the fire then for a while, or a sniff and gulp from Maude as she tried to control herself. And she did. Eventually. Though each time she looked at her sister's profile wedged into the pillow, the tears started up again. She tried not to. But she couldn't help it. She felt so sorry for Kate. It was her voice more than her appearance; that dear face could never make her sad. But the voice, more muffled than ever now because of the head cold. It made Maude realise how difficult it was for Kate. How difficult it had always been.

Once when they were children Maude had thought it was her fault: a notion that came to her one day in June and pulled the summer out from under her feet. She remembered quite suddenly how she used to lie on Mama's stomach shortly before Kate was born, her head pressed in tight, the heel of her hand occasionally pressing against a protrusion that would withdraw at her touch to the other side of the great pliable shell that was Mama's stomach. Then and there, as the memory came into being, Maude had stood up and walked away, leaving behind the lawn and their game spread out. She had hidden herself alone with her shame for the rest of the afternoon, weeping. And saying to herself again and again, 'I did it, I did it. I must have been lying on her face all the time and squashed her little nose all up.'

The guilt was huge for a while, almost impossible to bear; she hadn't even been able to look at her little sister without it pinching and burning through her. And then something happened to cause a diversion, then something else, and the guilt began to fade. Until one day it just wasn't there any more and she could look Kate straight in the face again.

Now hearing her speak for so long. On and off all afternoon in fact, growing familiar again with the voice that had been so much a part of her childhood. Now listening, really listening to it move, with its careful old fashioned tones, through the past. She realised how quiet, how introverted Kate had become.

That her voice should seem to be no more than vaguely familiar. Almost like an old friend that had emigrated years ago and had only just returned.

Kate turned her face back. 'You've finished then?'

Maude nodded as positively as she could, though her sister's smile almost started her off again.

'It was fun though wasn't it?' Kate asked her.

'Your wedding? Oh yes. It was.'

'No. No. I mean shopping in London that time. Just the two of us.'

'Oh yes. That was. That was the best.' She lifted her hands in praise. 'And what a trousseau. Unbelievable!'

'Ah yes, you could really get clothes then, before the war.'

'And with your beautiful taste.'

'My beautiful taste?' Kate rolled her eyes upwards.

'Well, so you have. Just like Mama. But so fussy. Goodness my feet that time, I'll never forget it. Every shop in London before you were happy. And that awful sales woman in Harvey Nichols. How we laughed at her. Her terrible accent – "*robe d'intérieur*". It took her forever to say it. Do you remember? How she said it? And how she kept comparing your trousseau to Princess Augustine something or other – every time, for every outfit – who has purchased one just like it for her own trousseau, don't you know.' Maude squealed and clapped her hands. 'And then I said, after we had let her go on and on showing us I don't know how many different things, "Thank you so much, you've been most kind, but my sister always likes to be original and would rather die than dress like anybody else. Besides, we wouldn't like to cause any confusion." Do you remember?'

'Yes.'

'Oh her face! And we went dancing too. Wasn't that such fun? All those funny new dances. What were they called again? What's this they were?'

Maude held her hand out towards her sister and beckoned an answer from her. 'The turkey trot,' she obliged.

'The turkey trot. Yes. Yes that's it. And that other one. The – the bunny hop. Will you ever forget it. Wasn't it so …? I ruined my new gown I remember. I was dancing with that young man we met through the Fleetwoods and only because, before I could stop you, you were up on the floor with his brother. We couldn't stop laughing for even a second. I just kept thinking *me* supposed to be acting as chaperone to *you*. And there was the pair of us like kangaroos hopping about the place with complete strangers. And me a married woman and you engaged to be married within a few weeks. If Papa had known.'

Maude stopped to take a breath, pushing one final gasping laugh out of herself to keep the mood going. But the mood was gone. It wouldn't stay.

There was a light tapping on the door then, a diversion Maude jumped to welcome. Maura walked in. 'I just came to take the tea things out of your way.'

She lowered her voice and raised her step to cross the room.

'Can I get you anything else Mrs Pakenham?' Kate shook her head. 'Mrs Cleary?'

'No thank you, Maura.'

Maura was about to leave the room when Maude changed her mind.

'No, no, wait, Maura. Mr Pakenham is still out, I take it?'

'Yes, no sign of him yet.'

'Does he keep cigarettes in his study?'

'Well, yes.'

'You wouldn't …?'

'What? Are you jokin' me? You want to smoke? I most certainly will not. What sort of a –?'

'Oh Maura, please?'

Maura looked over at Kate, who nodded lightly in return.

'Well – he probably has them counted. I wouldn't be surprised. Just this once mind. And if I'm caught …'

'Oh go on, Maura. You won't be caught. Go on. Be a sport.'

'I'll be a right sport now, when I'm out on the street.'

Maura blustered out immensely, pleased by her own disapproval.

Maude laughed. 'What a card, your Maura is. She makes me laugh.' She stretched herself out across the end of the bed and rolled over on her stomach.

'We should go again. Just the two of us. As soon as you're better. What do you think, Kate? We could go to the theatre and visit Aunt Milly again. And go dancing even. Why not? We're not all that old. It would be such fun, Katie. What do you think?'

She sat up again and faced her sister. 'Come on, Kate, what do you say?'

'We'll see.'

'We'll see?'

Kate nodded.

'Very well then, Kate. Just as you like.'

Maura came in then, the cigarette and lighter hidden under her apron.

'Are you gun smuggling there, Maura?' Maude laughed reaching out to accept them.

'There you are and mind now you don't burn yourself.'

Maude put her lips around the cigarette and tightened them. She held the lighter away from her with her two hands and pressed down with her thumb. There were several sparks before a real flame emerged. She pointed the cigarette towards it and closing her eyes tightly began to puff and suck. Nothing.

'I'm still learning,' she apologised.

Maura reached out then and guided the lighter closer to the cigarette. At last smoke began to appear and at its centre a tiny red glow lit and stopped, lit and stopped; like a lighthouse in the fog.

Maude withdrew the cigarette and waved it extravagantly through the air.

'Don't you think,' she asked in her best London accent, 'I'm too chic?'

She pulled the smoke back into her mouth and rolled it around a bit before jutting it back out into the air.

'Oh I don't have an ashtray,' she said in her own voice again.

Kate looked up. 'Over there,' she said, 'on the shelf; there's an empty bonbon dish, you can use that.'

'She most certainly can not –' Maura began. 'I'll go down and get an ashtray.'

'Well, just till you get back then, Maura dear.' Maude smiled sweetly and then began to cough in such a way that it was difficult to know if she was play-acting or not. She walked over to the shelf and lifted the bonbon dish.

'You should get out more, you know,' she began. 'Travel. Do things. You know – meet people.'

'I have a cold.'

'I don't mean now, Kate. When you're better.'

'When I'm better?'

'It's only a cold, for God's sake, don't go using it as an excuse.' She paused before continuing, 'Come home with me, I'll have you up and about in –'

'No!' Kate raised her voice.

'All right Kate, I was only –'

'I mean, no thank you. I'll be fine. Really, I promise.'

'Oh Kate, I just hope …'

'You just hope what?'

'Well that you're not …'

'I'm not what?'

'Going to be the way you were before Greta.'

'I don't know which way I'm going to be. I really couldn't say.'

'Kate, can I just ask you?'

'That depends.'

'It's nothing about Greta.'

Maude stood by the bed and, balancing the cigarette on its rim, put the bonbon dish down carefully on the bedstand.

'You haven't …?'

'I haven't what?'

'You haven't – well – you know?'

'I haven't what, Maude? Say it. Why can't you for God's sake say it?'

'I don't want to hurt your feelings. I just thought perhaps ... It's always puzzled me you know. Why you do … did, I mean. And besides you have so much. So many beautiful things. You should get out more, show them off. Here, I bet that Princess Augustine one didn't end up with a wardrobe as fine as yours.'

Kate closed her eyes again.

'Kate,' Maude raised her voice. 'Will you at least answer me? I said, I bet …'

'Maybe I do have a bit of a thing about clothes,' Kate replied then.

'A bit of a thing? A bit of a –? Don't make me laugh.'

Maude's voice was high and bright. Too bright, she knew. Partly to keep Kate awake, to keep her from dropping off again. But also partly because she couldn't help it. All this joy, this gaiety she had been beating out of herself all afternoon, it had lost the run of itself now. It just kept rising up inside her and would no longer stay submerged no matter how hard she pushed down on it.

'A bit of a thing?' she repeated again, moving over to the ward-robes. One by one she flung the doors open and then ran back to the first one.

'Look!' She brought her hand down and plucked the skirt of the first dress on the rack. '*Soie*, dove grey,' she said smartly, imitating the London sales assistant. She picked up the second dress and spread its skirt out in a fan: 'Satin, shell pink.' She dropped it again. The next item had a narrow skirt and so this was brought over her arm-crook. 'Shantung silk, dull rose.' An increased speed began to unsteady her voice as she continued down through the rails of clothes. 'Crêpe de Chine, saxe-blue,' she cried. And then: 'Silk voile, grey with veiled rose. Oh and look' – here a feigned surprise was expressed – 'satin, cream, brocaded in gold. Never worn, if I'm not mistaken Well my, my, my!'

This one was pulled away from the rail and sent swirling through the air.

When she had finished this first round, she walked back and started again. This time as each dress, opera cloak, racing coat, gown, costume or tailor-made was lifted, the words – 'Look. Look. Are you looking?' – were shouted over and over as though Kate had never seen them before.

'When was the last time you wore this then? Hmm? Never, I'd say. Or this? What about this once, twice maybe? No no – look, we still have a tag here, this is another 'never'. Oh and here, how many shops did we try before this tea gown found us? How many others were rejected in its favour? And for what? So it could sit in your wardrobe and rot?' She lifted her arms to where the hats were kept.

Later when Sam arrived to collect Mrs Cleary, Maura made sure to have drop of whiskey ready for him, which he accepted, although he wouldn't sit down. She just had to tell him. Had to tell someone, and who else? Who else? How she nearly dropped the ashtray when she came back up to the bedroom. How she couldn't believe her eyes. How Mrs Cleary, who'd been in the best of form before she'd left the room, was now as mad as an inmate pulling the wardrobes to pieces. And Mrs Pakenham's beautiful clothes, in rag balls all over the floor. And hats.

'Hanging off this and that and trod on by Mrs Cleary herself, who needs lookin' at, if you ask me.' Here Samuel frowned in a way that made Maura feel she had to apologise for that last remark, although she quickly followed the apology with an explanation for passing it in the first place.

'Well, all I'm saying is she was screaming and crying and flinging God knows what else to the four corners. Well it's not normal, now is it Sam?'

Samuel continued to frown and began backing towards the kitchen door, his hand groping for a space to put the glass still bright with unfinished whiskey.

Then Maura, realising she was soon to lose him (and who else? who else?), very quickly began to tell him what she believed to be the most peculiar thing of all the peculiarities seen that afternoon. And that had to be Mrs Pakenham. He stayed then to hear her out, returning to his whiskey, but still not sitting down.

'What about her?' he asked.

'I'll tell you what about her now. Sitting up there in the bed, as cool as a breeze and smoking like a man – that experienced. And there on her face was the first grin seen since the Greta one slung her hook last week. Grinning if you don't mind. Like she was nearly enjoying it.

'And then the pair of them, laughing in the end while guess who cleans up the mess? Laughing like lunatics they were and probably still are, for all I know.'

Here Maura paused as it crossed her mind that Samuel himself might be on the point of grinning. But no, she decided, she was just a bit confused by the general carry-on. She asked him then if he had any idea where the likes of Mrs Pakenham would have learned to smoke like that. But Samuel just shrugged and finished his drink.

*

'I am twenty-two years old and the little church of St Mary's, in the Diocese of Leighlin, Baltinglass, Co. Wicklow has, according to the newspaper cutting, "never accommodated a crowd of such dimensions as assembled within its walls to witness the marriage of ..." my sister Maude to Patrick J. Cleary, only son of the late Henry Cleary and ...'

Kate felt herself being lifted backwards, the net of her over-skirt floating softly away from her bridesmaid's dress. She stretched her hand up to her hat to stop it falling away from her head and smiled. It was just a windy day after all.

'No, no, that's not right. That couldn't be right. I am twenty-eight years old and this bed is where I am living and these walls have only to accommodate me and my nightdress is cotton, not lace, and it doesn't move at all. And I am not in Wicklow, I am in Dublin, asleep, dreaming. That's all. Dreaming.'

The wind dropped and Kate felt herself fall and bounce back down onto the mattress. Her earlobes were pinching and when she went to rub them there was something bitten on to them. Yes, pearl and amethyst earrings, that's right – the gift of the bridegroom. Yes that's absolutely right. She felt herself being lifted again.

Behind her bells were ringing and there was laughter. The wind gusted into her stomach, bending her over like a hook. Her arms made flutters in the air and she was laughing softly now. Dreaming or not, it felt like she was flying. Just like she was flying. She looked down and the bed was inches away. She would stay up this time. This time she would have to. She would hurt herself should she fall down again, now there were so many things piled out on the bed, sharp things, hard things. What were they? She couldn't quite make out.

She twisted herself over to face the sounds. There now, she could see across the river, the wedding party move. In groups through the main gates or through the turnstile bit by bit. And stepping up the slight incline of the path that leads to the church door, where even from here she could see the abundance of flowers through the open door. And motor cars and carriages in shining blocks along the narrow roadway, from the old abbey next to the church to Stratford Lodge school at its other side. Where we used to play, where we used to play.

And where we came back today so that Maude could be married where our mama once was. And look there: Hubert Ovington adjusting the wreath of slipping madonna lilies around the harness of the bridal carriage. Checking first that no one has seen him. No one to think him 'soft'. Oh and I thought he had died – been killed in the war. Oh how lovely to see him. Dear Hubert, dear kind Hubert. And here are the Lannigan girls laughing and flouncing. So young. Could they really be that young?

She let her legs drop carefully, leaving them dangling. Now she had manoeuvred herself to an upright position. Now she could cross the river.

Kate looked down at the bed again. That's what they were then. So that was it. Snuff-boxes! Arrayed across the sheets and the pillows. Gold and silver, some embossed, some not. Some like sea creatures with claw legs at each corner. Others flat and lying at a tilt. And open-mouthed or shut they seemed to cover each inch of linen, each mound of counterpane, rising and falling over their folds.

Where had they come from? she wondered. Who had put them there?

She moved her legs then in smart little kicks and her hands in pats manipulated the space. She was off. Now passing over the weir spitting silver down into the Slaney, she heeled the river behind her. Nothing could stop her now. This time she would travel with the wind at her back.

*

Pat Cleary's best man had simply not shown up. When Paud went to collect him at the station not a sinner alighted except for a nun and a dog, 'Neither looking much like candidates for the job,' Paud said, delighted with the circle of horrified unwed women gasping as he repeated his tale.

What can be done? We mustn't tell Maude. Somebody find Pat. Oh heavens that's all we need. We'll see him flip now and that's for sure.

But he didn't flip. He didn't flip at all.

He just looked around, pausing for a second at his driver who declined without being asked by pursing his lips and moving his head in the slightest manner.

'Well, we'll just have to cancel the whole thing,' Pat shrugged then. The Misses Grahams and the Misses Currans shrieked with dismay. Then he turned to Kate.

'Well, come on, advise me. What are we to do?'

And her face steamed up with embarrassment and of course pride as every other female guest under the age of forty experienced for the first time a feeling of envy towards Maude's younger sister.

At first she was going to take the easy way out. Just a shrug, a worried look, a sympathetic nibble at the corner of her bottom lip – that would do. Why nothing even, no sort of a response at all, would also be acceptable, for Pat Cleary was far too happy to take offence. But then all eyes were on her. Openly on her. She decided to brave it out. Not to throw away the respect he had afforded her.

First she folded herself over her little brother and fussed at his clothes so that he would be the only person to see her face. Then she spoke.

'Well there must be somebody willing,' she said as clearly as she could. And she didn't even stop to examine the words just out of her mouth (to check if that last 'somebody' sounded more like 'dummody' or not). She just furrowed her brow, concentrating on a possible crease or spot on the little boy's collar, and sailed on with:

'We just need two things, a male. And half-respectable looking at that.'

Pat clapped his hands. 'By God, you're right, my Kate, all is not lost.'

(My Kate, ha! And nice and loudly too. Wouldn't that show of affection surprise the lot of them?)

He bent down quickly and said, 'What about this little fellow here. He looks quite respectable, hmm?'

Kate gave him the stern sister-in-law look she believed was expected of her, and commenced tidying the hair he'd just ruffled up.

'No?' he asked, surprised.

Braver now she stayed to face him, taking a deep breath.

'What about your new business manager – the Englishman?'

'Pakenham? But I hardly know him.'

Kate continued to look up at him until he relented.

'Very well,' he agreed, 'I am your obedient servant. Pakenham you say. And Pakenham it will be. Assuming of course that the fellow agrees. And if he doesn't, my Kate, let me tell you' – he raised his finger and wagged it at the crowd of giggling females – 'instant dismissal. And … and no champagne!'

He made shutters of his hands, and over his mouth flapped them open and shut again: 'Pakenham, Pakenham, oh Pakenham.'

But Paud was already walking back with Mr Pakenham at his side.

Kate could see the nudge of elbows passing through the girls. She didn't have to look to know there were fingers sneaking upwards to check hair, and faces he might never even get to see being placed into their prettiest pose. Slyly they watched Mr Pakenham move. And the chiffons and the tulles shuddered gently as he passed.

'Well Pakenham,' Pat shouted across to him. 'As my future sister-in-law has deemed you to be "half-respectable".'

Mr Pakenham's eyebrow rose and he thanked her with a bow.

'And as she has informed me that you are also male (which by the way pleases me no end).'

'I thank you again, Miss.' He bowed again and this time included a clicking of his heels as part of his gratitude.

Kate drew her little brother to stand in front of her, and tried to make light of the whole situation. So much giggling behind her and her face about to burst. 'Oh God strike me dead,' she prayed.

Pat continued: 'In short, my dear fellow, it seems that you are to be my best man. And before you say aye or nay I must warn you, my about-to-be-acquired sister has deemed it so. And she is a woman who will take defiance from no man.'

Mr Pakenham looked at her for a moment and then he spoke. 'In that case I accept the honour without question.'

And he smiled. At her, only her.

'Well that settles it. Inside quickly now.'

Pat put one arm around Mr Pakenham and the other around Kate and drew them towards the house.

'Inside for a glass of champagne, we must celebrate. I had a man and I found a better one and now he is the best man that I've ever found. And come, my Kate, you can leave the boy behind.'

Kate looked down and indeed in all the excitement she had been pushing the poor child, like a hand-cart, before her. She released him and then swallowed an immediate gasp. There on the collar rim of his good Greenaway costume was a stain. More a smudge really, but there nonetheless and obvious, where her sweating palm had mopped itself dry.

He danced with her three times that day. Once in late afternoon, twice towards nightfall. And each time again the smile had shone down on her. It occurred to her that it may have been staged. As though from behind a tripod she had called out 'listen to the dickie-bird' and he had responded with those clean cut lines.

She wasn't certain if she liked him or not. What she did like was the sense of power he seemed to give her, and the sudden popularity she found quite amusing too. All the other girls wanting to be, if not exactly her friend, at least in her company. Even the Currans were chumming it up, each time they whirled past.

'Oh, hullo, Kate, isn't it the most …? Ha ha ha ha. Aren't you enjoying it? I'm having a ripping time, hee hee hee,' and a keen little dart of the eyes towards Mr Pakenham, as they tried to sound as English as he.

Kate smiled to herself and let her steps be led round and round and they danced well together, she could feel that. Both tall and straight-backed, both unafraid of stumbling. Then it was over.

The days passed and Maude's honeymoon with it. By day Kate painted, patting colours into stories on her canvas. By night she dreamed. And in her dreams she wandered through the paintings. On the frill of ocean water she almost drowned, and once inside a cottage door she dropped a cup and cut her hand, the blood trickling beneath the half-door. Next morning she checked the painting. Yes there was the trace of Cardamon all right. Had it just appeared or had she put it there herself? Of course she had. She was getting worse.

Then Maude came home in autumn, her happiness like a disease contaminating them all. And Pat said this and Pat said that and up to Dublin and back again and helping her to furnish the new house and dances and parties and race meetings and Pat saying more and thinking more and invitations to beat the band. (Who were all these people?)

She saw him too, here and there and always nice to her, always taking a dance or two. Seeking her out, rather than her making herself available. And again that feeling came over her as they moved together, tall and sure. Of power, of hidden ability, of having something desired by others.

In wintertime she dreamed she walked through snow. Following a woman whose cloak she thought she recognised, the snow squeaked under her feet and houses and shops darkened at either side of her. The woman walked to the end of the street to a flight of steps which rose and disappeared behind columns. As the woman climbed the steps, trinkets started to fall from beneath her cloak, dotting the snow with their intricate gleam. She seemed to be shedding them unknown to herself and so Kate called out to warn her.

'Madam, Madam, you are losing your treasures.' And then so slowly the hem swung around and two white hands gently turned a hood down into a fold. 'You call me Madam, child,' she laughed, 'when once you called me Mama.'

Then the woman turned and began walking away. 'Where are you going?' Kate called after her. 'Come back. You can't go there. Please stay. I don't want you to go.'

'Come with me then.' The woman called over her shoulder.

'Where? There is nowhere.' Kate began to cry. 'There is nothing. I have not yet finished. It is an unfinished painting.'

And then in early spring the painting stopped. The colours had become too bright, too often. Not the colours on the palette, they were just as they had always been, just whatever way she made them. But colours, in general. So that she could not take the shortest walk without her eyes being tormented by their variety; on the dullest tree bark or half-hidden through the plainest patch of grass; they would not let her be.

Pat Cleary's car had been the end of it for her. 'It's black,' she told herself, ' just plain old black.' But as it slept in wait all day under the drawing-room window it called to her again and again.

See my whites above and my silver higher and beneath my greens and insidious reds. And yellow. Ha, I've caught you out there. That's one you weren't expecting.

And just when she had all that arranged in her head the sun would take a shift in the sky so that with the changing light, the black car became another spectrum altogether.

'How is the painting going?' Maude began, just as the men came into the drawing room for tea. And without waiting for a reply, turned to Mr Pakenham. 'Oh you should see Kate's paintings. She is so clever you know. I'm trying to get her to exhibit, you must help me to persuade –'

'I didn't know you were an artist,' he said, 'I should very much like –'

'Oh I'm hardly that. It's more a hobby really.'

'She's an artist,' Maude insisted. 'I'm trying to cadge a painting for my own. She's got a very nice summery one with miles and miles of poppies. It would look so well in my dining room against that new pale green paper. Come on, Kate, what do you say?'

'Oh Maude, really,' she turned away and walked towards the window, 'you can't choose a painting simply because it matches a wallpaper.'

'You see!' Maude was delighted. 'Isn't that such an artistic thing to say? Why only an artist would come out with something like that. Isn't she marvellous?'

Kate listened to the praise her sister was lathering onto her talents. So obvious what she's at, she thought, I should really be humiliated.

She looked out the window while the talk continued behind her. If she would just take one moment, one glorious moment out of these endless days and walk past them all to the far end of the room to climb, first onto the foot rest, and then onto the arm of the sofa. And jump from there down onto the floor, run across it; a skip onto this window seat and one more onto the sill. Where outstretched arms could push and propel her through this plate-glass window.

She closed her eyes and imagined herself soaring through the air, the applause of shattered glass bursting out around her. Oh the freedom, the one second of pure sweet freedom, out of all these endless …

'Well supposing we were to commission something for the dining room,' Maude was still at it, 'would you then? Kate, are you listening?'

Kate looked down at the black car, the twilight, weighing down on it, had dampened the gleams away and for the moment they had subsided into hints, mere hints. But soon the house lights would be up and silver traces would come to lie across it, and gold and yellow and purple maybe and …

'I've decided to stop painting for a while. I've been overdoing it a bit. I need to take a break.'

'What a pity,' Mr Pakenham said. 'Let us hope the break shall not be too long. Although you may come back to it refreshed. I'm told that often happens.'

'Indeed.' Kate turned around and walked out of the room.

Mid-spring sees him coming more. But to sit in Papa's study, not with her. Some sort of business deal between the two of them with Pat attending the first meeting and then Mr Pakenham completing the task. He stayed to dinner here and there and Kate wishing her brother were old enough to dine. So that she could be distracted. ('Eat up, now. Have you had enough? And pay attention when Papa is speaking to you.') As if she were a child and he her doll.

Just the three of them so and nothing really to say. Papa going over and over the business details they had earlier taken the trouble to discuss in private and Mr Pakenham confirming and reconfirming slowly, patiently as if Papa's confusion was part of the procedure. And always polite never impatient. Kate had never met a man with such a patience.

One night Papa turned to her for help after Mr Pakenham had explained some point or another several times.

'Can you fathom that at all, Kate?' he began. 'Pakenham says I'm to still own the motorbuses after I sell them. How can that be?'

He turned then to Mr Pakenham. 'Katey will understand, never you fear, Pakenham. She's a clever one you know, she'll have us sorted out in no time.'

'Oh Papa, Mr Pakenham doesn't need sorting out,' she found herself blurting out and then Mr Pakenham smiled, his hand moving like a blessing, encouraged her to commence.

At first she thought she hadn't swallowed her food, that it was still stuck in her gullet, everything felt so tight in there, so overstrung. She picked up a glass of wine and took a wallop of it into her mouth. That should wash it down, clear the passage. But it had solidified somehow; turned into rubber. She continued to gulp, pushing it downwards as hard as she could. There now, it was through, now she could try.

She smiled back at Mr Pakenham and then spoke to her father.

'Papa, what Mr Pakenham means is that the people you have sold the motorbuses to have agreed to share with you a precentage of the profit that they make.'

'I know, I know. So he keeps telling me. But why? What in the name of God will they have to do with me once they're sold? And why should these people keep me, a complete stranger, in profit? Are they imbeciles or what? And besides, Kate, I can't understand the price they're paying. After all it's just a few old motorbuses and the worse for wear at that. Can we be sure they're not making some kind of a mistake? Supposing they think the house, the land even, is included in the sale.'

Kate put her cutlery down and began to explain. 'Papa, it's not the old motorbuses as such, it's the right to them.'

'The what?'

'The right to use them or rather the routes that they take. You see you are the sole licence holder. I suppose really you could say, they are paying for the licence. Without the licence a thousand motorbuses would be useless to them. In other words you are doing them a great favour, as you could object to them picking up your passengers.'

'Object? But what good are passengers without the motorbuses? Why in hell should I object?'

'In fact, Papa, you could probably stop them if you wanted to.'

'But this is the thing, Kate, I don't want to stop them.'

'Yes, but they don't know that, Papa.'

'Yes, they do. I've told them so. I've given my word they can fill it up with Fenians for all I care once they're off my property.'

'Papa,' she passed an apologetic glance over to Mr Pakenham. 'We are talking about extremely wealthy people. Who would rather pay and take no risk of bother later on. And they need your routes too, not only for the passengers along them but also to gain access to other places. Places that are growing bigger in population every day. As to the share in profits, well why not? It's not an enormous percentage and you have put a lot into introducing and providing motorbuses to this area. Don't worry about it, Papa, it's nothing that you haven't earned. And anyway if they make a mess of the business you will only be entitled to a percentage of nothing. So Papa, please stop fussing so and sign whatever it is you're going to sign eventually anyway.'

She lowered her eyes and resumed eating just as before. 'Yes. She's right I suppose, Pakenham. You see? I told you Kate would put us right. I shall do what she tells me. What do you think of that then?'

'I think I'm most grateful,' he said and then turned to her. 'Thank you, Kate,' he added.

She nearly fell off the chair. *Kate*. It was the first time he had used her Christian name. That put her in a pickle and no mistake. How on earth was she supposed to address him now?

While the orchestra retuned he asked for her hand. It was during a ten-minute interval at the Paget's ball.

It was after a day at the Punchestown races. They were now in the Royal Hospital, Kilmainham. It was 29 April. It was 1913. After the interval she had four other dances scratched onto her card. None were with him.

These were the details she checked over and over in her mind while his question ticked in the background.

He had asked her as he might ask her anything – politely, clearly – there could be no mistaking the question. She looked away to compose herself; to stop herself from crying out with shock. Across the room she saw Papa, sitting straight-backed in the midst of the full-skirted chaperones: a stem amongst the petals. He kept glancing towards her and seemed very much on edge, as if he was struggling with the demands of inward anxiety and outward sociability.

So, he had been spoken to first.

She searched the room again. This time for Maude's white brocade dress. Yes there it was alone by the door. Waiting for Pat probably. But why hadn't she come over? She could see them clearly. They were in full view. Why stand alone when she could have company?

Because she, too, had been informed. That's why. Whatever about Papa knowing first, but Maude – surely not?

The orchestra began to shuffle and fuss again and all around there was a general fidgeting of gowns and feet. And still she had made no reply.

'Would you like time to consider it?' He bowed his head suddenly towards hers, an urgent movement that made her realise that, yes, he, too, had seen her partner for the next dance starting across the floor. What was his name again? She looked down at her dance-card. Ah yes, Major –? She couldn't quite make out the writing – Ferrety, was it? Had been in the company earlier? Good-humoured man – backed four winners, hadn't he? No wonder then.

'Kate?' She heard his voice, a little anxious.

She blinked her eyes, forcing herself to deal with the situation in hand.

'Well, I have to say,' she began, 'to my mind a proposal is something that would, yes, would … well, require a little longer than five minutes to give it the consideration that –'

'I do apologise,' he said. 'You are quite right of course. Take as long as you –'

He spoke hurriedly, one eye on the figure of the Major meandering slowly through the crowd.

'However – ' she interrupted, 'I can tell you now.'

She looked up at him and saw that he was ready; then keeping her eyes on his face for a few long seconds: 'My answer is …' She reached down for her fan with one hand and with the other clasped a corner of her dress. 'No.'

And lifting herself away from the chair, she finally added before walking away –

'Flattered as I am.'

The dancers had begun to drift again towards the centre of the floor and through them she could see Papa stand and strain his neck. All that was left for him to see was Pakenham and some chap in uniform; two men of equal height standing close together, exchanging words. And splitting again, straying awkwardly to their separate ways.

Outside she wandered for a while upstairs and down. Through the supper room in the officer's gallery, on through the rooms decorated with an *Arabian Nights* theme. She kept her steps brisk, as though she were heading somewhere definite. As if at the other end of her walk there was a rendezvous, someone she didn't wish to keep waiting. She smiled and nodded when she passed a familiar face and sometimes she heard herself speak – 'Yes, wonderful isn't it?' and then a few steps later, 'Thank you so much, I had it sent from London actually,' and a few steps more, 'Papa? Oh he's fine. He's in the main ballroom: why don't you –? He'd be delighted, I'm sure.'

At the end of the corridor she saw a door opening. A soldier and a red-faced girl sneaked out and, checking that no audience was in attendance, hurriedly made their way back to the public rooms. She waited for their steps to slow and their voices to rise to a suitable level of innocence.

Darker inside than anywhere else although the lights from the lawn allowed her to see, at any rate, crates and boxes built up against the walls; from one, a spout of straw grew like hair. Kate stroked it for a moment as if it were. She sat on the window ledge and looked around. Spare chairs, thrown in the centre of the room, locked legs. Through them, she could see, beside the starched stacks of linen, a basket of injured drinking glasses. Some were stemless, others merely cracked at the brim; one or two seemed to have whole bitefuls missing.

Next to this was an arrangement of four plump linen bags lying on their sides; one across, three down. And dented with head and body prints; so this had been where they had lain. The soldier and the red-faced girl. This had been their temporary marital bed.

And now back downstairs were they standing as though nothing had happened, nothing had passed between them. Perhaps at this very moment discussing the next quadrille while each contemplates the consequences of their earlier passion?

Or maybe they've already forgotten it, distracted now by that family group, clenched beside them. A father, a daughter, a son-in-law and an Englishman. Who judging by the controlled and hushed voices are in the middle of a crisis.

And she had almost said yes. It was on the tip of her tongue. What changed her mind? Was it pride? The thought of them all knowing in advance? The thought that for all she knew, at that exact moment, while an answer tried to articulate itself inside her head, while Papa fretted and Maude withdrew into the shadows, Paud at home may well have been pacing the kitchen floor, unable to settle himself for the night until he heard the outcome of what had evidently been the talk of the house for God knows how long? The talk of the county too perhaps. And maybe even the ball itself, by the time Maude would have finished tipping off her flurry of 'exclusive' confidantes.

For all she knew. For all anybody had bothered to tell her.

But no, her pride was not so wounded; grazed perhaps because she had been the last to be consulted. She didn't love him enough for pride to enter into the thing. She didn't love him at all in fact.

And yet in her mind whenever she had dared to rehearse the possibility, she had never said no. She had asked for time – yes, on several occasions. She had even said 'yes' outright another time. Once, she had even taken it as far as 'Yes, my darling' (just to hear what it sounded like). But with all the possibilities, all the variations, an outright, unequivocal 'no' had never been an option.

It was the smile that did it. Or rather the preview of it. Yes that was the truth of it. That's what it was. For when she looked up at him to give him an answer, she saw that he was arranging his face for a smile. Poised for action, it was ready. Ready to slice itself neatly between his cheeks and, unwaveringly, hang there for as long as it took for her to turn away.

And in that one preview, she saw so much. It was as if someone had taken her by the upper arms and, staring hard down into her eyes, had squeezed and shaken her until she was made to understand something she had been refusing to see. But she could see now. Now she saw. She saw him carrying around with him all day his intentions, his proposal, and it having not the slightest effect on his demeanour.

She saw them all, a gay little party, alight at Sallins from the Dublin train and then he, being the calm one, supervise their transfer to Punchestown Racecourse. She saw their open carriage rush up to join a string of others. Above, the talk of the day's racing, the talk of the night's dancing being passed backwards and forwards along the line in haphazard bursts. Below, the uniform beat of trotting horses, holding steady to the ground.

And he knew. All the time he knew. Watching the tremble of motor-bonnet veils in the carriages and motor cars all around them, he knew. Studying the swaying rumps of horses on parade until he was satisfied with his bet, he knew. Sure-handed, plucking bottles from a hamper basket and then passing them out among the ladies, he knew.

He had kept it with him all day long, safe in his inside pocket, kept it there with his smile to use when the time suited him. Well this time he had miscalculated, this time he had been wrong. Preparing a smile that would not be needed.

When she hadn't even called for 'cheese'. When she hadn't even told him to listen for the dickie bird.

Kate reached down and pulled something out of the box of straw by her side. Something that had been catching her eye since entering the room. She held it on her lap where the light from outside could get at it.

It was a statue of an Arabian woman; brown feet bare and chained with delicate gold; legs softly swathed and cuffed at the ankle. The slight blink of an imitation jewel from the clasp of her exposed navel. She turned the statue slightly so that she could study the face. Large and sloping eyes whispered out at her, beneath them a carved drape of voile covered the remainder of her face.

'Ah yes,' she said, 'I was born in the wrong country.'

She stood up and stretched herself, the statue rising up with her arms like a trophy. She was tired, completely fagged. What a long, long day it had been.

Sitting down on the layout of laundry bags, she stretched again. How soft the top bag looked, like a bolster there; already dimpled for her head, how soft it felt too. She lay back into it then, the statue still in her hand and, half-wondering why it had been excluded from the display in the Arabian rooms, she closed her eyes.

*

Samuel was the one to finally find her, curled up on top of a load of old washing bags, with not a care in the world and the whole family sneaking around trying to locate her without making it obvious that they were worried. He looked down at her while discussing with himself whether or not he should wake her or whether he should simply go and look for Mrs Cleary. But thinking then of the crowds outside and in, and where to begin looking for Mrs Cleary looking for Miss Kate, he finally decided there was nothing to do but wake her. He wouldn't touch her. No. That might startle her into screaming the place down and that wouldn't do at all. Perhaps if he were to –?

He began towards the door with a view to leaving the room with a slam, which ought to wake her, and then re-entering with a gentle knock that should prepare her for his intrusion. He took another look at her. Sad little monkey. What was she doing in here anyway? Was she ill? And what had the rest of them so worried? Had something happened? Perhaps she'd had too much punch.

Nothing had been said to him except that he should take the top floors and search without inquiring. Well he'd searched and he'd found and he'd better see about waking her now, he supposed.

A sudden frantic gasp told him that would no longer be necessary.

'It's only me, Miss Kate – Sam. I've been sent to fetch you, Miss. You must have dozed off.'

Samuel removed his hat and stepped backwards.

'Oh yes, Sam. Of course, yes.' She was sitting up now, her hands instinctively rearranging hair and gown.

'I'll just go and tell Mrs Cleary I've found you, Miss.' He made to walk away.

'No! No, Sam, please. I mean couldn't you? Please. What I mean is –'

Samuel stopped and looked at her. What was she saying? She was speaking very quickly. And he sometimes had difficulty getting the full grasp of … *what* was she saying?

'I'm sorry, Miss?'

'Sam. I would really appreciate it if you didn't tell my sister I was here.' This time she spoke carefully, taking one word at a time.

'Well, Miss, I have to tell you – she is worried. To leave you here and say nothing … well I just couldn't do that, I'm sorry.'

'No Sam, I don't mean that. You could –' she began.

'Yes, Miss?'

'How far are we from Maude's house, Sam?'

'Only down the road really.'

'Well couldn't you take me there?'

'Without saying anything to the others, do you mean?'

'You could come straight back for them?'

Samuel stayed silent for a while not knowing which way to look. Now and then he caught her hopeful eye and turned away again.

Finally he spoke. 'Tell you what, Miss. I'd be willing to put you in the motor and take you home. But first I'll have to find Mr Cleary and explain to him. I'll tell how you're all right but not feeling too well and would rather be alone and if he could pass on the message to Mrs Cleary that you'd be grateful.'

Kate made no reply. He could sense her disappointment, and after a moment came back with another possibility.

'Look, the linkman's a friend of mine, I suppose I could – well, it depends on how busy he is of course. But if he gets a couple of minutes between calls I could give him the message to pass on, I suppose. Ask him to give us five minutes' grace before telling Mr Cleary. Though what he'll make of it …'

There was silence for a moment before he concluded: 'I'm afraid that's really the best I can do, Miss.'

'Oh yes, Sam, that's fine. And thank you.'

'Miss.' He held out his hand and she took it, pulling herself up onto her feet again. Then he opened the door and peeped outside. They sneaked out into the light.

'Oh Sam,' she said suddenly. 'Could you wait here? I've forgotten something, I'll be back in a minute.'

Samuel nodded and slowly started to walk back down along the corridor.

He could hear outside the long low whistle of the linkman calling out towards the rows of mixed carriages; linking them to their rightful passengers now waiting in groups to leave. They would have to hurry. Another half an hour and he would be too busy to oblige.

It only took Kate a minute before she was back by his side. Samuel looked down at her hand.

'A doll, Miss Kate?' he asked. 'I'd have thought you'd outgrown such things by now.'

'Oh Sam, it's not a doll, more a statue, a memento.' She held it up for him to see.

'Very exotic. Where did you get it?' he asked.

'It was a gift.'

Like two old friends then they walked, along the corridor taking them to the back stairs and the quadrangle outside, and chatting of this and that; the orchestra, the starry night, the day's racing gone by.

*

And she had intended going home to Wicklow, she really had. Settling herself the next day on the first morning train, she never meant to do otherwise. She thought about the two letters she had left on the hall table; one addressed to Papa, the other to Maude. She thought about writing them the night before, having to wait until silence finally took over house, until Maude stopped tapping at her door – 'Kate, Kate dear, are you asleep?' For twice she had come and twice had left disappointed.

The train relieved itself from the platform, leaving a gash where once it had stood. Through its window she saw Sam, his eyes flickering until he found her. They looked at each other for the few seconds that it was possible to do so. Neither waved, neither smiled. No acknowledgement of any sort was expressed.

Kate caught the final tip of his elbow before he shifted completely from sight and pulling off her gloves, slow finger by slow finger, hoped she hadn't gotten him into any trouble. Well, *too* much trouble at any rate, for she knew well Maude would give him hell. ('What do you *mean* you took her to the early train? Why didn't you wake us?')

The train began to loosen out as it increased its speed over the bridge, cutting through rooftops, sliding right into the city sky, and she began to realise; yes it was likely, no – more than likely – certain, in fact, one could nearly be positive, as soon as Maude realised what had happened she would make Samuel take out the motor car again and drive her to Wicklow. Pat would probably have to come along and Papa would be forced to break his Dublin appointments. Indeed if there were any delay at all, no motor bus or hackney available for any length of time, there could very well be a welcoming committee waiting on the steps for her. Oh horror of horrors, was she never to have peace?

By Sandymount strand she re-read the letters in her head. 'My dear Maude, I'm sorry but I'm not staying in Dublin after all. Please don't worry about me; I just want to spend a few days on my own. I shall come back for the children's charity concert next week. Yours, Kate.'

'My dear Papa' was much the same except for it made no mention of the concert and apologised for leaving without him.

The stations seemed to come and go, and still she could not think what to do. The restlessness that had started up with the first snail-line of distant ocean was growing. She moved to the seat opposite and now she could see what was behind her.

I cannot go back. I cannot go forward. I cannot face the questions, the concern. I cannot. In Kingstown the sea had widened into a band of baby blue; a bounce of careless yachts and boats. The mail boat. Yes. That's what she could do. She could get the mailboat and go to London. Look for a position, never come back. Why not? Why not?

Over shaky fingers she stretched her gloves and half-stood before sitting down again. If more than three people pass to alight then I'll take it as a sign, and London it will be.

Five people passed and then a sixth and still she sat, till the whistle blew and the train moved off.

Once more the gloves came off and the empty fingers were pulled and stretched and finally laid to rest.

How many miles from Dublin to Wicklow town? How many miles an hour goes a train? A motor car? High walls tucked her in now, protecting her from any outside views. Sandycove then and still she could not calculate. If a train ... if a train travels thirty-five miles an hour and the journey to Wicklow is how many hours and then on to Rathdrum, add another half? No? Three-quarters ... Oh I don't know. I don't know. If a train ...

It's hopeless. I haven't a hope; they'll beat me to it. Even if I were to call on Mr Carton, beg him to take me at once, say I'm not feeling well – even then they'll probably be there before me.

'My dear Maude,' she thought again down Dalkey way. 'My dear ...'

And a sudden burst of sea and cliffs and houses perched from a terrace made her forget her troubles just as long as it took for the walls to rise again. Locking her in, making her think.

And County Wicklow now upon them. But in a motor they would travel without interruption, no stops. No waiting each time for the blow of a whistle or the loading and reloading of parcel and passenger. Of course they would be much quicker. And even if she did get there before them. What of it? They would still get to her. They would still find her. There was nowhere to hide. 'My dear Papa, My dear Papa ...' The buckled houses now, all roof and no body; we must be coming into Bray. Yes, here we are. The glance of sea and promenade trying to catch her eye through the gaps between taller houses. She moved back to her original seat.

The train came into Bray station and along its body, a mimicry of door-slams. A railway uniform passed her window carrying boxes and began to load upwards to a pair of hands reaching down. Kate got up to the window and twisted her head to see. No use. She released a clasp and the window collapsed and disappeared down into the door. She stuck her head through. Now. The uniforms were working from a stack of boxes over by the wall. Why that would take all day!

She sat down again. All right, that's it. I've had just about enough. Five minutes and if we haven't moved by then, I'm off. The International Hotel will do nicely. I'd hardly be recognised? Yes that's what I'll do. Five minutes …

And ten minutes later she was still sitting there and fifteen minutes later the Sugarloaf mountain was soft and purple and well deserving of its title. And her head hung out the window until a determined tunnel told it otherwise. She sat down again. Yes she had made the right decision, no doubt. Too many people by far in Bray. Why almost everyone she knew, at some time or another. Yes, best avoid it altogether. And besides Papa would be so worried if he didn't find her at home.

And it came to her then, with Bray Head passed. Of course. She hadn't actually said that she was going home. She hadn't mentioned where she was going at all in fact.

She crossed the carriage to the seaward window; plush hills outside, easy on the foot. A row of boats, bottoms up, curving into the bed of the alcove. And grey sea slapping grey stones darker. Yes.

This time she didn't bother with the gloves. This time, she just stuffed them into her pocket and swung her travelling bag down into her arms.

*

It was in this room of the Grand Hotel in Greystones that she first made friends with the sea. In this room with its long french windows opening out like wings. And on this balcony, with wooden rails to hug her in, that the friendship grew. With each day, a longer chat, with each night another confidence.

Downstairs they called her Madame de Laisse and asked no questions. The first time the manager addressed her he spoke in French. Her French being better than his, she remained un-discovered. She complimented him on his accent and he shivered with delight.

The first night she dined downstairs at a table by the window. Poached salmon and bald potatoes. She had ice-cream afterwards and something else beforehand, but for the life of her she couldn't remember what it was. She remembered the salmon, though, because the manager had sent a message to recommend it, on a fold of hotel stationery. The waiter had nearly fallen onto her lap in an effort to read over her shoulder. '*Puis je recommender la saumone Madame, s'il vous plait. C'est une specialite de la maison. Merci Madame.*'

'Please,' she looked up at the waiter, indicating with her hand that she would like a pen.

'A pen? Is it, Madam, a pen?'

'*Oui, oui*, apen.'

Again she could feel him strain behind her as she wrote her reply to the manager. '*Bien sur, Monsieur, je serais ravie de l'essayer.*'

She folded the paper carefully and handed it to the waiter. 'Please to …' she pointed vaguely outside.

'To? Oh yes, Madam, certainly Madam.'

That meal her mouth saw more of the napkin than any piece of cutlery. Up and down it went blotting the grin from her face. When had she ever had such fun? She couldn't remember that either.

Her glass was refilled several times (the waiter being familiar with the habits of these foreign women). *Merci*, she said, each time a little giddier.

By the end of the meal she had forgotten to regret not having had the foresight to accompany herself with a book – something to hide behind, to confirm her indifference towards her fellow diners. She had forgotten also her resolve to take one with her the following night, for by now, what had started upstairs as a nodding acquaintance had developed into something else. She had had a most pleasant evening conversing through the window to the sea at the end of the long green lawn. And she would never be so rude as to ignore it, now they had become such friends.

For the next three days she scarcely spoke an outward word, though inside every thought that had ever crossed her mind had been recalled to give account. There was only silence inside her whenever she slept, which was often, for despite being a late riser, an afternoon siesta and an early night quickly established themselves as part of her routine. When she went walking she kept to the coastal road, winding her steps around with it so that she might never lose sight of the ocean, so that she always had its company.

Whenever she had to wander away from it to make a purchase in the village, she made her way back to report on whatever she had seen: the railway bridge with the lily sprouts beneath; the afternoon tea at an inland establishment; the woman in the chemist shop that had asked her where she was staying, stretching each word out to eternity so as to accommodate a visiting foreigner.

She had decided against dining downstairs again, the manager being a little too eager to greet her. And the rest of the staff too, hovering about her like wasps. She overheard the little chambermaid ask the housekeeper: 'Do they all look like that in France?' And felt sorry for the reprimand the poor child fell under. She was only asking after all – how was she supposed to know? She spoke to the manager, explaining that from now on she would prefer a tray in her room. *Naturellement* he understood.

On the fourth day she was ready to leave. When she settled her bill the manager kissed her hand and said (in French of course) that he hoped he would see her again.

Her tips were generous and the housekeeper divided them out in the room which had been hers. 'You can always tell the continentals,' she said, 'by the cut of their clothes,' and then looking behind her towards the open door, whispered wisely, 'Far superior.'

'Yes,' said the little chambermaid, fingering her half crown and frowning at the empty space above the bed where she was sure there had been a painting of the view outside.

'Yes,' she agreed then, 'probably buys them in Paris.' And smartening herself up, she continued to strip the bed, deciding that it must have been her imagination. That there had been nothing there after all.

SEVEN

Easter Monday night and Ballyboggan safe and sound, the sweat scraped off his coat and a hero's rest now on new crisp straw. And doubtless unaware that winning the Grand National meant more than just being first past the post, its effects going way beyond that.

Leaving aside the negative aspects (all those poor buggers whose day had been spoilt, cycling home with not a tosser) and concentrating on the brighter, the opened possibilities for certain discerning young turf-followers who had had the foresight to place a hand in Algie the stage-manager's hat in such a way that the slip of paper with all those lovely syllables had just crept up into his fingers and curled there, crying 'Papa! Papa!' The discerning young turf-follower (you could hardly say turf-goer, not yet, although maybe next week?) with pocket-book lined, standing now before those opened possibilities and saying, which one, which one am I brave enough to walk through?

Easter Monday night and bumper houses both times with people turned away from the doors – 'Though you could have fit a few more onto the grin on Masterson's face, from ear to ear, that pleased,' said Algie, scampering around the curtains and appearing now and then at intervals like a seaside puppet, to check all was in order, props and cast.

Easter Monday night when Masterson had called him 'Son' and told him he was doing just about as all right as anyone could do without actually singing. And his feet had felt so momentarily light that he couldn't even consider the stairs and had taken the banister sidesaddle, to land clean and even before floating through the stage door out to Sycamore Street.

And always intending to walk, like a normal person. A little better dressed than some perhaps. But walking just the same, just like anybody else. Even seeing his footsteps in advance – oh a little lighter than most, but footsteps walking just the same.

And the route too, like an opened map across a table, that clear: the upward left-hand glide and sweep, the quick nudge right with Christ Church sleeping on its side. And then straightening out again into High Street, where Cleary's bottle green-glassed stout under the supervisory eye of 'Pat the busy-bee-in-law'. Bottles for horses to draw north or south or wherever it is that Cleary's stouted bottles eventually find themselves. There would be a road to cross at this point before narrowing into Francis Street.

And glancing goodbye to Cornmarket about to join Thomas Street on its way out west. And quite a sharp turn left too, which always is temptation, the sharper the turn the greater so and especially the left one, when by nature right wants to compensate and steer it round: bang bang abang.

Problems yes, but not insurmountable to him, with his feet made of air.

And straight on now through the St Nicholases, Without from Within. Skip over Dean Street and then take the length of New into Clanbrassil, all in his stride. One more left turn and another little bit to go until he was standing before the familiar door and no hurry yet. Not even yet.

There would still be time to wonder how such a little latchkey could manage such a heavy panelled door. When a grown man would be wasting his time, wasting his strength. A grown man depending on something small enough to get lost in his pocket, so that he could sleep in his own bed of a night.

Yes, he could see that far in front of him and further on then even to the other side of the door and the hallway shaky with its feeble night light. Here he would slowly part company with his greatcoat; a last little shake here, a deft brush of the hand. He seldom shed himself, yet seemed to gather other dustings, other moultings from God knows where, despite the fact that he would have had taken the usual precautions before leaving the theatre with the big stiff mahogany brush from wardrobes. Always available to him these days now that he was doing so well and never bawled out of it any more. A little blow then skimmed across the top of his hat. And all could be settled on their rightful wooden coat-hooks – almost obscene there protruding from the hallstand.

The stairs would come next. And still nice and easy. Easy enough to notice things, like the thoroughness or not of that new servant girl. This was not so much to satisfy any potential disapproval on his part, but rather to allow a way to get to know her, to familiarise himself with her little ways.

Yes, there would be time for all this. And more. Even that nightly question that he found himself repeating as he turned the doorknob to the east. Did he now, at this moment, regret taking lodgings instead of accepting his sisters' invitations, either one?

And as much as he would have liked to solve the problem of the whereabouts of Mrs Gunne's kitchen, winding himself downwards on back stairs (for smells and clatters told him this was the general direction) to make himself something hot to drink; or much as he would have liked to be in a position to intrude upon a household for a nocturnal treat – either by pulling on the tapestry cord that activated a puff-faced servant into motion (as would be the case in the Pakenham household) or by accepting an anxious older sister's offer of servitude despite the hour (as would be the case in the Cleary household): yes, Maude would wait three nightfalls for an opportunity to mother him – he had to answer himself in truth. No, no regrets.

Yes, Easter Monday night. And a fellow could resist most things. Most splashes, slams, swishes, squeals, or even clippidy-clops. Even if all these things should come together in one swift and highly evocative arrangement. But if the same fellow's got the happiest heart he's ever had and the fullest wallet he's ever likely to have – well things could get a little complicated.

And he got as far as Dame Street, turning out of Sycamore. And his feet crossed the tram lines, without any extravagance, just one step forward and one step following at a gently walking pace. And all the time his route mapped out inside his head down to the very last detail when his bedroom door would click shut under his careful hand.

And he came along by City Hall as normal as you like with just the slightest glance allowed to climb the stepping stairs that led to its big majestic door. Nothing untoward, nothing strange; just a well-dressed young man strolling home, no less.

And then it happened. Over there. At his right-hand side. Probably at the top of Parliament Street (for it couldn't have been much further, every sound was heard so clearly). And although he didn't look, not for one second, he could identify the exact activity if he wished. Just by the sound that hit him as quickly, as mercilessly as a virus: a woman alights from a carriage with a whisper of gown. Her foot misjudges and slaps a fat puddle where they both can feel it. She squeals. The door bangs behind her. The driver clicks. And then … oh then … Clip clip clop. Clop, clippidy clop.

And all this bursting into the night from the time it took him to walk from the beginning of the hall's steps to their centre point. And even though the woman, the driver and horses went their separate ways, leaving nothing but the puddle stunned into silence, their music was left behind.

And over and over, the beat repeated itself in his head going all the way down to feet, greedy to mimic and imitate, eager to show these sounds how they might improve themselves with a little more thought, a little more grace, a little more time.

Down there, as from the bottom of his eye, he noted the speed of his shoes teasing the City Hall steps time and time again without ever actually completing ascent. And up there as the corner of his eye noted a right hand and a right foot, both of which appeared to be his, pushing themselves simultaneously off a wall, as if it were the trampolino Algie kept in the cellar 'in case of acrobats'. With speed and sound egging each other on, till he was beating the life out of his feet against anything that would take them.

Was it there between the up and the down? There that he felt a twist, a contortion of a sort; a pain even? And if it was just there, just then: where were the mechanics? Why did they not even cross his mind?

Backstage the capstan had been pushed, a wheel was shifting about to turn, the scene about to lift. Behind it another one was waiting.

II

THE WAR YEARS

EIGHT

Mrs Gunne's granddaughter was a particularly ugly child. So much so that Greta had to keep coming back into the front parlour for another look. This was misconstrued as admiration, a mistake that, as it happened, was to work to Greta's advantage – for Mrs Gunne's granddaughter was finally to provide the means of escape for which she had been searching since first entering the household.

The child's name was Beatrix. Beatrix Bumbury. A name which suited her very well, Greta decided on reflection. You couldn't really call such a child anything else.

She was almost two years old, certainly well past the sitting-up stage, and could walk, although this was not an option she often preferred. She was not a 'handful' as Greta knew other children of this age to be: she would sit for hours in the corner on the floor or propped up in her perambulator without showing any inclination to do other- wise. Indeed her only activities seemed to be eating and orchestrating a surge of bubbles from her raw little mouth. There was a sound to accompany this last pastime which seemed to come from deep down in the child's chest. This sound consisted in the main of one ever- lasting, elongated 'eeee' with the occasional pause for breath and was in any case designed to send all but the deaf off their heads.

Mrs Gunne proved to be a most affectionate grandmother, plying the child with endless sugary titbits and emitting loud exclamations of astonishment and admiration any time she came within sight of her.

On the first morning of her arrival Greta walked into the parlour and found the baby amongst a profusion of mauve and pink frillies on top of which her pale flaccid head seemed to have been abandoned. She had to rearrange the gasp that escaped from her mouth to make it sound like one of delight rather than horror.

'Can you believe the cuteness of her, Greta, in that outfit?'

'No indeed I can't, Ma'am.'

'Have you ever seen anything like as nice?'

'No indeed, Ma'am, I have never seen anything quite like her.'

'Do you hear that? My dear sweet baby, Greta thinks you're a picture. How I adore you. Don't I just adore her, Greta?'

'You most certainly do.'

'See even Greta knows how much I adore you.'

Indeed there was no length Mrs Gunne wouldn't go to to express her love of this baby. However, any washing, feeding, dressing or night-time attendance was seen to by either Francie or Greta.

Mrs Gunne had agreed to take care of the baby for ten days, while her daughter was in Kent accompanying her husband on leave. Her daughter then planned to continue on to London to do some shopping and to spend some time with her husband's family. Ten days. And by the afternoon of the first day it was clear that Mrs Gunne was already finding her nerves straining at the seams.

There had been the young gentleman's accident of course. And that didn't help in the least. Him laid up in hospital with his leg in a sling and that sister of his drawing inferences. 'Did it happen in the house? In *my* house! How *dare* she? Just because her husband has a few measly shillings she thinks she can ... Well!' As far as Mrs Gunne was concerned all very well having the shillings, but what good, without the breeding?

It would be at this point that she would stretch her hand out graciously towards the baby. For it had to be said Mrs Gunne's granddaughter had a father who was a captain. He in turn had a mother who came from a family in possession of two surnames, connected each to each by a most distinguished hyphen.

During those late spring days, there were endless complaints brought on by the straining nerves that had come to dominate the household. Mrs Gunne had started to confide all to Greta, since she had been helping her to wear her hair more in keeping with her position. That is, she managed, with the aid of a transformation or *en-tout-cas* as Mrs Gunne preferred to call it, to exaggerate Mrs Gunne's hair into a pile that coincidentally resembled the coiffure of her son-in-law's dear mother. Greta had also begun to advise her on dress, especially when a visit to the hospital was about to take place. These visits occurred now on a daily basis and were sometimes followed by an invitation to tea at Mrs Cleary's house, which gave Mrs Gunne ample opportunity to keep Maude Cleary informed of the captain, his hyphenated mother and the dear sweet baby girl left in her care.

On her return, she detailed each fault and flounder of Maude to include every stitch she wore, which Maude could never seem to get right. On an evening when Mrs Gunne had opted to be 'informal' Maude had arrived on her way to a reception. 'Who does that one think she is putting on the swank in a *hospital* with herself decked out like a Christmas tree!'

On the following day when Mrs Gunne had sworn not to be outdressed Maude had had the effrontery to arrive 'informal'. 'Having *walked* to the hospital, if you please. Like a parlour maid she was. Too plain by far. At her age she ought to be making more of an effort. Not less.'

She also gave out about Pat Cleary. 'Oh I'm not so keen on that fellow at all. Too sweet to be wholesome by far. Bit of a dash-the-lad, if you ask me.'

Even Pakenham failed to go unnoticed. 'The sour old face of him, as if there was a smell off of one of us. Hasn't a word to throw to a dog.'

She even gave out about them collectively. 'The poor boy doesn't want them there, you know, between yourself and myself. Oh no. He never opens his mouth when they're there. Has no time for them whatsoever. Why before the accident he never even visited their houses. Can you imagine – never visited his own sisters? I'm telling you. How else do you think he's never set eyes on you, Greta? Doesn't go near them and wouldn't neither if he could get up and walk away from them. Such a shower. Who can blame him? You'd want to see his little face light up when he sees me walk through the door.'

Mrs Gunne mentioned everyone. And everyone in detail. Not once, however, did she mention Kate.

Neither did Greta dare to ask. Not yet. It hadn't taken her long to be promoted from the back stairs to the upstairs, acting now as a lady's maid to a lady who scarcely seemed to notice this graduation. For it had been a gradual, if speedy process, sparked off with little discreet tips on appearance. In no time at all she was practically running the household. Mrs Gunne couldn't take enough advice from Greta; it became an appetite with her, which increased its voracity when she learned that Greta had worked in London before joining Mrs Pakenham. In a household in Mayfair, no less, as a young ladies' maid, if you don't mind. And that these young ladies as well as having a town house had a country house, a chauffeur and their very own hunting horses, possessed – as if there wasn't enough evidence already of the fineness of their breeding – two surnames apiece. Strung together by a hyphen. 'Well, isn't it a small world indeed?' Mrs Gunne said, beside herself with happiness.

After a few days when Mrs Gunne was feeling better, the baby having settled down nicely, and her hair looking very smart indeed, she began to take stock of the situation. Francie now wore a cap and had ceased calling her Missus every two seconds. Now it was Ma'am with the occasional little curtsy. She was like a different person, having taken to her new position as parlour maid surprisingly well. Mrs Gunne was pleased with her progress. Although for a while she had found the new rule of knocking only on the upstairs rooms a little startling. For Greta had told her that was how things were done in London and if anyone should know … Nonetheless for a couple of days there was, 'Oh good God almighty, Francie, you're after puttin' the heart crossways in me,' every time another downstairs door was burst open by a gleeful Francie. Still as Greta said, 'One shouldn't be doing anything downstairs anyway that needs to be interrupted with a warning.' And indeed one should not.

Mrs Gunne took out a piece of paper from the drawer of the what-not, resolving as she did so to try to sell that dreadful piece of furniture and wondering just what it was that had possessed her to buy it in the first place. She sat down and started to do her accounts. There was a small drop in income with the young lad in hospital and there was the extra expense of the new kitchen maid. For what with serving Greta and herself with dinner and afternoon tea, Francie couldn't very well be expected to see to the cleaning and scrubbing as well. They were well down on last month, but no matter. She had made up her mind and that was that. She would send a telegram to her daughter urging her to invite her mother-in-law on a return visit.

She began to dip mentally into the money her husband had left her. A new wardrobe would be necessary, a spring wardrobe. For, as she had said only this morning to Greta, what was the point in having your money fattening itself up if you couldn't have a new spring wardrobe? Or was it Greta who had said it to her? Well no matter which, the fact remained. A new wardrobe would be necessary. The back parlour would have to be decorated and renamed the dining room; the same must go for the front parlour which now could call itself the drawing room. A dinner party would have to be organised. Greta could advise her on that. Which reminded her – Greta? Well that was a problem that could keep for the moment. Until Twinkle-toes got out of hospital, at any rate, for you could be sure that after that there would be an invasion of relatives and Greta would most certainly be discovered.

In the meantime though, as long as she was careful ... Although it might be wise to start to refer to her as something else, stop using the name Greta altogether, just in case, as a precaution like. Now what would be –? Ah yes – what about Gray, Mrs Gray. Ideal. She could tell Greta it was Pakenham's idea. She would start on Francie straight away, get her into the habit, so that if anything should slip – well, who *was* Mrs Gray anyway? Only Mrs Gunne's personal maid. And why shouldn't she have one? Indeed. There should be no reason not to hang on to the girl for another while yet. Why it would be cruel to do otherwise and the poor thing so happy since she came here. After all her misfortunes too, why put her through more?

Still if Pakenham were ever to find out that his instructions had been disobeyed. Mrs Gunne reached into the back of the whatnot and drew out a large envelope. She peeped inside, hesitated and then began fingering the contents. Good Lord, was that all that was left? There had been enough there for Greta's passage to England, a month's salary in lieu – plus her own expenses for all her trouble. Well you wouldn't feel it going and no mistake.

Five days he had said Greta was to stay, not one minute more. She was to be out of the country by the time he and Kate had returned from London. Supposing he was to find out that when it came to it Mrs Gunne had simply been unable to let Greta go? Or supposing *Greta* was to get wise to the facts? Realise that instead of being trapped in this house she could be swanning around London with a few bob in her pocket. Not that she should mind really and her living these past weeks in the lap of it. Though just the same, better if she didn't find out.

Mrs Gunne drew the last two banknotes out of the envelope. Then a smaller envelope – the reference that she was to have handed over to Greta on the day of her departure. Supposing she should find it? Mrs Gunne chewed her bottom lip and tapped her fingers for a moment in a cavalry march on top of the whatnot. Yes supposing now …

'Oh supposin' supposin',' she sang to herself impatiently then and rolled the envelopes into a ball which she popped daintily into the fire grate behind her. She folded the banknotes over carefully and placed them in her housekeeping pouch.

Now where was I? What else? Redecoration of the spare room? No, too small in any case. She would move out of her own room, which was large enough for any mother-in-law and any amount of luggage. And what if she brought a lady's maid with her? Yes she could put Greta into the young fella's room and shove the maid into Greta's room. There, all eventualities covered. Except a motor car. Good Lord, where would she get a motor car? Perhaps dear kind Pat? But it was possible the mother-in-law would take her own car across. People like that often did. And then there would be no need to ingratiate oneself with those Clearys. Still, they would have to be invited to the dinner party. Oh yes. Oh yes, indeed they would.

NINE

Greta pushed the perambulator up the South Circular Road and cursed. First she cursed Maude and then she cursed Kate. She cursed that Lottie one as well. And every suffragette that had ever existed. Past, present and to come. Why couldn't they have just left her alone? What harm had she been doing? For years she had been hard at it, years of bowing and scraping, learning and copying. And watching. Always watching for some little crack of light to squeeze herself through. She thought at last she had found a resting place; at last she could just relax, enjoy life and good fortune. Forget about improvement, as there was nothing left to improve … And then just like that and through no fault or desire of her own, the quest had to start all over again. She had happened to agree with something somebody had said, something she hadn't even been paying much attention to. And before she knew where she was she had been pushed right into the middle of another obstacle course of 'self-betterment'.

It was all their stupid idea. She thought she was in paradise as it was. She never wanted to be a clerk, working long hours and never meeting anyone. Never getting out or wearing nice clothes. It had been Kate's notion really. Said she hated Greta being a lady's maid, wanted her to be an equal. Wanted her to have – what did she call it again? Ah yes, the dignity of work. Oh for God's sake. What do these women know about the dignity of work? Sitting on their frilly backsides all their privileged lives and then just because they become bored with themselves and their lot, decide that they'll play at something else. But note that nothing was done to improve their own lives. Oh no, by God! It was her life they decided to change instead. Her life. That was already perfect, thank you very much indeed for asking. And now what? What was she supposed to do now? Spend the rest of her life walking up and down the South Circular Road in the vain hope that Kate might pass by?

At least the ban on Stephen's Green had been lifted since that queer fish had broken his ankle playing hopscotch or whatever in the name of God he was up to on the steps of City Hall. Now that it was accepted that his sisters would be more likely to spend the afternoon at the hospital than strolling through the Green, she was at least allowed that far. But no further, really. With the fat turnip instructing and reminding her and only agreeing to let her cross the door at all so that the baby could get out: 'Greta dear, avoid Grafton and all its environs; you never know. And come to think of it – anywhere near High Street might be a mistake. I know I can trust you not to attempt a step in the Kilmainham direction … and you would have more sense than to direct yourself anywhere near your aunt's shop or the squares, dear. Forget about the squares. Oh and Greta – otherwise feel free and enjoy your walk. Excluding the canal of course; too open. And I don't have to remind you – Sackville Street and all that belongs to it … Make sure darling Beatrix inhales all she can, for you know me, a divil for the fresh air I don't mind telling you.'

And so that was it. The South Circular only as far as Dolphin's Barn and back again. And Stephen's Green, as long as she flew there, seeing as most routes were prohibited. Small chance then of ever bumping into Kate. For she daren't go to the house. He could be there. And who else? Where else could she go? Maude's house? No. Supposing Kate has shown her the letter? Seeing it in her handwriting she would believe everything. Maude would refuse to see her. Mr Cleary maybe? He never seemed to mind about anything. But where would you find him? The office? The public house? The bottlery? And even if you could find him, there would be the risk of Pakenham walking in at any time. Oh how could she have gotten herself into this situation? A situation which, hateful as it was, hadn't even got the decency to be permanent. For as soon as Pakenham decided, she would be thrown out to the dogs. To start all over. To start all over again. Oh no. The very thought of it was to be avoided. The very thought of it was making her feel sick.

But she sat down on a bench and, one hand bouncing down on the handlebar of the perambulator, thought about it. Meat only for father or only on Sundays when the juice from a fawn's pluck would run pink on the plate. Father said the men from the shooting-party gave them in gratitude, that and the two dead rabbits swinging by the ears from his bloody hands. And hip hip hurrah, Christmas had come early.

On her own hands too, Saturday traces would remain. Lines ensconced with blacklead that refused to go. Blacklead used to treat the stove, whose care was her job. And it would look well all right, sitting there like Queen Victoria, the shine of its fender discreet again the black, like a bright collar on a sombre dress. And despite the scrubbing the evening before in the tin bath, bits of it, indelible, having sneaked into creases on her hands, on her arms, to couch there like stowaways. You'd have to settle for a certain amount of stains in the end. Even if you were allowed to use any more soapcake, your hands would be too raw anyway from the emery-board used on the fender and could hardly continue.

That's what the beginning meant to Greta, raw hands and no meat. And that was just the one place she had no intention of going back to. Not again. Not this time. She had gone too far this time.

There were other times of course when it might have been possible to take a couple of steps backwards, after Aunt Florence's perhaps, the Gresham too, even after London. For up to then it would have been a small movement. And like a painting then viewed from a measured distance, better savoured, better appreciated. Too late now for that sort of thing.

Kate had treated her too well. Before Kate she had always shifted with the dividing line. That cut between 'your position and mine'. That slid and wriggled depending on the mood of whoever it was you were inferior to at the time. And Greta could move with it, nimble-footed, high stepping, she could even anticipate its speed. No matter how quickly it might swing. No matter how fast the wrist that flicked it. Kate had stopped all that. With her she could be a wallflower. Dancing only if she liked, jumping only when she chose. From the first Kate had made her feel on par and then – what then?

'I want you to be my equal,' Kate had urged. 'Equal? Equal?' she had felt like saying, but that would be going backwards. Six months ago, yes, I was your equal – but I don't dance backwards any more. It wasn't that she felt ungrateful exactly. Now it was a question of feeling more – entitled to her many privileges.

Among which she hadn't counted German lessons …

She sighed, stood up and sighed again. The baby was awake. Best move on. Get the walk over with.

What did she care about it? German. She couldn't care less if she never spoke a word of it. What had Huns got to do with her? Unless she was going to become a spy – I suppose that's what they'll be saying next.

And then locking her into a room with a foreign man. Well really what did they expect? She was only human after all. Locking her up with a … *Der Mann, die Frau.* Him with his musician's hands.

She cursed men then, leaning in towards the child and pulling out from behind the pillow a piece of linen which she dabbed queasily over the small leaking mouth. 'Oh shut up,' she said, her voice cavernous, lingering in the hood of the perambulator.

Every time she got on her feet one of them came along to knock her back off them again. First that Groom of the Chambers in Hafton House, then that other one. And as for –

Well that was an end to them. Never again. She was done with men for once and for all. If she never saw another one it would be soon enough.

She pushed the handlebar determinedly away from her, as though the perambulator was full of them, leering men, each one bursting with his own dishonourable intention.

That's one thing the suffies are right about. Men. All after the one thing. Say anything to get their way. And who needs them?

She reached out and pulled the handlebar back towards her again.

And cutting across Clanbrassil Street, she made sure to make no right-hand glances. That's where he'd been staying, down there somewhere, the filthy get. Taking advantage of me like that. Wouldn't you think a man with a name out of the Bible would be too holy for that sort of thing? And where was he now, for all his trouble? In prison? Or deported? Good enough for him after the way he … Silent black-eyed creature.

'Disgusting he was.' She poked her head in towards the baby, 'Like that mauve on you.' The baby squirted a row of bubbles out of her mouth and began to emit her special sound.

Greta straightened her self up, fumbled under the mattress and found a brown paper bag. She pulled a broken biscuit out and handed it in. 'Here,' she said. 'Stuff that into your face for a while, so I can have a bit of peace.'

In the distance she saw a brace of soldiers walking towards her. You'd be sick of the sight of khaki, you really would. Absolutely sick of it. Though it suits some of them very well. That one on the inside for instance carries it well.

Oh yes – she remembered now. There was that corporal too. Another selfish, heartless – and an Englishman at that. No morals.

Expect all women to be as fast as their own. And after Aunt Cath inviting them into her home too. Poor boys, she'd said, must be homesick. Bottles of stout and brown fruity cake. And singing for them at the piano: 'Goodbye, Dolly Gray' and 'Two Little Girls in Blue'.

As it happened she'd been wearing blue herself that night. 'Where's the other one?' he'd asked.

'The other what?' she'd asked back.

'The other little girl in blue.'

'I'm no little girl,' she said.

'I can see you ain't,' he said then, slow as molasses. Well no more. That's an end of them. I'll get out of this mess and it'll be the last I can tell you that. And the next man I look sideways at will be one with a ring for me finger and a feather for me nest.

Their paths were about to cross – the soldiers and the perambulator. She knew they were looking at her. Could feel their eyes … Well the nerve. She could be a married woman for all they know. This could be her baby (God forbid!). She could really be Mrs Gray.

She turned her head slightly and looked up at the clock on top of the barracks across the road. Then slowing down a little (goodness was that the time?) so that she could hear their soldiers' bootsteps.

'I shall tell your mother what a good little girl you've been,' she blurted suddenly at the baby, dipping her head in towards the child. So unexpected it was, so loud, that from inside the perambulator the little mouth stopped working for a second and Beatrix stared out of the darkness, her beady eyes gleaming with terror. And then she wailed. Her mouth as wide as her face, she wailed as though she had been bitten.

Greta felt herself jump and quickly began to rock the handlebar up and down. 'Oh shh, shhh, shh,' she kept saying, reaching inside to redirect the biscuit into the open mouth. The two soldiers stopped. 'Is everything all right, Ma'am?' one asked.

'What? Oh yes, perfectly fine. I mean I don't know. She was all right a second ago and suddenly –'

'Perhaps she's been stung,' he continued.

'Stung?'

'Yes. You know, by a wasp or something?'

'At this time of the year?'

'Well, it's warm enough.'

'Yes I suppose. Perhaps I should turn back and take her home? She's not mine you know, and if anything happened …'

'Oh well, perhaps that would be best.'

Greta waltzed the perambulator around. Now she was facing the same way as the soldiers. The baby continued to wail.

'I've never heard her do this before, shh, shhh, shh. Now there's a good girl. Bickie? Want a bickie?' She began to walk alongside the two men.

'It's very kind of you to stop. I'm most grateful for your concern.'

'Not at all.' It was the one beside her who spoke again. 'Wouldn't like to see any harm come to the –'

And then another voice joined in. Gruff, uninterested.

'Why don't you let the hood down?'

Greta looked over at him. She had to strain her neck a little to do so as he was lagging somewhat behind. Oh, he really was good-looking. Most attractive …

'I beg your pardon?' she smiled at him. He stepped over towards her then (oh dear) and reaching up to the hood an arm stretched out on either side of it like an embrace. Slowly he released the clasps and folded the hood down into itself. The crying cut off in an instant.

'Well – isn't that something!'

'No wonder she's been crying – must be like living in a cave in there.'

'Yes. Oh how clever of you. Oh now why didn't I think … I feel so foolish – lack of experience I suppose.'

They crossed back over Clanbrassil Street, the baby contentedly looking around. Now and then she raised a fat little finger and cried out, 'Dook. Dookadat!'

'Oh yes, look, Beatrix; that's a motor car. Isn't it lovely?'

They were across the street now, continuing on. Perhaps she would take the baby on a bit, down to the Green or – well just for a walk at any rate. Such a lovely day, pointless going back already. It was nice to have a bit of company for a change. Have a chat. The soldier next to her made pleasant conversation, playing with the baby and all. She'd walk on with them a while, see how far they were going. 'Dook, dookadat!'

'Yes dear, that's a horsie.'

She could hear their boots scrape the ground as they moved and still he hadn't opened his mouth. It would be nice to see what his teeth were like. The baby began to sing her 'e' song.

'Oh, funny little thing,' Greta laughed, 'always singing that song. She seems in good form now, indeed.' She leaned around and looked at the silent soldier. 'Thanks to you.' He nodded and looked ahead.

'I don't know what I would have done, her not being mine and that. It's so difficult to know, when you're left in charge. You certainly seem to have a way. I just can't get over it –'

The friendly soldier interrupted. 'And well he should too – him with four of his own.'

'*Four!* Well now!' Greta smiled until she thought her face would break. 'Well now fancy. No wonder. Four? Isn't that something? Boys or girls? Oh look, here we are. Thank you so much again. Good bye now. Thank you.'

She swung the perambulator around on its heels, dipping its handlebar to the ground. 'Day day, Beatrix. Say day day.'

And pulling her load backwards up the garden path, she hauled the back wheels up and over each granite step. When she reached the top she paused before ringing the bell and, gasping lightly to herself, watched the two men walk away, crossing over towards St Kevin's church.

Yes, he had a shape to him all right. No doubt. You could see it from behind. Especially when he walked.

But four children. He hardly looked old enough. One a year, she supposed. His poor wife, must be difficult for her to say no. How many more would the poor woman have to endure before he had lost his charms?'

TEN

The first time Greta stood outside her Aunt Florence's shop she knew she had landed right on her two old-fashioned 'reach-me-down' boots. And nothing mattered now. Nothing at all. Not even the hat that moments ago had been such a source of humiliation. Scuttling tight to the walls from the railway station to here, she had felt as though she was carrying the Botanic Gardens on top of her head. And despising it, first for preventing her from the joy of first sights, and then again for its general unfashionableness (which, she feared, could very well leave her labelled forever in Dublin). She tried to peer out from under it at the address clutched in her hand. To no avail. But of course she knew the address off by heart and upside down anyway, ever since she had learned that she would come to live at it. Still and all she would have liked another little peep.

And now here at last and not a worry. For what were they after all, but a hat and a pair of boots? And who was she to scorn what once had probably been the most important things in poor Mother's life? Greta felt humility drip all over her as she stood and stared through the glittering window panes at the promises inside.

She scolded herself then (but not unkindly): imagine believing people would recognise her again, just because she had walked a little way dressed like a country clod. Why this was a city – you could be someone different every day. She squared her shoulders then, pleased at the amount of sophistication already acquired in such a short time. What would she be like at the end of a month?

Then the door opened suddenly, tickling a bell under the chin. It was Aunt Florence.

'Is that you, Greta?' she asked from the doorway, without actually coming out onto the street.

'Yes, Aunt Florence; it's me.'

'Well come in child. Come in. Standing out there like an urchin.'

She spoke in a whisper and beckoned urgently as though there was danger in the street. Greta glanced over her shoulder before stepping into the doorway.

As soon as she was in reach, Aunt Florence grabbed her by the sleeve and pulled her into the shop. The bell giggled again and there was silence. Greta tried to look around her, but Aunt Florence was blocking the view, standing right in front of her now and unpinning the Botanic Gardens from her head. Using her hand she instructed Greta to take off her coat. When she did so she fluttered her hand again, indicating that she wished Greta to turn around.

Aunt Florence didn't look at all pleased. She stepped towards Greta again and hooked her hands tight into her waist. She then pinched her bosom.

'Owwwww.'

'Are these your own?' she asked, crossly.

'Well, yes, Aunt Florence.'

'You're bigger than I expected. I mean I was expecting a child.'

'I'm sorry, Aunt Florence.'

'Don't be sorry,' she said, turning away towards a curtain at the back of the room. 'It's not your fault.'

She beckoned again, this time for Greta to pick up her travelling bag and follow her. Greta did so, ducking under her aunt's arm into the room behind the curtain. 'Stay here,' she whispered. 'Until I think what to do.'

'Yes, Aunt Florence.'

'Oh and Greta?'

'Yes, Aunt Florence?'

'Less of the "Aunt", if you know what I mean …'

'Oh yes, I know what you mean.'

Florence let the curtain fall down lightly between them.

Between customers Florence popped her head in: 'Your bed – over there in the corner,' she said once. 'Pictures, over there under that shelf – study them,' she said the next time. After about an hour the curtain parted a little slower than before and this time Florence came in carrying a tray. 'Something to keep you going. You all right in here?'

'Oh yes, Florence, I've never been happier in my whole life.'

'Let's hope you'll always be as easy pleased.'

Throughout the morning Greta floated, soundlessly tipping and touching all that surrounded her. For the first time in her life, she felt as though she knew what it must be like to be in love. A discreet gap in the curtain allowed her peep-access to the shop outside. She took a corner at a time, wishing to remember, to relish every detail. There was a long wooden table at the other side of the curtain, just beneath her view. It was almost as long as the wall. Across it lay a roll of cloth, tightly wound into itself, and then falling loosely at the bottom into a huge flowing ribbon where a sample had been unfurled. It looked so strange, so foreign; Greta longed to touch it. She had never seen anything like it before. On a shelf above the table other rolls were packed together; different colours, different textures but none looked quite like this. A scissors winked silver at the far end of the table under the light of the window. There were pattern books and drawings and one huge leather-backed book that looked like a bible. It even had scarlet threaded markers falling from between its pages. The window itself was the best: It had a step leading up to it like a stage. And a curtain too, which she watched Florence draw back to adjust something inside. And the setting: how funny it looked from behind. Out front she had thought it looked so real: two ladies off to the races, picture hats and parasols. But from here you could see it was just a couple of wooden dummies, strips of cloth pinned across them, pretending to be clothes. How clever it was, how delicious too, to be able to fool all those people on the outside.

In the far corner was a sewing machine. Surely the most beautiful thing Greta had ever seen. A musical instrument, more like. And Florence's right hand spinning its wheel and her foot playing on its pedals and her other hand guiding material through its tight little teeth. Its music was pleasing too. Steady, unobtrusive. If she wasn't so excited it would probably lull her to sleep.

When a customer came into the shop, the machine was abandoned and Florence became someone else. Sometimes she measured, moving like a puppet, sort of stiff, the tape stretched taut between the span of her hands. Heel to hip and round to waist, up to bust, then wrist to shoulder and on to neck. She tottered between the subject and a notepage on the table. And jotting down whatever it was the tape had told her, she made wise little noises, 'Ah ha' and 'hmmm' as if it were just as she had expected all along and was really only using the tape for confirmation.

Once or twice she held up pictures for inspection. More often her hand swaggered a pencil over a piece of paper and made a picture of its own. When this happened the customer invariably smiled; the drawing was of a figure that was gracious and shapely, discreetly elegant. And Greta noticed that while the pencil moved Florence's eye kept returning to the customer as if it were a portrait she was drawing and not a wishful thought.

By the end of the day Greta was able to surmise that once a roll of cloth was dragged from the shelf down to the table with a triumphant thud, a sale was usually made and the bible book would be opened out. In time she would come to equate that thud with money and success.

Greta sat on the side of her bed and smiled to herself: so this would be the bonnet room then. 'I'm afraid she'll have to sleep in the bonnet room,' the letter had apologised. Afraid? – no need. If this was how bonnets lived, she wouldn't mind being one at all. On the opposite wall a series of wooden trees was arranged in a row. The first one hung, untrimmed and sometimes unbrimmed, bonnets from its wooden hooks. It was almost like a forest. A forest of skulls. Tree by tree, she was able to follow the progress: first the baldy tree, the one with the skulls, then the half-hung tree, where brims had been added. Finally the one nearest the door, in full bloom with hats hidden by tulle and ribbons, netting and bows, feathers and frills.

Why it was better than a nature study book. 'Out of little acorns,' she thought, picking a sandwich from the tray. And would you look at that, little lace cover and all, so the sandwiches wouldn't get dirty. And a tea cosy – how pretty. Hard to believe they were sisters, Aunt Florence and Mother.

She parted the bread slightly at the seam. And – what? It couldn't be … Mmmm it is, oh gosh, mmm.

It was her first taste of beef and she vowed there and then it wouldn't be her last.

At six o' clock Aunt Florence locked the shop and came into the bonnet room. 'I needn't tell you,' she began, 'I'm pure and utter exhausted.'

Greta sat bolt upright, trying to appear as though sitting was not what she wanted to do at all and was prepared to get on her feet at any given moment.

'Is there anything I can do to help, Florence?'

'No, not today. From tomorrow, I'll start to train you. We'll go inside in a moment and have a bit of dinner. And then I'll explain.'

'Inside?'

'Yes, I have rooms at the end of the hall.' Florence picked up Greta's hat and turned it in her hand. Carefully she studied it. 'A parlour, my bedroom, a small kitchen,' she said.

'I don't mind if you throw it out, Florence. I mean, I know it's not – to tell you the truth I can't stand it, myself.'

Florence looked up at her and continued: 'We have to share a bathroom of course, which is a nuisance, but what can you do?'

She stretched over and pulled a pair of scissors from a drawer.

'There's another tenant on this floor, a Miss O'Grady, works in the post office down the road. A nice woman, quiet enough. And upstairs –'

She turned the hat upside down on her lap and using the scissor points began to loosen the grips inside. 'There is a family called Sheehan.'

She turned the hat over again and began to pull the flowers away from the brim. According to colour and shape she dropped each flower into one of the boxes under the table. 'A dreadful lot, by all accounts. Except for him. He's a gentleman.' She lifted the hat to her mouth and began biting at threads. 'How he ever got mixed up with … I'll never know.' Unwrapping a misty bandage of tulle from the crown of the hat, she ravelled it towards her into a tight little ball; this was dropped into a long flat box which lay snug in the drawer. She continued: 'He works in the Gresham – the hotel, you know.'

'Oh yes, I know. I mean, I've heard of it.'

'Of course you have.' She had picked up the scissors again and this time, using its finer point, gained entry into the thick part of the hat where the crown met the brim. In a moment both were separated. Each with its own identity. Florence leaned across the table and carefully hung the crown on the first wooden tree. She then, bending a little at the knee, aimed and threw the brim, like a hoop, over an erect pole which had been fixed into a piece of wood at the back of the room. It looked as if it once had belonged to a barber.

'Two things, Greta, you must learn, if you are to succeed in this business.'

'Yes, Florence?'

'Never waste anything.' She straightened herself up then, shaking out her skirt and beckoning Greta to follow her.

'And there is no such thing as an ugly woman.'

Amongst the many things about which Aunt Florence had been right, Mr Sheehan being a gentleman was the truest. And yes it was impossible to associate him with that awful family on the first landing. What was even more difficult to understand was how he managed to emerge, night after night, from those filthy rooms and look so immaculate. He never passed the shop without a pleasant remark or two for the ladies, though he wouldn't linger, not Mr Sheehan. For as Florence pointed out, 'He wasn't the sort to outstay his welcome. And besides which his wife would gut him.' Once though, she made him stay for tea, after a new customer had placed a most lucrative order, thanks to a recommendation received by 'that waiter fellow at the Gresham who tells me he hears that all the best-dressed ladies in Dublin are so because of your talents'.

He sat between the ladies and the dress cloth, accepting just the right amount and refusing just when he should. And not a stain on the cup after him and not a crumb from the iced dainties either, Greta noticed later, while drawing a soapy cloth across the loops of spilt tea hanging like beads over Florence's cup. And indeed her own.

That wasn't the only thing she was thinking of as she washed up, she was also thinking of something he had said. Something which could be said by any amount of people and mean nothing. Indeed Greta had heard such words uttered before. But somehow when Mr Sheehan said it, you could nearly believe him. They had been chatting mildly away when Mr Sheehan had asked politely how Greta was coming along. 'Fine,' Florence said. 'Learns quickly, I'll grant her that. But do you know, Mr Sheehan, she's looking for wages on me now – what do you think of that?'

'Oh well now,' he laughed bashfully. Florence laughed too.

'Wages, if you don't mind.'

But Greta was furious: how could she make up a lie like that? To a stranger and all. What must he think of her? Why the bare-faced –

'I don't –' she began.

But Florence was too quick for her. 'Wages, if you don't mind. Why I know those that charge their apprentices for the privilege. A roof over her head. All the nourishment a body could need, the finest clothes – even if I do say so myself,' she laughed again.

The finest clothes indeed. Where was she going with her 'the finest clothes'? In the shop, yes. But Florence was the one who wanted her to wear them in the shop. Said she had the carriage for them, could show them off to the customers. But there was nothing fine about her street clothes.

'Oh now would you look at her, Mr Sheehan, all red in the face and fuming. I'm only ragging you dear.' And lightly, she laid a hand on Greta's knee before curling it back, pinkeen-first to the tea cup.

'Isn't that so, Mr Sheehan?'

'Indeed,' he smiled. 'Still, it's only natural for the young to want a few bob in their pockets. That's the modern world, I'm afraid Miss McNiece.'

'But sure, Mr Sheehan, I wouldn't be in a position … not yet in anyway. It's not out of meanness you understand.'

'Oh of course not, Miss McNiece, of course not. I tell you what, leave it with me. I'll see what I can do.'

'Oh, Mr Sheehan, that would be very kind of you. Thank you so much. More tea? I hope you don't think I was …?'

'Oh not at all, Miss McNiece. Not at all. I'm making no promises. As I said, I'll see what I can do. I'm making no promises,' he repeated, closing his fingers over his cup like a dome.

And he did mean it. Two days later he came into the shop and said he had managed to find something for her in the evenings. They were often short of waiting staff for the bigger functions nowadays, he said. Old boys' reunions or charity balls, that sort of thing. And now with the war started, there was such a shortage of young men to wait on table. 'The tips are good,' he concluded. 'You can let me know.'

'Oh Florence, how could you?' she wailed, after he had left. 'What must he think? I mean what am I supposed to say?'

But Florence just shrugged it all off. 'You'll say – when can I start? Thank you very much, Mr Sheehan. That's what you'll say.'

'But you lied to him.'

'Lied to him! Don't make me laugh. I got you what you wanted, didn't I?'

'What's that?'

'Money.'

'I never said I wanted …'

'You didn't have to.'

Maybe it was the Gresham itself, all rich red and sparkles. The fact that it had a grand piano for every drawing room ('Eighteen grand pianos? Ah you're joking me, Mr Sheehan.')

Maybe it was because waiting on tables in the Lord Aberdeen room and listening to the accents (they couldn't be Irish, surely they're not Irish?) made her feel as if she were in another country. Where evening dress was alive and moving rather than trapped in one of Florence's drawings or on the pages of her style pictorials. And the careless slap of gentlemens' gloves into upturned silk hats or the rustle of slow gowns were just what you might expect to hear. The uniformed officers moving across the floor left their impression too (oh what must it be like to wear a gown whose cloth stroked off their khaki legs, round and round).

Maybe it was the line up of polished silver on either side of a place setting and the platters of meat slices, thick and warm, resilient to the pinch of her serving tongs. ('Would Madam like some more?')

And maybe, too, it was the walk back home with Mr Sheehan by her side, looking every bit as much the gentleman as any she had served tonight. And the discreet envelope passed to her before the bridge. 'Your share, Greta, well done.' Maybe it was all these things together, each one like a single thread in a tapestry. But from her first evening at the Gresham, Greta felt a happiness which up to then had been unknown to her. These are my people, she had thought, even after only one hour under its roof. And for no good reason at all really, unless of course, by some miracle, she had been a foundling, had been adopted. Something like that. The similarity between her mother's features and her own had first to be wiped from her mind before this last thought could formulate itself into a smile. 'And there's a girl who's happy in her work.' A red-faced man had smiled back at her. Handing her a coin which he had eked from his waistcoat pocket.

Up Westmoreland Street her hand was busy in the pocket of Florence's good coat, fondling the envelope of money all the way home. Oh to rip it open, to count under a street lamp the coins that shook out onto her open palm. To see if she would regret or not having handed over to the kitty the coin given her by the red-faced man. Mr Sheehan spoke gently to her, pausing only to take her elbow lightly over a road. Sensing her delight, he answered unasked questions with an anticipation that Greta could scarcely believe.

On Nassau Street, a gentleman stopped to ask directions. He spoke to Mr Sheehan as an equal. But in an accent, strange, as if he had fur growing inside his mouth. (Later Mr Sheehan told her it was French.) The Shelbourne Hotel was where he wanted and Mr Sheehan invited him to walk a little way with them. They parted at the corner, and the man thanked them; first Mr Sheehan, shaking his hand gravely. And then removing his hat, he took her hand. 'Madame,' he said.

For the rest of the journey home, she could feel the embarrassment walk between them like a ghost. That man thought they were married, thought they were man and wife. Imagine? The very idea. Although it had to be said, he also thought they were quality. Quality man and wife.

And why not? she thought later, after she had counted her share of the tips and hung Florence's good coat away. He wasn't old after all. He was, if not exactly handsome, refined and well spoken. And she, well, she could easily be mistaken for his wife. A little young for him perhaps. But, why, he wasn't old. He wasn't even nearly old.

Under the baldy bonnet tree, he said he loved her. The pates of would-be hats looking down on them. And the eiderdown from her bed smoothed out beneath them. 'And because I love you, I can go no further,' he said, pulling down the skirt she had pulled upwards.

And at first, furious, because all the way home he had led her on. All the way home and for weeks beforehand. Driving her to the frenzy that had made her act this way. Pushing her to it, bit by bit, since the first night in fact, when the Frenchman had put the idea into her head. Until she could think of nothing else. The cut of his clothes and the way that they fitted him. The turn of his fingernails always white beneath. The fact that he could carry a coat better than any gentleman she'd ever known. That people looked at him in the street. His cleanliness was what she liked best of all. 'Spotless,' is how her mother would have referred to him.

And now to think he had humiliated her like this. Offering his arm to her on the walk by the College wall. Where her fingers felt over his man's cloth of cashmere, soft and yet thicker than any she had ever felt before. And in Clare Street then, in a doorway, pressing her to the wall. His arms, his mouth, his shaking legs, all for her. 'Well really, Mr Sheehan,' she had begun, her mouth nuzzling until it found his.

And her nose into his neck, that she knew to be slightly pink above his collar from a heavy-handed wash. 'And really, Mr Sheehan,' she said again, jutting her bosom up into his chest and leaving a little gap between their bodies, so that his hand could fit through and touch; his fingers could close over like a dome.

'But really, Mr Sheehan,' she was saying now. This time with another voice. 'I don't know what came over me – I really don't. What must you think?'

And no longer furious. Not even annoyed. A little bored perhaps. And anxious, in case Florence might come in. To take that risk for what? To have her fingers kissed and listen to his endless apologies? His endless excuses, his endless reasons for not completing the job.

'Florence could come in at any second,' she began, lifting the eiderdown at the edge and holding it there till he removed himself.

'Of course,' he said, 'yes, I should go.'

Next morning his wife came down and gave a little knock on the hallway door. Greta nearly jumped through the window when she saw her there. But Mrs Sheehan was smiling, shyly almost. 'I was wonderin' love,' she said. 'You wouldn't be any chance have the loan of two and truppence till me husband gets back. It's just that I'm stuck. I'll give it straight back. Into your hand, the minute he comes in like.'

'I'm sorry,' Greta said. 'I have no money, I'm afraid.'

The shy smile twisted and became a snarl: 'I might a known. You people wouldn't give out a spit. Oh yes, I know your type, not long up but well up.'

Florence walked in behind her. 'What seems to be the problem, Mrs Sheehan?'

'Why dontin you ask her? I ask for a miserable two and truppence for a half an hour, an' she wouldn't oblige. Give nothin' but take plenty.'

'Now, Mrs Sheehan, I'm sure if Greta says she hasn't got it –'

'And is that all she says? Huh? Is it? Ask her what she says about my husband. Go on. Ask her.'

'Now, Mrs Sheehan, really! Such a thing to say. Greta is just a child.'

'She doesn't look too much like a child to me.'

Florence unlocked a drawer and from the cash box removed a handful of coins. She sifted them on the palm of her hand and walked back over to Mrs Sheehan.

'Here you are now, Mrs Sheehan. I'll lend you the money. Here's three shillings. How about that? And you can give it back whenever. You hardly expect a poor apprentice to have money to spare now, do you?'

'She has her nights at the Gresham.'

'Something has to pay for her bed and board now, Mrs Sheehan. We can't have these young ones thinking they can live for nothing, now can we?'

Florence had one hand on Mrs Sheehan's back and was guiding her towards the door as she spoke.

'I'm telling you though, Miss McNiece, that one is up to something with my husband. His clothes was hangin' off him last night when he came up them stairs. I knew it. I just knew there was somethin' goin' on. I was waitin' for him, I was. And Miss McNiece – excuse me for sayin' it, but he was …' she had a quick peep about her before mouthing the final word: 'unbuttoned – you know.'

'Ah aren't you the ticket now? Mrs Sheehan! The things you say. Such a notion. You're a scream so you are. Goodbye now.'

Mrs Sheehan stopped at the door and looked back over at Greta.

'Thanks for the loan, Miss McNiece, the minute he comes back in. I swear.'

'Take your time, Mrs Sheehan. No hurry. Neighbours after all. Bye now. Bye bye.'

The door closed behind her and shuffles from her feet sounded long over the hall linoleum and then choppier, making their way up the stairs.

'Oh,' Greta began, sitting down and gasping, 'I can't believe that awful woman. Who does she think? I've never been so humiliated in my life. Such a horrible – Oh I don't know what to say. I feel quite weak. I really do. I mean *imagine*? The cheek of it. To accuse *me*. I don't know what I would have done had you not come in when you did. I really must thank you, Florence.'

'Oh you're very welcome,' Florence said, lifting the curtain to the shop outside. 'Now I'll give you a week to get your bag packed and out of here.'

ELEVEN

The thing Greta learned from Mr Sheehan was that she liked a clean man. Well-dressed too. Though it was no use having fine clothes if he couldn't carry them. She also learned that she didn't care for a man who was too fond of speaking. A weakness that, as it turned out, Mr Sheehan had been inclined towards. She also could not under any circumstances tolerate the smell of male sweat. Unless of course it had been freshly produced. And preferably as a result of her presence.

'The things I've learnt from my last position? Well quite frankly, Miss Sellars, I wouldn't know where to begin,' said Greta aloud. 'I believe I know all there is to know about dressmaking and I have been told I have a flair for – perhaps it would be better if …' she reached into her bag and pulled out a letter, 'if my reference were to explain.'

Greta handed over the letter and waited for Miss Sellars to read it.

'I'll be back in one moment,' she said, folding the letter over and disappearing through a dark brown door in a darker brown wall.

Greta sat back and listened to the noise of Bond Street outside. Where, oh where, did it all go to, that lovely noise, come night-time? This was her biggest disappointment with London, the lack of noise at the end of a day. She had imagined it would be so different: taxi doors that slammed through the night, revellers, in neat little bunches, pouring out laughing and talking to this dance or that party. Or earlier when on a city-lit street, snatches of orchestral music strayed out over tall windows as you walked along slowly, your step adjusting to match a tune. And then falling asleep nightly to the honk and hum of restless traffic, distant or passing, but always there, until dawn and further, when it would be time for it to start all over again, before it even had a chance to stop. Well lying these past two nights in the dormitory of the young ladies' hostel, there was nothing like that; the rise and fall of stranger's sleep-breath and that was your lot. Otherwise, you might as well have been at home in your own bed. Except there, the silence was never complete; in the country there was, at least, the nocturnal cry of wildlife with all its variations, and then later on in Dublin, a different sort of nightlife was not without its song. Sounds that once had made her tut and turn she longed for now. Anything, oh anything, to break the blackness of those awful London nights.

Ten minutes later she was coming down the narrow steps on to the street outside, her heart light with relief for another ordeal over, and repeating to herself the last few moments of the upstairs interview, muttering the conversation; this time with the inclusion of answers she had earlier declined: 'We'll be in touch. Good day to you.' (Don't bother your barney, you oul bat) and 'I have to say, not having French does go against you.' (Oh really? Well, that's why I came to London and not to Paris!)

Ah but the daylight is another matter, she admitted then as she came out under it. A different matter entirely. And she took her hat by the brim and steered it slightly westways before moving on.

Up Bond Street then at not too brisk a step, slow enough in any case to pause at shop fronts and smile to herself at what may have looked to the untrained eye like a fine display of elegance being really nothing more than cloth spread and pinned around the back of a wooden block. (Well mercy me, you have to laugh, you really do.)

And before continuing on, pulling her vision back out a little and balancing it then between the dummies and the window-glass to examine a spectral image of herself. And pleased with it sufficiently to just for a moment envisage herself, her excellent carriage and her inside information walking backwards, down a few doors and into Fenwicks showrooms. To ask there and then – and indeed why not? – if there would be a vacancy for one such as herself?

But then sternly, she had to remind herself – no. Unfortunately not. A live-in position was essential. And Fenwicks would hardly be that. Pity poor Fenwicks then! She reached the corner that turned out into Oxford Street. Here suddenly she stopped to take delight. There it was again, the bus full of swanks, off to the Ritz for lunch. How funny they looked all stuffed in together like that, done up to the nines. An absolute scream. Well that's their war for them now. There it is. And the best of luck to them. Hope they're enjoying it.

She crossed over Oxford Street, skipping up on the kerb for her final step. And the shops seemed to be doing well enough and no mistake. No shortage of money about the place. The cleaning lady in the hostel had said it was on account of them all being scared to spend the summers as they usually did, abroad. Still it gave a nice carnival flavour to the streets though, well dressed throngs getting their shopping and entertainment in together. Spending their money on whatever was available before it would be too late and there would be nothing left to buy. Or before the curfew at any rate, when the streaks of light come out to play, chasing each other in great big lazy semicircles, growing out of the horizon on one side and swooping back down again further along the line. Skimming the night sky of navy blue. And searching, searching. Searching for what? Something that's hiding? In the crack of a wall or tucked inside a window frame? Behind the stars? Or under the moon? Or was it for all that absent sound?

It was nearly the turn for Baker Street and Massey's domestic agency. But it was also nearly time for her dinner. What should she do? Eat now or carry on? Climb another stairwell, sit before another desk, hands in a clasp, answering the questions just as she planned. And all the time think of what she would like to eat rather than what she would probably end up eating? It would give her a distraction, she supposed, help her not to care about the little pause that inevitably followed each of her careful answers, as if an opportunity were being given her to break down and confess: No. No, it's all been lies. I'm sorry. I'm so, so –

('And what have you learned from your last position, Miss, eh?')

(That there *is* such a thing as an ugly woman actually, now that I've seen you.)

She swung herself up onto an omnibus and minutes later back down again at Clarence Gardens where she thought she had seen a little place just past and down from the entrance to Regent's Park. And yes. She was right. There it was. Just another few steps and a rest at last.

A pie and peas and a seat by the window, lips rotating in a rosebud knot. And congratulating herself on having found this place; table to yourself, nice and quiet. And reasonable too. As for the food? Well if not exactly the Gresham it was certainly filling. All in all, a grand discovery indeed. She then had a cup of tea and an apple slice, and settled back to have a little think about her plans for the afternoon.

Back to Massey's and then a little walk. Up towards Picadilly just in time to see them dribble into the tea-rooms on Swallow Street. Formosa Oolong was the name actually. She had seen it the first day and couldn't resist the tiniest peep. Orchestral music and an old-fashioned layout and, Madam, may I help you? Standing back to admit her if she wanted. 'I'm looking for a friend actually, doesn't seem to be here yet. Pop back in half an hour. Still got some shopping to do.'

'Of course, Madam, as you wish' and a perfect little afternoon bow.

'Formosa Oolong, Formosa Oolong, Formosa Oo-oo-ooolong,' she kept repeating to herself, thrilled by the very sound of it, and elasticating the 'oo' sound to various lengths as she walked on back to the hostel. She promised herself the moment, the very moment she had herself settled, she would go, flapping her gloves down onto the side of the table and ordering with a smile that indicated a nice little tip might just be on the cards. Yes that would be her treat, her reward for all the terrible traipsing around, for all those shy smiles and that careful diction. And nice to know she would be perfectly acceptable too, as good as any in there.

And she didn't mind crediting Aunt Florence either at this point, for having at least had the decency to throw her out properly dressed. So that she could make her mark in public without being shown the door. Three very nice outfits she had given her. And a very nice reference too. And an even nicer five-pound note.

Which was all very decent really, but the least she could do after the shabby way she had treated her, and after the ordeal with that awful man, not to mention his tenemented wife.

'You Irish?' the waitress asked her, lifting her plate and dabbing beneath it. And really – these people. They don't mind asking you your business. Not a bit of it. 'Yes, that's right. As a matter of fact I am.'

'My old mum, she's Irish.'

'Now. Imagine that.' And they don't mind telling you theirs either.

'Well she used to be. She's dead now.'

'Oh how awful.'

'Don't really matter. I didn't know her that well.'

'Oh?'

'Yea, I lived with my other ol' gran. She weren't Irish.'

'How interesting.'

'Nah. She was from the other side. You know, my dad's side.'

'Ahh.'

'You lookin' for work?'

'Well, yes, as a matter –' Greta was relieved that no one else was in hearing range of this conversation. And no wonder the place was so quiet, if this was procedure with every new customer.

'What sort of work?'

'Em, lady's maid.'

'Ye wha'?'

'Lady's maid,' she repeated, this time a little more clearly.

'Oh yea? Any luck?'

'Not so far. Though this is only my second day …'

'Well, you wouldn't, dressed like that now, wouldya?'

'Excuse me, but these are very high-quality clothes. I don't mind saying so.'

Greta was fumbling with her money. Well really …

'Yea, I know. That's not my point. A lady's maid, not supposed to look better than the lady. Know wha' I mean?'

'Oh. Well, I didn't know that. I mean I assumed …'

'Nah. Rule number one. My sister told me. She were a lady's maid.'

'Yes?'

'Yea, that's right. The one that lived with my other gran. The Irish one.'

Greta held out her hand for the change and moved towards the door. She paused then and turned back.

'Tell me,' she said. 'Your sister, can she speak French?'

'Nah!'

'She can't?'

'Nah.'

'Well I just happen to know that French is essential if you want to be a lady's maid.'

'Yea, that's right.'

'But?'

'She didn't go tellin' them the fru, you know.'

'The what?' (Where did these people learn to speak?)

'She told them she could speak it. Her. She couldn't 'ardly even speak English, never mind nuffin' else.'

'And they believed her?'

'Oh yea. She took a couple of lessons later like. Just in case. But she didn't never need them.'

'No?'

'Nah. Nice girl my sister. Pity you couldn't meet her. She tell you all about being a lady's maid. Yea, that's right. She used to say to me: "Betty. Betty," she used say, "you couldn't never be a lady's maid, account of you being such a looker."'

'Absolutely,' Greta said hurriedly after a rather long pause. 'I quite agree.'

'Yea? I dunno. Never could see it myself. Here, I know! Why don't you come back Sunday meet her for yourself. Come about this time, I got the afternoon off. We could all go off somewhere.'

'I'd love to. Thank you so much for asking. Well, I'd better be off now.'

'Sunday then.'

'Yes Sunday. Can't wait.'

You must be jokin' me, Greta thought, pulling the door behind her and giving a little wave in through the window as she passed. I'd rather eat the cat.

The following morning she sat in Massey's, from head to toe in plain navy serge. 'And tell me, Miss, eh …? Do you speak French?'

'Yes, yes I do, actually; my mother is half-French. As a matter of fact. Now that you mention it. That's right. Half-French.'

'Really?'

'Oh yes. They say that's where I get my interest in clothes.'

'Do they indeed?'

Miss Massey put Greta's reference back into its envelope and pulled a long box out from a drawer in the desk. Resting it on her knee she began to crab-crawl her fingernails across the cards packed tightly inside.

'You're much too young and inexperienced to be a lady's maid. I don't know who or what put the idea into your head. The idea!' She gave a little laugh.

Greta didn't know what she should do. Ask for further explanation or just stand up, thank her and leave? She was about to do the latter when a fingernail stopped and, with a little 'Ah ha' from the owner, pulled a card up out of the box.

'A young lady's maid. That's what you want. You have to crawl before you can walk, dearie.'

'A young lady's maid. Do you mean a nursemaid?'

'No. No. Two young girls. Miss Annabelle and Miss Lucille. Thirteen and eighteen years old. House in Mayfair, room shared with undermaid. House in Bucks, room shared with parlourmaid. House in Ireland, own room.'

'Ireland?'

'Yes. But I shouldn't worry about that too much if I were you. They rarely go. Twenty per annum all found.'

All found. All found? What did she mean? Did you have to search for it. Like hide and seek or something?

'When can you start?'

'When can I start? Oh, em, what about tomorrow?'

'What's wrong with today?'

'Nothing, it's just that I have an old aunt, I promised my mother I would visit.'

'She French too?'

'Mmm.'

'I see,' she said, tapping the card on the side of the desk before handing it slowly over.

'All right then, tomorrow at ten o'clock sharp. Make yourself known at this address. I'll let them know you're coming.'

She was the first into Formosa Oolong's that afternoon and almost last to leave. A pot of tea as big as a toddler, every drop all to herself. She had to take Chinese steps for the last few yards back to the hostel to hold it all in. But, as she told herself that last night in her silent bed, it was the highlight of her whole life put together, Gresham and all. Peeping through palm fronds like a sly child peeps through his fingers, she took it all in. First, viewing the afternoon parade, identifying each cut, each piece of cloth the way Florence had taught her and every now and then looking down at her own costume to verify its suitability. And then listening while the exchange of easy greetings gave way to the more complicated business of gossip being traded.

And although not a word was spoken to her and she spoke not a word to anyone (and she was hardly going to count waiting staff, not in this hat she wasn't) it was the sense of equality that made her tingle.

She could have had three pies and peas for the price of a few crustless sandwiches and a fruit cake rather lacking in fruit. But every mouthful was relished, every crumb a treat to be remembered; even if, in all honesty, the tea she had chosen tasted more like boiled rose water than anything else.

Eighteen months later she was back in Massey's. This time it wasn't necessary to exaggerate her talents; the sixpence a week she had forked out on French lessons had not been wasted. She had been to Paris twice and had negotiated her way about with only slight difficulty. She made all the underlinen for her ladyship and the two girls with materials purchased by herself on these trips, and bust bodices or petticoats, you had to search for Greta's neat stitches before you found them. Her accent had passed that tight-lipped stage when it had tried too much to conceal its origins and had only succeeded in making her sound 'common'. She had the balance just right now, for one of her position. Her ladyship had counted herself lucky to have discovered Greta, or more particularly, Greta's knack for furtively copying and later detailing the most complex of gowns. Indeed, her reputation and her wardrobe had greatly improved since Greta's arrival. It hadn't been too long before the young ladies were passed onto a lesser talent and she had claimed Greta for her own.

She could handle anything to do with dressmaking from a gopher iron to an embroidery needle. She could handle anything to do with ladies from melancholia to a massive tantrum. Her wages were about to be lifted to twenty-four guineas per annum and yet here she was back at Massey's willing to take an inferior position for inferior money.

'And would you mind my asking why?' Mrs Massey asked.

'Indeed I would not, Mrs Massey. It's on account of my poor old mother.'

'Your mother?'

'Yes. You see, she hasn't been very well and to be honest, she's not getting any younger. Frankly, I'm worried about her, Mrs Massey, and would now like to return to Ireland to be nearer to her.'

Mrs Massey looked down at the letter on her desk. 'These really are most excellent references,' she began. 'You would do a lot better if you were to stay here, you know.'

'I know, but as I said …'

'I see. Well, I do have something actually. In Dublin as it happens, travelling to London every six months or so. For health reasons.'

'An invalid?'

'No. No, nothing like that. A medical check-up, that's all. I only mention it because it would mean you would have plenty of time to see your mother. Your presence not being required on these trips.'

'Oh yes. That would be very convenient.'

'The husband is English. He was in with me yesterday actually and is anxious to have something settled before returning at the end of the week. His wife is Irish. But most refined.'

'Well, that's a relief.'

Mrs Massey gave a little laugh. 'Oh I do beg your pard ...'

She handed Greta a card with the name Pakenham written across the top.

'I could do a lot better for you, if you were to stay. You know, if there was anything worrying you about your last position, I mean anything at all, you could tell me. In the strictest of confidence, naturally.'

'No, Miss Massey. I can assure you. My reasons are genuine.'

As Greta's mother had been dead for almost three years now, the reason given could hardly be less genuine. However, since her arrival in London, and more particularly since entering into service, Greta had found a mother lurking in the background to be an in-dispensable convenience, one she wasn't about to surrender. And besides which – how could she tell the truth? She had been asked to leave by the housekeeper because rules had been broken. An excellent reference was offered in return for a quick and painless exit. But the more Greta thought about it, the clearer it became: she had been asked to leave not because she had broken the rules (she could have wiggled out of that part all right) but because of where she had broken them: the 'pug's parlour'.

Across its floor Greta lay with the Groom of Chambers blowing hot air down into her ears. He stuck his tongue in once or twice too, which put her right off. But his smell was fresh and his hands were clean and it was all like a dream really, bits of reality or irrelevancy making the odd appearance through the pleasure. Like: why do they call it the pug's parlour? Such an ugly name. And implying too that they are pugs, the senior members of staff. And what in the name of God is a pug? And speaking of ugly, he's taken it out. What is it like? I just don't know.

Long ago a baby brother had a little bulb, with a tiny finger curled and sleeping over it. And she used to think, ahhh, how dotie. But look what happens to dotie, when dotie gets to manhood. Like a tree with bumps of wrinkled bark at the bottom. Or something old, grey and old. Hard to believe it was where life comes from. Just another piece of old grey flesh. Except the mess it makes – the smell of it, oh God. Greta wiped her leg with an antimacassar. While he lit himself a cigarette.

He used one hand to lift the cigarette back and forth from his lips to the fire grate and the other to stroke the bits of her that were still showing. In the end there was only the back of her hand left, all else having been redressed. And he slid his fingers over and across it, taking as much care with its crevices and corners as he had done earlier with other darker regions. He could never keep his hands still, this one. Which was what had attracted her in the first place.

It was his job to organise the weekend card games for the house guests, could play a pack like an accordion so that you could hardly see the air between each card. With the cigarette at the side of his lips and one eye half-winked against its smoke, he practised at the kitchen table until dinner was over, when he would be called upstairs to deal: pull, release, pull again. His hands running the cards away from and then into each other with that dry clacking sound as they collapsed and then were rescued again.

Her first weekend at Hafton House and she had noticed him. It took a lot longer though for him to notice her. That was in the days when she wasn't allowed to even enter the pug's parlour. When she was still confined to quarters fit only for the junior staff. And even now that she could walk in any time, any time at all, she still found a lick of pleasure in sneaking through a darkened house, anticipating as she crept the touch of him, the feel of him, his inscrutable face crumbling and twisting into the mask of the devil, making him say things he did not want to say at all. Making him powerless in her hands. He was too fond of taking unnecessary risks. Was he still prone to them, she wondered, after they were caught and he had been forced to enlist?

That last evening, unable to wait. Unable to resist. Another hour or so that's all and the house would have been sleeping. Stupid man. All his fault. She could have waited. She liked that. To hold the thoughts of it fat and safe and under her skirts all day if needs be. That's why she had rubbed off him in passing in the first place; so that she could keep it on a simmer. But not him. Oh no. He had insisted.

No self-control. It was his fault they were caught.

Even the housekeeper had said it. 'I know, Greta, that it was all his fault,' taking a hankie from her pocket and handing it to Greta. 'Taking advantage of you like that. How dare he? I know what men are like. And in the pug's parlour. How could he be so ... so disrespectful? You are the victim, my dear. I have no doubt. But what else can I do?'

Once she sat in Hafton House on late spring afternoons watching the hazy light hang over the lawns and down to the stables where her young ladies played and further on past the tiers of coiffured trees, to the slope of fields, the twist of a river. And tea taken to her by a maid whose curtsy she hadn't even bothered to acknowledge, too busy with the chat, all grown up and worldly. And where will 'Good-time Greta' be off to next week when her ladyship returns? They laughed without malice.

Now. Now she sits on a window sill of the South Circular Road, looking out at houses across a street where there is nowhere for the hazy light to hang or be noticed. And Good-time Greta goes nowhere now, except to push a baby carriage along the only decent gap in the rows of houses on this side of town.

Seeing no one, going nowhere, all alone. Except for this afternoon, when a soldier's walk had led her backwards for a time, giving her an outing for a couple of hours. Out of all that time.

But then, thought Greta, rising as she heard Mrs Gunne's key in the lock. What else is memory for, if not to be a friend, in times such as these?

III

THREE PATIENTS

TWELVE

In the corner stands the dancer; darkness snug about him, like a smell. And yet he can see right across the plane on which these rows of strange things grow. But first there is a hem of footlights, planted by an exact hand, in even shapes and spaces – only in colour do they differ – a blue here, a red there, but mostly yellow he sees, along this the beaded line. Beyond which is a sudden drop, a dip filled with different shapes, again in rows, though no two shapes are quite alike. Some have foliage piled and balanced on the top; others have a tight sprouting at the front. They move in a disorganised fashion, flopping or wagging lightly. He thinks perhaps they have been allowed to over-ripen.

His eye travels upwards. Further again along sloping hillsides, there are more rows, climbing abundantly. It is too far to see if they can move, too dark to catch more than a blur. For wild, unweeded, they have blocked the sun.

There is a muttering of sounds, high and low, throughout the rows, in the plane, on the hillsides; a fussy rustling, a sort of rumbling. It is almost as if they are communicating with each other. A nudging sort of language without a rhythm of its own: nothing to distract or interfere with what he is about to offer.

The dancer grips his cane a little tighter at the neck, lightens his right foot, but for the moment will not lift it. When it is weightless as a snowflake on the floor. Then. When the spotlight is ready to take his lead. Then.

And when the introduction loosens and finally unties his name, yes then.

He is listening to it now, that introduction, slow and firm, bellowing out like a warning. The beam drops, an impenetrable slant filled with silver. It hones into a circle, staying on the salt which he has sprinkled in advance. It waits now, only for the touch of his feet.

Now, the final syllable of his name is being cast off. He can see Masterson wrench it from his starchy chest and squeeze it into a fistfold. And unfurling that long arm, his hand springs open and bounces it out from the tips of his fingers.

His name has been released, let out to the air. Where it lingers for a while before swooping down to settle onto the dancer's outstretched palm, caught.

These are the sounds now that crack open in the stalls: the teeming rain, the trotting horses tearing through it. The bustle of a thorough-fare, the scram of traffic, mechanical and human.

The bash of it! The enormous unbearable bash of it. He thinks about putting his hands to his ears, but what to do with the cane? He must be ready when the time comes, not one second behind. No time to put it down and then pick it back up again.

Then it cuts. The noise. In two and then in two again. And now in smaller pieces until there is just the occasional clinging screed, which one by one the silence sucks away. Now it has stopped completely. And he can hear at last the tune, his tune, sauntering up from the pit – where it has been loitering all the time.

The dancer feels the fuel rush through him, rushing into his centre and holding fast there. Squeezed and trapped, there is a spark: one tight explosion and he is ready. To come out of the darkness, to glide towards the moonbeam, to enter and to take it with him over the whispering salt.

His cane is up, his elbow pointed and now his foot is the weight of nothing.

He is about to move off when he notices the moonbeam has already started moving. Without him it is moving, without his lead. He looks around for Algie's explanation. Across the way in the other wing, he sees him finally, smiling with pleasure at the empty stage. Enjoying what? Nothing? How can he be smiling at nothing?

The dancer looks back to the capering moonbeam, bouncing now, soft and jaunty; a sudden glide taking it off to the right. And now jigging back a little to the left before moving over to the right again, it swings in circles: tight and small.

It is then he notices the salt, thinning slightly under the silver rays. Slipping away from its mass, it has started to fray at the edges. As if. As if.

Down in the dip too, there has been a change. A lazy swaying from side to side and softly a song wanders up to Masterson who, standing at the front with arms outstretched, conducts, guides the rows down there. He takes them through it, filling in the gaps with questions and bringing his hand up to his ear so that it can trap the cheerful answers.

'I know she likes me.'

'What do you know?'

'I know she likes me.'

'How do you know?'

'Because she said so.'

When they get too loud, he shelves his hands out at them, as if to say, 'Shh shh, shh shh.' And shh shh, the salt goes rustling, but how? And who?

The dancer looks out from his veil of darkness and sees nothing.

Just the print of the moon shifting itself in time to a tune. He hears the shuffle of soft shoe and salt. And pause-perfect; the sounds come and go just they should do. He can hear the hollow slap of a knee and the tap-thin-tap from a foot or a cane. But still he sees nothing. Nothing at all.

When the noise breaks out again its strength is reinforced. Now shrill whistles and calls for encore spin up from it. A feeling comes over him, unfamiliar though instantly recognisable. It is a feeling of envy, rejection, a feeling of abandonment. So that was it all the time, that's what it had all been about. It was never him, his feet, his steps. It was the moonbeam they had been after. Or was it just so they could hear themselves sing? Of a girl called Lily and the lamplight she stands under? Perhaps there's never been a moonbeam at all? All the time he has been dancing – was it as an intruder? Moving beneath lamplight that belongs to someone else?

And Masterson walking towards it now, parts his clapping hands and breaks through the shaft of light. 'Ladies and Gentlemen,' he proclaims, the warning tone gone from his voice. Now it is triumphant, grateful; it gloats a little, as if ready to say, 'I told you so.'

He asks for more; he begs for it. He rolls his hand behind him to urge support from beyond the footlights, as he begs them to beg with him. They do.

They implore an empty stage. But that is not all. They are using the dancer's name. They are calling to the stage and using his name.

Some among them have sprouted up from their stalks and scream for it. Their heads enlarging puff by puff, like air balloons.

More, encore. Encore, more.

They are leaving the dip behind, growing up through it, filling it in with themselves. With each cry of encore they grow bigger. And bigger. He can see the swell of their heads rise over the footlights. He can see them dwarf Masterson who, unaware of these distortions, continues to beckon them from over his shoulder. More. More. They will not stop until he gives it.

How can he give more? More of what? For here are his feet still with him in the wing. And heavy now, too heavy. They have grown too heavy for his legs.

*

When he opened his eyes he could still hear his name. He looked upwards first as if that was where he would find it, flitting about in search of an exit. The early evening light was there all right, all the way up at the top and rubbing itself drily against the dust on windows that would never be reached.

He brought his eyes slowly down along the smooth expansive walls, watery green. And down onto the screens stretched out with more green, thicker this time, enough to lend a sort of privacy to the beds on the other side of the ward.

But not to his. His privacy had been removed, that space now otherwise occupied

They were all there. Standing at the bottom of his bed. It was like a finale; they could almost be expected to take a bow. There was Matilda, a little plainer in her street clothes but smiling more than she usually did. And Algie – smaller somehow without his neck, his collar and jacket seeming to be pulled right up over it, to just below his ears. And bashful Carabini beside him, smiling shyly as a maiden. And there was that other fellow, the one that hid an orchestra in his mouth and could produce an entire symphony when he opened his small baby's lips. Castle the contortionist next, the feet he usually had dangling over his shoulders or tucked up under his armpits now firmly on the ground.

They all gave a little cheer when he looked down at them.

'Well he's not dead anyway,' Algie said, and behind the nervous laughter he heard them all agree.

'I brought you some lemon drops,' Matilda said then, pushing a paper bag out in front of her. When a few seconds had passed, she stopped smiling and said, 'Will I put them away for you?'

She moved towards the locker before he had a chance to reply and first patting the bag under its bottom, she then pushed it into the open slit. 'There now,' she gasped. 'Any time you feel inclined, you just have to slip your hand in and help yourself.'

'Oh God now, Matilda. How come you never say nice things like that to me?' Algie said, and Castle laughed through his teeth.

Matilda made great play of ignoring the last comment and slipped out of her gloves. She pushed them into her handbag and then clapped it shut, loudly enough to make herself wince.

'So how are you feeling pet? Sure, God love you. You poor unfortunate.'

'Ah sure, the rest'll do him good,' Algie said and then, clapping his hand off his knee, continued: 'What were you up to at all? Were you noodled or what? Or maybe he was climbing up a ladder to me lady's chamber? Come on, you have to tell us, all the details, exactly as they fell out.'

Matilda rolled her eyes skywards. 'Don't be so foolish Algernon,' she sighed.

When Castle stopped laughing, he leaned towards the bed. He sounded worried. 'What's the grub like? All right?'

The dancer shifted himself upwards a little and cleared his throat.

'Well ...' he began.

'Oh ho ho, say no more,' Algie said, tipping his nose with his index finger and tossing his head like an over-bridled horse. 'If they don't kill you one way, they'll kill you the other. I tell you – I was in one time a few year ago. A small job, not serious. Well be the – I'll never forget it. I tell you, as I said to herself: "It wasn't the surgeon's knife that I was weary of, it was the cook's one." Sure they near killed me with it. Pure poison, and nothin' else. Shit, shite and shilacky breakfast, dinner and tea. Ah you never seen the like of it. Unbelievable. And mind you, I'm no grouser. Herself'd tell you that.'

Mr Carabini stood red-faced and beaming, his eyes sprightly, trying to follow every word. Up his sleeve, he had a few sentences of his own arranged, perfected on the way up Dame Street – some in groups, others in single file. However, despite his confidence in them – their structure, tense and conversational possibilities – he would prefer to get them over and done with. When he found a gap he slipped the first of them in.

'I have brought you these flowers. Daffodils. Don't you find them most beautiful?' The dancer looked at them, their full yellow, blinding against the dark suit and complexion of Carabini. He smiled.

'Yes I do. I find them very beautiful.'

'Oh they are absolutely just gorgeous. Now aren't they? Just gorgeous.' Matilda took them gently from Carabini and held them up for inspection like a newborn baby.

'In water now, straight away with them. You can't delay with the daffs.'

She bundled them to her breast and carried them off with her up the ward.

Carabini was thrilled by their success. He had felt a little nervous about producing the flowers at first, sensing Algie and Castle may have been laughing at him. How glad he was now that he hadn't given into the inclination to linger behind and abandon them in the hallway outside. He decided to continue with his second line. A single one this time.

'Are the nurses kind?' he asked casually, as if he'd only just thought of it.

'Kinda what?' Castle asked, nudging Algie and winking.

'Kinda gamey,' Algie answered, taking over the joke. 'I tell you I wouldn't mind her taking me temperature.' He nodded his head towards a nurse bent over a bed at the top of the ward.

'No,' said Castle, 'nor would I mind giving her an injection either.'

The weight of his own laughter caused him to double over.

When he straightened himself up again he was surprised to see that Algie had remained unamused, cross even.

'That's enough of that, Castle,' he said sternly. 'No need to be vulgar.'

'*What?*'

It was then Castle saw Mr Masterson standing at the back of their little group. His face flushed the colour of red tea.

'Good evening, gentlemen,' Masterson spoke. 'Miss Telford,' he nodded coolly beyond the bed and they all turned to see Matilda return with a vase in her hands and her chin bearded by a ruck of sunny heads.

'Mr Masterson,' she returned the nod and carefully set the vase down on top of the locker where she stayed with her back to the group, preening and re-preening the flowers with the utmost attention.

'And how is our patient today?' Masterson inquired, slowly stepping through the gap that had been made for his benefit.

'Oh you know, not too –'

'Good, good. Most unfortunate though, I must say. Most unfortunate indeed.'

'Oh wasn't it just, Mr Masterson?' Matilda sprang away from the vase and made herself a little perch on the side of the bed. 'I was just saying as much. Why if it had have been any other part of his body. But his foot. I mean to say for a dancer.'

'And what other part would you suggest he break, Miss Telford? To my mind a dancer needs all his bits. Unless you were thinking perhaps of his ear?'

Matilda turned pink and, stroking her handbag, gave a little laugh. 'I suppose ...'

Behind her Algie laughed out loud. 'Or his nose maybe? He could still dance with that in a splint.'

Castle clapped his hands. 'Oh now, wouldn't that be the sight?' And Carabini roared with delight without knowing exactly why.

The dancer gave a little cough. 'Actually,' he began, 'I could manage to practise at least with just my feet. A broken hand or shoulder, arm even, wouldn't stop that. I mean I often do, you know. Trap my hands behind my back into my braces and … Good for the balance you know.'

'Indeed,' began Mr Masterson, taking note of Matilda's hand reaching up to disguise her grin with an invented itch. 'It's a pity you didn't do it that way so, on Easter Monday night – you might have held onto your balance a bit longer.'

'Perhaps,' the dancer quietly replied.

An awkward little silence then, hanging like a canopy over the bed. Inside each head a suitable farewell was being searched for, while each waited for the other to take the initiative. Masterson, who rather liked these little moments, accepted the chair the symphony man was pushing towards him and waited to see who would be the first to speak. He might have known.

'We miss you, like I don't know what, I needn't tell you.' Matilda wriggled as she spoke. 'And not just because we have to go down for our own buns and biscuits either.' She tapped his hand playfully before continuing: 'I was just saying to the girls, Wouldn't you miss him somethin' terrible about the place? And they all said, Oh God you would. Didn't they, Mr Carabini?'

'Excuse me, Miss Telford?'

'I was just telling him about the girls, how we were saying about missing him, like …'

'Oh yes, yes, yes. All are saying it. Who's supposed to go for our bloody buns now?'

Matilda gasped. 'He's only coddin' you. I swear. Honestly do you hear him?'

Algie and Castle exchanged looks and grinned. The symphony man coughed.

'You might do as well without the buns and biscuits for a while,

Miss Telford.' Masterson picked up a newspaper which had earlier been abandoned and left to the floor. He studied it carefully. 'There might be a bit less work for wardrobes, in refittings – if you get my meaning.' He lifted his head to the dancer then, before she had time to recover from her shame: 'I see you're getting fond of the horses.'

'Oh I wouldn't say that. Just passing the time of day really.'

Algie was grimacing like a monkey behind Masterson's back.

'That'll be your influence, Algernon?' Masterson spoke as if he had eyes in the back of his head.

'Me? Ah not at all. I'd contradict you flat there, I'm afraid. In any way, he isn't even backing them. Are you sonny boy?'

'No, just picking at them, you know.'

'And seeing how you judged the next day, I wouldn't wonder,' Algie prompted.

'Yes, seeing how I've done.'

'Oh a dry bet. The lad's got the right idea about horses. He won our little draw for the national you know. No bother to him. Stuck in his thumb and pulled out a plum. That's the way to do it. Never even been to a race meeting in his whole life. Am I right?'

'That's right,' Castle answered on his behalf. 'And better off too. What a farce Easter Monday turned out to be. The crowds. You could hardly see the light of day and a shilling a bottle a stout. An outrage is what I call it. Why no wonder people lose their shirts, trying to win that kind of money. A fellow would nearly *have* to back a winner at that rate.'

'And then there was the hailstones.' Algie jumped back in. 'Don't forget the hailstones. Fellas catching them in their caps, that big. Knock ye out till Sunday. No joke. Oh no, this lad has more sense than to be wasting his time at the races. And I'd have to agree with him. That's why I seldom go, not any more. Herself'd tell you. You just ask her.'

'Yes,' said Masterson. 'Perhaps I will – if I ever get to meet her.'

Castle glanced at Algie sideways and gave a little laugh. 'Now as for me, the Baldoyle quid is the only bet you see me risking. Twelve coppers – just for an interest, you know yourself. And well what's the harm in that?'

'Harm?' Masterson stretched his gaze lazily up and down the apparatus that held the injured foot in place. He took a pair of spectacles from his inside pocket and brought them across his eyes. His brow puckered and his hand moved, tracing the bandaged arrangement. 'Worse vice of the lot,' he said. 'In my opinion,' he looked up at Algie and smiled.

He began to rise. 'Worse than the drink. Worse than the …' he paused before continuing, 'well, than anything else.'

Up now, he folded the spectacles over and returned them to his pocket. And bringing his hand down, began to fumble inside the pocket of his ulster. 'Oh yes. You can only drink so much you know. Before you drop. But the gambling. You can shove your home and hearth on the back of one fickle animal. Am I right or am I wrong, Miss Telford?'

'What? Oh absolutely right, Mr Masterson. Why there's nothing really worse. Nothing at all.'

'Except for the buns and the biscuits,' he smiled at her, not unkindly.

'Oh, Mr Masterson,' she bowed her head and between her pinkened cheeks squeezed back a grin.

He pulled his hand out of his pocket and placed a brown paper bag on the side of the bed. 'Oh I almost forgot. I brought you some lemon drops. I thought they'd be refreshing, I find them so.'

Algie winked. 'Watch out now you don't turn into a lemon,' he said.

Masterson looked at Algie until the grin fell away from his face.

'Well I don't know about the rest of you,' he said then, 'but I have a show to put on. If anyone would care to join me?'

Standing back from the chair so that the symphony man might take a hold of it and return it to its place, he concluded: 'Look after yourself young fellow. And let us know how long you'll be.' He waved vaguely towards the hoisted leg.

They began to loosen then, the tight little group at the end of the bed. Matilda struggled back into her gloves and gave his hand a special little squeeze. Algie waved and managed to wheeze in another sally or two. Castle, reluctant to get caught again, stuck to a formal farewell, adding as he walked away, 'I'll be passing again.'

The symphony man approached him then and shook his hand. Pressing a paper money ball onto his palm, he whispered: 'Compliments of Algie and he said to tell you well done.' He then muttered something about him taking care of himself.

Masterson stood away from the end of the bed allowing each one to pass as goodbye after goodbye was delivered. Carabini was the last. He cupped both of his hands around the dancer's fist and shook it gravely. 'I were so sorry for your foot. How happy I were to be here and we will meet again, you see.' And then with affection equally divided, he touched him first on the cheek and then turned to tip off the daffodil bonnets before taking his leave.

Masterson sliced his hand up and down, as though patting each one on the back as they filed past although in fact he didn't touch them at all. He followed then himself, lagging a few steps behind Algie: he would have to have a word with him about his appearance. He was like a tatterdemalion there, the get-up of him. Algie moved on and now it was Matilda he had immediate view of. Yes, she was getting hip-heavy. No doubt about it. And that baby-girl way she had of going on made her look ridiculous. Her voice was at its peak, though, and that's what counted; she could still draw the tears from them with 'When All Was Young'.

Of course that would finish too, he knew. That day would come.

He'd seen it so many times before. The crack comes soon after the peak. And what would happen to her then? How would she face that, he wondered. Still at least she had lost the dependence on him. Had realised that whatever small thing had been between them was in the past. And yet he knew in his heart that he could revive it with half a word or the hint of a smile. And it annoyed him that he sometimes felt more pleased than vexed by this. That little blush there at the end for example, a sign of what could be rekindled. No respect for herself really, would have left the company long ago if she had. Hanging about for so long, waiting for any little titbit he might throw her. Still she wasn't bad looking he supposed. Which was the problem. A fellow could weaken, if she hung about long enough. Could catch him on a hungry night. And then what? He'd find himself back at square one. Tears and implorations. Oh look at her, trying to make him jealous with Castle. Pathetic. Only made him despise her. Less inclined to feel guilty should he happen upon her some night after the show. Less inclined to reproach himself for using her. Should it ever happen again.

As they came to the door of the ward, Masterson watched them all turn and wave one last time. He was debating on whether or not he should do the same when his attention was taken. There was a woman standing there in the corridor talking to a nurse. He slowed up to allow himself that extra moment or two in which to study her. Yes, a fine figure indeed. Nice and tall. And a good big head on her. He liked that. Couldn't be doing with these penny-farthing faced ones at all. He stood back to allow her through the door and he raised his hat as she passed, taking a quick look into her eyes. Now that's what he called a woman, he thought, watching her walk away, nearly looking better from the back than from the front. A sign of breeding, he always maintained. He walked through the door and was about to turn the small sharp corner that gave way to the corridor when he changed his mind. The others were out of sight, half-way up the corridor and tittering away like half wits. (Don't tell me they're still laughing at Algie's nonsense about turning into a lemon.)

And no one in the ward could see him from behind the door either. Not that they would notice anyway, by the looks of things. Were they all dead or what? They must be, not to look up as she passed. Being unobserved, he decided to linger awhile and let his admiration wander in after her.

She had a slight sway, nothing overdone, and a nice slow walk to go with it. He couldn't stand a woman with a busy-body waddle.

And beneath the merest touch of evening sun, her hair seemed to be, well … alive. Who was she? Somebody's daughter? Some-body's wife, more like.

She stopped then at the end of the dancer's bed and, stepping up, leaned over and kissed him. Ahh so that's who she was. One of the famous sisters.

Right enough there had been a family resemblance now that he thought of it. Though obviously she had got all the nourishment. The other fellow being a bit of a consequence, by comparison.

He watched her then pull over the chair he had only just vacated and, drawing her hand over her skirt, sit herself down and wait for her brother to wake up.

Wait for him to wake up? How could that be? He was barnaby bright not two minutes since. He couldn't have dropped off already. The little scut was pretending. What the?

He felt himself jump when he heard Algies's voice creep up behind him. 'Eh, Mr Masterson the lads were wondering like. Any chance of a refreshment before …?'

Without his consent or knowledge, Masterson found that his hand was flustering all over his coat and trousers. 'I'm sorry, Algie. I think I may have lost my wallet. I've been looking every – Ah no, thank goodness, here it is.' He pulled out the wallet and waved it. 'You see? I usually put it in the other ...'

Algie looked at him and said nothing.

'You were saying?' Masterson began, pulling himself together and guiding Algie away from the alcove and back out onto the corridor.

'Ah yes,' he answered himself, before Algie had a chance. 'Refreshment did you say? Wasn't that it?'

'Well, now,' began Algie, 'to be honest it's all the same to me, one way or the other. You understand. They just asked me to ask you like. I'm easy meself. If you'd as soon get back, now I'm all for it.'

'Are you indeed, Algernon? Well, of course you must do as you wish, but I think – yes, I will accompany the others. The Irish House, I think. Isn't that the premises of the boy's brother?'

'Brother-in-law,' Algie gently corrected.

'Ah yes, brother-in-law. Well a good choice, I feel; let the family know we bother with the members of our company, no matter how minor. Besides, we might as well get as near to home before the journey lengthens, you understand?'

Algie understood perfectly; it wouldn't be the first time they had cut it fine and had to hail a taxi to take them back in time.

'Well seeing as it'll be somewhere handy, sure I suppose I might as well join you. Be able to keep an eye on them there. And maybe offer my sympathy to Mr Cleary, should he be there.'

'Mr Cleary? Is that the brother-in-law's name then?'

'That's right. Cleary, Pat Cleary.'

'I see. Oh and Algie –'

'Yes, sir?'

'The lad's not quite dead yet, don't overdo the sympathy. We don't want them thinking we are somehow responsible for the accident.'

'Oh indeed. Oh I know. I meant – Well, you know. Leave it to me, Mr Masterson. Never fear. So!' He clapped his hands smartly together. 'The Irish House it is. And now. I'll be warning them: just a couple, no more, mind. I'm not having a last-minute sprint. Half an hour at the very least before first call and we'll have to be home,' he concluded, taking Mr Masterson's example in always referring to the theatre as 'home'.

The two men came together down the corridor where the others waited in a clump at the opposite end.

'Doesn't Mr Masterson look in great form now?' Matilda said to Carabini. 'Sort of springy?'

'Springy, Miss Telford?'

And indeed he did, that one last backward glance before leaving the ward left Masterson with an invigorating picture: Maude, raising the brown paper bag onto her palm and weighing it there gently, and then stretching its paper mouth open, first finger, then lift one of his lemon drops into her mouth.

He hoped she would find it refreshing – as he would. While at the same time he couldn't help wondering if, at that very moment when he joined the others and led them to the stairs and the street outside, she had finished rolling it about her tongue and was now quietly sitting and licking the lemon dust clean from her lips.

THIRTEEN

Maude lay down on the bed. Bony fingers tying knots inside her. Tighter and tighter they pulled and then took out a blade, flicking it off the sinews, like a bow across a string, until the gradual blood came through, drop by tiny drop. One thing for certain, every month the pain got worse. It was almost as if nature was punishing her for her lack of co-operation. Thirty years of age and nothing to show for it. Thirty years of age and barren.

She placed the bed jar, wrapped in flannel, on her stomach. And yes the heat eased, melting a bluntness into what surely must be thorns? She pressed it in and rolling it over and back felt the chill subside in her womb. Oh but too hot now, beginning to burn. She pushed it off her stomach back onto the bed.

Lightly laid, her hands touched each other across her bloated stomach. If she were pregnant this is what she would look like at what – three, two months maybe? This is how it would be with a tiny sleepy handful being organised inside her, mixing a bit of this with a bit of that, until –

Well at least this time, she didn't have to worry about *that* on top of everything else. This time she knew she wasn't pregnant. There had been no need to cope with that oh too familiar feeling, to have to stand there and take it, slap after slap.

Oh yes. She mightn't know too much about the ins and outs of matters gynaecological. But this much she did know. This much at least. You had to be with a man before you got pregnant. No matter how fertile you were. And Pat had very kindly taken that little worry away. By removing himself, he had removed the possibility. And maybe she should thank him. For after all what was it really but a self-induced agony? A hope that you will not allow to go away.

You seize it, wanting it, needing it despite its fragility. Despite its struggling against your embrace. Nothing else can come into your head. You will say anything, do anything to keep it with you for as long as possible. You will tell yourself any lie.

Oh perhaps this time? Perhaps the miracle has happened. (Running to the lavatory a hundred times a day to check, just check.) Nothing yet. Oh thank God, nothing yet. Still clean, still beautifully clean. Oh no. What's that? I felt something there, as I coughed. Oh no, don't tell me … 'Will you excuse me just a moment?' Oh it's all right. Thank God, it's all right. This swelling in my breast not necessarily a bad sign, it happens too in early pregnancy. And my stomach nice and round and the smell of those onions – surely making me feel quite queasy?

And then from its secret place you take the newspaper cuttings; a woman in Italy, barren for nearly twenty years of marriage, suddenly conceives and gives birth to a healthy baby girl. At thirty-eight years of age. Thirty-eight!

And then that other woman in County Cork. Taking her brother's orphans into her childless home to find now three years later that she has two more to add to her household. Two more. Both of them her own. And she had been married how long? Ten, eleven years. And others too. Plenty others.

Oh the snippets she has kept with which to feed her hope.

And then it comes, usually just as you have begun to be sure. Just as you have determined to make an appointment with the doctor, or as you are shyly wondering if you should tell him (for of course, by now, you know to wait, not like the first year or two when every month, you knew this was it. 'Pat darling, I can't be sure, but I almost am') and his joy gets a little thinner month by month, until six have passed and then, 'Well, let's just see what the doctor says.'

How annoyed she used to be with his lack of enthusiasm for her false pregnancy. How dare he not mention it. And then after another half-year or so, praying that he wouldn't, knowing by then that a disappointment shared was doubled and not halved.

On the breast of a snowy bed. Or a wound on silken underlinen. It comes. During an interval at the theatre or when you've left a crowded room in full spirits to return ten minutes later, as good as dead.

When you've dared at last to look at somebody's child, to touch its cheek and lift its hair; to think 'Perhaps, perhaps this time, I can have one for my own.'

It's only when it's all over, when all possibility has expired, you realise how awful it has been, this anguish. What a fool you've been, yet again.

Maude turned on her side and drew her legs up to her stomach, sore: too sore. When did it start to hurt her this much? After she was married surely? When she was a girl – a mild discomfort, nothing more. But then the pain began to visit. Yes. Sneaking back month by month, growing a little stronger each time. And not a visitor to be deterred either, no sending out to say, 'Madam is not at home today.'

And now it owns her body fully, now that it knows this is a body without purpose. Nothing to light the way. This womb is an empty tunnel, its walls packed up with congealed blood. You must walk barefoot through, wandering, with nothing to guide or mark the progress. Except, of course, the passing of time itself.

And how long more, I wonder? How many years has it been so far? Thirteen years old, was I?

In Baltinglass, it was. Vanessa told us. Busy little cousin. Always the harbinger of bad news. First about Father Christmas. Then a year or two later about 'the secret'.

Mama died before there was time to tell. Would she have though? So many mothers leave it up to nurses. Nurse Flanagan would never mention any such thing. Not she.

Oh the day Vanessa told us. The day we heard! 'Blood,' she said, 'comes out of –' and her finger pointed downwards.

'Where? There? Do you mean, down there? Don't be so rude!'

And she stopped giggling then and became a little frightened. Yes, down there. That's what she meant, she really did.

Maude had started to cry. 'But I hate blood, I can't stand the sight of it. I don't want it to happen. I won't let it. Why should I? I'm going to ask Papa. You're lying, I know you are.'

But spiteful-eyed Vanessa shrugged. 'Every month,' she said, 'and every month after that. Until you're old. So there. And there's not a thing you can do about it. It has to happen. Otherwise you can't have babies.'

'Well then, I won't have any babies.'

'It'll come anyway.'

'*Anyway!* But why?' Maude was weeping now, angry tears. 'But why? Why me? What have I done? It's not fair, it's just not fair.'

'And as for asking your precious Papa, you can forget that. You're not supposed to tell them.'

'Them?'

'Men. Ever. Or it gets worse and worse and you will bleed to death. My mama says.'

Maude had wiped her tears then began to pout and with folded arms flopped herself down on the garden bench. 'I don't believe you. You're making it up. You're nothing but a liar.'

Now it was Vanessa's turn to be angry.

'I am not. Don't you dare call me a liar. I'm telling you the truth.'

Maude could still remember her sister Kate, sitting on the other end of the bench, swinging her feet so that she could watch the buckles of her new moleskin shoes gleam back and forth. And Vanessa standing in between facing them, her fists dug into her waist and her angry little face pushed up, screaming at them: 'I'm telling you the truth. I'm telling you the truth, I said. I'm –'

And only stopping when she heard Kate quietly say, 'I believe you, Vanessa.'

She rolled over on her stomach and pressed it hard into the bed. She could feel it ooze and bubble from her. Three more days of it at the least. And then what? A week of peace before the first of the appetites appear. This was the pattern of her life, predictable as wallpaper. Once a month there was the blood, twice a month the longing.

The first one came ten days or so after the bleeding had stopped, a whimsical sort of a thing, whispering and seductive. It lazed around for a couple of days, whinging slightly when it did not get its way and finally sighing off so that it just became a memory of itself inside her head. The longing for his weight on top, to feel it shift and shift again. To feel herself beneath it in the dark, his skin, his man hair, her teeth grating against these things.

Lottie told her this is the time that pregnancy occurs. And was she sick to the teeth of warning the women that come to her clinics? 'Time and time again I've warned then: when you feel you really want to for God's sake don't. It means your eggs are ready and nature wants you to have them fertilised. Remember: abstinence, abstinence – the only thing that keeps baby out of the cradle.' She mentioned it to Maude in passing, listing it in with the rest of her complaints; lack of hygiene, inability to exact respect from husbands, a general disinterest in the coming vote and, sighing grandly, she apologised in the end. 'I'm sorry Maude dear, to go on about it but at times I feel I might as well be howling at the moon.'

It was as if she were explaining the foibles of another race. One so alien that Maude could not possibly be expected to understand.

But she understood all right. She knew exactly what she meant.

For Maude it had become an extension of 'the curse'. Another form of punishment. Oh once it was different when he was there within her reach. When she only had to move a little closer to him, to look at him a certain way. Or to ensure he caught her dressing or, better still, undressing. To sleepy-limbed brush off him in the middle of the night, as if she couldn't guess the consequences. To make out that he had woken her and melt loosely into him as if she were still asleep.

But now? What was she supposed to do now? To lie clenched alone. The bed that once seemed too small for them, now as wide as a field? And him tucked away at the other fence, unreachable. Never moving towards her. Not once now in over three, no, four – this will be the fourth month now.

What if she were to move first? To touch him there. Oh to be brave enough. What would he say? What would he do?

And it doesn't seem to dawn on him either. He doesn't seem to mind that she sees him dressing or, worse still, undressing. As if it should have no effect on her. Perhaps it shouldn't, perhaps this is another of her flaws? Oh just a few days ago, the sight nearly killed her. It was during the time of the second appetite, the one that screams for it, kicking and howling when it does not get its way. The one that comes just before the blood. Just as the gnawing has started again and the iron fist tightens up into her, wringing the entrance that was once used for joining them, husband and wifeways, together.

And there he stood, his cruel chest bare, his arms stretching out as they fumbled across newly ironed shirts. And snug in his armpits his hair mocked out.

Through the mirror she had watched, the curve of his collar bones leading down to the place that once was for her. For her face to rub, her nose to smell and her hair to mingle and spread itself across. Frictional, the pleasure and the pain contradicted each other, and as she watched him draw the shirt over his body and pull the beauty out of her sight, hiding it first beneath linen and then taking it with him outside the bedroom door, she felt the appetite come on, making her long beyond reason. Oh with such ferocity that let her know this monster must be fed before it bleeds.

Is that why she has been so bad lately? Dissatisfied appetites griping in the background. Prowling past each other, up and down. Nourishing each other's dissatisfaction. (Come on, let's get her. Let's get her now.)

And making her mad, unable to control herself. There was that carry on last week, in Kate's bedroom, throwing all her clothes like giant butterflies about the room.

And what about that row with Pat this morning? How she disgraced herself! Losing her reason in that way. But all she wanted was for him to find out, please, please, please, where Greta had gone and why? She asked him just to inquire from Pakenham. Just one little inquiry that was all. But he wouldn't. Said he thought it wouldn't be right. A chap's domestic disorder was his own affair. All that rot.

'But Kate, what about Kate?' she had cried, jumped up and angry. 'I don't know what to do with her. She won't leave the house. She's been telling me the most awful stories about Pakenham. I just can't believe –'

'All the more reason why I shouldn't interfere.'

'But what if she's telling the truth. What then? I mean I don't disbelieve her. It's not that. It's just she keeps talking. I can't manage her. I tell you, I need Greta's help. Surely you can ask? I need to know what happened.'

'Well, you must ask Kate,' he replied.

'I have, I have. Why can't you understand she just won't tell?'

'I am not interfering, Maude,' he said, preferring her christian name to one of the usual pet ones. 'And that is that.'

'That is that, that is that. Is that all you have to say? Very well then, I shall ask Pakenham myself.'

'Do as you wish. Look I have an appointment. I'm already late as it is,' he said then. 'I can't stay and listen to this.'

And he walked out of the house. Simply because he could. Because he was dressed and ready. He walked out of the house because he was a man and he had somewhere to go.

At first she sat back down again, ready to weep and nothing more. But then the fury started through her. And she shot back up to her feet again and ran out into the street after him. Running so fast, she caught up with him. He had been turning into the back lane to search out Sam.

So he hadn't been late at all. Couldn't even wait for Sam to come around to the front of the house. And Sam was always on time, five minutes in advance at least. Had he been in that much of a hurry to get away from her?

'How dare you!' she had screamed at him, pulling at his arm. 'How dare you walk out and leave me like that when I was trying to speak to you. How dare you treat me like this.'

She was swinging from his arm now, the tears spilling out all over her cheeks. And only slightly aware of a blurred face or two passing by and looking at her. She hadn't time to do her hair and there it was trailing across her face, clasping itself over her mouth, as if trying to shut her up. Oh what a sight she must have been!

She could remember now his face, the startled look giving way to anger and then, as he noted her deranged state, trying to hush and to soothe her, guiding her back towards the house with an urgency he kept well disguised.

'I'm sorry, my dear, I had no idea it meant so much to you. You're distraught now; come on. Come, come.'

'No,' she continued to cry, to struggle against him. 'No, you care nothing for me, you treat your bottle washers with more respect. You expect me to go to that man, after the way he has treated my sister?'

'I'll do it for you. I'll ask him.' His voice was low and steady now, keeping a level tone in the background, a banister she could hang on to, distracting her with its quiet strength, while he organised the other details, those necessaries that would get her off the street and through the door. The key in the lock, his hand on her elbow, his will behind hers, ushering it into the hall before anyone else on the street became aware of her state. 'I'll see to it, but first you must rest. That's it my dear, that's it my sweet. I promise, yes I promise.'

In minutes he had soothed her to sleep. A sleep that as it happened lasted only a snatch. The front door wakening her again, despite the lightness of its touch as it clicked itself back into the wall. She looked over to the mantel clock. Five minutes. She had been asleep five minutes. That was all. And already he had left. And Samuel sitting outside, the car turning over and ready, right on time as prearranged. And why should it be otherwise? Had something happened after all to interfere with their morning routine?

And now the doctor has been and gone and she is alone. Already the messages have been sent, the appointment with the dressmaker cancelled. The 'war fund' luncheon too. And in the afternoon, tea with Mrs Gunne, to honour her daughter's mother- in-law. (Thank God for that escape at least!) And the message to Kate, delivered too by now. No visit today, no fruitless hour to be passed trying to coax her out of doors (A little fresh air perhaps?) and then later the tentative suggestion that she accompany her to the hospital. (Oh come on, Kate, come with me. Your little brother after all in hospital almost a week. Isn't it time to stop this coolness between you? What better time to do it? And he asks for you every day, I swear he does.) No lies to sell today at least.

But lies or truth Kate will not go. Kate will not budge. All Kate wants to do is talk. With those slow and formal words of hers, as if she is writing a letter or a private journal that may one day be read.

After all the years of wanting her younger sister's confidence, all the years of covetousness – 'Talk to me, Kate, why don't you talk? Give me what you have in there, give it to me please' – she finds herself wishing only for silence again. Once Kate started there seemed to be no end of it. She could not seem to stop. Telling all now, relieving herself day by day. Handing them over, one by one, laying confidences in her sister's lap; things Maude cannot bear to hear. Making her long to cover her ears and shout: 'Oh stop. *Stop!* Enough, I have had enough.

She tells everything, except the one thing that Maude wants to know. Where is Greta? Where in God's name is Greta? I need somebody to stand at the other end of this, somebody to help me carry this load.

Maude sips the sweetened tea Philomena has brought her. She would like to wash her hair, to comfort herself with its clean feel, its smell. She cannot even bear to brush it when it's like this. Dirty. She would like to take a walk then, alone. Down through the park where the soft-backed deer crouch dun among the trees. But to go out would mean she was well enough to visit. Kate, the hospital, Mrs Gunne. Was well enough to receive too and had no business sending that man from the theatre away (what was his name?).

She picked up his card again and read it. Masterson.

Now that she knows she will be alone, there is already a feeling lightening up her edges; a feeling of relief. And a stranger's concern for her younger brother is not reason enough for it to be spoiled.

She has today, nothing to dread. Except the embarrassment when Pat comes home, but even that she can avoid. Pretend to be asleep.

She has nothing new to contemplate tonight. Nothing more foul than has already been given her. She might have a chance to clear a space or two inside her own head for a change. Make some room for other thoughts. She might at last be able to think what to do.

She would give it a few days and make no mention. By then if Pat had left the subject untouched, she would go herself to see Pakenham and make demands, for Greta, her sister and her father's wishes. She would dare him to defy her.

Maude put the cup down and rested her head back on the pillows. That dreadful man – who would believe it? And yet she could do little about him. Not without Pat's help. And Kate had made her promise, not a word. She must make Kate understand. She must make her unashamed. None of it had been her fault. How could she have known? She must get Kate to release her from this vow of silence. Greta could help her. Greta had more influence on her sister than anyone she had ever known before. She would find her. Yes. With Greta and Pat. Between the three of them, they could help Kate.

Why should she have to live with a man like that anyway? Why should she have to add further to the misery?

And Papa? How could he?

Maude had imagined it time and time again. That awful honeymoon. That awful time her sister had been forced to endure. By now it no longer broke her heart; by now she felt it so strongly that: 'It might as well have been my own experience,' she said aloud. 'I might as well have been there myself.'

On a soft winded night, dressed in the best of the trousseau's tea-gowns, my sister sits opposite a man. There is a small table set between them. A breeze strays around the shutter and into a room, lit only by fire-flame and the fractional light of candles. It ruffles this light a little and kisses her hair with its summer breath. She waits for the man to make a move.

He smokes silently a cigar and gazes towards the fire. She knows he has done this sort of thing before, probably quite a lot. But she prefers it that way, a man of experience: no point in the pair of them depending on innocence to take them through their first night together.

Their meal has long since finished and still he has not moved. Perhaps it is up to her? Perhaps she is supposed to leave first, to prepare, make ready for her wedding night. Yes, she thinks, that must be it. It is almost midnight, after all.

His eyes seem a little clouded as he looks into the fire, as if he is not quite sure just what it is that he is looking at. Perhaps he is a little drunk? But no, that's not how drunken men behave, they shout and sing, they tell amusing stories – often more than once. Sometimes they brawl. They don't sit and stare into their own silence.

It's the length of the journey, that's it. A long, long day. And she knows he has been up before the dawn. She saw him after all.

Perhaps he is nervous? No, surely not. But how is she to know the way a man might think? The way a man might feel? She decides to move.

Fidgeting at the hem of her tea gown, she says, 'I – I think I'll …' She nods towards the door.

'What? Oh yes. Yes. Goodnight.'

She stands up and slips away, the cinnamon cloth that I can remember helping her to choose breathing around her legs as she moves. She leaves the door ajar and prepares herself. Depending on the shy hints that I have given her and her own womanly instincts to guide her.

She slides beneath the covers, shivering now a little with the cold, a little with the nerves. She hears his step move across the room outside and the shivering increases. Perhaps this is it?

But the step goes the other way, turning towards the fire; where she can hear now the poker levelling coals and then restacking them again. The step comes back to the centre of the room and then stops. There is the sound of glass touching glass. He is pouring himself another drink, a nightcap to take with him when he comes to her? She only has to listen now for the step to resume and his shadow to stand in the doorway. She waits.

After a while her eyes start to close and the shivering stops. After a while she sleeps.

When she awoke, it was to the snarl of an opening curtain. A maid stood with her back to the bed and picked up a tray she had left down on the table. 'Good morning, Madam,' she said, nudging the tray across the bed and onto Kate's lap.

Kate sat up and looked to her side, where a pillow lay plump, untouched.

'Has my husband gone out?' she asked. 'Oh yes Madam. I met him on the corridor about an hour ago. He asked that you weren't to be disturbed and said to tell you that he would see you later.'

All day she waited for later. The first hour gave her pleasure, taking her bath and then carefully changing into her Ascot outfit. Just as I had warned her, she couldn't manage those tiny crystal buttons that fastened at the back and had to call the maid to help her. She had begun to panic a little at this point, terrified that she wouldn't be ready before his return and that he would be kept waiting. But the maid calmed her, staying with her to the hat and gloves and gasping with genuine approval when the outfitting was complete. Kate looked at her reflection and yes, she too was pleased, always preferring those big picture hats in any case and the way they covered her face. She chatted with the maid for a short time while sipping the tea she had insisted that Madam take before Sir returned to fetch her. Then the maid left and she waited alone.

By two o'clock she finally accepted that Sir would not be returning. Not on time to take her to Ascot anyway. She changed her clothes – an afternoon frock this time – and sat near the window busying herself by writing letters to those wedding guests whose gifts she could recall.

She ignored the hotel stationery and used her own, taking the trouble to postdate – for after all who has time to write thank you notes on their honeymoon?

Once in the afternoon when she knew the maid had finished work, she went downstairs to take afternoon tea. But in the foyer she became overwhelmed by the fear that he might return to the room and think she had gone out for the day. She went back upstairs and ordered tea up to her room.

Six o' clock and still no sign of 'later'. She had spent the rest of the afternoon sitting on the side of the bed, feet up first and then feet down. She changed her clothes several times, each time hurriedly in case he should walk in.

Then there was a knock at the door causing everything to dip inside her. She ran to answer it and stopped then for a second, hoping that one deep breath would somehow be enough to compose her. It wasn't him.

The porter handed her the theatre tickets that had been ordered for this evening. Now she had something to work on. The theatre. And then there was that restaurant Pat recommended they should try. 'Quite *the* place,' he had said. 'Just the place to spend your Ascot winnings. And you can dance there too; has a nimble little orchestra.'

And he had said. 'Oh yes. I'll reserve a table, first thing. For Wednesday?' looking over at her. She remembered nodding and trying not to smile. (Dancing? – oh yes!)

'Well that's settled then,' he reaffirmed, 'Wednesday after the theatre.'

At least now she knew how to dress. She chose a suitable gown and arranged her own hair; as she always does.

He was back on time.

'We're dining up here,' he said, the moment he set eyes on her. And so she changed back into her second tea gown, ignoring the fact that his voice sounded strange, as though he had borrowed it from someone else.

This would be her first time to see him drunk. The first time to encounter those habits with which later she would be so familiar. The reluctance to be seen in public after six (the hour when the drink usually began to manifest itself). The silence. The refusal to have it broken, unless he had something particularly savage to say. But all that was the future. For the moment this was also to be the longest conversation they would ever have. Perhaps that is why she remembered it so well? Its filthy words and all the background details that surrounded it.

He gave no explanation for his absence, although he took care to mention that the crowd had been ample at Royal Ascot. And that he had had an excellent day. What was to have been their first outing together as man and wife, he had enjoyed alone.

Nonetheless she made no remark on it. No scene, nothing to disgrace herself. She just sat on the edge of the chair as she had once sat years ago on the edge of a garden bench. And accepted it. Except this time no bright buckles on childish shoes could distract from the situation.

The meal was much a repeat of the night before. Similar food, identical crockery. This time he sent for an extra bottle of wine, and a decanter of whiskey. The room was much the same as well. Except now the tickets for the theatre lay on the chaise longue where she had left them. And no fire burned in the grate; it was June, after all.

They served themselves as honeymooners do. And she made no effort to disturb or to cajole him. Again towards midnight, she thought she had better be the one to make a move. This time she had no doubt that he was drunk, his eyes not clouded now, but completely hazed, expressionless. As she put it herself, 'They were there in his head – open but not necessarily looking out.'

'Well, I think I'll go in now. I'm feeling rather tired,' she said to him.

He looked up suddenly, startled, as though she had woken him.

'I'm sorry, did you say something?'

'Nothing, I'm just tired. I think I'll go to bed now.'

'You're tired, is that what you said?'

'Yes. That's right. I'm tired.'

'Ahh.' He picked the decanter up again and, pulling its head away from its shoulders, turned it on its side and into an empty glass, as if it were made of paper and had no weight to it at all.

'You see,' he said, 'I wasn't quite sure. I thought you said, "Ein dired. I mant do doe do med."'

He smiled then and laughed into her face, pleased at the shock he had exacted.

'I mant do doe do ded,' he repeated, in a singing tone, pressing his hand down onto his nose until it squashed to a stump. And he laughed again.

The honeymoon was over.

'Ahh,' he said then, 'Are we sad on our honeymoon? We're not going to cry now are we?'

It was those exact words that stopped her from doing just that. Calmly she looked at him and then stood up.

'Tell me my dear,' he began, 'what did your dear Papa give you for a wedding gift?'

'A piano,' she said, answering him because she did not know what else to do.

'Yes, and ...?'

'A dressing bag.'

'Anything else?'

'With silver and ivory fittings?' (What was it? What was he getting at? That Papa's gifts were inadequate?)

'No no. I don't mean that. Come on now. Think, there must have been something else?'

'He gave me a cheque, actually.' (Was that it? Was that what he was after?) 'You can have it if you want. I was going to tell you.'

'Going to? I knew about it before you did, my dear. As if I'd take your cheque from you. No there's something else. Something you've forgotten. Come now. Come on. You're not thinking. *Think.*'

'I don't know what you mean.'

'Oh dear, oh dear. Poor Papa. Spent all that money on a wedding present for you. The most expensive one you got too, I might add. More expensive than the whole lot of the others put together. We won't bother to include, of course, those given by your Papa's peasant relatives – My God, how pathetic ...' He paused to fill his glass again. She tried to speak.

'I –'

'*Plus,*' he interupted, 'plus of course, the cost of the wedding. And you can't even remember. Well I'm ashamed of you my dear, I don't mind saying it.'

He lifted the glass to his mouth and she took the opportunity to move away from the table.

'Where are you going?' he asked.

'To bed,' she answered.

'Well, what are you telling me for?' He was becoming irritated now; her calmness provoking him. 'You needn't tell me about your, your – bed.'

'I am telling you because you asked me.' She walked away.

'Yes, yes. You're quite right. I apologise, I did ask you. Please forgive me. Yes, you go on now. You must be tired.'

She walked to the bedroom door. And then he spoke again: 'Oh Kate, dear, I feel it really ought to be said. I mean, there's no point in our starting out by being dishonest with each other. It's a mistake made by so many couples, don't you agree?'

And he sounded so sensible, that for a moment she forgot the past hours and was caught by his sudden shift of mood. She stopped to nod and say, 'Yes. Yes of course.'

He then continued: 'I married you because your half-wit of a Papa paid me to. Yes that's right. I'm your wedding present. It's me. He bought me for you. Devoted Papa that he is. Of course, like all people of his particular class, one step up from the peasantry, he thinks anything can be bought. And he is quite right too. Or so it would seem. But really, my darling – to expect me to share your bed? Well now…' and he laughed a little before filling up his glass yet again. 'Be reasonable.'

And Kate, with all her strength, managed to look straight at him. 'I don't want you in my bed,' she said. 'I don't want Papa's present. You can keep the money, if it means that much to you. But I don't want you.'

'Don't want me? Oh how hurtful. And tell me my dear, what do you propose to do with me?'

'Divorce you.'

'Ahh. Well I'm afraid that's not a very good idea. You see, I don't want a divorce. I will never leave you, my dear. I promised your Papa and I promise you.' He pulled a cigar from his pocket and bit on it before smiling at her and whispering, 'Never.'

He leaned towards the candle flame and puffed slowly into it until the cigar took life.

'But let's not dismiss your options out of hand. Let's think about this, shall we? Just supposing you were to decide to take matters into your own hands. What would you say? I want to divorce my husband. Yes, but why?'

He walked towards the fireplace, continuing as he moved: 'And they do ask why, you know. And that would be the problem, as I see it. What would you say when they asked you why? I mean, would you stand in the dock and say, "Well, your honour, it's like this: my husband couldn't bear to sleep with me. Couldn't bear to *look* at me."'

He swung around then to face her, a feigned look of bewilderment on his face. 'I mean everyone would know. Absolutely everyone. It would be bound to get out. No, I really can't have people laughing at you like that. Or worse still, feeling sorry for you. And I can see no other way around it. Can you?'

He walked towards her sighing heavily. 'Still, let's not talk about that now. We have the rest of our lives to talk about that. You go and have your rest. You look all done in, poor dear.'

Kate remembers him leaning towards her, his arm stretching behind her to open the door to the bedroom.

'Goodnight my sweet,' he said, kissing her lightly on the cheek.

At last she was behind the closed door of the bedroom.

Things were much the same here as last night too. The flowers that had been waiting for them. The bed made up for two. The evening gown she had earlier left lying across it. But this time the door was firmly shut and the key turned fully in the lock.

She cried all night, the same evening gown stuffed into her mouth. This was not to prevent him from hearing her – he had already gone out – it was so she couldn't hear herself.

By morning she was quiet again. The tears all dried. All put away.

It would be a long time before my sister would cry again. And neither death nor loneliness could induce her to. Almost five years would pass before they would return.

On a Good Friday morning, unseasonably warm. When a letter would bring them rushing back to her. A letter from a friend.

FOURTEEN

On Easter Saturday morning Kate ordered an early taxi and dressed hurriedly to be ready for it. She refused breakfast. No, she said. Thank you but she would breakfast out. Maura asked if it were wise of her to go out with such a cold on her but Mrs Pakenham seemed to be in such fine spirits that she decided, after all, not to nag. Perhaps she was going out to meet Miss Greta off the train.

'Are you going to meet Miss Greta off the train?' she asked.

Mrs Pakenham appeared not to hear, coming down the stairs behind a great big lump of a box and humming to herself as if she were alone.

She then handed the box to Maura, drawing her attention to the envelope lying on its lid: a note addressed to her sister.

'Will you have this sent around to Maude for me, please, Maura?'

'You're not going racing then?'

'Oh no. I don't feel up to it. Monday maybe. Fairyhouse. We'll see.'

Maura weighed the box in her arms gently.

'Something nice for Mrs Cleary?'

'Yes that's right,' Kate said, 'a hat with four corners, would you believe?'

She straightened her coat about her shoulders.

'All very well,' said Maura, 'as long as you've a head with four corners for it to fit on to.'

Kate took up her bag and smiled. 'I'll call into the doctor and then take it easy for the rest of the day.'

'You're not going shopping then?' Maura asked her.

'Shopping? Oh no, I hardly think so.'

'Well I'll see you later so,' Maura called after her, laying the box awkwardly on the hall table, so she could close the front door after Mrs Pakenham.

In Bewley's Oriental Café Kate found a nice dark corner to fit herself neatly inside. First thing after coat and gloves, she saw to the withdrawal of a notebook and fountain-pen box from her bag. She opened the notebook and firmly pushed down on its pages, allowing a moment to see if there would be any defiance. The pages remained flat. She opened the pen box and extracted the pen daintily from its velvet belly.

Then she ordered an almond bun, a piece of toast and a pot of Indian tea. Her tastebuds, having already been dulled enough with the head cold, were hardly likely to be amused or soothed by tea from China. Something stronger was needed this morning.

She laid her hand gently onto the fresh new page. 'Brown Thomas' she wrote at the top and then slid her hand downwards. After a second she moved upwards again and carefully added in 'No. 1' just before the 'Brown'. She moved back down again, this time starting with No. 2 House of Switzer. She stopped for a moment to admire her handwriting; yes this new pen suited it very well. Very well indeed. She carried on – No. 3 Roberts & Co.

The waitress returned, pulling the crockery up from the tray and rearranging it all in the exact same order on the table.

And what a pity somebody doesn't invent a tray that slides out from under and just deposits everything, ready for use on the table, Kate almost said to her, as she watched the poor girl lifting and replacing, and keeping to the pattern too.

'Will that be all, Madam?'

'Mmm? Oh yes, thank you.'

Already Kate had forgotten about the tray and was lifting the milk jug to a more accessible spot. She rested the pen on the thick parting of the pages, while she attended to the butter and jam, the tea and, finally, the merest touch of milk which was her preference. She took the pen up again, checking her hands first for crumbs or grease spots which might spoil the look of the page.

No. 4 – West & Co. She took a bite from the toast, ragging it at the corner.

Next she left a nice space and in large copperplate letters spread the word 'Luncheon' evenly across it. Now. All nice and organised.

She continued a little down the page and wrote No. 5. But where could No. 5 be? Where to start after lunch? She checked the list again. Any shop in Grafton Street that interested her was already listed. She would have to cross the bridge. Where to? Instinct told her Clerys – but no. She couldn't bear Clerys, not since it had been moved to that Metropolitan Hall; altogether a too depressing substitute for what once had been her favourite store. Two years now almost to the day and still no sign of them returning to their former premises. Two years since the rebellion. What were they waiting for? Another one?

With strawberry jam she moistened the well-sprung flesh of the cut almond bun, smearing the knife off its yellow sides and softly remembering.

Up the stairs with Mama's hand swinging beside her head and close enough to whisper to like a friend. And under the toplighting they would go, where Mama stopped to think. Should she get this? Or maybe better get that? It was part of their shopping routine. Mama would look at everything the store had to offer and then take five minutes on the balcony while she made up her mind. And while she stood tall, her long fingers clawed over the banister, a nibble of inner discussion sometimes leaking out onto her lips, Kate would wait. Tucked down near the ground, her chest pressing against her thighs. And over her folded legs, the muslin frock dropping full, into a midget woman's ball-gown.

And looking up first into the corona where the lights grow down from brass stalks. (You can take their sparkles from them, if you stare hard enough. Draw them into your eyes and then carry them away behind closed lids, anywhere you like, to sprinkle when you blink again, like seed pearls onto the crowd below.)

And looking down to follow their course, one small hand flat against a pillar whose curve she'll never catch, the other hand playing loop the loop fingers up and around the curls and hooks of the fine metalwork balustrade. And thinking with a different mind now up here, seeing things differently since the stairs have been climbed. Adults for example, how different they looked. How different the distance can make them. Nothing to be frightened of, not in the least. For what were they after all, but children playing games? (Good day to you, Madam. Now what can I do for you? Oh good day to you too. I think I'll have forty-nine pairs of merino underwear please. And I want them very large, thank you very much, because I have a very fat bottom indeed. Yes, Madam, indeed you do. Would you like an osprey feather to make them look nicer? You could stick it in just like this. Oh how lovely, do you think it goes? Oh thank you very much. Good day. Oh thank you very much. Good day as well.)

And other things too, seemed altered from up here: hats moving flat amongst the wiggle-waggle feathers and every other minute it seems as if a hope might be realised, that just once the little money trains bustling past each other on cable lines, streamered across the ceilings, would suddenly snap and drop, smashing into a burst of coins on top of some unsuspecting head.

And all she would think of was what she could see. Not remembering why they were here in the city at all. And not thinking of what was to come either, until the stairs are passed again and well behind them and Mama with renewed energy has retraced the counters down below, her address now jotted into little books with promises of postage.

Then it comes back to her as they pass out through the doors into an afternoon that is beginning to thicken. Oh that's why she is here in the city. It was for her quarterly inspection. With that man who pokes his sausage finger into her mouth, prodding his thumb up against her palate, going, 'Hmm aahh hmmm' and then sending her to sit outside all alone while he whispers secrets to Papa. She should have bitten it and then said: 'Oh I *am* sorry, I thought it was a sausage.'

Then other things come back to her too, like Noblett's sweet shop before the journey home. And now everything has returned to where it was before: the past, the future. And the present which had started when Mama took her hand from Papa's and they climbed together up velvet steps and under lights which grew brighter as you neared. Turning for a second half-way up – 'Bye bye, Papa' – to see if you can pick out his head zigzagging through all the others, towards the door. That present is over. Gone. It ended when they came down the stairs again. Back into the adult world. Where she walks again, frightened amongst the flat tops and the wiggle-waggle feathers.

No. 5? Kate rested the pen down once more and finished her breakfast. She lifted her hands up and away from her skirt and rubbing them lightly off each other dispersed any crumbs lurking between her fingers. She would fill in the rest of the list at luncheon, she decided. It would give her something to do.

It was after half-past nine when Kate pushed through the doors of Brown Thomas. It was early yet, a straggle of shoppers. Even so she invited little attention beyond the expected courtesy. She walked to the handbag counter first where a sales assistant stepped forward to greet her. Kate shook her head. 'No thank you.'

She moved on then down through the aisles, looking out from under her hat at the lay-out of the various counters, so that she might get an idea of what was available. They'd changed the position of the glove counter, she noted. Or maybe she was thinking of Switzers? And a new sales assistant too. Such a long time since she had been in here. She'd forgotten what a lovely shop it was. And the range of goods. Changing all the time. So modern. Yes the glove counter …

As she moved down towards the back of the shop she replied politely to the 'Good morning, Madams' drifting out from behind the various counters as she passed. But it was hot. Wasn't it hot? Her collar felt so tight and inside her gloves she felt trapped heat melt. Her heart was at her too. Must be the heat. Thumping away like that and making her feel quite giddy. Somebody told her that since high collars were no longer in fashion, women's necks were actually growing larger. Could that be true? Was that why now she could feel hers throb as if it were bulging to get out of her collar? But she wasn't wearing a high-neck – was she?

She brought her hand up and gave a hurried pat. No, of course she wasn't. Must be the head cold, she decided then. Although I feel surprisingly well.

Upstairs then back down again. They still had that old bat in fur and millinery anyway. She'd be taken out of here in one of her own hatboxes. And that other man over there with the tape around his neck – oh what was his name? She felt sure she could remember him here as a child, when Mama came to be outfitted. In fact, now that she had had a good look around, almost all of their staff looked familiar, except for –? Back to the gloves.

'Good morning, Madam. Can I help you, Madam?' the girl at the glove counter asked.

'I'm looking for a gift actually. For my sister. Gloves I thought.'

'Oh yes, Madam, you can never have enough. And we have a lovely selection, just in. Skin or fabric?'

'Oh well I'm not sure really.'

Kate looked vaguely at the boxes of gloves built like bricks into the wall behind the sales assistant. She smiled a helpless sort of smile. The assistant understood, ducking under the counter and coming back up with a large box of assorted gloves marked 'sundry'.

'There now,' she said, 'if you'd like to have a browse through these, you can pick what you fancy and then we only have to worry about size.'

'Oh goodness, where to begin?' Kate peered down into the box as though it were crawling with live things.

'Take your time,' the sales assistant smiled, moving off to see to somebody else.

Kate gently laid her hand into the box and using a blind man's touch patted around, feeling the different textures beneath her palm. Doeskin and, yes, suede. And that one there with the yellow lining and two buttons? She picked up one or two loose ones, holding these boneless hands in hers. She pulled off one of her own gloves and replaced it with one from the box, stretching her hand out and up, turning it a little bit this way, a little bit that, lingering for a while to admire. With her free hand she ran her fingers over the tiny nut buttons of bone and porcelain. And shivered the soft skin of dovelet grey into the tiniest ripples. The sales assistant returned.

'Have you had any luck, Madam?'

'Yes, I'd like to see this one.' She raised her hand again to show she meant the one she was wearing, and removed the glove, dropping it down onto the counter. 'And I'd like to have a look at – ah yes, here it is – this one.' She smiled at the assistant.

'Certainly, Madam,' she heard her say as she began to slide the box off the counter.

'Ah ah ah ah,' Kate wagged her finger.

'I beg your pardon, Madam?'

'My glove – it's in your box.'

'Oh I beg your pardon, Madam,' she repeated, this time with a different tone. She returned the glove to Kate, smiling apologetically.

Up along the stack of wooden drawers then, Kate watched her fingers climb and stopping then when they found the number and colour label they had been looking for. A long box was pulled out, leaving a small square cave in the wall. The sales assistant then came back down and laid it cautiously on the counter. 'There we are,' she said, 'the dove grey. Double-dome suede finish. And double-tipped fingers. We also have them in drab or pastelle?'

With her fingers swimming down the length of the drawer, the tissue paper loosened. And then slowly it parted and its contents were revealed. Nestling, finger to finger, dozens of them, soft, untouched, their fine bone and porcelain buttons seeming even smaller in a crowd.

'Ahh,' Kate heard herself say.

'I have a feeling this other one has been discontinued.'

'I'm sorry?' Kate asked.

'This one,' the assistant held up the second glove.

'I don't think we have it. It's certainly not up there.'

'Oh no,' Kate said, 'what a shame. And I had decided to take both. I liked it too. It would have made a lovely second pair for my sister. Give her a choice. You know.'

'Well, there's a small chance we may have some left in the storeroom. I could check?'

'Oh would you? How kind. That would be absolutely marvellous. Save me having to make up my mind all over again.'

The assistant smiled and then hurried off.

When she came a few minutes later, a pair of gloves triumphantly in her hand, there was no one at the counter. And Miss Graham from haberdashery was replacing the drawer, trying to manipulate it back into the wall in the clumsiest of fashions.

'Where's my customer?' she asked her crossly.

'She was in a hurry. Said she had to meet someone and couldn't wait. But if you held onto the gloves she'd be back in.'

'Well, now. I've heard that one before. And isn't that just great. After all the trouble I've gone to. It took me ages to find this pair. Horrible old-fashioned things. Who'd want them anyway?' She flung the gloves huffily onto the counter. 'Did she buy the grey ones?'

'No,' Miss Graham said. 'She didn't buy anything.'

'Well that's the last time I'll strain meself, I needn't tell you. Typical. Just typical.' She scowled until the sight of another customer smoothed her face back into a smile.

In West & Co. a large man stood facing Bart Tully. He was blowing out of him like a bull because his blasted binocular glasses weren't ready yet. And what did he expect anyway, leaving them in at five o'clock on Holy Thursday and then demanding them first thing on Saturday morning. Had the man never heard of Good Friday?

'Shouldn't be too long now, Mr Belton. Only another few minutes,' Bart nodded reassuringly.

'Another few minutes? I'll miss the first race.'

What was he talking about 'miss the first race'? It was only half-past eleven, plenty of time, and him with a driver waiting outside for him. In a hurry to get more liquor, more like, judging by the whiff of him. Yesterday was probably too much for him and coming so soon after the publican's strike too and Sahara week. Honest to God, the whole city seemed to be making up for lost time. And where the hell was Higgins? Ten minutes he'd sworn over thirty ago.

'And you couldn't get a nicer day for the races, Sir. Hasn't the weather only been …?'

Mr Belton glared at Bart and pulled a copy of the *Irish Field* out of his pocket.

Bart tried not to look down at the glass counter. I'll end up saying something, he said to himself. If he doesn't stop, I'll say it straight out and I don't care who hears.

The man was pawing his counter. It was that simple. No point in being nice about it. A fact was a fact and this was it: he had his big paws making smudges on the glass that Bart had spent the last hour buffing up to the hilt. Only finished the job not twenty minutes since. And look at it. Looking like the glass on a kip's window. The dirt of it. What if Mr West should walk in? What then? Who was he going to lay the blame on – Belton? I don't think.

And here he was off again asking where the hell were his bloody binocular glasses so that he could go off to the bloody Park and what in the name of Harry was keeping them. A simple adjustment, that's all. What had they to do, send to bloody Gallipoli for them?

'Our Mr Higgins will have them for you in plenty of time. Never you fear.'

Our Mr Higgins indeed. And where was he now? That's what I'd like to know, me stuck here with this baboon while he sits up in God knows which shop nursing a small one that might steady his hand so that he can do an hour's work. Oh yes all very fine for me laddio, leaving me here with this mitt-slinger.

'Damn and blast you and your bloody Mr Higgins.'

Oh and that's lovely talk. That's just lovely, and a lady just after walking in too. Satisfied now, I hope, with himself and his bad language.

She was standing half hidden behind Mr Belton at the side counter. Bart tried to give him the billyo, let him know there was a lady present. But by the time he had the sense to see it, a dozen more swear words had been flung around the place. No respect. That was the trouble with these so-called 'gents': no respect. No wonder the women of the country were losing the run of themselves.

'I'm looking for a gift,' she said, when he walked around to greet her.

'For my father.'

The girl looked timid, obviously embarrassed by the language she had been forced to witness. She wasn't well either, a bit of a cold. And God love her but she had one of those noses like the chappie on the door knockers. He would serve her promptly, exercising the discretion that he had been complimented on more than once.

'Had you anything in mind, Madam?' he asked lowering his voice, as he usually did for lady customers. Though this time he found himself dipping an octave or two lower than usual.

'I thought perhaps a snuff box,' she replied.

'A snuff box? An excellent idea, I always think, for an older gentleman.'

'Yes, as long as he takes snuff. Otherwise it's a damned stupid idea,' said Mr Belton, after he had turned around to interfere with their conversation.

The young lady gave a little smile. Out of politeness. Bart knew and understood straight away, giving a little smile of his own. One that said, 'There you are, your joke is acknowledged. Just don't expect *us* to be amused by it.'

'And does he take snuff?' Bart asked, so gently, it was as if the words were made of blades and likely to cut his lips.

'Oh yes, of course,' the lady replied.

'Of course,' Bart confirmed, giving Mr Belton one of his looks which he rather prided himself on.

('I just gave him one of my looks, Mother.')

('Did you son? Good for you!')

'Well whatever you do, don't get him binoculars. Unless he

doesn't mind not being able to see through them.' Mr Belton turned away and returned to his copy of the *Irish Field*.

Bart continued to stare at the back of Mr Belton's head for a few seconds, just to let the lady know he wasn't used to, nor did he approve of, such manners.

'Now what were we saying? Ah yes, snuff boxes. If you'd just like to come down to the end here,' he made to move, intimating that she should meet him at the further end of the L-shaped counter, 'and I'll bring them over to you.'

Now that he had managed to manoeuvre the lady as far away as possible from Belton, he could let her have a look at the snuff boxes without intrusion. She'd buy all right. Bart could always tell. He'd show her the expensive ones first and work downwards. He could tell she had a few bob. Best of stuff on her back, no shortage there. Still he wouldn't try to force anything on her. That wasn't the way with Bart Tully, a fair man according to his own lights. As anyone would tell you. Sometimes a little bit too fair perhaps, for his own good, Murphy outselling him nine times out of ten. But that was the way God made him, and anyway Murphy wasn't in till this afternoon. He'd guide her and well – who knows? Maybe he'd be in the way of having a bet himself before the day was out?

He saw himself then just for a moment, standing up at the bar of the Moira and chatting casually to Higgins and that Murphy with the pasty face on him. Always bragging about how well he cuts it.

'I knew it was just going to be one of those days, Higgins, you know?' he could start as he gave the barman the nod. 'First the sale and then backing those couple of winners. Mr West came into me himself. He says to me, he says: "Bartholomew, how do you do it? The best sale we've had this year. Nothing worth talking about for months and then up you come on the outside with something like this. Oh yes," he said, "you certainly know how to make up for lost time."'

And then as the barman comes down, he could say, 'Give the lads whatever they're having, there's a good man.' And Higgins would hop to it with, 'Ah you're not off already Tully?'

'Indeed'n I am. I like to keep a clear head. Besides I have a rendezvous.' A bit of a wink and out he'd walk, leaving the two of them gawking behind him.

And then Higgins would turn to pasty face and say, 'Did you ever notice that Murphy?'

'What's that?' says Murphy.

'A man who doesn't drink. Well he's often more of a – of a success, if you like.'

And Murphy then depressed as doomsday.

'Yes, I see what you mean. And often in more ways than one.'

Cheerier now, Bart walked back to the front counter and stooped down. He began sliding and unsliding doors until he hit upon the required cabinet. He heard Higgins returning through the back door into the workroom. And not before time either. He'd be reading the note left under the binocular glasses by now. 'Please see to this immediately. Customer (Belly-ache Belton) in shop waiting. V. annoyed. Says he's coming in to strangle you. And I won't be long behind him.'

He raised his voice (just to let Higgins know that he wasn't exaggerating and that Belton was still here):

'So do you fancy anything yourself today, Mr Belton,' he asked, cheerily picking out a selection of boxes to place on top of his lap-balanced tray.

'No!' Belton boomed back at him, as if he'd asked for the loan of a quid. Bit of a waste then going at all, Bart thought, unhinging himself upwards and returning the set of miniature keys to their hook on the wall.

'Oh well,' he said, dividing his voice loudly between Belton and the workroom. 'Maybe when you get there, *Mr Belton*, you'll find something you'll fancy.'

'What would be the point?' Belton leaned over the counter slightly and raised his voice to match Bart's: '*When I won't be able to bloody see 'em!*'

Bart tightened his lips and took his selection tray away. He moved down to the other end of the counter and placed it down in front of Kate. It was bold of him he knew; even while he was doing it, he knew it was risky. After all the world was divided between those on this side of the counter and those on the other. But the next time Belton tutted loudly and gasped out another 'Oh for the love of –' Bart found himself catching the eye of the lady and rolling his eye upwards. He was not unrewarded; she verified her sympathy with a small but definite smile.

'Now,' Bart began, much cheered with this little show of support, 'this is a bit expensive but I'm sure you'll agree …'

'Oh yes.' She held her palm open and Bart gently lowered it down as if it were a baby bird.

'Don't you think –?'

'Oh yes,' she said again.

'Open it,' he said softly.

She looked up at him nervously.

'Go on,' he urged.

With the merest touch of her hand, she tipped the lid over and together they peeped inside.

'You won't find another like it in the country. Or indeed anywhere, except maybe Boston. Which is where it comes from.'

'I was in Boston once.' Belton was turning around. Bart could hardly believe it. 'Here let's have a look at it.'

Now he was walking down towards them. Who would believe the nerve of some people?

'Oh yes,' he said. 'See – they've made it like a little tea chest.

Very clever I'm sure. On account of the Boston Tea Party, you know.'

'I was about to tell the lady that.'

Mr Belton looked up at him. 'Well you won't have to now, will you?'

'How much they looking for it?' he asked Kate, while stretching his little finger over and lifting the tiny price tag.

'Robbers!' he said. 'You could go to Boston for that. Buy a half a dozen snuff boxes *and* a real tea chest.'

Kate continued to look down at the snuff box as if it were about to fly away.

'It is an antique,' Bart spoke as slowly as he could. He was going to say something, he really was. If that man lost him his sale …

'Yes well, whether it is or it isn't, it's no bloody good.'

'Excuse me, Mr Belton, but –'

'Well, look.' Mr Belton reached down and with a flick of his finger opened the lid. 'Opens too easily; snuff'd be all over the bloody place. You could get it fixed I suppose. It's a nice little thing all right. But it's not worth that money.'

He was addressing Kate as if Bart didn't exist. Oh yes, thought Bart, this one knows which side of the counter he's on and no mistake. I've a good mind to say –

'It's an interesting city, Boston,' Mr Belton continued. 'They take things very seriously there. Like women for instance.'

He looked perplexed for a minute, hesitating before he continued. 'Yes, they're fond of education, you know. Do you know they have this club for graduates. Girl graduates. Oh yes, they'd have enough of them to make up a club all right. Anyway, they have to swear to postpone marriage until three years after taking a degree and then to husbands whose income is not less than £1,000. Did you ever hear the like? *A thousand quid.* Some of them'd be lucky to get any sort of a husband at all, if you ask me. And waiting three years is not going to improve their chances much. They should be paying a thousand quid for someone to take them. Buck ugly some of them Americans. Too many teeth. Still that's Boston for you.'

'Yes, very interesting,' Bart said as pleasantly as could be expected, 'but if you'll excuse me a minute.'

He had to get out for a second, he really did, he had never been so embarrassed in his whole living. Talking about such things. In front of the poor – well, she was hardly going to agree with him, was she? With her looks. No sensitivity. None whatso–. It seems nowadays all you needed was a few bob to pass yourself off as a gentleman. And where were his bloody binoculars anyway, so he could get the hell out of here and off to the pub or the Park or bloody Boston or wherever he was going.

Bart walked into the backroom determined to stand beside Higgins until he had the job finished.

'Robbers,' Mr Belton repeated before turning away from Kate and back to the front counter. 'If I were you dear, I'd take me business elsewhere.'

*

There were the things she had found and the things she had lost. Where had they gone? And what's more, what exactly were they?

It was making her weak all this groping, this searching. Think, she told herself, think, where had you got them last?

There had been Maura at the front door.

(Oh my God, you look wretched. Get up to bed this second!) And something else. She had said something else.

'Did you go to the doctor?' Yes she said that all right, but something else. 'Did you go to the doctor, Mrs Pakenham?'

'The doctor ... oh yes, of course.'

'And what did he say? Mrs Pakenham, what did he say?'

'Bed. Not to be disturbed.'

Her arms came out of the coat Maura was holding; her head came out of the hat. Maura's hand reached out for the bag. 'No, no, I'll keep that. Medicine. Sleep now, doctor says.'

It was then Maura said that something else.

There had been Maura through the bedroom door: (A little something? Are you sure?)

'I said, "No thank you, Maura, I'm not hungry."'

'Just the tea then maybe?'

'Nor am I thirsty.'

The next thing she could remember was waking up on the floor under the front bay window. How long had she been asleep? And the bedroom door left wide open like that. She had shut it, she was sure. He must have come in, must have seen her. Who else could it have been? Maura would never have left her lying there like that. Yes, that was it: he came in, saw her and left the door open, so that she would know. Know that he had caught her.

Strange: she knew where to find her handbag. Instinctively she knew, crawling under the bed for it the moment she could sit up. And she couldn't remember hiding it. Yet she knew where to find it: strange.

And now here she was in the attic room, kneeling beside that trunk. A long time since she had seen it. So long. Were those the things she had lost inside? She opened it slowly and – no. Those were the things she had found. She pulled the handbag towards her and reached inside. No medicine as well she knew. Something else – her notebook. She pulled it out first and then went back in, this time feeling something that almost made her heart stop. She opened the bag and looked inside: a bundle, wrapped in a linen cloth.

'Oh no,' she said. 'Please God, not again.'

So that was it. Yes that was it. She'd had a relapse. After almost a year of being well, she'd gone back again. Oh how could she have been so stupid, so weak? And he knows, he knows. Would easily have guessed.

Slowly she took the package onto her knee and opened it. She pulled the napkin away, emptying its contents out onto her lap and shielding them with her hands as they fell, in case they slid onto the floor. She opened the lid of the trunk fully and spread the napkin out over several other bundles that were packed inside. One by one, she removed the items from her lap as if they were iced dainties. She began to restack them carefully on top of the open napkin.

A small round … what? Pill box, she supposed. A soft grey pair of ladies gloves trimmed with buttons that appeared to be porcelain; another pair of gloves, this time for evening wear, black satin with lace inset. A mouth organ? What in the name of –? *Where?*

A fountain pen. Wait, this was her own. She looked in her handbag. No, her own pen was still there, snug in its box. This was just an identical one. Senseless. It was all so …

It had been half-past nine when she went into Brown Thomas. And later? Later she could remember in West & Co., wondering about the time and looking at a row of carriage clocks that answered in unison. Half-past eleven. Half-past nine and half-past eleven. But in between? What had happened in between?

At least she knew now what she had lost, not things at all. But time: fragments of time.

She looked back down at her lap and lifted the tiny tea chest.

'Oh yes,' she said first in a whisper and then, 'Oh God!' out loud when she caught sight of its price tag fluttering from a string. She threw it then on top of the pile and hurriedly reparcelled the napkin.

About to slam the lid of the trunk shut, she changed her mind suddenly. No, too uneven, sticking out like that. Too bumpy; not suiting the surrounding bundles at all, with their longer mounds and softer curves. She lifted it gently and moved it over to the side where the larger unwrapped items had been set into the sides of the trunk to form a wall. There she made a space for it. Much better; over here. Balancing out the corner at the other side and fitting in nicely beside a statue of an Arabian woman and a painting of a seascape which looked soothingly familiar.

She was growing sleepy again; best get back to her room. Maura would probably be up to check on her. And she mustn't find her here. It came back to her then thinking of Maura: that was the other thing she had said. Of course, that was it: 'Mr Pakenham said Greta is not coming back. Is it true?'

And poor Maura, looking so anxious. How rude of me not to have answered her.

Why didn't I? Really. When all I had to say was: 'Yes, Maura, of course it's true. Greta is not coming back. Ever.'

Kate gave her answer now to the empty room. Out loud and quite cheerfully. Closing the lid of the trunk, pulling the darkness back down over the bundles.

IV

FOUR PROMENADES

FIFTEEN

Another fortnight and the dancer didn't have to be told, he already knew. And despite an easy mastering of the crutches, his steps progressing from baby to man in a matter of days, giving rise to a general approval from staff and patients alike, he still knew. He couldn't avoid it. He only had to look into his heart and it winked back up at him.

'In time,' Doctor Hamlyn began, 'in time, you'll hardly notice a thing. The slightest limp perhaps, if you've tired yourself out but … We're very pleased with your progress, you know. Very pleased indeed.'

The patient made no response, just stood there staring as if waiting for something more. Doctor Hamlyn felt obliged to elaborate: 'As I said,' he continued, 'there may be the smallest irregularity.' He raised his hand and began moving his fingers as if twisting a rather large knob. 'But absolutely nothing to cause –' The patient hobbled forward and was now peering intently at his gesturing hand. Doctor Hamlyn dropped it abruptly back down to his side.

The young man sighed impatiently. 'Yes,' he said, 'but will I be able to dance again?'

'Dance? Why yes, I don't see why not – in time.'

'But I already know how to dance in time,' he said and turned away.

Doctor Hamlyn watched him go, in slow even swings down along the centre of the ward. 'Ah yes, I see it now,' he half laughed behind him. 'Very good, I'm sure.'

That was the trouble with these private patients; you had to laugh at their jokes. Had to tell them everything too. Every blasted detail. Fancy worrying if he would be able to dance or not, at his age.

'Remind me, Sister,' he said to the woman standing behind him.

'That young chap. He is a civilian, isn't he? I mean, he's not just back from the front or anything?'

'Oh no doctor. Not at all.'

'Thought he might have been a bit …' He brought his finger up to the side of his head and tapped it. 'You know?'

'Shell shocked? Oh good God no.'

'Tell me, Sister, do young people really have nothing more to occupy themselves with other than dancing? Wouldn't know there's a war on or anything? Might disturb their recreation, I suppose. Still perhaps I shouldn't judge a whole generation on one?'

'Not that one anyway, doctor,' she smiled.

Sister Clancy took her smooth brisk step down the ward. Now and then a badly hung counterpane might slow her up. Or the tilt of a medical chart in need of realignment, and the nods she gave, left and right – 'Good morning, Mr Clarke. And how is Mr Binn today?' – caused no more than the slightest stammer to her course.

However, the closer she got to the dancer, the slower her step became.

What was he up to now? Sitting like that, his back to the ward, in the middle of the aisle. Under a window that was far too high up in the wall for him to possibly see out of. And yet from here it looked as if that was exactly what he was trying to do.

She wanted to walk up to him, to put her hand on his shoulder, ask him if he were all right. But with him, it was difficult. She would give him another few minutes and then perhaps …

Three beds away she stopped and looked around for something with which to occupy herself. She landed on the chart of a snoozing patient and busily began flicking the pages back and forth, so that she could keep an eye elsewhere. How could it be, she wondered then, that after all these years, one slip of a lad could have knocked such a dent in her professional confidence?

For already the dancer had gained a reputation as being somewhat of an odd egg among the hospital staff. For one thing he could never seem to hold on to a present. Any gift he received was given away at the first opportunity. And not that the nurses minded his passing on these treats to them, but it did at times make Sister Clancy feel somewhat uneasy. After all somebody had taken the trouble, spent good money. But really at this stage, he had given her no alternative other than to allow the staff to accept. Otherwise, he would either leave them there to grow beards on (as was the case with the chocolates and the figs) or else, now that he was able to make his way about, throw them in the bin. How awful it had been the first time she had spotted a bunch of the juiciest red carnations, head-first thrown in amongst the rubbish. Just awful.

The only thing he had shown any appreciation towards was a few old daffodils, insisting on them, way after their poor old heads were hanging with exhaustion and their stems had slimed with age. What a time she had trying to get him to part with *them*.

And then there was that peculiar routine of his, for it had to be said that for one of his young age, he had an old man's love of habit. Getting up at 11 a.m. and then hopping about the hospital all morning. Twice a week demanding a bath at noon, a most inconvenient time. And then refusing to take lunch at twelve like everybody else.

Refusing to do *anything* like everybody else. He was the most peculiar case. Whatever was going on in that head of his.

But inside the dancer's head, the world was crystal clear. He got up at 11 a.m. because that was the first hour of his day. That was how he did things, his way. He saw then to his toilet, just as he had always done, just at that exact time.

Before the accident he went strolling out until luncheon, and he would continue to do so now. Only this time instead of the South Circular Road onto Harcourt Street it was the ward out onto the corridor. Turn after turn he would take until, after a while, the night stiffness would have left his limbs and the sticks that appeared to have grown alongside him wouldn't matter quite so much. Two crutches, one good foot and somewhere in between was that big white knob always hanging mid-air, struggling to keep pace with the rest of this unfamiliar walking apparatus.

And what he saw out there then, were his own feet, the feet he could remember, smacking smartly the pavement of Grafton Street. And not the tiles of a hospital ward, the colour of carbolic soap.

By this time, the complaints from his fellow patients would usually have started up. Gone were the early days when initial cries of delight would sound through the ward, gone were the cheers, the pleasure. 'Gangway, gangway, here he comes. Now watch him go. Look at him, Sister, watch out now, it's Woodbine Willy, go on my son. Go on.'

Now, like a joke too often told, the novelty had worn: 'Oh Sister, that tapping noise is getting on me nerves, it's like a bloody funeral march – tap, tap, bloody tap.'

And he, quite agreeing, could only empathise with the complaints. The tap being the dullest imaginable, with neither tempo nor variation to its credit. He would gladly take it outside into the corridor to continue on his way. Up and down, until he had outwalked the morning.

And true on Tuesday and Thursdays, he ordered a bath. But that was because those were the days when he took his Turkish bath in Hammans Hotel, Sackville Street, 1s 9d the hour. He always put it aside, never missed. And he wasn't about to do so now.

Besides, what nicer way to take him hungrily up to lunch? Which was for him, one o'clock and one o'clock dotted.

And it seemed to Sister Clancy, watching him now, a lone figure looking so very harmless, so very fragile, the more determined she was to bend his will, the more he seemed to get his own way.

The first time he had ordered a bath, for example, and she had said, 'No, I'm sorry, it's quite out of the question,' even going so far as to laugh at the temerity of him, the very idea: a bath at lunch time! And he just stood there at the bathroom door, for nearly an hour. Balancing on his crutches and looking like a crane or some such bird, strange and somehow balanced. His face drab and shrunken from the strain of it. And staying there, too, in full view of anyone who came into the ward, be it visitor or doctor. She had to give in. She really had no choice, in the end.

And then there was the matter of luncheon. 'I'm sorry,' he said to her, as if there had been some misunderstanding on her part.

'I never eat before one o'clock.'

And this time, there would be no nonsense, she convinced herself, smartly replying to him, 'Well you'll just have to do without it then, won't you?'

'All right.' He smiled back at her as pleasantly as anyone could. 'As long as I'm not expected to eat before one.'

And she relented gradually; at first telling the staff to leave it on a tray for him and pity about him if it was cold. But then she felt guilty at the sight of him eating cold mashed potatoes as politely as a child, and softened. Now his food was kept warm until one o' clock. All the trouble she had gone to, not to mention her under-mined authority – and had he said even thank you?

He hadn't said thank you because he didn't feel grateful. It made no difference to him if the food was hot or cold, on his tray or not at all. It just didn't matter.

One o'clock was the hour when he had his two-bob lunch in the Cafe Cairo and that was the fact. He never bothered with breakfast, finding it a silly meal and having failed to date to come across one that pleased him. Preferred to wait until something decent could be had, something worth the bother. But he couldn't touch a mouthful until one o' clock. And if by then the food was cold and congealed, he didn't mind that much. So long as he could stick as near as possible to his routine – then he was a happy man.

After luncheon, just as always, he spent an hour in Samuel's company. Just as always – in reverse. This time, instead of him sitting at the side of Samuel's workbench, Samuel sat at the edge of his bed. They spoke intermittently and on subjects various, Samuel enjoying his afternoon smoke, taking or leaving the silence as it came. He brought whatever books had been requested from the library and sometimes, if there was time before returning them, he might have a look at one or two himself, and that took care of another discussion. At three o'clock Samuel went home.

From three to four had always been his floating hour. The hour he allowed for eventualities, unavoidable appointments or necessary errands. Now since he came to the hospital he found himself dedicating this time to the studying of horses. What had started out as a mathematical equation he found he had rather an aptitude for, had now been well and truly integrated into his regime. And with the help of Castle and Algie had also become a way of accumulating a tidy little profit. But nothing too extravagant. The money saved from his Turkish bath, his Cafe Cairo luncheon; little incidentals such as these were used for his stake. His winnings were a separate purse. And the two could not be mixed. As a man who believed discipline and extravagance could not survive under the one roof, he choose discipline every time.

Besides the money never meant that much to him. He didn't see it as the point. It was the challenge, the mathematics, the feeling that he had taken on the forces and, with his own intelligence and perhaps a little divine inspiration, had beaten them. It made him feel unique – almost as if he had been chosen. So that when Castle came and passed him the envelope, he hardly looked at it. What concerned him now was the list he was handing in return, the marked card so to speak, with his selection for the next meeting. The card that represented tomorrow, along with the stake that would secure his selected horses, the stake that would make them temporarily his.

Sometimes he tried to imagine what they were like, this ream of names and numbers, sires and dams, weights and jockeys. What did they look like, out there on the field? How did they do it? Did they run in a bunch, nosing and dunting each other out of the way, until the strongest won? Or was it in a curve? A splay of shapely legs, like a chorus line bending as they came into the home straight and then one breaking loose and flying to the finish before the rest. When he got out he promised himself he would see, he would put flesh to these names. When he got out.

Five o'clock had been another of his designated hours, the hour for his warm up (if he had a spot that night) or for his solitary rehearsal (if he had not). But now five o'clock was also the time for his evening visitors. He had, however, also managed to overcome this problem. Just before they came, he simply got back into bed and waited.

When they arrived, he sliced a part of himself away and left it there to deal with them, to reply or respond as was necessary. While the other part of him, the real part, the part that he wanted, went with him, down Dame Street and, turning left then into the narrow alley, slipped in through the side entrance to the theatre inside. And climbing again those tiny side steps that led to the stage, there before the sea that had been drained, there before the winter fields where nothing grew, he began, tucking his hands behind him into his braces: And Exercise 1, Exercise 2, Exercise 3.

Meanwhile, by the bedside, things could appear to be as usual. ('Not too bad today, thank you for asking' and 'No sign yet – they haven't told me when.' 'Well it's edible anyway.' 'Like a top. Every night' and 'Not too bad today. Thank you, again, for asking.')

After a while when the visitors began to turn away from him to concentrate on each other, he could close his eyes for this, pretending to have fallen asleep, and hearing the voices adjust to a whisper, he would continue, this time using all that he had learnt and all that he had thought about and taking possibility and permutation he would go, stomping and spinning, round and round and slapping the silence until it came back up in bruises.

He read then after supper until he tired. And the problem this had once been had now also ceased. Now that he could get about and no longer had to worry about Sister Clancy turning off the light above his bed. Now when she took his light away, he just looked for another. Out to the corridor, down to the lavatory. Wherever there was light he wasn't far behind it. But even on this, their tightest struggle to date, she was beginning to weaken. Fed up with following him about, the pommel of the crutch squeezed under his armpit, a limp hand holding a book, not altogether successfully, so that she had to keep bending down to pick it up, just to stop him from trying to retrieve it himself. Now even as she looked at him, she was wondering if there was a way to screen him in, him and his light: would it disturb the other patients, she wondered. Or more to the point would it disturb them enough to cause them to complain?

Sister Clancy looked over Mr Toohey's chart and made up her mind. That was it, she didn't care. She would give him one more minute and then she would jolly well make herself go up to him. Decided now, she hung the chart back into position and pointed her toe in the right direction. She swung herself around then to follow and – Oh my goodness! It was the young man's afternoon visitor. 'Excuse me, Sister,' Samuel said, stepping around her and continuing on his way.

Well that was the end of that then. There'd be no need to do the ministering angel bit after all. Thank God. She turned herself back to face the ward again and 'How are we feeling now, Mr McCracken?' she asked, choosing a bed half-way along.

Samuel hooked one elbow under a hospital chair. Then at a slant –
the books weighing him down on the one side and the chair lifting
him up at the other – he made his way up to the dancer. Clumsily,
he swung the legs of the chair around to land in line. And placing
the pile of books on the floor, he sat himself down, facing the wall
beside his companion. For a while the two men sat in silence.

And would you look at the pair of them, Sister Clancy said to
herself. You'd think they were sitting on a pleasure pier or at a picture
show. What are they like at all?

'He thinks I'm your father,' Samuel spoke first, 'that doctor
fellow.'

'Ahh,' the dancer said.

'Why he should think it, I don't know.' Samuel reached into his
pocket to arrange his afternoon smoke.

'I mean it's not as if I'm paying your bills or anything, is it?'

He peeled tobacco threads from his tongue and then continued:
'We don't even look like each other, do we?'

Samuel manoeuvred his chair around so as to look at his friend.
The lad looked old today, he decided. It was as if his face had lined
during the night. Perched up on those two crutches like that, as if he
were leaning on a country gate, you'd think he was an old farmer. But
Samuel knew he'd probably be back to his young self again tomorrow. It happened like that sometimes. He had seen it before.
One time when he was about nineteen, he saw it in himself: looking
in the mirror one morning, his face looked back out and it was forty.
He never forgot it. A preview, that's what it was. The face giving you
a preview of what it will be like.

'I'm not old enough to be your father?' Samuel asked him.
'Am I?'

The dancer looked up, but made no reply.

'I suppose I am,' he said finally, opening out his hand to a
sprinkle of ashes.

After a while, it was the dancer's turn to speak: 'So you were talking to him then?' he asked. 'The doctor?'

'Yes. Yes I was. Stopped me on the way in.'

'I see.'

'Yes. Seemed to have been some confusion about your dancing.'

'You put him right?'

'Yes. I did that.'

'And what did he say then? That I could forget about taking dancing as a career.'

Samuel gave a second drift of ash to his hand and took a few more pulls.

'It seems you did it some damage by not going to the hospital straight away. Making your own way home like that, and waiting until the next day to have it seen to. Why did you do that anyway?'

'Who knows?' the dancer shrugged. 'I suppose there's no point in maybe consulting someone, an expert?'

'No. No point.'

'Yes. That's what he said – the doctor.'

Footsteps came by them: an old man's shuffle, the spring of a young nurse's step. The dancer cocked his head to listen. When the steps turned to go back the way they had come and had gradually tapered into silence Samuel spoke.

'What will you do now?' he asked, standing up to go.

'I don't know.' The dancer gave a little laugh, as though Samuel had said something vaguely amusing.

*

That wasn't the only visit Samuel had to attend to that week; that wasn't the only bad news he was to carry. In the hospital he hadn't had a choice, the doctor having nabbed him on the way in. And even then he hadn't taken the initiative himself, had only really answered questions. There had been no way out. No alternative. But now?

Samuel looked at the numerous doors, all ajar. He looked at the windows too, doubled down to the sash, all open. No shortage of exits and what was he doing? Scuttling away into the darkest corner. Tripping himself up in his eagerness to get there. And once in – he reminded himself for the hundredth time – there would be no way out. Once in, he would be trapped. He walked up Infirmary Road, from Parkgate to the North Circular, and wondered why. After all these years of counsel-keeping, why bother now? All these years of blind-eyeing it, why choose now to see?

And Samuel had seen it all in his day and had rarely if ever felt compelled to act. Seen it all and still had managed to keep to himself. There had been those two chaps he was drinking with that time in Liverpool, all getting along splendidly, all cheek by jowl. When suddenly a fight broke out between them. Before Samuel knew what had happened a knife had been drawn and slashed a face, split down the length of one cheek, like an over-ripe tomato. He may have been able to prevent it. He may have not. Perhaps sacrificing his own face in the effort. To this day, he still didn't know what the argument had been about, nor did he know how far it went. He never stuck around to find out. It wasn't his fight. Nor was it his face.

There was that other time as well, in Egypt, when he saw a man beat his old mother to within an inch of her life and then stab himself in the neck. And at the other extreme of it, there was the foetus he found when he was still a boy himself, thrown in a bin, in a back lane down the East End. Still beating softly – or so it had seemed – still trying, refusing to give in.

He'd even seen two men doing it like dogs one time, when he was driving for the nobs, the two of them looking back around when he walked into the room and the one in front grinning at him. And the next day then on the steps of the great hall as he helped the gardener pass around baskets of flowers for their derby-day button-holes, the two of them again. As though nothing had happened and the one that had been at the front calling out, 'Come, darling, you help me choose,' to his newly-wed wife.

He'd seen it all and this would be the first time he had put his own head on the line. In all the thirty-odd years it had taken him to realise that there is little, if any, good in mankind. Little point in trying to rectify its ways. For if you had to intervene every time you saw an injustice or an outrage, where would that leave you? Worn out with frustration. With little time left for your own sins.

He crossed over the road and he could see her house from here. Under a snowfall of cherryblossoms he moved and thought how easy it would be to turn back. Who would know the difference? Who would be the wiser? Just walk on by. Keep well out of it.

And his shoulders shrugged clear again of the flimsy blossoms, and his hat unpinked and back on his head. Keep walking, he reminded himself, walk on by. And yet somehow, he found himself stopping outside the house next door, where he could easily survey his destination.

He reassured himself, and not for the first time, that Pakenham wouldn't be home. How could he? Pat was away in Kildare for the day. Someone had to look after things. No, there was no chance of being caught as long as he remembered not to delay.

Quickly he ran through the calculations: a half-hour's walk from Kingsbridge Station to here, another half to get back. One hour. Hop into the motor and up to the hospital to collect Mrs Cleary. Back down to collect Pat from the Kildare train. And as long as some clever Henry railway porter doesn't say, 'You back again?' all would be well. It would take no more than twenty minutes to spill the beans. Her choice if she wants to make anything of it. Twenty minutes. 'And that,' he muttered, 'is as far as I go.'

Through the wagging bush leaves he looked up to the window where the curtains were drawn. That must be her room. Ten minutes should be enough really. It would hardly take more than that. Time for another smoke? Of course. Plenty. He walked back down the road a little way and lit up a cigarette.

How would he begin? What would he say? How do you tell somebody something like that? She may not believe him. Well that was up to her, he supposed. He checked his inside pocket then to see if the newspaper cutting was still there. Of course it was. Where would it have gone in the two minutes since he had checked it last? Well here goes, he thought, throwing the cigarette to the ground and twisting the sole of his shoe across it.

He remembered then how, when he was a child, he hated the rule that said you had to eat the head of a fish or the head of a beast during the New Year Festival. He didn't know which he hated most: the minutia of fish cerebrum moving around his mouth and always wondering, is this the eye? is *this* the eye? as each new jot broke under his reluctant teeth. Or the heavy smell of a sheep's head boiling. And afterwards, its naked skull, the holes it once used for eating grass, for smelling it, for seeing it, like caves on a dark grey cliffside. And through his tears asking Aunt Esther, 'Why do I have to eat any head at all?' and she answering him, 'Because this is Rosh Hashanah. How else are you going to be sure that in the coming year you will be a head and not a tail?'

Well, it had finally happened, he said to himself. After all the years of turning his back on Judaism, it had caught up with him. All those heads he had omitted to eat and now he was a tail. The biggest tail that ever there was. He could nearly see Aunt Esther's gleeful finger wag into his face.

Maura stood in the doorway and whispered across the room, 'Mrs Pakenham, Mrs Pakenham ...' And wondered was she sleeping. 'Are you sleeping, Mrs Pakenham?' She stepped forward to have a better look and felt sure that was the snap of a closing eyelid that she had just spotted.

'There's a man here to see you, Mrs Pakenham.'

Kate's voice was slow, reluctant.

'Tell him I'm sleeping,' she said.

'I did that already, Mrs Pakenham.'

'Tell him again.'

'It's Mr Cleary's driver, Ma'am. That Samuel chap.'

Yes. That opened her eye for her all right.

Kate turned around in the bed and raised herself up onto her elbows.

'Sam?' she whispered.

'Yes.' Maura began and then she noticed that Mrs Pakenham wasn't looking at her. She was looking beyond her, to the doorway. Maura turned around. Well the nerve!

'I have to speak to you, Mrs Pakenham,' he said. 'It can't wait.'

He glanced over at Maura.

'You'll have to wait downstairs. Mrs Pakenham isn't well.'

Kate spoke. 'I'll see him Maura, it's all right.'

'Well,' she said, 'you just go down to the drawing room so and Mrs Pakenham will be down when she's dressed. Go on now. What are you waiting for?'

But Samuel wouldn't budge. He just kept on looking at Mrs Pakenham and she just kept on looking back at him.

'Leave us, Maura,' she said at last.

'Leave you?'

'Yes Maura, please.'

He began to speak the moment the door was shut, reverting to her maiden name as he did: 'Miss Kate, I want you to listen to me and listen very carefully,' he began. 'There's a place called St Edmondsbury in Lucan in West Dublin.' He walked to the window by the side of the bed.

'It's a hospital for people with mental … illnesses. More especially for ladies with mental … problems.'

He stuck his hands in through the chink in the curtains and, pulling them roughly apart, concluded.

'Your husband intends that you should go there.'

'What?'

Kate sat up in the bed, wincing at the light from the window. Samuel walked towards her. 'You can read about it for yourself,' he said, laying a piece of paper on the side of the bed.

She glanced at it. It was a newspaper cutting, a hand-written note on the margin.

'What are you talking about?' she asked him. He pointed to the paper. Kate picked it up and read. Yes it was an advertisement for a hospital for ladies, offering 'curative treatment for mental cases'. The writing on the side was a name, presumably that of the medical superintendent, and a sum of money had also been noted down, presumably the fee he was asking. There could be no mistaking the handwriting; she recognised it immediately.

Kate looked up at him. 'How could you know this? How could you possibly know?'

'I eavesdropped,' he said. 'I make no apologies nor excuses for it. They started to discuss it in the back of the motor and I picked up on it. Then I followed them inside and –'

'They? They? Why do you keep saying they?'

'Your husband, Miss Kate, and Pat Cleary.'

'Pat Cleary?' Kate's face twisted. ' I might have known. What did they say? Tell me exactly what they said.'

'I can't remember exactly, Miss Kate, not to the word. As I said, I was taking them to the factory last Sunday, to look over the new machinery. And they started to talk in the back. The new motor is not as noisy as the last one, but they don't seem to have realised that yet. Well I gathered it had something to do with you, in some form or another. And I'm afraid I followed them into the factory.'

'Yes and then?'

'Well, let's just say a voice would travel far on a factory floor on a Sunday and I heard the whole thing. And later when I went into Mr Pakenham's office, well, I found this, just thrown there on his desk. I knew then when I saw it, there was no mistake. I hadn't taken them up wrong.'

'And tell me whose idea was it? My husband's or Pat Cleary's?'

'Oh your husband's. Mr Cleary was dead set against the idea at first.'

'At first?'

'Well, your husband told him about things that have been happening –'

'Things? What things? Things like my stealing. Is that what you mean?'

'Well, yes, and other things besides.'

'Like what?'

'Like you refusing to leave this room, see anyone, eat – those sort of things.'

'And what did Pat Cleary say then. "Oh well in that case you go ahead and what a perfectly splendid idea"?'

'No, Miss Kate, it wasn't like that at all. He made Mr Pakenham promise not to do anything for another fortnight and in the meantime, he would have a man of his own look at you and if ...'

'He would give his blessing.'

Samuel walked to the back of the room and sat in the seat attached to the big bay window.

She looked wretched, he thought, maybe she was in need of

treatment after all, her face a little handful against the big white pillow. She looked sick, really sick.

'Does my sister know about this?' she snapped.

'No, Miss. I heard them agreeing not to tell her until –'

'Until what? I was safely behind bars?'

'Oh please, Miss Kate. They were talking about Greta.'

'Greta?'

'Yes, Mr Cleary said his wife was anxious to trace her, thought she'd be a help to you.'

'Oh yes, I'm sure – great help she'd be!'

'Mr Pakenham said he had no idea what happened. She'd just upped and left, he said, leaving no message. Nothing.'

'For all he knows.'

Kate rolled the newspaper cutting through her fingers till it began to break. 'Oh damn that Pat Cleary to hell.'

Samuel sighed. 'There's no sense in blaming Pat Cleary, Miss Kate. He's got nothing to do with it.'

'Exactly. He has got absolutely nothing to do with it. Nothing whatsoever. He's not my father. What happens to me has got nothing to do with him. And you. You even less. Why did you have to come here and tell me all this? Why didn't you just mind your own business?'

Samuel stood up. 'Don't think I haven't asked myself the same question every other minute since the notion first came to me. And don't think I'm not asking myself again now. I didn't have to come here. I didn't have to take the risk. Just as you don't have to do anything with it. You can just lie there and wait for them to come and get you for all I care.' He turned to walk away.

'No Samuel, please. I'm sorry – it's the shock. I'm so very very sorry. I just don't know what to … I mean what can I do?

'I don't know, Miss Kate.'

'You mean you're not going to help me?'

'I don't know that I can.'

'But I have no one else, I can't tell Maude. She'd have to tell Pat and –'

'What about your brother, Miss?'

'No, Samuel. I turned to him before, you know, nearly two years ago, when he came to Dublin first.'

'And he didn't help you?'

'No. He sent me away. It was stupid of me to go to him like that. I mean what could he do? Hardly more than a child.'

'Is that why you two are strange with each other? I mean, I wondered ...'

'Yes. He walked me to the stage door. Said he was sorry that my marriage had been a disappointment and that was the last time I purposely saw him. Oh we're civil, if we should happen to meet, but ... I haven't seen him this long while. And we were very close, you know, at one time. Very close.'

'Yes,' said Samuel, 'I can imagine.'

Kate nodded and smiled across the room to him.

'You'll think of something, Miss,' he said.

'Sam, I am sorry. I mean it. I shouldn't have spoken to you like that. After all you've done.'

'Don't waste your time apologising to me, Miss Kate.' Samuel reached behind him and pulled the curtains of the bay window apart. When he turned around she was leaning over the mattress and pulling something out from its grip. It was an envelope.

'Would you please?' She was holding it out to him. 'Nobody must see it, ever. I can't leave it here. Not now and you're the only one I can trust.'

'Shall I burn it for you, Miss?'

'Yes, Samuel,' she said. 'Perhaps it would be best.'

'I'll see to it, Miss.' He hesitated before continuing: 'There is something I'd like to ask you though. A favour.'

'A favour?'

'Yes. I took a risk in coming here today. And now I'm going to ask you to do something for me in return.'

'Yes, Sam?'

'Don't run away, Miss. Not this time. Stay and fight it.'

'Oh Sam, how?'

He walked towards the bed and softly patted the end of the mattress before leaving the room.

Sixteen

She walked with the waves each morning for a week. Where they recoiled from her, she followed, crossing the turbid expanse that had been left behind, feeling it flab beneath her feet, step after step, until she had caught up. And at last they could hear each other think.

By the fifth morning her legs felt strong again and the colour had come back to her skin. This time she hardly spoke to the sea at all; this time she listened.

At first Maura was all against the idea. Going out alone after such an illness, sneaking out the back way, catching two trams. She refused to promise silence. In fact she threatened to tell: 'You step outside that door, Ma'am, and I mean it. I'm straight tellin' now. Do you hear me?' And when Mrs Pakenham came back three hours later, the colour of porridge and fit to fall, she said, 'You ever do that again, and I'll tell, I will. Mind what I say, I mean it.' The next day it was: 'I've a good mind to tell on you. A good mind ...'

By the third day, she was willing to commit herself only insofar as she agreed not to say anything unless she was asked. But after another two days when she could see these little excursions were doing some good, she began to get more into the spirit of the thing. By Monday morning it was an adventure not to be missed, and when Mrs Pakenham went to leave through the scullery door, Maura insisted on running ahead and, taking up a look-out position at the corner of the back lane and the side street, had beckoned an enthusiastic 'all clear' to start her on her way.

Later that morning when Mr Pakenham called back to the house to pick up some papers he had forgotten, she looked him straight in the eye. 'Sleeping,' she said, just like that. 'Still sleeping. I've looked in not two minutes since.' Maura was relieved to see he must have believed her, the way he was taking care not to cause any disturbance, not to be his usual noisy self, managing to not so much as slam one door. And no one could slam a door like Mr Pakenham. It was as if he wanted his wife to sleep, and sleep, and sleep.

She peeped down through the landing curtains and watched him hop, two, three, down the steps and back out through the gate where he picked up the whistle he had dropped on the way in.

Maura wasn't the only one to have a share in Kate's little secret. Samuel knew as well, having spotted her the second morning while testing the first of the lorries intended for the Cleary fleet. At first he thought that she was going to do something foolish. Walking out to the sea like that. Alone and in defiance of such a breeze.

He found himself suddenly jumping into life like a marionette, out from the lorry, his feet scuttling heedlessly down onto the exposed strand. He took a few steps over it, with the intention of bursting into a run as soon as his feet had calmed a little. And the only thing he could think of was at what point he should start to call her name. But then he looked again and it came to him. No, it was all right. She had nothing like that in mind. She was here to regain her strength. She was here to be cleaned and decoded, just like an engine.

He made it a point to drive by after that, parking for a moment to watch her silhouette, small and dark against the sea and sky. Spilt ink – he thought the distance made her look – a series of elongated stains, with her head, happed tight into a motorhood, the round one at the top, where the flow eventually comes to rest.

By the end of the week all the lorries had been passed and were now lined up waiting for the signwriter's hand. All creamy white and even, like sheep in a pen, they needed only to be branded. It was on this day, too, that he walked into the hospital and saw her sitting there, her straight back making the top half of the chair look unnecessary. He was walking behind Pat and Maude, carrying an armful of what he knew to be unwanted goods – a cake, an assortment of garden flowers, a bottle of lithia-water, an adventure novel that they might as well give to the cat – when he heard Maude's cry of joy. 'Oh Kate! I don't believe – How lovely, lovely to see you!' And rushing over to kiss her sister's face, 'Pat look – isn't it wonderful? Kate's here.'

Pat stepped forward then: 'Kate, my Kate. Welcome back to the land of the living.' He bent down to kiss her too.

And Samuel couldn't be sure but it certainly looked like she picked that exact second to stand up, leaving Pat's lips with nothing to land on.

Maude was crying, just a little. Squeezing back the tears as best she could. 'It's so lovely,' she said, 'to see the two of you talking again. Like this …' She smiled then at sister and brother, each in turn. 'And you – here.' She squeezed her sister's arm.

'Oh Maude dear, really, there's no need for tears. I had an influenza that took its time leaving, that's all. Listen – I had my invitation to Mrs Gunne's dinner this morning. It made me feel quite strong again.'

'You're going?'

'Certainly I'm going. I wouldn't miss it for the world. I can't wait to feast my eyes on this illustrious in-law of hers. I've been practising my curtsy.' She walked over to her brother and kissed him. 'Friday week, did you say, before you're out? Well, I shall come and visit you again so. And after that at Mrs Gunne's, I suppose. You are going back to Mrs Gunne's?'

He nodded

'You mind yourself now, do you hear me?'

'Friday week?' Maude asked. 'You mean you won't be out sooner? But that means you'll miss the dinner party. Oh what a shame.'

'Hmm?' said the dancer.

'Mrs Gunne's party, you'll miss it. I said, it's a shame.'

'Oh yes,' he said 'a shame.'

'Couldn't you ask them to let you out a little earlier?'

'Oh no. No, I couldn't do that, oh no,' he said before closing his eyes again.

'But –' Maude began before Kate distracted her.

'Goodbye, Maude dear. I have to go now. I'll see you tomorrow?'

'Go? Oh no, surely not yet. Wait a while, we'll give you a lift,' she said, blinking against the tears. 'Won't we Pat?'

'Yes, of –'

'Nonsense. I won't hear of it. You haven't had your visit yet. I shall be perfectly all right.'

Kate stopped then and gave a mildly disapproving look at her sister. She pulled a handkerchief from her pocket and handed it to her. 'Dry them up,' she said, and then spoke to Pat without actually looking at him. 'Pat, if your wife is going to carry on in this emotional state, you're really going to have to have somebody look at her.' She smiled a little then to nobody in particular, to show that she had been only joking. A measure which Samuel didn't find quite convincing.

Their eyes met as she passed him, standing at the wall a respectable distance from the family gathering at the bed.

'Be careful, Samuel,' she said tipping the bouquet in his hand. 'Your flowers are slipping.' He almost laughed out loud.

There was silence for a second as they watched her move away. Then Pat spoke: 'Quick, Sam, go after her. Bring her wherever she's going. We'll walk home from here. If that's all right with you, Maude?'

'Yes. Yes of course. Go Samuel. She can't go home alone.'

Samuel struggled with his armload and nearly dropped the lot. Eventually through sparring with Pat he managed to offload it, piece by piece. And then for the second time that week, he found himself moving faster than he was used to. This woman will be the undoing of me, he thought to himself, as he made for the door where he hoped he would catch her before she reached the stairs.

V

PRANDIAL

SEVENTEEN

Mrs Gunne pulled the napkin up by its neck and for the umpteenth time shook it out. 'I'm going to scream,' she warned it, 'if you don't fold properly.' She tried again. But the napkin refused to oblige.

'All right, have it your way,' she said, twisting it into a ball and flinging it onto the floor. She looked around the table, all beautifully laid out and sparkling except for those wretched napkins lolling about the place, like fat lazy lumps they were, fat lazy … 'Gret-taah, Gret-taah,' she called at the top of her voice, rushing out to the hallway. 'Greta – where in the name of God? Francie, where are *you*? Has everybody upped and left? Is there no one in the house at all?'

Francie came up the back stairs with Beatrix affixed to her hip like a saddle. Mrs Gunne looked down at the sight of her grandchild, face bloated and pink with the strain of a recent tantrum. 'Oh and that's all we need now, a screaming baby and who does that one think she is anyway? Out galavanting and leaving the child in my care? Out shopping – if you don't mind – with her mother-in-law. While her own – her own mother – well. I just might tell that other one she's a grandmother too. When she gets back in. I mean really, she's hardly looked at the child since she arrived. Since she arrived – with one arm as long as the other, mind you! Didn't even bring the poor child a little something. It's well she might have it. Not that we've seen too much of her money over here, I might add.'

Mrs Gunne turned on her heel and walked back towards the dining room shouting over her shoulder. 'Francie, where's Greta? I mean Mrs Gray. Where is she? Find her for me now, do you mind me?'

'She's upstairs packing her bags, Ma'am.'

'Her bags? It is only one night, you know. She'll be back to-morrow. And take that infernal baby downstairs and out into the back garden with her.'

'She won't stay, Ma'am, I've tried.'

'Won't stay? Nonsense. You must make her.'

'How, Ma'am?'

'How do I know? Give her some toffee and tie her to a tree or something, just keep her out of the way until everything is sorted.'

'Yes, Ma'am.'

'Mrs Gray, Greta, will you come down here to me this minute please? Greta ...' Mrs Gunne had come back to stand at the end of the hall stairs and, with the lungs she had once used to win a silver medal in the contralto section of the Feis Ceoil now opened full throttle, she gave it one more try: 'GRET- TAWH!'

There was a knock at the front door just at that point and Francie stopped midway down the kitchen stairs to return to answer it.

'No, no, Francie, it's all right, that'll be the flowers, you carry on with the baby,' and walking towards the front door continued: 'Don't bring her back up here anyway whatever else you do. And for God's sake go and find Gret—'

It was Samuel, standing there, an envelope in his hand. Mrs Gunne nearly slammed the door shut in his face with the fright she got. 'Samuel. Oh. I thought you were ...' (Had he heard her calling Greta?) It dawned on her then that Greta could very well be making her way down the stairs. She couldn't ask him in. Supposing she was half-way down when he came into the hall? 'I can't ask you in, I'm afraid ...' she began, reprimanding herself almost immediately for being so obvious. When had she ever asked him in? 'Floor's just been polished, you know.'

'That's all right, Ma'am. I was just delivering this message from Mrs Cleary.'

'Mrs Cleary? Oh no. Don't tell me she's not coming. That would be the second time in a row she's let me down at the last minute. Bad manners I call it. Simply –'

'No, no I don't think it's anything like that.'

'Oh. Well, thank you.'

And he just stood there – what was he waiting for?

'Well thank you, goodbye now.' Mrs Gunne gave a little laugh and began drawing the door to a close.

'What about a reply?'

'Yes, yes. I'll see her tonight.'

'There's one expected.'

'Oh yes, a reply. Of course.'

She could hear Beatrix plodding, knees and hands, up the kitchen stairs. Oh that Francie one. When I get my hands on her …

'Geta, Geta,' the baby voice called out.

Mrs Gunne ripped open the envelope. 'Let me see … now … Dear Mrs, yes, yes, yes. Looking forward to hmmm hmm mmm and hope it will be all right if Kate comes after all … *Kate*?'

She looked up at Samuel. He was waiting for his reply. What could she say? She had only asked the Pakenhams out of politeness, never imagining that they'd accept. Still what could be done about it now? And besides what harm? Greta wouldn't be here in anyway. Still it made her feel uneasy. Such short notice, such short – no time to think.

Beatrix had reached her skirt by now, pulling at it and wiping a pale brown froth of toffee and cocoa dribbles onto it. 'Geta, Geta,' she called up to her grandmother while pointing back up towards the stairs.

'Dear sweet child,' Mrs Gunne laughed. 'Isn't she adorable? Yes, angel, we'll get it in a minute. She wants me to get a … Well yes, Samuel, you may tell Mrs Cleary that will be no problem what-soever. Goodness me, certainly not. If our little household can't run to one or two extra … I take it Mister –?'

'Oh I would think so.'

'Oh how nice. Yes. Well as I was saying, if our little household can't accommodate without confusion a couple extra … I mean to say … Delighted.' She scooped Beatrix up into her arms and closed the door smartly. 'Goodbye,' she remembered to say, after it had been shut.

Oh my good God of almighty. Another two places to set and that Pakenham definitely coming. With the sneery oul' face on him, watching every move. What Mrs Bumbury will make of him …

Let's hope we have enough of whiskey. I'm nearly sure I'm missing a soupspoon.

Greta stepped out of the first landing shadow. 'Was that Samuel?' she asked.

'Yes. Would you believe? I hope he didn't hear me calling you that time. I had my voice raised just a little, you know.'

'What did he want?'

'Oh nothing, it was just something about tonight.'

'Did I hear Kate's name being mentioned?'

'Kate? Oh heavens no. It was something to do with …'

She walked into the dining room. 'Come and help me with these blasted napkins, please Greta. Francie, *Franci-eee*, come up and take the baby.'

Greta followed her in. 'So she's not coming?'

'Who?' Mrs Gunne asked. 'Where are those flowers? They should be here by now. I mean really.'

'Kate. She's not coming then?'

Mrs Gunne stopped and looked at her. She had about enough of this. 'No, Greta,' she said. 'Mrs Pakenham is not coming tonight. She's not well. But Mr Pakenham *is*, which is why you can't be here. If he finds out that you're … He mustn't know you're – I mean they *all* mustn't know – in case they tell Kate. Francie, ah there you are, come and take that baby now and out from under my feet.'

'Yes, Ma'am.'

'Yes. Day day, bye, bye. Oh do hurry up, Francie.'

Mrs Gunne turned to Greta. 'Dear Beatrix, such a darling – but I don't know what's wrong with me today, I'm finding her just a tiny bit nerve-straining.'

'What do you mean, he mustn't know I'm here?' Greta asked. 'Of course I won't be here. He gave his instructions, didn't he?'

'Who?'

'Mr Pakenham.'

'Oh yes, yes. He said – send her off for the night, he said, yes. That's what he said. Absolutely.'

Mrs Gunne walked towards the window. 'Oh still no sign of the flowers. What am I to do?'

'Perhaps you should have bought them from a proper florist shop and not be depending on an undertaker's surplus.'

Mrs Gunne swung around and faced Greta. 'It's not as if they'll be used, Greta. I mean they won't have been on a coffin or anything. And I'm not so sure I like your tone either. Will you see to the napkins please?'

'No. I will not.'

'What? What are you saying to me girl?'

'I'm saying there's some things I need to know.'

'Like what for goodness sake? Really, Greta, I'm appalled at you – such frightful carry-on!'

'Like what exactly I'm expected to do once his nibs comes out of hospital? I mean, you don't think Maude is going to stay away, do you? She'll be here every afternoon, just as she was at the hospital. And how do we know Kate won't be here too?'

'Now you're being ridiculous. Mrs Pakenham never comes here, as well you know.'

'Anything could have happened; maybe she's made good with him again. And what am I supposed to do if she has? Hide in the scuttle every time there's a knock on the door?'

'Good Lord no. Besides, there's no need for you to worry about his highness coming out of hospital. I'm looking after all that, Greta. I'm going to tell them tonight that he can no longer stay here. They'll be delighted, of course; can fight for him between themselves.'

'They?'

'What?'

'They, you said they.'

'Yes. Yes. Pat and Maude, yes. They. Of course. That's what I meant.' Mrs Gunne's eyes were flying about the room, from corner to corner and up the middle, everywhere except to the space where Greta stood.

'Look at me please, Mrs Gunne.'

'I am looking at you. Really, Greta. I have so many things to do. What's gotten into you at all?'

'What does Mr Pakenham say I should do about all this?'

'Mr Pakenham?'

'Yes, Mr Pakenham. I mean, isn't he the one pulling the strings?'

'Oh yes, dear. And a very serious string-puller he is too. We must do exactly as he says, otherwise – well it just doesn't bear thinking about. And I wouldn't put anything past Mr Pakenham, you know. He'll do as he threatens. He will. Oh yes, without hesitation. Time and time again, he's told me.'

'But he can't expect me to stay here forever, undiscovered?'

'Well, why not dear? With the lad gone, they'll have no reason to come calling. We'll have seen the back of the lot of them. The whole seed and breed.'

'But he can't make me stay, I won't let him.'

'Don't be silly, child, where else would you go?'

'Back to London.'

'Oh no, dear, not without a reference. Oh dear me, no. Besides haven't you the fine position here?'

'Mrs Gunne, to my mind a position is not a position without a salary.'

'By the month, by the month, Greta. How many times have I to tell you. By the month and a back month too. That's how we've always done things in this house. And you're almost there my dear. Before you know where you are …'

'Yes, but –'

The door swung open behind Mrs Gunne and Beatrix crawled in around it: 'Not *you* again.' Mrs Gunne ran over to the door and had to stop herself from kissing the child with gratitude. 'Well, Greta, we certainly can't discuss all this now. We'll sort everything out tomorrow. I agree we should talk. Yes, indeed. But tomorrow, when we have more time. All right dear? And we've still got to discuss your terms of employment, don't forget now.'

'No, Mrs Gunne, I won't forget. God knows you've reminded me enough times.'

Mrs Gunne laughed. 'Oh you're the hard nut, Greta. You really are. I tell you what – why don't I give you a little something on account? Just to show there's no coolness. Yes that would be best. I'll pop something extra into the envelope with your hotel money. That's what I'll do. In case you want to treat yourself to a little cake or something, a nice fruit slice maybe?' She walked back to the table then and beckoned Greta to follow: 'Now come and help me, there's a pet. I mean look at these napkins.'

'What's the matter with them?'

'Just look at them,' she wailed, her nerves beginning to get the better of her. 'Look, they're all floppy.'

'What do you mean – floppy?'

'Look, when I try to stand them the way you told me to, they flop. Look. Flop, flop, flop.' One by one she slapped the offending napkins, till each one had limply collapsed. 'Now do you see what I mean? Now are you understanding what I mean when I say *flopping*?' Mrs Gunne was shouting again.

Greta leaned over the table and snapped up the napkins until she had the whole lot lifted. 'I'm sure there is no need to get so excited. I showed Francie how to iron them. Doubtless, I shall just have to show her again.'

'Francie hasn't the time to be ironing. Not now. And not a bit of starch to be had anywhere. For one thing, she's got all that food to see to.'

'Mrs Gunne, the cook will be here in a half an hour, all Francie has to do is prepare the vegetables. I really should be –'

'Are you sure though, Greta? These agency cooks, are they really reliable?'

'Mrs Gunne, she's been coming here every day for the past week at the exact time we've agreed with her.'

'Oh I don't know. I don't like the look of her.'

'Well, don't look at her then.'

'And there's the baby, the baby. I really wish you could take her with you. It would make things so much easier. I'm sure the hotel could make arrangements. Wouldn't you just love to go with Geta, hmmm, with Aunty Getty Wetty? Wouldn't she be a bit of company for you?'

'Mrs Gunne …' Greta began. (She would have liked to say, 'You must be joking me. For a start it's hardly a hotel, a cheap little lodging house more like. And for another, I wouldn't be seen dead five seconds longer than I have to with that dreadful child.') Greta would have liked to say it, but didn't. Despite feeling the weight of the words bouncing on her tongue, she took a nice deep breath and reminded herself of her philosophy – everything could be slithered out of if you used your head. And so: 'Mrs Gunne …' she laughed good-naturedly at the very idea of it, 'now what would be the sense in that? Depriving your guests of little Beatrix – after all she's such a credit to you. I mean look at her.'

Greta pulled a handkerchief from her pocket and began sponging up the various leakages of Beatrix's face. 'And what would you tell her mother and grandmother? Hmm?'

'I'd tell them Mrs Gray has taken her on a little outing. What could be more natural than that?'

Greta bit her lip and took a little breath before continuing: 'But that means your guests won't get to see the baby? After you inviting them early especially. That means Maude Cleary will never see her. Is that what you want?'

'Well I …'

Greta concluded, deciding on a final ace as she did. 'What about that lovely lemon dress you've spent all that money on? When else is she going to have such an opportunity to shine. She'll be the talk of Dublin. I know she will. And all down to you, Ma'am, if you don't mind my saying so.' Greta smiled happily to herself at the notion. 'All down to you. Give her to me here now – come on you sweet angel – and I'll take her down to Francie and sort out this napkin business. And then I really should be leaving.'

And she disappeared out through the door and down the kitchen stairs before Mrs Gunne had time to say, 'Dear Greta, why I'd be lost without you. What I'd do, I just do not know.' She did, however, have time to shout after her. 'Oh Greta, will you send Francie up to me this minute please? And don't forget your hat on the hallstand, we wouldn't want to leave that lying around to get itself recognised, now would we?'

'Yes, Mrs Gunne,' came the muffled voice from below the stairs.

When she had finished instructing Francie, Mrs Gunne walked into the front parlour and had a good look around. Oh how well it was all looking – like a new room. And that's exactly what it is, she reminded herself sternly – a new room. A drawing room. For goodness sake don't go saying, 'Would you like to come through to the front parlour?' Remember: front parlours don't have antimacassars that cost the same as a Sunday dinner. Nor do they have boxes of dun-coloured cigars stacked like logs that cost – well, best not think about that too long. She looked at the empty vases and frowned. Oh what if the flowers were too late? What if they didn't arrive at all? What then?

As gently as she could she placed herself on the side of the first newly chintzed armchair and gave a gracious little laugh across to the empty sofa. 'Why thank you, Mrs Cleary, how kind you are. She's a wonder, the new cook. Why I'd be lost without her.' She stood up then and crossed over to the sofa, sitting back into it, to check its comfort and looking up suddenly to the door. 'Ah here's the gentlemen now.' She sat forward again. 'I trust you enjoyed your port?'

She lifted herself up from the sofa and rearranged the seat covers, brushing her hand across the roses and tugging the frills back down into place. Then she turned suddenly to the sideboard lamp and brought her hands up to her bosom. 'Oh dear me no, Mr Cleary, I couldn't. I mean my singing days are long since. Oh no, I couldn't possibly … well perhaps if my dear Marguerite would accompany me. Would you dear? Yes, yes, say you will. I will sing but only so our guests can hear you play.'

She moved elegantly towards the piano and, with bashful eyelids lowered, cleared her throat. She opened her mouth then and closed it again, looking over at the photographs on top of the mantelpiece. 'Why thank you,' she bowed her head, 'you're too kind, I'm sure.' And moving her hand backwards to the piano stool: 'Please, credit where credit is …' As she started towards the mantelpiece, she began to speak: 'Now, Mrs Cleary, would you do us the honour? I'm showing myself up, I know, asking you to perform next, but I do wish you could hear her, Mrs Bumbury – a delight.'

Now at the fireplace, she studied the layout of its overmantel. From the rank of framed photographs, she pulled out her late husband. 'Dear William,' she said, holding it up to look at it. 'What would you think of all this, hmm?' With the photograph still in her hand she sat down again and looked around her. 'What a good job you're not here tonight,' she said, with a little giggle. For Willie wouldn't approve of spending money on the likes. And buying it spanking new at that! No. Willy, wasn't a man for novelty. 'Why waste good money?' he used to say, 'When I'm bound to have one just like it, or near enough to it, somewhere in the shop.'

It was the 'near enough to it' that used to upset Mrs Gunne so. Why Willy would think an eggcup and a porter barrel were twins if it saved a few bob. And much as she missed him, and much as it did her heart good to see how like him little Beatrix was, she did at times find herself taking pleasure in things that simply would not have been possible while he was alive. It was so nice to be able to go into a real shop, a shop that sold new goods, and demand whatever you wanted still in its wrapper. And then to buy it, take it home and run your hand over its unused, untouched surface. And to know that, be it a chair or a coat, it came to you clean, with no history, other than the one you were about to give it. She sighed.

He was a good provider though; she couldn't take that away from him. Sending Marguerite to the best schools and name an accomplishment, just you name it, and Marguerite was its mistress. No expense had been spared in that way – why no wonder she did so well for herself, marrying into a family with well-got relations. Yes you wouldn't find a better provider than Willie Gunne, no doubt. She just wished at times, well, that he hadn't made such a song and dance about it.

Those advertisements for example. The humiliation of them.

Half the city laughing at her. It's not that she objected to business people advertising their services, goodness no, in a commercial world, after all what can one expect? But it was the way he did it – telling all his business like that. She was thinking in particular of the advertisement he ran in a weekly paper, introducing himself as Honest Willie Gunne, mentioning his lady wife and lovely daughter by name, then inviting himself to the homes of the readers to inspect their second-hand furniture. And to price it there and then for no charge other than the 'kindness of a cup of tea'. A cup of tea! You'd think they hadn't a kettle in the house. Instead of about eight – all of them seconds, needless to remark!

When he used to sit there opposite her of an evening, composing those advertisements and reading them out to her with his lovely Ulster drawl – God bless it – she used to die inside at the thoughts of another one. And him, delighted with himself.

'What do you think of this, Girlie?' ('Girlie', he used to call her. Bless his soul.) 'Listen to this one: "Send for Willie Gunne for unlimited price for furniture and let-off clothes. Why have it sitting when it could be paying? Honest Willie Gunne – I'm your man."'

'Let-off clothes,' she had gasped. 'You can't possibly be serious?'

'No, no, of course not. What would I want with let-off clothes stinking out the shop? Have a wee bit of sense, Girlie.'

And she sighing with relief until he continued: 'That's just a ruse to get into their homes, where I can spot the real pieces. Half of them don't know what's valuable or not. Need to have it suggested to them, if you know what I mean.'

'So you'll still put that bit in your advertisement then?'

'Yes, of course.'

'But what about our friends,' she wailed.

'What friends?' he asked, mildly confused, before returning to his composition.

Mr Gunne didn't think too much of socialising either, considered it to be a waste of money, feeding people you didn't even like. A waste of time too, which in his opinion was just another way to waste money. Why, only for a few oul' charity dos for the war effort and his Unionist meetings he'd have never crossed the door. Twice a week, Tuesday and Thursdays, nothing could stop him. Spick and span off with him, down to Molesworth Street (and not a let-off stitch on his back either). Though why he bothered she sometimes wondered, coming back in the foulest of moods by times. Swearing and roaring, and him normally such a mild-mannered chap. Mostly it was on account of this 'Unionist Call' business – him all for it and others against. His idea it had been really, he said. And she believed him too, especially the bit about putting it in advertisement form in the newspapers – who else but him would have thought up *that*?

Mrs Gunne looked down at his placid, stilled face, looking out of the frame as if it was looking out of a Sunday window. She could remember when it wasn't always like that; she could remember when it was florid and angry, steaming with the temper, on account of those blasted meetings. Oh how he would go on, her nerves in tatters by the time he'd quieten:

'Put it up to them, says I. Advertise in the paper, call them out, every Unionist in the country, and have them report to headquarters. I tell ye they'll be in their droves, says I. We'll soon show the world our number, says I. But do you think they'd listen? Answer me now that, Missus? "It might be a bit –" says that lily-livered wee granny of a chairman. A bit what? says I. "Ah well now, ye know nowww, I'm afraid –' says he. What are ye afraid of? says I. They're a disgrace to the crown, the whole sorry whimperin' bunch of them. Well now I'll tell you …'

Twice a week, she'd to listen to it, the ranting. Until she had to take to the bed early on those evenings, so as to avoid him.

And what did they do in the end? Wait'll he had died on her

before they had carried out his wishes. Poor Willy, after all he had done for them, supplying them with free umbrellas for the Unionist march that he had bought in bulk from the Railway Lost Property Office. Why only for Willie Gunne they'd be all going around soaked to the skin and dead the half of them from it too.

How much had he paid for those umbrellas? A damn sight more than that floral tribute they all bunched in to buy for him. Orange blossoms if you don't mind. Had to make their point no matter what, even in death. It looked more like a fruit than a wreath, truth be told. And not a one of them bothered to make the trip up to Antrim to deliver it themselves. Sent it on the train, all alone, like a scaldy orphan.

Mrs Gunne stood up and walked back to the mantelpiece. Carefully she set Willie back in line. 'Everything's new now, William,' she told him. 'Everything is mine. I hope you don't mind dearest'

'I'm-your-mon' they used to call him behind his back. Oh yes, she'd caught the children sniggering and laughing at him. And where would the children get it, if not from their parents? That time at the War Fund Dance in Dr Crystal's house, stepping out of the ladies' room towards the stairs, she saw the doctor's children peering down through the banisters at the guests below and something had them in stitches. She had smiled a little at them herself for a moment. Then she saw Mrs Crystal come up to shoo them away and she hid in the shadows. 'Look mother,' the smallest one said. 'It's "I'm-your-mon, Honest Willie Gunne". Nancy said she's going to go down and ask him if he'd like a cup of tea.' And they all giggled together until another one said: 'He's been looking at the coat stand in the hall – I think he wants to buy it.' And more laughter then. Next she heard their mother saying, 'Children, children, shush this minute, if anyone heard you. Mr Gunne is an extremely generous man, one of the best contributors to our fund, you know …' and then hurrying them on back to bed with her own giggles added to the racket and as loud as the giddiest of them.

And that's what it had all been about really, the donations he made to Mrs Crystal's war fund. That's why they were invited in the first place, that's why they were invited anywhere. It wasn't for their social standing anyhow. It had taken her a good five minutes to compose herself sufficiently to come from behind the door and back downstairs. And when she finally did what did she see? Willie, true to form, squinting at a table in the hall and feeling for woodworm beneath its top lip! Oh she could have killed him, she could.

Well, time to return the hospitality at last, Doctor and Mrs Crystal. Let you meet the Gunnes at home. And you won't be asked to empty your pockets before you leave either – not in this house. War or no war. We'll show them, Willie boy. We will. She patted the photograph one more time and her eye began to wander.

Behind him stood another photograph, one taken on Marguerite's wedding day. There was her son-in-law, in his captain's uniform, Mrs Gunne standing beside him, wearing her feather and marabou necklet that cost a fortune. On the other side of her stood another officer, his best man and first cousin. And wasn't he the business? The refinement oozing out of him. And behind them was a stretch of brick and glass as big as any hotel, spreading out way beyond the reaches of the photograph. This was the cousin's house in Kent, where the wedding took place, so that the poor boys could make the most of their leave. The size of it. Why you'd fit the Cleary's residence into it a dozen times and over. And as for them Crystals? The same again and more so.

She lifted the photograph taken in Kent and smiled at it. When she replaced it, she found much to her surprise that she had changed its position to the front rank and there was dear Willie in the back row, against the wall, where you would have to strain to the tip of your toes to be able to see him.

EIGHTEEN

Greta picked the iron back up from the stove and pressed it firmly across the first napkin. She lifted it again and returned it to the heat. 'This is a waste of time,' she said, 'a complete and utter ...' The last bit of starch, which she had been saving for herself, had ended up going to Francie to use on the napkins. For all the good it did. Of course, if Mrs Gunne hadn't been too mean to invest in a few decent napkin holders, none of this would have mattered. The fact that the napkins were 'floppy', as she had put it, wouldn't be noticeable. But no point in thinking about that, now was there? Mrs Gunne's meanness was simply a fact of life. And would ruin everything she put her cheap little hand to in the end, you could be sure of that.

She tried again. This time flicking a few drops of water across the linen and applying the iron with a little more pressure. No, no, *no*! It wasn't working; all that handling, grubbing them up and making them droopy as ...

'Francie,' she began as soon as she spotted her coming back into the kitchen. 'Are you sure you used that starch I gave you on the napkins?'

'Me, Miss Greta? Of course I did, Miss Greta. I don't know what you're hintin' at. I mean to say –'

'Oh stop it,' Greta snapped. 'I'm only asking you. There's no need to have an asthma attack over it.'

Greta put the iron back down on its heel and shook her head. There was something bothering her, something that didn't quite fit. At first she thought it was because Mrs Gunne was probably lying about

Kate coming to dinner. Why else would Samuel call and she was sure, nearly sure, that she'd heard Kate's name mentioned at the door. Besides Pakenham would never come here on his own and if Kate was really unwell he would have an ideal excuse not to. But he was coming. She did say he was coming, didn't she? Pakenham. Yes.

Was that what was bothering her? And why? She couldn't quite put her finger … It was making her cross. Pakenham? Hot and cross, she would love to have taken Francie and given her a good shake for herself. Or pinched the fat on the baby's leg. Or slammed a few doors. She would have loved to do something. Pakenham, Pakenham, Pakenham. She shook her head again. But he was still in there. He wouldn't get out.

What difference did it make if Pakenham was coming or not? He knew she was here. Didn't he? He was the one who brought her here in the first place. It wasn't on account of him that she had to leave the house for the night. It was on account of Maude. Or Pat. Or anyone else who might tell Kate. Wasn't it? Wasn't that his whole intention – to keep her away from Kate? And if Kate herself was going to be here – all the more reason that they would want her out. Yes, all right. That was sensible enough.

She tried the napkin again, turning two of its corners into each other so that it stood like a portly *maitre d'*. Now, there: stay, now stay. Slowly she took her hand away and – down it lurched again. She flung it aside and picked up the next one. Mrs Gunne must have made a mistake. Yes that was it. A mistake. She meant to say: 'and if *they* find out you're here' (they, meaning the Clearys). That was it. 'They mustn't know you're here', yes that was it. She had just got flustered from all her lies about Kate, it had made her muddle-headed. That's all. She hadn't meant Mr Pakenham mustn't know she was here. Because Mr Pakenham already knew. Didn't he? Of course he did. And since bringing her here, it was him that was in control of her every movement, wasn't it? Yes. Well through Mrs

Gunne of course: 'Time and time again, he's told me.' Hadn't she just said that upstairs, not more than half an hour since. 'Time and time again, he's told me.' What? What has he told her though? That Francie must call me Mrs Gray? That I'm to stay on here? Be given no money, no reference? Why though, it doesn't make sense. Sooner or later someone will find out and his game will be up. But those are his orders. Aren't they? He gives them to Mrs Gunne and she passes them on. Yes but when? *When?* When does he give them to her? Not at the hospital surely? No. It wouldn't be possible. Anyway he hardly goes. Here? No, he never comes here. Well she must go somewhere to meet him then. No, she hardly ever goes out alone. The post maybe. Maybe he writes to her? No. She opens the letters in front of me, commenting on every one.

Greta closed her eyes and let Mrs Gunne's voice come back in. 'He mustn't know you're here ... if he finds out you're ...' Oh stupid woman – she had meant something else. Well if she'd meant something else why hadn't she said something else, like – like what? Like ... Greta covered her mouth with her hand and gulped. Oh she would never have. No. No surely not. She would never have dared. Oh surely not?

'Are you all right?' Francie asked her.

'She meant, Mr Pakenham mustn't know you're still here. If he finds out you're still here ...' Greta said aloud. 'He thinks I've left. He meant me to go long ago.'

'What? Who does? What are you talkin' about?'

'Oh nothing,' Greta said, picking up the iron and examining it casually. It still didn't fit though. Not yet.

She looked up to the mirror hanging on the wall facing her. Too far for her to see her own reflection, but there was Francie, back bent over the sink, fiddling with potatoes and humming to herself.

Francie stopped then for a second and, bringing her fingers down to her backside, pinched and pulled at her skirt so that she could readjust the underclothes beneath. She wiggled her bottom happily then before resuming her work. Unaware. Unaware that Greta had been watching her.

That was the thing with reflections: they were so disloyal – giving you undivided attention one minute and the next sharing your secrets with, well, anyone who happened to be passing by. It was the second time a reflection had whispered to her in this house. Yes. That first day; that first moment. When she stood alone in the hallway, it had whispered then to her as well. Come have a look at this. Here, over there in the parlour. Then it had been Mrs Gunne. Mrs Gunne and a wad of money, one, two, three. Now. Now it was beginning to add up.

Greta smartened herself up a bit then, returning the iron to the heat and arranging the rest of the napkins in layers. She was feeling a lot better now although she wasn't finished yet by half. There was still the matter of Kate to be sorted. Was she coming to dinner or not? She would have to be sure.

'What did Mrs Gunne want, Francie?' she asked.

'Mrs Gunne? Oh nothin', nothin' at all, well not nothin' at all. Somethin',' Francie gave a casual laugh, 'about the celery actually.'

Well now, there was a start. Something to get a foothold onto anyway. Francie's answer had been too breezy, too friendly by far.

'Oh of course, the celery,' she gasped. 'How is it?'

'Not a bother on it. It's goin' to be just –'

'I'm sure it is, Francie. I'm sure everything is, after all your hard work. And I'm going see to it now that you're given some of the credit. We won't let Cook take all the bows, now will we? After all she is just a temporary measure. She'll be gone out of here as soon as Mrs Bumbury has had her last dinner in this house. And it's only right that Mrs Gunne is made aware of your contribution to the success of the household during her sojourn.'

'Wha'?'

'I'm going to tell Mrs Gunne you were a great help.'

'Are you serious, Miss Greta?'

'Why certainly, Francie. Tell me, will there be enough?'

'Enough of wha'?'

'Enough of everything – you know, vegetables, meat, fish.'

'Oh yes, we'll be grand. I'm sure no one will go hungry.'

Greta frowned; that one was hiding something. She could tell, even down to the smug swing of her backside as she peeled the potatoes into the sink. That one knew something all right, something she was holding on to like virtue.

'Are you though, Francie?'

'Am I wha'?'

'Are you absolutely sure there's enough. I wouldn't want Cook putting the blame on you – should there be a shortage.'

'On me? Why me? It's nothin' got to do with me.'

'Well, you know what these ones are, Francie. They're hardly going to take the blame onto themselves, now are they? Could you imagine, though, the embarrassment if the Canon were to ask for another spud? Oh it doesn't bear thinking about.' Greta gave a little horrified laugh.

'The Canon hardly eats a thing, since he came back from the front. He says it turns sour in his stomach; he says when he thinks of all them poor lads eating muck and drinkin' petrol, he just –'

'Oh yes, of course, the poor man. It's a pity, though, Pat Cleary couldn't show such compassion. Honest to God, Francie, if you could see what that man eats at times. It's disgusting. It really is. Why I've often seen him clear eight potatoes at the one sitting. Where he puts them, I just –'

Francie stopped turning the potato in her hand and looked

around at Greta. Yes, she was beginning to scare a little. Greta decided this might just be the moment to change tack.

'Oh Francie, you've just got to help me – have you any suggestions as to what I could do with these napkins, I mean, would you look at them?' She turned a pair of imploring eyes on Francie, as if she were well used to relying on her in times of trouble.

'Suggestions? Me, Miss Greta? How do you mean?'

'Well. Say if we had napkin holders – which we don't – they would be rolled up and would look fine. I wonder if there's anything we could use instead? Let me see, let me see…' Greta tapped her forehead and looked down at the table.

'What if you tied something around them?'

Greta's head flew up. 'Francie, you are an absolute genius! Of course. Now why didn't I think of something like that? I could kick myself, I really could. Now when you say tie something, you mean something like that nice red ribbon in the sewing cabinet, am I right?'

'Yes, yes, that just what I mean.'

'And I suppose, you think maybe I ought to add some sort of a trim?'

'A trim? Oh you'd have to have a trim.'

'Yes, Francie, I suppose you're right. A pearl, do you mean? Or something sewn in the middle?'

'Yes, yes there's pearls in the cabinet. I seen them, I did.'

'Oh just wait till I tell Mrs Gunne about your marvellous idea!' Greta clasped her hands together and shook them joyfully before moving over towards the sewing cabinet. 'It's little ideas like that gets one noticed in a big house, you know, Francie. Little gems that have you flying up the ladder quick as Jack. Before you know where you are, your place would be at the side of the Mistress.'

She patted Francie on the back as she passed by her.

'Now let me see.' Greta stooped down and started to rummage.

'Ribbon, yes, here we are. And … aha – got you! Sewing basket and what else now? Scissors. Yes.'

She sprang back up and over to the table. 'It's an awful pity though you couldn't give me a hand, Francie, seeing as how it's your idea and all, but I suppose you must have so much work – how many portions of veg are you doing?'

'Oh more than enough, Miss Greta, never you fear.'

'Is that right?'

There was silence then for a few moments longer, Francie's work being the only exception, the sound of scraped potato flesh and the slobber of water as she dipped each one into the bowl to clean and take it back up beaming like a seaside stone.

'I know!' Greta sparked up suddenly, walking towards Francie. 'Why don't you help me with the napkins. And then when we're finished *I'll* help you with the vegetables. Now isn't that an idea?'

Francie paused and looked up at her. 'You'll help me?' she asked carefully. 'Are you sure?'

'Of course I'm sure, Francie. Come on, between the two of us we'll be no time. No time at all.'

'You'll peel potatoes?'

'Yes,' Greta laughed.

'Promise?'

'Absolutely.'

Francie dropped the half-naked potato from her hand down onto the sog of thin brown skin that was growing up the sides of the sink like a disease.

'Will I then? Will I give you a hand?' Francie was beside her now, her face flushed and excited.

'Hands, Francie, give the hands a wash there.'

'Oh right.'

'Have we much to do on the veg?'

'Oh I have them nearly all done.'

'No extras to see to?'

'No. None.'

Greta looked at her. Yes, Mrs Gunne had certainly warned her well. She would just have to keep chiselling away until she made a hole.

'All right so, Francie – the napkins. I'll just show you. You cut them, like this …' She unravelled a section of ribbon and stretched it out on the table. 'About this size, would you say?'

'Yes,' Francie rolled her index finger along the stretch of ribbon. 'About that size.'

'Good,' Greta continued, 'and I'll roll the napkin up like …' She curled the napkin up into a scroll shape and laid it on the ribbon. Tucking the scissor blades up under it, she snipped. 'Now pay attention here. A little bow like this, and then I'll sew the pearl button on in the centre to secure it. You leave a piece hanging down here, so that when you pull it, like this – it comes undone and the napkin is ready to use. All right?'

'Oh Miss Greta, how pretty.'

'Yes, isn't it? My last employer loved this idea. Always had me do it for special occasions.'

Francie looked up slyly at her.

'Did I say my last employer? I mean, of course, the one before that. This is a very English idea. As you probably already know.'

'Oh yes, said Francie, 'it's very English altogether.'

'Now, Francie, off we go, fast as we can. We'll have our own little factory down here. A factory for making fancies.' Greta squeezed Francie's arm and laughed. 'Where's baby?' she asked then.

'She's out the back.'

'What's she doing? We don't want her in annoying us now do we?'

'Oh no, she won't be. I tied her to a tree.'

'You *what?*'

'Wha'? Wha'? Why are you looking at me like that, Miss Greta, what's wrong? I only did what Mrs Gunne told me to.'

'She didn't mean …'

'She didn't mean wha'? Oh God, Miss Greta, am I in trouble? Will I go out and get her?'

Greta smiled. 'Have you tied her up very tightly, Francie?'

'No, no. I used the long rope. She's seemed happy sitting down at the tree, playing.'

'We'll leave her a few minutes so, seeing as she's happy.' She handed Francie the scissors and rolled the first napkin into shape, 'I'll just get the pearl buttons organised so. Have them ready. How many do we need, Francie?'

The tip of Francie's tongue was sticking out like a third lip. She caught the ribbon between the scissor blades and it fell away from the rest of the coil. 'There,' she smiled with satisfaction.

'Francie, how many buttons will we need?' Greta repeated.

'Hmmm?' she looked up.

'Buttons – how many will we need?'

'Oh ten,' Francie answered, spreading out the second piece of ribbon and poising the scissors to see to it.

'Ten? I thought there was to be only eight guests. Sorry, I was forgetting about Mr Pakenham, if he shows.'

'Oh he's coming all right. Definitely.'

'Is he now?'

Francie was about to snip again, when she stopped and looked up.

'So let me see, that's Mrs Bumbury, Marguerite, Mrs Gunne, Maude and Pat Cleary, Canon Prior, and Doctor and Mrs Crystal. And Mr Pakenham. Why, Francie, that's only nine.'

Francie blushed and looked away.

'Mrs Pakenham's coming isn't she?'

'Mrs Pakenham? Nobody told me nothin' about Mrs –'

Greta grabbed her by the arm and swung it around to her back, taking Francie with it as she did. 'You tell me the truth now, unless you want me to tell Mrs Gunne you stole the starch.'

'I did not. How dare you!'

'Are you sure now, Francie? Are you absolutely –?'

'All right, all right! Let go of me! Let go!'

'Will you tell me?'

'If you promise –'

'Yes, I promise I won't say anything. Not a word.'

Greta released her arm and Francie told her: 'There's to be another two guests. And she told me I wasn't to lay the places until you leave.'

'Did she now?'

'It mightn't be Mrs Pakenham – I mean she never said who it was.'

'She didn't have to.'

Greta pushed past Francie and made for the kitchen stairs.

'Oh no Miss Greta, you promised you wouldn't tell, you promised.'

Greta prised Francie's hand away from her arm. 'I'm not going to say a word about Miss Kate. And Francie, you mustn't let on you told me, now do you hear me? Not a word.'

'No! Are you daft? What would I want to tell on meself for?'

'And you better untie that child before she strangles herself.'

'Where are you going then?' Francie whispered up the stairs after her. 'If you're not going to tell.'

'There's something else I've got to see to that's been on my mind this while. Nothing for you to worry about.'

'But the veggies, you promised you'd help me with the veggies.'

Greta stopped and turned around. From the darkness of the narrow stairway Francie saw her stoop, her face dropping suddenly, pale and strange. 'Ah now, Francie,' she said, 'I can't keep all my promises, now can I? It wouldn't be natural.'

'But I helped you with the napkins.'

'More fool you, then,' she said, her face lifting back up and out of sight.

Francie turned into the kitchen muttering away to herself and turning her hand over her arm in soothing rubs. I might have known not to believe her. I should never have believed her. Imagine the stupidness of me: believing her.

And ignoring then the rubble of potatoes on the side of the sink piled up like a Galway wall, she made her way back to the napkins where she began attending to the finer points of the evening, the little gems that get one noticed.

NINETEEN

Samuel had been right of course, there really had been no point in Maude coming along as well. Leaving Mrs Gunne's dinner party like that in a flap. Bad enough they had to practically carry Kate out without her leaving too. Now there would be two empty spaces instead of one, two pulled teeth around the table. And now, there was Kate, after causing such a scene, sitting up front beside Samuel, cosy as you like. And him making no objection either; as if that's how they had always done things. And what am I so? Maude asked herself sullenly. A stranger to be carried along in the back seat, in case Samuel needed someone to call Ma'am, or his hat might need doffing before the journey's end?

'I don't know,' she answered Maura on the doorstep, 'I simply do not know. One minute she was fine and the next …'

The two women stood in the hallway watching Kate and Samuel walk past them to the staircase.

'Are you all right, Mrs Pakenham?' Maura called after them.

'She's fine now. I have her,' Samuel answered on her behalf.

At the bottom of the stairs the two women exchanged glances. Maude meant to follow, but found herself delaying, making no further progress than a light foot on the first stair and an undecided hand almost on the banister, to fill Maura in on details which might just as easily have waited until later. Why she did this, she wasn't sure, but had the vague notion that to follow them, Kate and Samuel climbing together up under the darkness, would be some sort of an intrusion. She turned back to Maura. 'Yes, one minute she was in the best of form,' she began, 'chatting away to Mrs Bumbury and the next. I just don't –'

'Was something said that might have upset her?' Maura asked.

'I don't think so. She was saying how much she was looking forward to dinner and discussing with Mrs Bumbury how awful the bread in London is – putty colour and putty taste. Then they began talking about ... Well, magpies.'

'Magpies?'

'Yes. Apparently they've flown over in droves from France to escape the guns, or something, and have settled in a marsh in Kent. And now the local graziers are planning to shoot them ... I think. Oh I don't know exactly what they were on about. Except that something or someone must have upset her.'

'The magpies, Mrs Cleary?'

'Oh no, Maura, I hardly think so. She was just making conversation. No. I don't really know what happened. Shortly after that, she excused herself for a minute, but cheerfully like there was nothing the matter. She was fine, just fine. When she didn't come back after ten minutes or so, I went looking. After all it was almost time to be called into dinner. Marguerite said she thought she had seen Kate go into the dining room a few minutes before. I looked but she wasn't there. Eventually I found her.' Maude looked warily back up the stairs.

'Where?'

'On the second-floor landing. Sitting on the floor, Maura.' Maude lowered her voice to a whisper.

'But why, Mrs Cleary? Why? What did she say?'

'She didn't say anything, not a thing. She was hunched over and clearly very upset.'

'And where was Mr Pakenham?'

'Hadn't arrived yet, still hadn't up to the time we left. He's probably there by now.'

'You mean the dinner is still going on?'

'Oh yes. It was just about to start, and we could hardly expect Mrs Gunne to turn everyone out. Not that she had any intention of that. In fact, I had to promise I'd go back as soon as I had Kate settled.'

'And Mr Cleary? Where's he?'

'That was the thing, Maura. The strangest. She wouldn't have him near her. She started to wave him away, whimpering to herself and carrying on like a pup expecting a beating. And she was – *is* – so fond of him you know. Yet the minute she saw him coming up the stairs, she started. Just wouldn't have him near her. Luckily enough Samuel was still in the kitchen, lifting a pot for Mrs Gunne. Would you believe he was the only one she would get up for? Once he took over she seemed fine, more exhausted really than anything else. Tired and in need of sleep. But before that? Well quite frankly, I was more than concerned. Oh Maura. What are we to do with her at all?'

Maude finally removed her foot from the bottom stair and lowered it back down onto the floor. She walked over to a hallstand and slowly sat down onto its ledge, perching herself between the coats on either side. 'One thing's for certain,' she said, 'I'll have to forget about asking Pat to take me with him to London tomorrow. I'll have to stay home. I can't leave now. And I was hoping … ah well.'

She closed her eyes: what had she been hoping, exactly? That in different surroundings he might soften towards her? That seeing her in a different room, under a strange light, he might …? They might …? And she'd badgered him until he had agreed to take her along, brushing aside his excuses, one by one.

Tied up with business all day. (I can shop!) And at night dinner with the stockbroker or the banker; these Americans never bring their wives you know. (I can amuse myself.) Won't finish until late. (I can wait.)

But supposing he didn't soften. Just tipped a kiss off her forehead and said, 'Goodnight, my dear.' It would be the first time that they slept away from home and had not been with each other. It would mean facing up to the possibility that they would never … again? Was she brave enough to take that risk? Better maybe to stay at home and never know. Keep it in reserve. To continue being able to say, 'It will be better once we get away.'

In the background Maura was mumbling away to herself a quiet supplication to the sacred heart. Her bits of prayers were soothing to Maude; she would have liked to take a little snooze with them trickling away in the background like rain. To listen and to sleep here, behind the forgotten winter coats, strange textures brushing off her face.

Suddenly Maura called out to her: 'In here, Mrs Cleary,' she heard her say.

'Yes, yes. What? What is it?'

And pushing back the bunches of coat sleeves then, she saw Maura beckoning to her from the doorway of the study. Slowly, she stood up and followed her. She crossed to the window where Maura was standing and looking out onto the street as though she was expecting to see somebody.

'That Greta one's just been here,' she whispered.

VI

PREDATORS

TWENTY

The minute Aunt Florence set eyes on Greta, she knew there was trouble. She took one long look at her travelling bag and sighed. 'Go inside, I'm just locking up.' And well really, Greta thought to herself, you'd think I had it loaded with manure, the face of her. While at the same time demurely saying, 'Thank you so much, Florence,' as she squeezed past her aunt, under the awning and into the cool interior of the dress shop.

Florence left her sit in the back room while she locked up the shop. And nothing had changed, nothing at all. The same baldy hat tree, the same labelled boxes bearing the foliage that would eventually make them decent: ribbons, bows, feathers-osprey, feathers-ostrich; four boxes of trimmings – sundry. And over there behind the door, paunchy with bolster cushions, the same divan that had once been her bed. And as she looked down at it she saw again her hand of long ago lift the tiny meat sandwiches from their lacy nest. And her feet swing her mother's reach-me-down boots back ways and foreways, rubbing off the coverlet she would eventually spread on the floor to lie with Mr –? (Oh what's this was his name again – that man that took advantage?) Nothing had changed in this room, except for her. She had outgrown the girl that once had been so thrilled by all this. The girl that had been convinced by every scrap of lace and fold of ribbon, each detail sartorial, that she had reached it – the limits of life. And nothing but nothing could possibly look better, except perhaps for heaven itself. That girl was gone now. Gone the way of the old-fashioned boots and the high neck collar: she would never be coming back.

Greta sat down beside the ghost of herself and felt the tears haul themselves up from her chest and into her eyes. By the time Aunt Florence came in she was weeping steadily. 'Oh Florence,' she began, 'whatever am I to do?'

Aunt Florence, her order book fat under her arm, paused before dropping the curtain and settling it back into place like the skirt of a gown. 'Well, you can stop that nonsense for a start,' she said. And then pulling chair to table, cleared a space onto which the order book could be slapped. She sat. The book was opened at the appropriate place and a pencil slid out from behind her ear. 'Well?' she said to Greta without looking at her. 'Come on, let's have it then,' and for a moment Greta thought she was going to take notes of her troubles, the way she had her head bent over the open book like that. But no, she remembered then, that was how things were always done. As soon as the shop closed it was time to calculate the business of the day: cloth, measurements, costs, profits.

Greta hesitated for a moment, wondering if this evening might be made exception and if any second Aunt Florence would postpone this summing up just for one day and look back up, close the book and lend her undivided attention to her niece's problems. But when she heard Aunt Florence turn another page while at the same time say, 'Well? I'm waiting,' she realised she would just have to compete with the order book for attention.

Greta took a deep breath and began speaking: once started, she was glad that Aunt Florence wasn't looking at her – it was so much easier to confess like this if you weren't being watched: the lack of response or reaction giving a peculiar impression of privacy that caused her to tell perhaps a little too much. Certainly more than she had intended.

And no wonder the Catholics go to confession, she remarked to herself, after the first few sentences had been uttered and she was beginning to gain speed, telling all their secrets to the dark, no judging eyes to make them hesitate or retract. And even later, if their priest were to scold them for their sins, so what? You'd never know the face that disapproved, never see it wait in anticipation of your shame. And then off with you with your new soul all fresh and clean and knowing that should you dirty it again, you could always come back, like The White Swan Laundry – sort of. Oh well for them, indeed, with their absolution and their endless second chances. And who was going to absolve her now? Aunt Florence? Why Aunt Florence wouldn't even give you a second chance the first time around.

And yet, into that room, padded up and muffled by bales of spring-coloured cloth, she let it all out. In there amongst the calico and cotton, she danced up close to the truth. In that secret room, with no one to hear, but a frozen aunt and a guard of dressmakers' dummies. In there amongst the crisp, the untouched, she told. Everything, or almost everything: the German lessons she had been forced to take, the Jewish man that had compromised her. Pakenham making her go to Mrs Gunne's and blackmailing her into writing a letter that was so full of the most horrible lies that Kate would never have anything more to do with her. The dreadful Mrs Gunne trying to hold onto her for her own gains and keeping – no *stealing* – the money Pakenham had meant for her exile. And no reference either, mislaid she said it was: lost! Here Greta started to cry again for a moment or two before concluding angrily with: that ugly baby that had caused her so much humiliation every time another person assumed it to be her to be the little horror's mother. Not to mention the Francie one whom she suspected was really one of those tinker people.

Greta told all this to her aunt, or rather to the crown of her aunt's head, Florence never quite taking her attention away from her sums.

Except once when during the discourse on Mrs Gunne, Greta happened to mention how much she hated liars. If there was one thing she hated – she began but stopped then wondering why that particular statement would be the only one to distract Aunt Florence; causing her to raise her head, and her eyebrow too, in that vulgar way she sometimes had before returning to the price of poplin.

When she had finished there was silence for a while, Greta sitting still and waiting for Florence to say something. She in return concentrating on her work. Eventually a satisfied 'there', and the clap of a shut book set things moving again. Aunt Florence stood up.

'Well, best have our tea then,' she said. Greta followed her out of the room and before entering the hallway hesitated. And just about to ask if that awful woman still lived upstairs, when she thought better of it (no point reminding Aunt Florence of *that* particular incident). She would just have to brave it out. She rushed behind Aunt Florence into the kitchen, asking, 'How's Miss O'Grady?' as calmly as she could. For she had, despite her rush to be safely out of the hallway, noted the door at the far end of the corridor had been painted a brighter colour and the glass of its peep window was flounced with new curtains, the cloth of which she seemed to recognise as once belonging to an afternoon dress rejected by an 'expanding' client (the term Florence used to describe the fuller ladies who had managed to get yet fuller between the initial measuring and the final fitting of an order).

'Oh she's dead, poor thing,' Florence said from behind the growl of a kettle being filled. 'Found in the bathroom. On the floor, God help her. Still I have it to myself now.'

'What?'

'The bathroom.'

'You mean her room hasn't been let?'

'Oh it has. To me. But don't get any ideas, Greta. I use it as a fitting room.'

'Ideas? Why I wouldn't dream –'

'Good.'

They had cheese sliced thinly and bread cut in triangles. Aunt Florence served the tomatoes separately so they wouldn't bulge through the bread. Afterwards they shared a slice of cherry cake and the apple tart that Greta had seen fit to bring with her.

'Oh I enjoyed that,' she said, after her third cup of tea.

'I wasn't expecting company, I'm afraid.'

'Oh what does that matter, Florence. That's your knack, isn't it? Making the simplest of things seem special.'

And Florence looked at her that way again and gave the tiniest snort. She lifted the teapot.

'So how long are you gone?' she asked.

'Gone where?'

Florence made no reply, her eye kept busy on the bow of brown tea thinning down first to one long drop and then, after she had given it a little shake, to nothing. She frowned – the teapot was empty and her second cup not yet filled.

'How long am I gone where, Florence? From Kate's do you mean?'

Aunt Florence put the teapot back down slowly and looked up.

'Greta,' she said. 'I have been fitting women long enough to know better. And the corset that can fool me has not yet been invented. So now, do you want to tell me, how long are you gone?'

And Greta began to cry again. 'Oh don't say that. Oh please don't tell me that. It can't be true. It just can't be. Oh Aunt Florence, what am I to do? Please tell me what am I to do?'

'I would have thought that was obvious,' her aunt began, holding to the light the napkin she had just finished using, refolding it then patting it softly at the side of her plate. 'You must find yourself a husband.'

*

Find myself a husband indeed. Greta raged inside as she crossed over College Street with Maura's fat shocked face still blanching in her head. Oh why did I go there? Telling that one all my business. Filling her mouth for her. And her pretending to be all sympathetic too and thrilled with herself really. Ooooh Miss Greta … oh you poor unfortunate … What'll you do-oooh, Miss Greta? Why find myself a husband, of course, Maura. Didn't I mention that? My Aunt Florence says they grow on trees, so they do.

Find myself a husband indeed.

She came up by the college railings and, between two of its stems, squeezed in her foot, scowling at her shoe laces as she did. And just how does she think I'm going to do that then? How? Or more to the point, where? Will I find one on a church pew that someone has left behind? Or on the floor of a tram rolling along under the seats with the rattle of movement and being turned over in the dust by blind feet.

Or perhaps I should try that place where Mr Gunne used to get so much of his stock – the Railway Lost Property Office. 'Excuse me I was wondering if you had any unclaimed husbands that I could buy?'

Now her feet rejoined and tightened up for the rest of her walk, full span of the college undergirth up as far as Lincoln Place then over and onto the shop where Florence would be waiting. Oh I can just imagine her standing there with the huffy mouth on her:

'Was she there?'

'No, just Maura.'

'Well, did you do as I said?'

'Yes, Florence.'

'And did you mention –?'

'Yes, Florence.'

'Good. I hope you told her-?'

'Yes, Florence.'

'Excellent. Now the next thing you have to do is ...'

Just before Trinity main gate the other shoe came undone. 'Well damn these stupid lace-ups,' she screamed inside, now lifting the right foot up to the squat thickset wall. These satin jobs are all very fine in the window, but no grip when it comes down to it. No staying power. Would Florence still have that ball of cord, she wondered, trying to remember which of the sundry boxes it would be labelled under.

Out from under the cave Greta watched two of them saunter, leaving the arch and nearing the gate. Hands deep in ducks that looked as if they could do with a good washing. Dirty gets, they're worse than babies. I wouldn't marry one of them, in anyway. Not if you paid me. And skipping along like schoolboys. Why they can't realise they're old enough to be men is beyond me. Chaps much younger, out earning their living, reach manhood years before these ones. Worst husbands of the lot, always acting the brat, too much learning beyond the necessary. And they always have hands like girls too. Never grow up.

Always be more like your eldest. No thank you, no college boy husband for me. Think they're it and no mistake.

One of them lifted his hat to her and gave what he obviously thought was a becoming grin. (Get lost sonny boy.) She nodded deftly, carrying on past them and sorry now she hadn't worn the nigger-brown wrap coat that takes a hold of her hips from behind as she walks, give them something to gawk at. Oh but soon it will be the hips taking a hold of the coat. And then coming through it.

Making a bald patch appear in the front like mother's one used to have, bits of stuff falling and sticking to it, always stained. Humpty Dumpty. Oh the thoughts of it. The *thoughts*.

Find a husband! What does Florence expect? Making me go there tonight like that. I told her Kate wouldn't be there. I told her she was going to Mrs Gunne's dinner tonight. But she still insisted.

'Go,' says she, 'you never know, maybe she changed her mind. If she's not there then all the better. Speak to Maura. Give her your troubles on a silver plate. She'll pass on everything, you can be sure. These people have to be made realise your predicament. After all it was under their roof.'

'Do I tell Maura about the letter?'

'Mention it, by all means. But not its contents.'

Aunt Florence was so firm about this that she actually stopped working for a moment, her hands keeping perfectly still, her eyes looking at Greta, and only at Greta. ' Say nothing about that. Until you've spoken to Pat Cleary. After all he's the only one who knows if it's true or not. If it needs denying then let him deal with it.'

'Yes but what must Kate think?'

'Let him deal with it.'

'But surely –'

'Just tell Maura the rest and make her promise not to say anything.'

'But I thought we wanted her –?'

'Yes, yes. Making her promise not to say anything is your one guarantee that she will.'

And oh that Florence one's mind. You'd want a compass to get through it. How anyone could be so devious – well quite frankly ...

And what did she mean in anyway with her, 'He's the only one who knows if it's true or not.' Didn't she believe her own niece? As if! Oh what a low opinion Aunt Florence must have. And him a married man. And not just a married man either; but Maude's married man: well minded. Still swinging out of him as if they were on honeymoon. Not that he's unattractive mind. No. Not half. But did Aunt Florence think she was stupid as well as everything else? Why the thought had never even crossed her mind. Never! Until Pakenham had made her write that letter about carrying on with Pat – Mr Cleary. Oh a chess move if ever there was, cutting her off on all sides. What better way to make Kate hate her? To make her keep silent too. Not the sort of confidence she was going to, after all, share with her sister, now was it?

And more fool me for writing it in the first place, I suppose. But he knew about me hiding Issac. And he knew about me and him together like that – I mean Issac making me be together like that with him. Against my will and better judgement. Pakenham had me cornered, no escape. And how many times has Aunt Florence warned me? Never put anything in writing except Christmas cards and bills of sale. Imagine. Me and Pat Cleary, the very idea! And to have written it down. 'For some time now, your sister's husband and I …' Why I never even thought of him at all. Never crossed my mind. Except for now, of course, a little. In retrospect. A bit.

For how could she help but think of it now? Pakenham having inserted it in with a pin-point. Right in, till it went trick-o'-the-looping in through her head, so that she was thinking about it now all right. Just a bit, just little things, just sometimes.

Like that time last summer. At the Henderson's picnic, when he lay back in the grass, his head resting in Maude's lap and she said something to make him laugh. And his teeth glimpsed out just for a moment from the darkness of his surrounding beard. Oh lovely and white. How she liked a nice set of delph!

And other things too: the way he spent money, for example, nice and careless. Is there anything more appealing than a man who can afford to be careless with his money – and is? And the way he knew everyone too. Everywhere he went. It was like being with the Lord Mayor, strolling out with the Clearys. It made you feel sort of, well …

But there was that other side of him too, the stern one. That time on the way to the races when he got Samuel to pull into the backyard of the pub just for a moment, and where, unexpected, they came upon two of his men burrowing large bottles into a sack. Drink poachers, no less. And he stepped down from the motor car, his mood swinging downwards with his heel. And there and then he dismissed them. Right on the spot. Even though one had started to cry like a baby.

'Well you should have thought of that before you started stealing from me,' she remembered hearing him say, in reply to some appeal about a sickly child, while Kate and Maude swapped schoolgirl looks with bitten bottom lips. And later as he climbed back in to take his seat between the two sisters, Maude trying to melt him: 'Oh Pat, couldn't you just have warned him? I mean to say, really, the poor man and what was it after all but a few bottles of porter, worth no more than a bob or two?' And him holding fast. 'Please don't interfere, Maude,' he said. 'It's none of your concern and I don't wish to discuss it any further.' Oh yes, he cut her off like a slice of cake. And she nearly died, was absolutely raging, turning her head and pouting out the window for the rest of the journey. While at the other side of him, Kate took to the opposite window, pretending to be deaf while dying of embarrassment really. But not her, well she remembered, sitting facing them on the dicky seat and looking straight ahead, seeing no need to duck or avert her eyes. For she quite understood. He had no choice. And now come to think of it, she could remember too glancing at him once or twice and fiddling with bits of notions inside her head, that may have had something to do with him. Yes. She had found it quite attractive, this surprising firmness of his. Was there, after all, anything worse than a man who let himself be trod on?

Anyway what was the point in even thinking about him? You'd never get him to look at another woman. She wondered though – they say they'll all stray if shown a brighter path.

It was between lights now; she'd want to hurry. Aunt Florence was an early sleeper. She probably should have taken the tram all the way, but she needed time to think. The way Florence would slap orders on you, you'd be living a different life before you had time to look sideways. And dare disobey! Two days was all she got out of her in the end. Oh she broke her heart all right – two lousy days. And what was she supposed to do then?

And yet Aunt Florence had the cheek to insist that she wouldn't be throwing her out to the streets. That two days was more than enough to sort something out. She said if needs be she'd call on Mrs Gunne herself, get what was due to her niece. Florence and Mrs Gunne – that'd be a match all right. Twenty rounds at the very least.

Greta turned off the curve just before the railings' end and positioned herself to cross the road. She reconsidered her position: anyway, how do I know I am? I haven't been to a doctor or anything. I bet I'm not pregnant at all. Of course I'm not. It's all a mistake. That Florence one thinks she knows it all. It's a bit of wind, no more. I'll dose myself stupid with Dr Cassells, that's what I'll do. Just the job for flatulence, Mrs Gunne says (and she should know). Yes that's it, Dr Cassells. Pregnant my eye. How could I be? A respectable girl like me.

She waited for a tram to drag itself heftily around the corner and then set one foot down on the street. Now I'll go straight back in there and I'll just say ... Then she saw her. That woman. That awful – Oh God, Oh God. What was her name again? Your man from the Gresham's wife. She was going to walk right smack into her. Greta looked sharply to her right and, raising her hand casually, waved at an imaginary friend that she had conveniently posted outside the dental hospital.

And redirecting herself, head down, she bustled around the corner and out of sight.

Now on Lincoln Place she examined her options: skulk or continue? For Mrs Sheehan (*now* she could remember her name all right; nothing like a good fright to jog the memory) might very well be still about, perhaps having gone no further than McCarthy's for her ounce of snuff – in case her beak wasn't brown enough – and flopped over the counter now gossiping away, this very minute, just waiting for something to divert her, like a familiar figure from the past sneaking by the window. And wouldn't that be lovely all right for warming Aunt Florence up to see her favourite niece banging on the door of the shop with that targer snapping at her heels?

Greta slipped into the tuck of the doorway between Gogan's and Butterworth's shops. She hoped to see Mrs Sheehan cross over the far side and make her way down towards Nassau Street. No fear. She must still be lurking about somewhere. Greta would just have to continue on to Westland Row. Take a detour back to the shop.

Half-way up Westland Row she forgot about Mrs Sheehan and Aunt Florence came back to mind. Find a husband. Why hadn't she found one herself if they were so easy got? Because the good ones were swiped the minute they poked their noses out the door, that's the why. Like Pat Cleary for example.

Public house and bottle factory. And God knows what else he has tucked away. America, I believe. That's where he has all his real money invested. Mrs Gunne says he's his mark on half the New York stock market. She paused in her stride to watch a night train slant over the bridge. Oh to be on it, to have somewhere to go, to be one of those shapes in the window up there; one, two, three, four ... But the squares of light slipped by too quickly to maintain a count. Her prompt step resumed.

He's all very respectable and that but he doesn't come from

money. Oh no. Made it himself, every bit of it. They say he made it out of petrol first. Before the war. Before most people had even heard of either. Buried it all in a pit in hundreds of tin drums until the price was right. Plenty of fuel now he has, in anyway, whatever way he worked it. Still, if he was my husband ...

I'd get a bigger house. One out Ballsbridge way or some seaside place, with big buxom windows to keep an eye on the view. Somewhere like Dalkey maybe or Sandycove. Somewhere a train might go. Certainly not Kilmainham. Heavens above. I suppose she likes to keep him close to his work in case he gets lost like, on the way home some evening.

She turned the corner into Brunswick Street and, this time stooping, gave her laces such a good tug and pull for themselves, adding two unbecoming knots that she knew would later give her trouble, but for the moment did the job.

But he's fussy I'd say, in private. Picking out her clothes for her and interfering in the household running. Likes his own way too. I wouldn't like to give him too much fat on his bacon. Oh no.

There were the lights of the Queen's theatre now, at the far side of the road. And: oh for God's sake – no. Not that pair again. She peered up the street to verify and yes. Definitely. The two she had nodded at earlier. Wouldn't you know the cut of them anywhere? And the darkness pushing their trousers forward so that they actually looked clean now. And here they were making their way down towards her. Oh for the love of what will they think? Passing her again. Oh why did she nod at them that time, drawing attention, making herself look like ...

She bent over her shoes again (although this time it was quite unnecessary) and peeping slyly up saw, to her relief, that they were jaunting across the road and into the theatre. Spared that embarrassment anyway. She was beginning to think there wasn't a corner of the city safe for her to pass. She stood up again. Typical of course. Typical. Them going late like that, to pick up a left-over seat at a fraction. Typical lousers, doing everything on the cheap, saving their fat for middle age. Always looking for something for nothing, their sort. Buy you a shovel of butterscotch and expect the works.

What was playing there tonight, she wondered first and then: oh who cares? The least of my worries, I don't have to say. Anyway they'd get on your nerves, those theatre people, always talking. And so sincere, I don't think. They never know when to stop acting. And dirty too, under the furs. Don't wash themselves half the time – a scum of make-up on their collars and necklets. That time when Maude had a few of them round from the Empire, taking the opportunity to try to soften the rift between Kate and the brother and at the same time have a look at the sort of company he was keeping. It was his birthday too. Can't remember how old. Waste of time it turned out to be, with him going home after half an hour. Leaving us stuck with his pals till the dawn, drinking their heads off and doing their little turns, giving each other glowing but hurried applause. No one really listening to anyone else, so anxious for their own performance to be called. Wouldn't you think they'd be sick of it, after a night on the stage. Poor Maude. Thought she'd never get rid of them.

And laughing at nothing when they had plenty to be amused by, starting off with each other.

He's different, I suppose. Though very peculiar. How old would he be now? Not as young as he looks. Or is it the other way around? I was expecting him to be much younger, the way they coo on about him; a baby I thought he'd be. But he's not. And never says a word either. Comes from being small for your age probably – 'Shut up shortie' all your life.

Though he's not that small. Just compared to his sisters, who are unusually tall for women. What would he be, about five – what?

Four, four and a half maybe. Five five? Maybe even six. About the same height as myself, I suppose. Wonder what he dances like? Never seen him, but heard him all right a couple of times, when I came to Gunne's at first. Thought he must be drunk, banging out of him like that in the middle of the night. But he doesn't touch the stuff apparently. And I believe he's just only a *spectacle* when it comes to dancing or so Mrs Gunne says. Big disappointment to her, him being out of action like that and unavailable for showing off to old bumble bee.

Back now at College Green, the repetition of Nassau Street to Lincoln Place had no appeal. No appeal whatsoever.

As she took her seat on the tram and settled her skirts, he came back into her mind. Dancing back in and looking quite tall now. (Six and a half maybe?) But you'd know by the walk of him that he'd be good, loose beneath the knee yet straight as a steeple otherwise. Even on a staircase, you could tell. The first time she ever clapped eyes on him, coming down Mrs Gunne's stairs. She could tell.

He's more like Kate than Maude really, come to think of it. Without the lack of lip, that is. He's good looking, if a bit baby faced. Though those sort of faces mature very well. Most attractive when they get into their forties. Quiet inside – deep would you say? I suppose. Or just stupid? Certainly his room is full of books. And spotless. He keeps his room spotless. His clothes too. You'd think he had a valet. Does a better job than any I've seen, Hafton House included.

At the first touch of Clare Street she hauled herself up and stooped a little to look out. No sign of the targer Sheehan anyway. Thank goodness for that. Must be gone to bed. As long as she brought that moon-faced husband of hers with her.

They say he'll never dance again. Not that that's much of a career for a man. Wonder what he'll do now? Still he won't go short. That's for sure. What his father forgot his brother-in-law will provide. Yes. Could be the making of him, in fact. Could well be.

Up at the platform now, nodding goodnight to the conductor, she could see the lights still on in the shop. Must have waited up, Aunt Florence.

Find myself a husband indeed. Yes. Indeed …

And lightfooted then she came down onto the pavement, a little hop expelling the surge of energy she found suddenly inside. And glad too, now, that she'd caught the straight tram home. The one that stopped right outside her door.

TWENTY-ONE

The evening after Mrs Gunne's dinner party, Maude was back again. And turning out of that same lady's gateway now, she walked down towards the crossroads to enter into what she hoped would be the final phase of her search. Where on earth was Greta? Maude felt as if she had put on three stones overnight; that tired, her legs that heavy to carry along.

What a day it had been, what a long and strenuous ... and as for Mrs Gunne! One hour in the company of that woman, one hour of sparring with her lies and trickery was about all a body could be expected to bear. Maude could still hear that dreadful voice struggling to keep itself beneath the level of a screech. And starting off with: '*Greta?* In this house? Whatever can you mean, Mrs Cleary? I don't know where Samuel came up with that notion. And you think that's why your sister had an attack last night – because we've kidnapped Greta? Well where is she then? Please tell me? I'd really like to know. Did you ever hear the likes, Francie? Mrs Cleary thinks we're hiding Greta in the house. I want an immediate search, do you mind me now? Starting off in Beatrix's perambulator.'

And she had that Francie one as bad as herself, backing up every lie. And so good at it too, the pair of them, that she had begun to doubt what she had heard from both Samuel and Maura and was just thinking about apologising when Mrs Bumbury arrived. And thank goodness too. At least there was some bit of truth to be had afterward. Now at least she knew that Greta had been living in Mrs Gunne's house (why there of all places? If I was in trouble, it would be my last choice), had been due back this morning; but as yet, had failed to arrive.

Maude looked across the street to the recruitment poster, urging Irishmen to do their bit and thought of what Pat had to say about it on the way home last night: 'There would be no need for that if every man in the kingdom was given a choice between an evening with Mrs Gunne or a trip out to the front. "Join an Irish regiment today – or join Mrs Gunne for dinner", it could say, with a portrait of Mrs Gunne on the side, standing by the piano ready to burst into song. The recruiting offices would be bulging with volunteers and conscription need never have even been heard of.'

Maude laughed now, where last night she hadn't even smiled. Oh how true and what an ordeal that woman is. And why my brother would want to stay there is beyond me. It really is. Even now, after his accident and everything, he still chooses to go to Mrs Gunne when he gets out tomorrow. (What has that woman got that I just can't see? – everybody wanting to stay with her. Everybody so keen to be under her roof?)

When she reached the corner she thought about just going home and postponing everything until tomorrow morning. All she wanted now was to take a taxi-cab home and once there to climb the stairs and into the bathroom. To fill her own bath and sit on its edge while the steam tumbled up to her. And then to feel the water, unbearably hot, pinch and nip her flesh. And to lie there, aah yes, while her skin sieved the heat into her, right through to her bones. Until Mrs Gunne and Greta and Issac, whatever his name is, became no more than a distant memory. Till everything Maura had told her had turned to steam. But then she remembered, wasn't tomorrow Saturday – the Jewish holy day? Yes. And that would probably make things even more difficult than they already were. Best get the whole lot over with now, while she was at it. She would sit on this bench and have a little rest before carrying on. Yes that's what she would do.

And besides with Pat in London seeing his American brokers,

what better time? There was no way he would allow this sort of an adventure, not unaccompanied anyway. And she hadn't even had a chance to confide in him. Hadn't really wanted to, truth be known. At least not until this morning. She had been annoyed at him, not even bothering to speak to Pakenham for her; after he had promised. How many days ago? Must be nearly a fortnight. Oh how angry that had made her. And the nerve of him, not even mentioning it to her again – the cheek.

Well that was the reason, until this morning, that is. When everything changed. And she could forgive him anything now. Now after this morning. When by the time they had finished – whether or not she had wanted to – she would hardly have had the time to tell him anything, except …

But she mustn't think of that now. She must hold that for later, when the business of the day is done. And she is alone.

Maude felt her insides tighten and fall again, the warmth of the memory still there, beneath her skin and down in her wrists where a lightness made her feel that her blood had been drained. By him perhaps, sucked away, into his own veins; to keep her inside him, as she had kept him. So that if he found the afternoon too warm, when sitting across a table from an earnest-faced American, or taking a banker's advice through cigar smoke and the waft of cognac, it would be her blood that would come slowly through, to cool him. To keep him calm and clear headed. And if he found the night too cold, walking back to the hotel after dinner, or alone on the ship deck, strolling with the push of the sea, her blood too would rise inside him, to heat all over, every inch – as if he was with her all the time. As if he were there, in the secret warmth of their bed.

At least it was over now. The distance that had been between them, at last no more. Though what must he think of her? she wondered – timid now at the thought of it – throwing herself at him like that.

But she couldn't help herself, it must be that time again. When the longing comes. How many days since she had – ten or so? Yes, the longing. The feeling had been too powerful for her, had reached behind her when she wasn't looking and closed over the book of rules, freeing her for the moments that it took to go over, to cross the divide.

And oh how good it feels – the satisfied appetite. Oh how good it feels at last. He had simply been too much to resist. And to her credit, she had at least tried to think of other things, as she was trying now. The events from the night before for example: Kate, Samuel, Greta. Mrs Gunne when she got back to the dinner trying not to show annoyance: 'Why, of course, we waited dinner for you, Mrs Cleary. Goodness, what must you think of us to imagine we would have done otherwise? Mind? Of course I don't mind. It's not me I'm thinking of. It's Cook, you know. And poor Francie. I know it's not fashionable to think of one's staff. But it is them I am thinking of – as well as my guests of course who must be ready to drop. Mrs Bumbury does be quite weak, you know, if she's kept waiting. But as to me? Well – whether I mind or not is im-material.'

And then later, Mrs Gunne singing and Pat stroking his beard to hide a grin. The fat baby in the lemon dress kept up way too late and screeching holy blue murder at anyone who looked at her. And the food (remarkably good as it happened). So good in fact that Mrs Bumbury was unable to speak at the table, stuffing all before her into her mouth and leaving room for no more than the occasional grunt of assent. Barely listening to anyone. And asking for butter, butter, butter, time and time again. And how bad things in London must be with this rationing business to ask for milk instead of wine. And how disgusted Mrs Gunne was too at the very mention. 'Are you sure, Mrs Bumbury? 'Tis the best you know. The finest French.'

'I'm quite sure it is, Mrs Gunne, but I have cellars of the stuff at home. Whereas I haven't tasted a nice glass of milk since I don't know when. One has to be under ten years of age to get any in England, you know.'

'Well if you're sure milk is your preference. Such a shame not to taste ... You wouldn't care to mix it I suppose? No, I suppose not.'

And even Canon Prior, seated beside Mrs Bumbury regretfully nibbling at a piece of bread and whispering things into her ear that would kill the sturdiest of appetites, could not deter the brave Mrs Bumbury. And another glass of milk if you please. And butter, she said again and butter she got again, to paint across another rather helpless looking little spud that was destined like his brothers to be swallowed whole, while the Canon, with more amazement than distaste, peered over his napkin. Yes, his napkin ... which reminds me ...

For even last night there had been something familiar in the presentation of them, the napkins. The little bow, the pearl button at the hub and Greta's name had sprung to mind just for a second. But the workmanship had been too clumsy to keep it there for long. For well she remembered similar napkins on Kate's table, devised by Greta to compensate for the shortage of starch. And how clever they had all thought it. How typically 'Greta' they had said, nodding contentedly at each other.

Had that been it, she wondered now. Had Kate peeped into the dining room on her way upstairs and recognised them. From the doorway, perhaps not realising the standard was not quite up to Greta's? Or had she found something else? A glove, a scarf, a piece of jewellery? Some small personal thing that had made her realise, had brought about the shock.

For if Samuel had seemed sure of one thing it was this: Greta had somehow become part of Mrs Gunne's household and last night Kate had been made fully aware of that fact. And where to find her now? Poor thing. Let's hope this Issac fellow knows.

Maude sighed: yes. Kate, Samuel, Mrs Gunne, Greta and now this Issac chap to add to the list: such were the little thoughts with which she had kept herself straight this morning, sitting up against the pillows and tapping the cup on the dip of the saucer. And she was managing all right. Keeping calm on the outside at least. Until she saw him reach into the wardrobe to search for the jacket of his suit. It was then that it got just a little too much.

Of course she knew it wasn't there; Philomena had taken it downstairs to give it a brushing. She knew that. But she didn't tell him. She wanted to watch him. Oh just a little longer. But he looked so fine, so real, still in shirtsleeves. Crisp white shirtsleeves. So white against his hair and the high colour that his face has lately had. Was she imagining it, or was he getting better looking? He began to cough again, his slight dry cough, just lifting his shoulders so that the cloth of his shirt was gently agitated – as if it were being caressed.

And a vision came into her head then. Without invitation, just came barging in without so much as … and remembering it now made her blush all over. Just remembering it was enough. It was a vision of him standing there in the formal clothing of the outward gentleman. And her reaching up to him, naked and pressed against him, so that the buttons from his suit nibbled into her skin. Her hair the only cover that she had.

He turned then to ask her: 'Have you seen my –?'

'Your …?'

'My –' He stopped and coughed again.

'You still have that cough?'

'It's nothing.'

'Its the dust from the factory, I told you. You should wear a –'

'Yes. So you haven't seen my –?'

'I don't know.'

'Oh?'

And it was then she found herself clambering out and over the bedclothes, the way a child might do, although there was nothing childish in her intentions. Oh no. And crawling to him, to where he was standing there at the bottom of the bed, her throat already scorched from a strange dry weeping, without any tears. And remembering how he stood there, puzzled, a little afraid even. Not knowing what to expect. Until she hooked herself around him and could see his face no more. (Oh my darling, my darling please I don't care if we never have any children. When I can't have you, what use? I promise I will never let it upset me again. Just please, don't deny me, my darling, please.) And her arms around him and her body pressed into him hard. And yes, she felt it at last. She felt it. He weakened, his face against her skin – only the thinnest cloth of her nightdress stopping her vision from coming true. Only the thinnest cloth between them. So that his hair could scrape, could graze as if she had come to him naked.

He put his arms around her and lifted her up off the bed and down she slid, her legs along his, until her bare feet rested small on his leather shoes, and he kept her there by her hair, bunched into his hand, and he kept her there by some sort of gravity she couldn't now in hindsight even begin to define.

Maude uncrossed her legs; she would have to stand up, to walk and stretch these legs that were fraying again at the thought of him. Three nights more, that was all. Three nights and he would be home again. Hers again. She would try not to think of it until then. After all she had work to do. She had set out with a task this lunchtime. And mustn't allow for any distraction. This Issac man now, for example. Supposing she does find him, what should she do? Ask him out straight if he knows where Greta is? And the pregnancy. Should she mention it? No. No, that wouldn't do. Might scare him away. Best keep that secret for the moment. Besides

Maura may have misunderstood. And anyway he may not even speak English.

Turning the corner into Clanbrassil Street, for the first time she experienced a feeling of regret that she hadn't taken a leaf from Lottie's book and learnt how to drive. What a nuisance this was, traipsing all over the city and having to organise taxis – all very well if one or two destinations were all that were required but any more and well forget it. You couldn't get them to wait for you more than five minutes, these days. Still what could she do? If she wanted to keep it a secret until she had all the facts, she couldn't use Samuel. Not if he was as thick with Kate as he seemed to be, as Maura seemed to be sure he was. She looked up at the shop fronts: Rudstein, then Buckhalter. Now Weinrouck. Their strange arrangements of letters let her know – yes – it must be down here somewhere all right. And yet none of the shops with the funny names was open. Why?

She began to realise the smell just then; cautiously at first it came over her, and then it was there all around her, overpowering, unavoidable. Oh God, what could it be? Down along the curvature of the street, she could make out the thick black plaits of horsemanure bumped up on the surface. But that wasn't the smell, surely not? Whenever had the smell of horses disturbed or repulsed her? And she a country girl. No it was something else. It had to be.

She continued watching out for Daniel Street, just as Lottie had instructed her to. Although she knew it wasn't time yet. Not yet. Lottie's directions were always so precise. (Which was why she had made hers the first visit today.) Lottie had such a sensible approach to things.

'First you must find the truth,' she said. 'Without it, all solutions are nothing more than speculation.'

'How do I do that?'

'You demand it. You speak to anyone who may have a bit of it.

And they all have, you know, you can be sure of that. Then you put all the bits together. I mean everyone, mind, Kate included.'

'Oh but I can't. She's not well enough.'

'Not well enough? Don't talk to me about "not well enough". Where you're going today there's people being wiped out with consumption. Which reminds me: *don't* go into the house on Daniel Street, in the unlikelihood that you should be asked that is. Her husband's next.'

'Oh dear God –' Maude began.

'As to your sister not being well, as you put it, that's exactly why you have to speak to her. If what Samuel told you last night is true, if it's true that her husband is trying to have her locked away, then she has no choice other than to pull herself together, otherwise, he won't have to try any longer. She'll end up doing it for him. She needs your help and Pat's, but she also needs to help herself.'

'Well whatever about me, I don't think she'll accept any help from Pat. She seems to have taken such a turn against him lately.'

'Why would she do that?'

'Why? Well I don't quite know.'

'Has he got anything to do with this plan to lock her up?'

'Oh no, Lottie. Oh Pat would never –'

'No I suppose. What exactly did Samuel say?'

'Very little, actually. He just said he thought I should know that he believed Greta had been staying in Mrs Gunne's house and that Mr Pakenham intended having Kate locked away.'

'And Maura? What did she say?'

'Just that Greta had been to see her and that she was in trouble; she'd been staying in Mrs Gunne's. And that German chap that you had arranged the lessons from –'

'Trouble? What sort of?'

'Oh Lottie, you know …'

'Ahh. Ask me if I'm surprised?'

'Lottie, really.'

'And does Mrs Gunne know she's – in trouble, as you say.'

'No. I haven't mentioned it to anyone.'

'I see. Strange, Kate taking against Pat like that. All the same if Kate dislikes someone, I daresay she must have her reasons …'

Maude looked up to see a man walking towards her. A dark, dusty suit of clothes and a plump trilby on his head like a button just asking to be pushed. As he moved, the sunlight clipped neatly at something in his top pocket. His spectacles, she supposed. And she found herself rehearsing an excuse for being here on this street, should he step this way. He turned into a side street before their paths crossed and a feeling of relief started on her, before she scolded it away. 'What absurdity. Why should you have to say anything? Why should you have to explain yourself? You have just as much a right as anyone to walk along this street as anyone else.'

On Daniel Street a group of small children sat in a circle. They were playing a solemn game. When they saw Maude, they stopped, as if ashamed. And gradually, as the focus of the game was lost and all attention was slyly turned on her, each one stood up. She tried to smile at them. But seemed unable. A moment ago, when they had been bent over the little bits of stones, chopped up leaves and broken glass that had been the essentials to their tight little world down there on the ground, they had looked different. From where she had been standing at the pillar-box, their smocks draped over their hunkers seemed to fatten them out into squat hens, hatching in a circle. And now unfolded, as each one stood up, their body size pared, their gaunt faces and enlarged eyes looking at her, she thought of Mrs Smyly's children, recognising the look from the portraits on the collecting cards used to appeal for that orphanage.

Except Mrs Smyly's children had a certain prettiness about

them, designed to almost please the giver. Whereas these children, well, there was little that was pretty here.

And again, although Lottie had told her, 'The third house on the right – Mrs Rooney, you can't miss it,' she felt as though she ought to say something, just as she had felt on seeing the man with the glinting specs. 'Hello there,' she smiled, choosing the girl that was the nearest and stooping herself down to meet the appropriate height. 'I was wondering …'

The little girl sucked on a ruck of hair, which she had caught into her mouth like a horse's bit. She stared back at Maude without replying.

'She's a dummy, Missus,' a voice from behind said. 'She can't say nuttin'. You can ask me but.'

Maude turned around and looked down at a small boy. And oh hardly there at all. His face was too old, too large for his body. How she managed not to cry out. Could anyone so thin be alive?

'What's your name?' she asked him.

'Mattie.'

'Oh well, Mattie, if you could help me, I'd be so grateful. I'm looking for Mrs Rooney.'

'Mrs Rooney?' the boy sounded shocked.

'Yes … This is Daniel Street?' The boy nodded and pointed to the third house. Maude took a shilling from her purse and handed it to him. He looked down at it, as if he wasn't quite sure what it was.

Mrs Rooney's head came around the door. The rest of her body, including her neck, remained behind. And so determined she seemed to be to keep it there, that for a moment Maude believed she must be naked behind the door.

The head moved up and down twice as it took a good look at Maude and then she asked: 'Did Miss Lo'ee send you?'

'Oh yes, actually she did. Yes. I was –' (How did she know?)

'Look I know I told her I'd go, but I just wasn't able. Sorry. I'll go the next wan. Promise.'

'I'm sorry?' Maude said.

'Mee'in'. I couldn't get to the mee'in'. But I got her little message. Tell her God bless. He's terrible bad these past few days and I'm just not goin' to have the time to be independent this week.'

Mrs Rooney's head looked as if it was about to disappear again and so Maude raised her voice to keep it with her.

'No. No, that's not why I'm here,' she said. 'It's nothing to do with the meeting.'

Behind her she could feel small shadows close in, yet she could hear nothing. It was as if the narrow street were empty. She would have looked around, but she was afraid to take her eyes off Mrs Rooney for a second, in case she would close the door.

'Lottie said you might be able to help me, Mrs Rooney. I'm looking for a gentleman, a Jewish gentleman.'

'Don't know none,' Mrs Rooney blurted before popping back behind the door. Maude had to push against it to keep it open.

'Please, Mrs Rooney, you must. Lottie said.'

'No, I don't know nothin'. Amn't I after tellin' ye?'

'His name is Issac, you recommended him to Lottie as a German language teacher. My sister and I. We sent you something for the children.'

'Oh tanks very much, I'm sure.'

'No. No, Mrs Rooney, I wasn't looking for thanks, I promise you, I only wanted to remind you.'

'Well, ye've reminded me. Good luck and goodbye.'

'Mrs Rooney, I must speak to him. It's so important.'

But the door was shut. And Maude knew that no matter how hard, how long, she knocked, it would not open again. When she turned back around the slower children were silently scuttling back to their game; the quicker ones were already seated. Maude said goodbye to them but no one raised their heads and so she walked back out onto Clanbrassil Street. As soon as she turned out of sight, she heard their voices resume, and the game continue just as before. It was as though her presence had made no impact on them. As though she had never been there at all. Oh what to do now. Ask someone else? Mrs Rooney had been lying, of that she was certain. How could she expect anyone else to tell the truth?

Now what? Go back to Mrs Gunne's and see about calling a taxi-cab? Oh God no. She would make her way on down to see her brother at the hospital. Yes, that's what she would do. Her last visit to him in that place. From there she could ask the nurse to make arrangements. To call Samuel or a taxi-cab, whichever. The hospital was at the other end of the long lane, which should be … Now where?

She was just deciding which direction to take, when she felt a tug at her coat. Oh my God! She spun around.

'Oh Mattie. You frightened the life –! Oh I'm sorry I shouted. Did I frighten you?'

'No Missus.' He laughed and waited until she had caught her breath before continuing: 'I know him, Missus. I do. Issac the Figgler.'

'The Figgler?'

'Yea. Ye know,' Mattie stepped forward and, lifting his elbows, mimed the motion of someone playing the violin.

'Oh yes of course, the fiddler,' Maude whispered to herself.

And looking down past the top of his head, through the gap his raised elbows had made, she saw that the toes of his small bare feet seemed to be groping for her boots as though they were curious to feel real leather.

'She's only lettin' on she doesn't know him,' he continued.

'But why should she do that, Mattie?'

'She lights their fires an' does their work for them on Saturdays. She has to keep in with them.'

'I see.'

'I know where he lives, Missus.'

'Could you take me there?'

'He's not in hes house now. He's in hes church. We can't go in there. I could show him to you but. If we catch him on the way back like – you might be able to talk to him.'

'Yes, Mattie, that would be fine.' She followed him across the street.

'We'll go up here, Dowker's Lane, Missus,' he shouted back to her as soon as they had reached the other side.

'Yes, all right, Mattie.' She hardly paid much attention to where they were going after that, the endless chatter from him keeping her more than occupied. Now and then he stopped to cough, a weak dry sort of cough.

The street widened a little here and she could feel stout cobblestones muscle into the soles of her most unsuitable boots.

'It's called a sinnygod,' he said suddenly.

'What is, Mattie?'

'Their church. A sinnygod. Because that's where they brin' all their sins. To God. Now do ye know?'

'Oh yes,' she said, 'of course.' And looked up to study the wrought iron name arched over the convent entrance like a handle so the poor child wouldn't see her grin.

He continued: 'They were all in jail, except the figgler. He escaped.'

'Jail?'

'See they were playing billards in the hall in Portybello when the police came in and they all run for their lives. Only he didn't get caugh'. He jumped up at a window like …' Mattie climbed up onto a wall, 'this.' And swinging his arms and dipping his knees he gathered momentum before he continued: 'And jumped offa it, like ...' Maude was horrified to see him leap through the air and down onto the ground shouting 'this way,' as he landed.

'Mattie! Are you all right?'

But he was back up on his feet in a second.

'And he hurteded hes hand so he did. That's why she was afeard to tell you as well. In case you'd tell the police and he'd be nabbed again.'

'Again? I thought you said he escaped?'

'Yea, he escaped but then he was caugh' later on. After the others like. Someone squealt on him while he was hiding. No matter now, they're all out again. No matter.'

'What did they do wrong, to have to go to jail, Mattie?'

He shrugged as though surprised by the irrelevancy of her question. He caught his breath, then with his cough, began rooting down into his lungs until he came back up with a mouthful. This he spat out onto the ground and paused for a second to admire the cluster he had just produced.

'Mattie,' she asked him, hoping he hadn't caught the look of disgust she could feel passing over her face. 'You said he was in his church. I thought it was only on Saturdays that they went to church.'

'Oh no, Missus, they start on Friday evenin' that's the Sabbat Eve. That's what they do. Friday and Saturday, either prayin' or stuffin' themselves, me ma says. Sure they have a great time altogether, she says. They even have a sing-song, she says.'

'Does she?' Maude laughed. 'And where is your ma now? Won't she be looking for you?'

'She's in the house, Missus, you're only after been talkin' to her.'

Maude stopped. 'You don't mean Mrs Rooney is your mother?'

'Yes, Missus.'

'Won't she be angry with you if you show me where he is?'

'Yes, Missus. She'll knock the shite out of me, Missus.'

'Oh, Mattie.'

'Unless, you give me another shillin', she mightn't be so bad then.'

'And if I give you a half a crown?'

'Then she'll prolly won't mind at all.'

Maude leaned down to him and gently pinched his rosy cheek.

'Where are we now, Mattie?' she asked.

'Blackpitts, it's called, Missus.'

She looked around. 'Yes, Mattie, I bet it is.'

Twenty-Two

Henry Masterson was a man well used to the sound of wagging tongues. They were, after all, at it, even before he was born, were they not? What with that slight discrepancy between his father's departure on tour and his own gestation period. And neither his father's success in the theatres of Rome – 'an unforgettable *tenore leggero*' they had said – nor his own subsequent birth and weigh-in of eleven and a half pounds of prime baby weight could distract the sudden spate of mathematicians and amateur obstetricians to be found among the theatre set that May of 1878. And he had no doubt that even after he died, and the last sip of sherry had passed the last twitching lip, the tongues would start again, finding they had not finished after all and had remembered something else to merit another wag or two. Not that he cared in the least. Not a jot. Not smaller than a jot's jot.

He padded his jaw with a lathery wad and swiped a diagonal from his ear to the centre of his chin. He then dolloped the razor into the bath water until it bobbed back up soap free and gleaming.

Besides which – he reminded himself – in his line of business, a scandal or two could only be considered to be advantageous (excepting of course, those concerning embezzlement or an appetite for young boys). All feathers being necessary to the cap of a man of the world. And no theatre manager should be less, he reassured himself sternly, now directing his chin to the left and cancelling the last soapy traces from his face.

And so what if people should happen to notice that Masterson had left the concert early and had failed to catch up with the rest of the party until a couple of hours later – say, just before supper? In tip-top form (with a bit of luck) and with an unusually large appetite (unlikely – but one never knows). And if people were to conclude that his absence might very well be due to pleasure rather than to duty, would that be his fault? Would it be anything to be ashamed of? Certainly not. Not with the woman he had in mind anyway. These days there weren't too many prospects that made the hair stick up on the back of Henry Masterson's neck. Not too much would cause a stir nor a tingle. Which is what happens – he ruefully admitted – when you have had premature access to the pleasures of life. By the time you're thirty you've lost the ability to be surprised. 'Wouldn't you agree?' he asked his squinting reflection, condensed in the shaving mirror, while returning his razor and brush to their bowl, set on top of a stool at the side of the bath. Now finished that task, he continued: 'To be thrilled utterly. To appreciate completely ...' When was the last time? He stretched his long arm over the side of the bath and placed the hand mirror on the floor.

Ah yes that season just before the war in London. Covent Garden and the Royal Opera House. That time around his thirty-fifth birthday it was. Yes, that was the last time he could remember being in the presence of something exquisite. *La Boheme*: Enrico Caruso and Nellie Melba. Rodolfo and Mimi. Did they have any business being so beautiful together? The blend of superbness, male and female. Masterson drew his legs towards his chin and unfolded himself up and out of the bath. Like a dog, he shook himself free of the looser drops.

Never could go out to the front of the house to look at them, all the same, preferring to listen. To close his eyes backstage and listen, soak it into himself. Ah yes. *Bello, bella, bellissimi!* Besides he saw enough of them during the day to realise that if he watched them on the stage, two plump turkeys, playing at beautiful consumptive and penniless garret dweller (and it would want to be a big garrett that would hold the pair of them) – well, the beauty would be gone. Thy 'tiny' hand, indeed.

He ruffled his legs with the bulk of the towel and with its corners tended to his ears and all of their redundant little alleyways.

To tell the truth he always thought Caruso was a bit of a – well. Egyptian cigarettes were one thing, but for a *primo tenore* to believe that slither of stinking anchovy he wore like a medal around his neck would protect his voice from harm – ridiculous! Chaliapin, now he was another matter. Could get away with foolish carry-on, for some reason have it put down to artistic temperament. Maybe because he was Russian or because he was a *basso*. He had the breeding of course or was it his height perhaps? A giant if ever he'd seen one, made Masterson feel quite the little maid beside him. That pet monkey of his though, Boris, wasn't that what he called it? Had more sense than the pair of them put together. A lot of old nonsense they went on with.

Would Father have turned out like them, had he carried on as he had started before his voice began to darken, had he survived his love of cognac and syphilitic women? Is that what would have become of him – sitting around between concerts in a flowered silk kimono feeding chocolates to a monkey?

His chest next: patted and scoured. And his belly – was it getting a bit? No. Just needs a little … He squeezed it in to himself and gave it a little tap. Tight as a drum.

Nor did he think that much of her. Nice woman, but – Australian. And, well, one shouldn't expect too much, one supposes. God knows, she couldn't have had much of a start. But sing and … Open their throats and … Oh they could be anyone, all powerful, all perfect. They could make you believe in God. Masterson sighed: and we are expected to believe that all men are born equal.

He stretched over to the sill where he had left his pocket-watch and, yes, better hurry along, patting the towel one more time up and over his legs and around his loose change. Then down under.

That was the summer; the last time he felt he was somewhere he deserved to be. The summer of his prime. With London throbbing and always in the background the singing voices, McCormack, Melba, Melba, Caruso, Sammarco. Melba: her voice would get to you all right, could leave you shocked. Stay with you in your sleep up to early morning then. And early morning then, no matter how long the night before had lasted, you'd never feel tired. No. Tiredness just didn't come into it. Five hours would do fine. And nothing better then than to rise with the dawn to hear them: Caruso's fellow countrymen taking up the queue outside the theatre. And singing Tosti choruses joyfully. All day they'd wait. All day in the rain. (For *I Pagliacci* wasn't it? Yes that was his first performance that season).

And then come early evening, when the tail coats and gardenias, the gowns and the fresh faces came strolling out, those privileged with reserved seats would sometimes delay to applaud the poor unfortunates. Quite the hoot they found them all right, quite the scream. Still waiting for an almost hopeless unreserved gallery seat. Still there, the salami meat and melon fruits that had kept them going since the dawn – still breathing on the air.

And yet seats or not, one got the impression that no one could enjoy nor appreciate as much as those poor beggars left out on the street. Missing a day's wages for nothing and willing to spend a month's given a chance. Even when the curtain came up and it was accepted that all seats were full, they'd wait, one eavesdropped snatch of *Vesti La Giubba* enough to fill their hearts to capacity. Yes you had to admire them. That you did. They became part of the pleasure that season, another of the features like Diaghilev's ballet and the late-night suppers in Pagani's.

Wrapped now in his robe, he strode through to his dressing room where, as he would wear them, his clothes were laid out, top hat down to shoes: a well-dressed man without a body.

And there were, of course, one or two other little features that contributed to the pleasure during those five weeks, yes indeed.

That nice black-eyed interest he had managed to acquire for himself, for instance. Making himself the envy of the backstage. A married one, unhappily so, wealthily so – always the best. No expectations nor desire to jeopardise her position. No endless persuasion either. Knows what's on the table from the start. Gets keener too, if she thinks you're losing interest, do anything then. Anything to keep you. And hardly a scrap of English, so none of this tiresome 'getting to know you' rot. As far as he was concerned there was only one way to get to know a woman, and that was ... Yes. She was a nice little specimen all right but ...

Wouldn't be a patch on this one. Wouldn't be in the same class at all. No challenge. This one would need all your senses at once. No half measures here. The mere thought of this one would make more than the hair stick up on the back of your neck.

He looked down to where, through a gap in the robe, he could see his interest beginning to manifest itself. No time for any of that now. No time for distractions, better get dressed quickly so. From beneath his trousers he slid the first garment and struggled inside. And the chance of success was slighter too. She could be the exception. Every persuasion would be called for. Every ounce of energy, every trick in the book. But what of it? He was fed up with making do. Wanted something exquisite in his life again. Wanted the challenge. Just one last worthy fling was worth the risk.

It wouldn't be easy. He knew. Careful planning, and well picked opportunity . Still can't be too much of a problem. He thought of old Tildsey then. An expert in the field of women, still drawing them to him like flies at the age of seventy-odd. Died in the saddle too, they say. 'Women,' he used to say, 'fall into two categories: unwed and wed. The unwed you avoid, because despite yourself sooner or later one of them is going to snare you and your life will never be your own again. The wed, you concentrate on. Unhappily married women – there for the taking.'

'But what if they're happy?' he had naïvely asked.

'No such thing, Henry,' smiled old Tildsey. 'No such animal. A women who has been married for more than two years is never happy. No woman with a ring on her finger gets enough attention from her husband, they are all neglected. And remember that's all you need to give them: attention, with a capital A.'

Well old Tildsey knew his way around his subject all right, but he'd go further than that himself. Attention from one man? Even if they did get it, honeymoon style for the rest of their days, they'd still be discontented. It's attention from all men they want, every last one on this earth. He picked up his shirt and rummaged for its entrance.

'What we are talking about here,' he said to himself, from under his shirt as he eased himself up through it, 'is a thoroughbred. Yes. Careful handling indeed. And we could be looking at time. And trouble.' (But no matter, there was always Matilda, he supposed, should he find the waiting a strain, the load too heavy to bear, so to speak.) She was no chorus girl, this one. No pony to be hacked out and forgotten.

All in good time. The longer the chase, the sweeter the meat. He lifted his suspenders and adjusted them to size. Snap.

But he'd heard she was happy, they were happy together. There was a general air about them, he'd heard it said. The exception to the Tildsey rule? No, it's a rule without exception. It's simply that she doesn't *yet* know she's unhappy and will have to be taught that for a start. Snap again, and both in place now, stretched and settled and nicely taut. Well known, too: wouldn't be all that easy to be discreet, to *stay* discreet. And yet …

If people remarked upon it, what did he care? He liked to be remarked upon. Made a fellow know his worth. Give them something worthwhile to remark upon, this time. Maybe.

He stood back and examined himself in the full length. Yes, even if he did say so himself – most impressive. Not a bad idea casually dropping in on her tonight. Let her see me at my finest. (Just happened to be passing on my way to …) Not a bad idea chumming it up with that bar hand at Cleary's shop either, privy to all her business now. Like the lack of a husband over the next few days and the fact that the brother is getting out of hospital tomorrow.

'So worried about your younger brother. If there's anything I can do for the little bastard. Like give him a good kick up the arse for example for being so stupid. The loss of such a talent … What a shame. Perhaps we could find him something else in the theatre. Believe he gets out tomorrow. Have a few ideas, like to discuss with you. Perhaps over lunch. Or dinner, even better? Bla bla and et-cet-erah!'

Henry Masterson leaned closer to his reflection and then stepped back to enjoy one final look: Yes, they say people have stopped dressing properly in the evening. Silk toppers on the wane and plaque shirt fronts just a memory without starch. They say it and perhaps it's true.

He pulled his shirt shell straight and played his fingernails lightly on it, enjoying the delicate beat. And pulling then a torpedo-shaped cigar from his top pocket. (Another thing he knew they catted about – where does Masterson get those torpedoed cigars? Thought they'd stopped making them long ago.) 'And wouldn't you like to know,' he told the world in general, slipping it gently into his mouth.

The trouble with most people was that they made no provision for the future, no plans, no aims, just took life as it passed over them, hoping for the odd titbit to land in their laps. Well that was never his way; he liked to see what he was after. See it and slowly creep up to it. 'Pounce,' he whispered softly to himself from behind the cigar.

He drew it then from his back teeth round to his front where he closed his lips over it before pulling it out with a pop. Then returning it to his pocket, he patted this temporary nest. Now. Where were his gloves?

'Algernon?' he called. 'In here a minute.'

Algie looked around the door as if he'd been waiting outside to be called. 'Off out are we?' he asked.

'As well you know, Algernon. It is Friday.'

'Oh of course, of course. And may I say you're looking very …' Algie stretched his arm towards Mr Masterson and began gesturing with it, up and down.

'Have you seen my gloves?'

'Oh I have them here – just giving them a sprucing up for themselves.' He held the gloves out towards Masterson. 'See?'

'Put them on the bed. Did you order the taxi-cab?'

'Oh indeedin I did. Ten after seven wasn't it? Or did I get it wrong? Oh don't say I did? You did say ten after?'

'Yes, Algernon. I did say ten past.'

'Thank goodness for that.' Algernon gave his chest a little pat of relief and moved towards Masterson, his hands outstretched and ready to offer assistance with Masterson's evening cloak. When he saw that this assistance would not be required, he stood back and lowered his arms again. 'No I have to say it – never saw you looking as well. Not in a long time, if you don't mind me tellin' you. No. I have to hand it to you.' He laughed quietly to himself.

Masterson was about to say something derisive, when he hesitated. Perhaps it wouldn't be a bad idea to, well, if not to be exactly nice to Algernon, to perhaps tone down the disrespect just a little. After all, supposing this venture were to come off? He'd need support, cover. She was, after all, a married woman and, if nothing else, Algernon was dependable.

'Thank you, Algernon.' He gave what came near to a smile.

Algie smiled back. Encouraged by this show of civility he continued: 'Would it be impudent to ask where it was that you're –?'

'Indeed it would, Algernon.'

'Beg pardon.'

'But you may ask.'

'All right,' Algie beamed.

'I'm going to a recital in the Shelbourne Hotel, as it happens.'

Algie gasped. 'Oh the Shel … Oh well now. No wonder.'

'And on to a supper party later. On Fitzwilliam Square.'

'Fitz …? Oh be the … Would you be up to you? And you'll outswank the best of them. I haven't the slightest doubt.'

'Yes.' Masterson took his hat from Algernon and arranged his gloves over its rim. 'I may be dropping in on a lady, actually.'

'After the concert like?'

'The interval – catch up with supper later, you know.'

Algie paused before asking: 'Someone worth impressing?'

'Yes indeed, Algernon. Someone very much worth it.'

'Oh ho ho, say no more.' Algie tipped the side of his nose, 'Officer's horse,' he added softly.

He began to tidy about the room then, grinning to himself and shaking his head in gentle disbelief. 'I don't know how you do it. I really don't! Oh now – the lord Harry.' He turned to Masterson and wagged his finger jovially: 'I knew you'd somethin' more than recitals on your mind. The minute I seen you. I said to meself oh be the –'

Algie was starting to enjoy himself a little too much; it looked as if he could very well slap his knee if he was allowed to continue. Masterson was beginning to regret his former friendliness.

'That will do, Algernon,' he said reaching into his vest pocket and pulling out a coin. 'There's no need to do yourself a mischief.'

Algie straightened himself up and held out his hand. 'Of course,

Sir,' he said. 'Beg pard … And thank you very much. Enjoy your evening.'

As soon as Masterson shut the door, Algie's hand sprung open to examine his tip. 'Ye miserable oul bastard ye,' he snarled, looking down at his palm to where a single shilling was looking back up.

*

It was near to half-past nine by the time the taxi carrying Masterson pulled up outside her house. Half past? He glared at his pocket watch. A little late to be calling perhaps? Perhaps, but with a flurry of excuses and apologies, he should just about get away with it. He had calculated on arriving at no later than a quarter to nine, having slipped out of the Shelbourne at half-past eight or thereabouts, straight into the taxi he had tipped in advance (the slithery bastard had insisted on it). But – blast that Lamont fellow anyway. And that jumped-up wife of his. Damn them both to hell and back again.

It wasn't often that Henry Masterson had occasion to reprimand himself but, tonight of all nights, he deserved it.

Really, how could he have been so careless? To let himself get nabbed like that. And he wouldn't mind but he saw Lamont coming, saw him twiddling through the crowds with his Aunt Sally walk. And to his credit he had managed to slip in neatly behind the Macken sisters and party. And seconds away from a clean getaway and the door to escape when – *she* got him. The Lamont wife. Spotted him with her cat's eye and down on him like a ton of it. And full of her charity performance next week and how many players could he spare? And please not too many comic turns. After all, for such a solemn occasion. And on and on went her royal fatness, bleat bloody bleat, tweet after tweet. And playing up to him as if she were a beauty. Enough to turn the stomach! And as if that wasn't bad enough the husband caught up with them and then he had to run through the whole bloody thing again, item by item.

Until the bell rang to call them back in and before he knew where he was, she had hooked herself onto his arm. 'You don't mind, Mr Masterson? Hoo hoo hoo. Do you know I was just saying to Mr Lamont, how did Henry Masterson escape marriage this long? A handsome man like he is. What can the women of Dublin be thinking of? Hoo hoo hoo.'

By the time he managed to slip back out without causing a disturbance, the recital had been almost over. *And* the damned taxi had disappeared.

Really, it had hardly been worth his while coming at all. Now he would probably miss his supper to boot.

He bent himself down so as to peer out. The windows of the house were black. All black. Black as his mood. Not a light in the house.

The driver was beginning to fidget. What to do? He could hardly say: 'Turn around, I just came to look up at the windows.' He would have to chance it. Get out and walk up to the door anyway, perhaps there might be some sign of life closer to the house.

'Driver, wait a minute, would you? Won't be a second.'

The driver nodded and Masterson dipped out under the door onto the pavement where he stretched himself out full length again.

He moved towards the gate. Yes, fine house. Not bad at all. She'd be nice and comfortable here, wouldn't be in too much of a hurry to leave it. Or her husband. Ideal set up. Yes indeed. He pushed the gate from him and stepped through, glad to note that he wouldn't even have to go as far as to pretend to push something through the letterbox, as the front door would be well concealed by a guard of assorted trees. He might even take refuge in between them for a moment, cut out the risk of being spotted lurking about the steps or door.

He moved forward a little more with this intention in mind.

Then he stopped. Was that somebody up there on the threshold? Somebody standing at the open front door?

He stepped back in between the trees. What now? Go back or continue casually on? For whatever way he chose to move, he would most certainly be spotted. That's all he needed now, to be taken for an intruder. Who the hell was it anyway? Not the bloody husband surely?

Carefully he prised open a gap in the foliage. He peeped through. No, it was female. A maid, by the looks of it, standing at the opened door and peering up the road.

Oh Christ. Masterson came out from his hiding place and took the steps up to the front door. 'Is everything all right there?' He said, 'I was just passing and …'

The maid didn't answer him. He took another step towards her.

'I'm looking for Mrs Cleary,' he began.

'Mrs Cleary? So am I, Sir.'

'She's not home then?'

'No. I don't know where she's gone, Sir. She's never this late. Not without Mr Cleary. Not even Samuel to drive her.'

'I see. Well, perhaps I'll call back tomorrow.'

The maid ignored him, craning her neck to look up and down the road. Masterson turned on his heel and went back down the steps. 'Can I give her a message?'

'No, that's all right,' he called back. He clacked the gate shut and climbed back into the cab.

Well! That was a nice bloody waste of time.

VII

STRANGERS AND ANGELS

Twenty-Three

He can expect the visits soon. As soon as it is possible. Already journeys are being planned. From the various departure points; Maude in her bed, testing the tea for honey Philomena may have forgotten. Kate at her window watching the drift of lives passing on the street below. And Pat? Pat across the water, fixing his necktie and smoothing his shirtsleeves before inserting them into the grip of his new business suit.

Already straws have been drawn. (I'll go on Mondays and Thursdays, so you take Friday and Wednesday. Mrs Gunne permitting, we'll all take Sundays – agreed? Maybe take him on a little outing.) This morning each one will have remarked, more than once: Today is the day. The day he comes out. Back to the real world. Time to start thinking. Time to face forward. Time to hang up his cane and fold down his collapsible hat. Time, at last, to be a man.

He can feel their relief in the wind touching off the back of his neck as he comes up near the river: a sigh.

While his limp takes him beat by beat through the city, they are stepping lightly through their morning. By the time they get to luncheon their minds will be twinkling; all that exercise, all that sport. For they have spent the morning playing with the possibilities, and are hungry now to get started. Hungry to embark on the first of the visits.

Already gifts have been planned. Nothing at first except perhaps the usual – they don't want to startle him after all. A bunch of grapes wiggling from their spine, a bag of best toffee slabs. And the smiles they bring will be the same ones kept over from the hospital visits. Their songs, too, at first will have a similar ring. A slight variation on words perhaps, but nothing too noticeable. 'So good to see you back again out and about. How are you feeling? Are you sure now? Wouldn't rather stay with me? (Or me?). You know you'd be very welcome at mine (and mine!).Tra la laa la laaah.'

They will fuss around him in Mrs Gunne's parlour, while she brings in the tea. 'Won't you take another cup? I got the impression this morning that you always went for two? Or was that yesterday afternoon? I get mixed up you know; so many visitors. So often. So much tea.' And turning to him then, the flush of begrudgery bringing youth to her cheeks. 'Bless me but how popular we are!' And when finally he offers to compensate her for any extra expense, her horror will be genuine, expressing itself for days to come, moving like a bereavement, in shifts. Every time she thinks of it: 'I can't believe you would imagine for one moment that I could possibly …' Until eventually he will leave an envelope under her door. 'I wanted to buy you a little something to thank you but wouldn't have a clue …' re-wording the thought behind it in such a way that she will be able to accept. 'Well, when you put it like that, I suppose …'

He crosses towards the bridge, a well-dressed cripple counting the stammers between his foot lifting off and his foot touching down. Back on the pavement again, he stops to take a rest, leaning on the balustrade, looking down to where unhesitantly the water sees to its business of the day. Passing under and away from him, efficient as a train.

Within a week the gifts will have taken on a different shape, the shape of his future. In wrappings various, suggestion and innuendo, keen or sly. They will tease up to it, bit by bit. Just for the moment, leaving it laid out in little pieces along a sill edge. Or on a flat outstretched palm coming slowly across the field to where he has cornered himself. Approaching step by steady step, the one hand carried out in front. The other pinned behind a back where the bridle and the bit try not to swing into the light, try not to jangle or to rattle. In case he might catch the tintinnabulum; the tintinnabulation. They will hold it under his nose. There's the boy, now, there's the fella. Nice and easy. See what I have now? See what I have brought?

Pat, standing before the hotel mirror of another city, is preoccupied with other things; the cut and cloth of his suit, the contents of his memory, asking it to verifiy all those new business words he has been using. (Convertible stocks. Bonds. Securities. Returns and risks.) Asking it then for reassurance; I did make it clear that I …? Yes, yes you did. And that I was only interested in …? Yes, they understood that all right. They were impressed, weren't they? Yes. Oh yes. They were. It's going to work. Yes. The United States of America is going to work for him. For her. Wait till he tells her. Might as well, he supposes, go and have that cough checked out so. Now that he's here and not ten minutes away from Harley Street. Waste of time and money, of course, him right as rain. But − might as well. Now that he's here. And seeing how he's made a promise anyway, to Sam. And wasn't that why he came here alone in the first place? So as not to cause her worry. To get it seen to on the q.t. Nip it now before he loses another night's rest from all that barking. Besides supposing they decide to go over? Have a look at it for themselves, and what better time to go? Now with an extra pair of hands going a-begging, now with an extra head, and a mechanical one at that. Shove him in with Sam till he learns. And shove him if he doesn't like it.

They'll hardly let him cross the doorstep, with a cough in his craw anyway. Not the Yankies. Terrified of illness. Over there. Might as well see to it now. Get a certificate anyway, to say he's in the pink.

By the time Pat sails home, all the preparations will have been carried out on his behalf. All the introductions will have been made:

'Pat and I were just talking before he went to London and do you know he has this marvellous idea ...'

Or: 'I know! Why don't you take a start from Pat? Oh now why didn't I think of it before. He'll find something suitable – the perfect solution.'

'You're interested in (motor cars, public bars, bottles washed well and lined up for inspection). Well why not help Pat out? Of course, that's it!'

'He has designs on America now, you know ... will be needing someone to hold the fort ... stir the soup ... mind the baby ... carry the can ...'

And then at last, the morning will have arrived: the day for the smiling face to come alone. Appearing at the doorway while, behind him, the whispering voices will coach him one last time before he walks through. And then coming towards him, behind an extended hand, impossible to refuse.

The dancer turns himself on the axle of the crutch until he is perched on the remainder of the bridge, the vague decline. And jerks over it bobbing along with the smoother motion of the crowd. He wonders about the ordinary things: if his bag has arrived yet at Mrs Gunne's? And his message too? And should he have sent a separate one to Samuel, in case he calls in this afternoon? (Rather than rely on Mrs Gunne to pass it on?)

He frowns. But then remembers the new maid or housekeeper or whatever she is. Gertie? No, Greta. She'll pass on the message all right. Seems the efficient type.

He passes over and into the mouth of the boulevard, glancing up along its parting of monuments: strangers and angels. How far it seems from here, the pillar, his destination. He stops and folds one leg up, balancing on the other unwaveringly. And releasing a hand then to pluck dust from his shoulder. How far it seems, he thinks again, before swinging the folded leg back down again and resuming the double clutch of his crutches. And one, and two, he takes the street rhythm up through his legs before moving off over its flow.

*

'He's not here, I tell you,' Mrs Gunne repeated to Samuel, raising her hands and her eyes in unison before adding, 'And yes, before you say it, I am quite aware of the fact that the suitcase you are looking at is his. So before you go running off to tell his sister that I've kidnapped *him* as well, let me repeat. He is *not* here.'

Samuel opened his mouth to speak.

'And no – before you ask me – I don't know where nor do I particularly –' Mrs Gunne put her hand to the back of the door with the intention of bringing it and the conversation to a close. Samuel put his hand to the front of it with the intention of keeping both open. 'Well really!' Mrs Gunne exclaimed.

'Did he by any chance send a message along, Ma'am? It's just that I've been told at the hospital that he was discharged this morning and I was to collect him this afternoon. And ...'

He looked at the suitcase again.

'And what?'

'And I'd just like to check on him, see if he's all right and if he sent a message.'

'Yes, yes, yes. Of course he sent a message. The suitcase didn't just arrive on its own, you know – knock, knock, may I come in, thanks very much, I'll just plonk myself down there. He's gone to see some fellow. His note said he'd be home later. I assume he sent a message to his sisters to that effect and that I won't have to – I mean I won't need to explain – what I mean to say is that I had hoped to go to a demonstration this afternoon: cooking by electricity, you know. I don't get out that much either. I certainly don't want to have to miss it. Well you know what I mean. I don't want them calling – I mean worrying. Anyway I won't be here.'

Samuel nodded politely. 'Well, you see, Mrs Gunne, if you can give me an idea of the nature of the message, I'd be pleased to pass on the news to Mrs Cleary myself. Let her know that there would be no point in calling today.'

'Oh yes, you do that. Good –'

'Yes but they'll want to know where he has gone.'

'I declare, our Beatrix gets more freedom than that poor chap. Really, Samuel, I know he's the youngest, but he's not a baby, you know.'

'I quite agree, Ma'am. But even so, he is, for the moment, an invalid. The nature of the message?'

'What nature? It didn't have a nature. It's only a piece of paper with a few words scribbled on.' She sighed: 'Oh very well, I suppose. But all's I know is that he's gone to see some fellow, like I told you.'

'Which fellow would that be, Mrs Gunne?'

'Some fellow called – oh let me see now.' She tutted wearily and stretched herself backwards more than a little. With a groan from her interiors she achieved the neat fold of writing paper from the hall table behind. And bounced herself back up to be once again in line with the door and the foot which she had left jammed at the bottom of it, by way of a door stop.

'There.'

Samuel was impressed with her dexterity. He looked away.

Unfolded now, she glanced at the paper and then at Samuel.

'Yes that's right – he's gone to see a Mister Chap– Chaptin is it? That's it. Mr Charles. Chaptin. Or something, I can't quite …'

Samuel was smirking, no less.

'Do you know him?' she asked.

'Of him, I'd say rather.'

'Really. Well I hope who ever he is, he has the patience of a saint.

That's all I have to say. To be able to deal with a member of that family and put up with their demands. Yes I hope he has nerves of steel, that's all I've got to say.'

Samuel lowered his eyes and bit his lip. 'Thank you, Ma'am,' he said, and with a slight tip to his cap he hurried down the front steps.

'Yes. I hope Mr Chap–' she hesitated, looking down at the piece of paper in her hand before raising her voice back up towards Samuel, now closing the gate behind him.

'Oh very amusing, Samuel, I'm sure. Very amusing altogether. I see it now – Charlie Chaplin. I didn't know you were so humorous I'm sure. I must remember to include you in my next dinner party.' She stepped back inside.

'And what could be apter, I ask you – one clown going to see another.' She muttered to herself then, closing the door with a satisfied snap.

*

It was a while before Samuel came to realise there was a life going on up there on the screen. He glanced at it once or twice as he rummaged and excused his way to a vacant seat, but that was just to distract himself from the complaints his intrusion had caused.

For the moment all that he could take from it was what he needed: the light, the still white light, guiding him in. There. He was seated. He was in the Pillar Picture House, surrounded by people whose faces he couldn't see and presumably couldn't see him. He was down and safe. And almost immediately found he had to move again. For now that his eyes had adjusted to the darkness, he could see the dancer seated over at the edge of the far aisle; the movement from the screen flitting onto his crutch first and then slower upwards to pass over and back across his face. Samuel stood up again, edging cautiously back into the laughter: 'Excuse … Pardon … Sorry. I'm so sorry.' He stopped apologising and stumbled on. These people could get dangerous, he thought to himself, relieved to be back on the aisle at last. He tiptoed up along it – as if that would make any difference with all this racket going on – watching the brash giant of himself spreading itself over the screen. There was an outburst of objections around him.

Sit down, will ye sit down.

Ah here!

Was his head really that shape?

He found another seat. On the outside of the row this time, opposite and a little way behind his friend. Now at least he knew where to locate him afterward, wouldn't miss him in the crowd. Or indeed, if the dancer decided he'd had enough before the end of the show. For that was the thing about him: you wouldn't know where or how quickly he would slip away out of sight. Samuel relaxed a little. How long was it since he'd been to a picture show? Not since London anyway. He'd never even seen this Chaplin fellow. Might as well have a look, he supposed. Now that he was here. See what all the fuss is about.

Up on the screen, at first nothing happens: there is just a lot of ink-black movement molesting that lovely flat light. Then a penguin in the far distance, no a man – a gentleman. No, not a gentleman, a tramp. Oh who cares? Wait … both now, both begin to take shape. It is a gentleman *and* a tramp. He means nothing to Samuel. A stranger. They remain strangers to each other. The tramp waddles, he gives a little skip (his cane might break at any moment). But that doesn't concern Samuel, that is none of his business.

Samuel leaned back and, crossing his leg, glanced over at the dancer, who seems intent on following whatever it is that's going on up there. He studied the young man's face, impassive. He could be looking at something, or nothing. As if he was sleeping with his eyes open. What's going on in there, in that head of his, Samuel wondered. What's he studying now? Samuel looked back up to the screen:

The tramp's hat hops, then drops, then he waddles again. But Samuel has other things on his mind. He uncrosses his legs. Should he do that to pass the time – think over his problems? Think over his (perish the notion) *feelings*? Yes maybe that's what he ought to do. Things will, after all, have to be sorted out sooner or later. Arrangements made.

And when the show is over? Just what should he say to the dancer?

What should he tell him about Pat, for instance? Pat had made him promise, that was the deal. 'I'll see the consultant if you promise not to breathe, not a word.' Straightforward blackmail, that's how they dealt with each other; himself and Pat.

But look at him over there, not a child, not a man. And he's probably always been that way, probably always will. Now more than ever they're going to want him, need him. Who else would take over, should the worst happen? He ought to be warned.

But a promise was a promise. Pat would keep his promise. Yet. The snow-white handkerchief with the clot in the centre. The child's jam in the middle of the bread, the endless cough, the peaches and cream complexion. But he might be all right. Yes, he might. It could still be early stages yet. Although he'll need treatment at least. And for how long?

He looks back up at the screen, thinking, what an idiot. What a fool up there. People were expected to swallow any canard these days.

He pulled his eyes away and looked back to the dancer. Nothing had moved, the crutch perhaps, had it shifted a little to the right? But the face was just the same. He'll know all about it now, poor chap, when they heap it on top of him. And no Pakenham to help out either. That letter business – they'll hardly keep him on now. Oh why hadn't Kate come to him sooner, he wondered, shown him the letter? Isolating herself that way, so unnecessary. He could have told her. He could have said: 'I don't care whose writing it's in. I don't care if it's got the King's seal on. I know. I know it's not true. There's nothing that man does that I don't know about. He can't even spit in a hanky without my knowing it. He's nowhere but I'm one step behind.' Him and that Greta one? As if he'd be bothered with her likes.

He reached into his inside pocket and took out his tobacco box: a smoke. Yes. He wished they'd all shut up laughing at nothing. Allow him to think about all that he must think. Holding his fingerfulls out towards the screen light, he used it once more to fidget a shape to his lot: a match now.

He glanced back across the aisle and said to himself, 'I won't tell him about Pat. I just can't. It would be forcing his hand, or forcing him to flee. You wouldn't know, with him, where or how quick. I'll tell him about Kate though. Give him a bit of warning. Confide in him maybe?'

Samuel looked back up at the screen. The sooner this nonsense is over … Utter tripe; he hadn't missed much staying away all this time. It'd give you a pain in your head, trying to follow. Samuel leaned back, took a pull on his smoke. Then heard himself laugh. Yes. It was him. After a few seconds, he heard himself laugh again. Then again. After another few minutes he found himself tutting angrily when the blot of a latecomer came clumsily on his view.

Now he has become one with the audience. Now he laughs with them. He takes a quick look over at his friend. Still the same. Why can't he see it's funny? Samuel laughs again. And he knows this little man too, by now. He knows the tramp. Why certainly he does. Knows him well. He can bring him up now in conversation, any time he wants. To that assistant at the Irish House, for example, rubbing the counter over and lifting his eyes to heaven with, 'Oh don't talk to me about that Chaplin fella. He's an awful man altogether.' They can discuss him as though any minute the door might part to let him come through. Right through and on up to them, his two butties, ready to confide his latest antic. Oh that Charlie boy, honest to God, he'd make the cat laugh.

He hears himself again, rather louder than before. He looks across: still nothing from the dancer. This time he turns to the man beside him. They laugh together, shared, like a bag of sweets. Samuel wipes the tears from his eyes. Oh what next? They shake their heads at each other. What can he possibly get up to next? Surely he can go no further?

And then there is one big roar, a gasp, a wave that's rising ... shocked. Frozen at the peak just for a second and then crash. It tumbles down into individual voices laughing.

Who would have believed it? How does he think them up?

The tramp is turning now, he is moving away; the laughter subsides. Waddle waddle skip, waddle again, his cane bends. Will it break? No it won't. An unbreakable thing, his cane. Propelling him along. It gets smaller, he gets smaller. The noise in the theatre gets smaller. And then, up there, on the screen hardly anything at all. Just a scuttle of black threads, a few wispy snags. It is as though the little tramp has unravelled himself into nothing.

It is calm again and under the house lights the crowd have become shy with each other once more. The man who has been sitting next to him stands cold-eyed waiting for him to leave his seat. The woman with the high-pitched laugh that had been screeching behind him, now whispering delicately to her friend. All gone, the common joy. All disappeared behind the long black letters of 'The End'. Samuel stands and looks across the way. His young friend, over there, waiting by the crowd edge for a gap so that his crutch can go unobstructed. He hadn't laughed at all. The only one. Not once. It was almost as if it might interfere with his concentration; intrude upon its clarity.

Although now that Samuel thinks about it, there had been someone else. Another one to have remained aloof. Somebody else who preferred to remain untouched, untouchable.

The narrow-shouldered man now disappeared behind the screen. Now gone waddle, waddle skip. Waddle again. They were the only two to have remained silent. The only two to have taken the whole adventure seriously.

TWENTY-FOUR

They left the red-brick houses behind and came out onto a narrow pathway which ran between a high wall at one elbow and an open area at the other. This space was what Mattie had referred to as 'the fields'. Green in the distance maybe, but here beside the pathway, where carefully she walked behind him, bumpy and bald. Diseased earth, a few loose hens picking at its sores. Now it was almost dark and the tall houses at the end of the wall suddenly started to take shape, their Dutch capped roofs and high narrow walls showing solid in the dim light. As they drew nearer she could see the strain of age and neglect; there was nothing solid about them at all, wood and brick, old and dry. Rotting away, from the inside out.

Facing these houses on the edge of the otherwise deserted fields was a row of stumped cottages, the print of an occasional light pressing out from them. There was a camp fire burning in the nearby hollow. Three people stood around it, almost as if they were perched on guard. Two more were huddled, nearer the flame. One of them, an old man, raised his face to look at her. Leaning back, he reached out with a stick to push the man standing beside him out of the way so that he could get a better view.

'Don't worry about them, Missus,' she heard Mattie say. 'Just keep on sayin' nuttin' and we'll be all right.'

Maude hesitated. 'Mattie,' she whispered, 'maybe we should just go back.' She could see his small face twitch to her in the firelight. 'Come on – let's go,' she said. 'Let's just turn back.'

Mattie stared at her for a while, and then: 'Wait there.'

'*Mattie!*' She watched him go like a young goat, across dust mounds and heaps of scrap iron, leaving her with nothing to do but watch the last of the light drain from the sky.

After a while he returned, springing towards her out of the darkness, his arms outstretched to help him balance.

'Mattie –' she began to call out to him. But he veered away and entered the doorway of one of the tall houses. Once there, however, he beckoned to her.

And Maude, who had been determined to leave the moment he returned, tucked herself in tight to the wall and followed his hand signals until she came to the house. She had almost reached the door when he disappeared again. Stepping inside, his voice hissed down to her from one of the stairwells. 'Quick, quick, Missus. Will you hurry yourself up now?'

He was holding a candle, its light disguising him fully so that, except for his voice, she had nothing to recognise, nothing reassuring to set herself towards.

'Oh Mattie, please … Let's go now.'

'You're all right there, Missus, come on. No one lives in this one. You're grand now, that's it, take your time.'

Maude climbed the stairs blindly. Guided by nothing more than a gauze of light and a raggedy boy she had never met before.

'Mattie, I must insist –' She put her hand out to take a hold of the banister.

'No, Missus!' he warned, *Don't.*'

She pulled her hand away and continued on unaided, trusting herself to this child. 'I must be mad,' she whispered as the light changed direction and turned for the next flight of stairs. She noticed then she was shaking all over.

They were on the first floor. Mattie turned into a small room at the front of the house and laid the candle down. He reached up to the window and pulled a hanging rag away. Then he called her over, pointing down to the field outside. 'Look, Missus, they'll be goin' in now. Into the watchmaker's house. See now.'

'We're going back, Mattie,' she said. 'I mean it, come on now. You'll get your half crown, like I promised. But this house is dangerous. This place – my God. Do you hear me?'

She took a hold of his arm. 'Mattie, come on …' and then she stopped.

There was a lighted room below in one of the cottages facing them; two windows blaring out from the black. She could see everything, right in. Nothing to stop her view, except for the slight interruption of bricks set between the windows. The front door was wide open and latched up to facilitate the stream of shadows passing through it. Maude bent closer to the window, shielding her eyes from any interference.

A woman stands over a table, two candles flicker before her. Her hands cover her face as though she is afraid to look. Reluctant, uncertain, her hands then leave her face and she looks down at the flames, two pear drops of nervous light. A brave face. Always brave? Or has she just found the courage in there behind her hands? The hands begin to move again, in and out – a slow silent applause. Her lips move too, as if they are singing. Or praying. Perhaps both. Beside her are two young girls; they join the woman, moving in the same manner, lips and hands. The faces on these young girls are flat and sallow, until they lean over the candlelight which touches them gently, giving shade and shape to their faces

At the second window a group of men begins to appear and the last of the black shapes pass through the front door, pausing, like the others before them, to touch something pinned over the door post. Now inside. Now all have passed through.

The men, darkly dressed, seem clumsy beside the white linens of the table and the delicate curves of candle-sticks and goblets. At first they are faceless men, only their clothes, legs or hands are visible. The windows are too short and no one has yet taken a seat.

Now they stand around the table. Only one man sits, an old man. He drinks from a cup, the tail of his beard tipped grey, the stamp of black on his skull when he bows his head. He is facing the woman and the two young girls positioned at the far end of the table. He lifts his hands to the woman, appears to be singing to her or in some way addressing her. He then passes the cup upwards. A hand reaches down and takes the cup. The cup disappears and then comes back down again. Now this man sits, and lifts the cup again to his lips, this time using his second hand, one that is heavily dressed in bandages.

Maude turned to the child beside her. 'Mattie?'

'It's him, Missus,' he said. 'Issac the figgler. Can you see him? Look – the one facin' us, beside the watchmaker. That's him. Can you see hes hurted hand? See it? Didn't I say I'd get you to him? Didn't I, Missus? Didn't I now? Didn't I not let you down? Didn't I not? Didn't I?'

'Yes. Yes. I see him. Shh, Mattie, shh.'

He drinks again. Lifting the cup to his lips, his eyes look upwards. The most beautiful man she has ever seen. The most. He looks like a Christ. A Christ man.

(Did he? With Greta? Did he, this man? With Greta? Was this the one? His baby now growing steadily in the dark? His child …)

'Open the window,' she whispered to Mattie.

'The windit?' she could hear Mattie say. 'It's freezin, it is.'

'Open it.'

'It'll break, Missus, these windits – you can't open them.'

'Mattie, will you just open it.'

Mattie struggled with a tight-fisted sash and then, coaxing it open, brought the window down creak by creak. Now she could hear them.

A strange-tongued song. A song of many different voices. But how sweet they make each other sound. How sad. How unnecessary man-made instruments would be.

Maude leaned out the window. The older man stands up again and slips an embroidered cloth away from something on a plate. A yellow cloth, fringed. Now he is holding an arrangement of bread in his hand. Flesh-coloured bread, like limbs plaited around and into each other. He breaks it and passes the bread on.

The Christ man now lifts it to his lips. It sheds blonde against the deep dark copper of his beard. He passes it on and with his unbandaged hand teases the flecks that it has left behind until his beard is clean again. (Did he? With Greta? Make her pregnant. And then leave her? Never intend to see her again. *Leave* her? Free. Forever free?)

He is singing alone; she hears his voice. Not tenor, not baritone, not anything definite. And yet when she hears it she can almost recognise it. It is no voice she has ever heard before, but she knows she can recognise it. If only she can think. Can listen to it long enough.

'Get him for me, Mattie,' she said.

'What? Are you jokin' me? I can't go in there, Missus,' he said. 'Are you gone soft, Missus? I'll be skinned.'

'Please, Mattie.'

'D'ye want me to get the digs?'

'Please, Mattie. Get him for me. You must, Mattie. Do you hear me?'

'Your hurtin' me arm, Missus.'

'I'll give you a guinea if you bring him to me. Two guineas. Just bring him here.'

Mattie picked up the candle and handed it to her.

'It could take me ages, you know. I won't be able to go in till they're finished. You'll have to wait. You might have to wait a long time.'

'That's all right, Mattie,' she said, holding the candle back out to him. 'I've already been waiting a long time.'

VIII

DEEPWATER QUAY: SEPTEMBER 1918

TWENTY-FIVE

Deepwater Quay: so that's where you've been waiting? All night. While I've married myself to a man I've never even mentioned to you. It is from here you will take me for the very last time. To your fingertips first and later placing me at your other parts. Tomorrow your belly, where I will lie small, feeling you breathe your deep sleepy breaths and moving with them, slow up, slow down, until I wake again to find myself at yet another part of your anatomy. I am an insect now, lurking on you, shifting over you. By the time I reach your toes, I will have been intimate with all of you. But none of you will displease me, none will offend. Not even the blackest spots the sun has failed to sweeten. How fitting that this should be our farewell, my last time to cross you. I can at least leave you that: the longest goodbye. Longer than those with whom I have shared my land life, those to whom I leave nothing.

Kate wiped the spray from her face and moved along the deck making room for an elderly couple; the woman trying not to cry, the man not to notice. She smiled. Will we be, Sam and I, one day, like them? Reversing the journey for the first time in – how many years will it be? Perhaps taking grandchildren who will throw out their questions to us in accents we have yet to become familiar with.

Yes, yes, I'll say. This is where your grandfather and I, all those years ago, left to make our new life, so that you could grow and live in a land that runs like a scar through the ocean. Yes, yes, he'll say, Grandmother waited on the deck, leaning on the balustrade, just like you are now, waving to people she didn't know, while I went off to see to the cabin and the passenger baggage, the little of it we had …

Will we look together at this same harbour view, with its layers of long-bodied houses rising up with the hill, with its unfinished cathedral (finished by then?) like a crown above. Getting larger as we near it. Getting clearer. Instead of the other way around? And will we glance at each other over the children's hats and smile. Acknowledging a secret, so deep, we never even speak of it.

Kate felt herself sway. The ship was awake. It grumbled and moaned: still tired? From Liverpool to here, bad enough. But now? New York, Boston. It stirred itself, lurching. Ohh, she heard the old lady say. Ohh; they were moving.

Now pull me away from it, Deepwater Quay. Now take me with you, hold me up, balanced on the palm of your experienced hand. For the first time in my life, I have no fear. And so I don't mind if you turn me a little – for I feel I ought to somehow be afraid. Make me afraid – just a little.

There now, the hotel, where last night I watched him sign his Mr, then his name and a 'and Mrs' inserted between. (That was me. Yes *me*.) Last night I followed behind him, a respectable-looking couple, we two. Step by step, to where a pinched-voiced boy turned the key in a lock and bade us, 'Sleep well now.'

'You must take the bed,' he said.

'And what about you?'

'I can –' and he turned to a settee in the corner of the room.

'No.'

'I thought you might like to wait until …?'

'Oh no.'

Until what? Until we could be married? As long as *he* (you-know-who and I'll never say his name again) still lives? But I am married to another now, as I was never married to him. We are married now. Inside ourselves, we are. Now I am his wife, his mate, his queen. (In

Queenstown, in the Queens hotel, she became his queen). Kate sang to herself and then laughed. Two runaways at our age. Really!

A room at the front, it was. Outside the vacant lights stared blindly in and the empty bandstand moped. And I could hear the American sailors come and go below, on the street, come and go from that public house there and that one too, most probably to the Consulate. Where? There. Could hear their accents move like music beneath our window. Which one was it? That one there? No that one (I think). Oh why didn't I stop to hang something from it? A glove or something. A banner.

Kate crossed the deck, siding with the ship, pushing with it, as it nuzzled for its course. Away from the tears, those weeping down on their past, displayed now in rows of waving, crying confusion.

She leaned over and bit at the air, ahhh yes. And looking out at the horizon and all around her to the other ships, loitering in dock and out. War, cargo, steerage. More war. Big guns. She bit again. Ahh yes.

You still taste the same. No matter who, no matter what, imposes on you. Still the same smell too. Do I? Now that you know.

All. All about Kate.

But I haven't told you quite all, have I? I haven't told you about the letters. Yes of course.

Were there letters? Oh don't you know? True to form. Have you ever known me to depart without them? And posted only an hour ago from this little place: 'My darling Maude ... My own dear sister. Please believe me when I tell you ...'

At first she'll think it's a joke, recognising my writing and frowning a little (Queenstown, Co. Cork? Whatever is she up to now? – I can almost hear her say). And then slowly realising that it goes further than that, further than Queenstown, to the outside world: America. Will she scream? No – faint more like. But I know what you're thinking: what a terrible thing to do to my sister, in her condition. And you're right. I know you are. But I'm hoping that her great happiness will compensate. Listen to this: 'God,' I told her, 'has blessed you with a child, to ease the pain of losing a sister' – was that all right do you think? A bit much perhaps? Will that do?

But it hurts me too, you know. The only thing I'll miss is the child that I'll never see. And never to be Aunt Kate to anyone. Not ever ...

Pat? Ah yes, Pat. He was my second letter. What else could I do? But beg his forgiveness for my stupidity. To have believed that he and Greta ... Oh it shames me still. But he'll forgive me. I know he will. It's his way. Too efficient to hold a grudge. He'll lie in his sanatorium bed, waiting to be well again (please God soon) unable to fully understand why there is nothing he can do, no string he can pull, no money he can pay. Nothing to command the situation or take it in hand. And looking out through the window, but never quite as far as the Dublin mountains backdropped there, too busy watching for ideas to come, to tease and hover like summer bees. And to catch them then. *Snatch.* To turn each one, straight away, into a memo note, before it has a chance to flit away. And somewhere in there between, I'll feature; between the business now and the business to come. And somewhere in there will be my mention. Somewhere, he'll jot: Kate, my Kate – forgiven.

My last one was to Mr Masterson. A bit forward I suppose, given the short time that I have known him. It was just a farewell note really, nothing lengthy. And a wish expressed that he would continue to be the friend to my sister that he has these past months been. And he has been.

How would she have otherwise managed? He takes her to see Pat every other day without fail, you know. Waiting outside on the verandah so that they can spend time alone. And cheering her then through the darker moments which will always occur during the long drive home.

A good friend, yes, he's been. A friend indeed.

And there were other letters too, of course. Written by my 'Mr' and handed to the hotel clerk just after mine. Three I saw; two I could identify. One to my brother (I left that up to him, after my fifth attempt to get it right had gone so terribly wrong).

'How's this?' he called out to me, from the desk in the corner. 'Kate says cheerio and good luck with the wedding?' Now could I have done it so well, I ask you? I was on the wrong track altogether; no need there for the gentle hand, nor the sweet consolation. Just a cheerful so-long. (I'm popping down the road, won't be long, just forty years or thereabouts ...) And the wedding a few more days, that's all. We could have waited I suppose, but – I wanted away, I wanted to be gone. And there was, I suppose, the slightest hesitancy on my part ... the slightest doubt. Now why?

Because Greta is to become my sister? I don't know. Perhaps. The wife of my brother. To take him as her husband. Her boy husband (I can't help thinking, I keep on thinking ...). To take him ...

Yes, I wanted away. Like the magpies. You remember the magpies – you must have seen them? Passing over you from France, quivering frantic shadows; in a million, across your skin.

His other letter was to Pat. I wonder which he used: 'Dear Pat' or 'Dear Mr Cleary'? I've a feeling, though, it wasn't 'Dear Sir'. As to the content, I couldn't tell you: he didn't offer nor did I ask. But I'm sure he found the right way. Insofar as one could be found.

Kate turned her head to look back at the diminishing town behind them: watch it now, smaller and smaller, shrinking with each knot passed. Shrinking until it disappears altogether. Soon gone.

Out there on the quay, the arms are waving, the tears are being shed. Now in the distance looking more like branches in a forest where no two trees look the same. And it is always winter: bare and black. Are we the only ones to have no one to wave at? Are we the only two to be completely free?

Ahh … he is coming now. Here he is. I can see him. Passing through the crowds to find me and, seeing now that I have moved, he searches for a colour that belongs to me. He searches for the turn of my hat, something, anything to do with me. His face anxious – oh look – when it appears between the shouldered clumps of voyagers. Look – worried. 'Don't move,' he asked me, before he went inside. And bending to my ear then, he whispered shyly: 'I don't want to lose you. I don't want to lose you …' Oh I know I should call out to him, raise my arm and shout out: 'Sam, Samuel!' (Which should I call him? – I don't yet know) But I want him to find me. To come and find me. As you did once. All that time ago.

And we have been such friends since then, have we not? So much the same, so much in common and yet … all that must be sacrificed. You must let me go. Let me leave you behind, along with the wardrobes thronged with unworn clothes (how well Lottie's fishwives and urchins will look this coming season).

And should you resort to your naughtiness to gain my attention, I warn you: I will stay silent. Should you go further and do your worst, I will say nothing: neither scold, nor speak up for you. And I know your capabilities, I know your worst.

How you calmly watched them wave from docksides as your victims climbed to you, in twos and threes. Hope, trust, futures: bringing you these things. Did you know what was before them? Did you plan? Did you perhaps say, I'll give you something to cry about?

I'll show you who decides what may be called 'unsinkable', what may not …

Tell me now, I want to be sure. Did you, in your very depths, *know*. Make a list perhaps? I will have that man and this child, the couple at cabin three in second class. That officer with the Dunderry locks …

Or was it an impulse that made you do it? Twice in a few small years (a few seconds, I'm sure, by your calendar). *Lusitania, Titanic.* Is it these names that make you cringe, out there? Make you buckle and fall?

And do you, like me, need to have been upset by something? Something to set you off – and later then, counting the hoard you've hidden beneath your skirts, shivers of horror and delight passing through you, shame and pride. Do you try to pass on the blame? It wasn't my fault: it was the war; the Germans. The wind, the moon, the piece of me that had frozen solid. Or do you prefer to justify, to plead your case, to whinge to the night. 'Am I always to carry this load on my shoulder and be expected never once to shrug?'

(Oh don't shy away from me like that, don't pout. I know the excuses, I've used them too, remember? I've used them too, to my own capacities.)

Perhaps, though, it is the pure greed that drives us, the voice that says, 'I want. Them. Him. Her. This. That. I want them all. *Now* … 'smine all's mine …'

And yes I may have used you, I suppose. From the first. Been using you all along to take me up to this. Do you forgive me? That hotel restaurant where first we met, that curved coast road, where I walked beside you. In my despair or indecision, you took all that I flung to you, skimming your surface with my endless stones. Blistering you at your thinnest parts, where you are most vulnerable, most delicate.

And yet if, after today, we should meet, I will not know you. If coming across each other by accident, where at the bottom of a hill I've yet to know, or rounding a bend as yet untravelled, we should suddenly come face to face. And somebody at my side should ask, 'Do you two know each other?' I will say: 'Only to see, only to see ...' In a strange land, I will not know you. I will look at you, untempted, no matter what trick you play, what sparkle, what wink. No matter how you call to me with your great kind sighs. For I have married myself to him in more ways than one. In all ways. I am giving him full measure. But I know you will understand that. You who have always done things by the utmost.

You see? How well we understand each other, you and I. You see the way we never lie. Come kiss me and let's not make our last a row. Come kiss me now once more.

Epilogue

There were consolations of sorts; the pub for instance, wasn't too bad. The music that played off it, in and around, as if it were a drum. The bells from the countless nearby churches, each with a voice of its own. The gibble-gabble river to the front. The rowdies passing along on its quays. Then there were the tighter gurgitations, those that played inside. In amongst the kirk wood and under the mellow light. Into the mirrors' slit-sharp eyes, reflecting and deflecting, starting and stopping. Maundering endlessly in that holy place. Yes there was the music …

In the yard a silent figure skulks about, one foot a little slow. They watch him coming across the cobbles under the rain to welcome the brewery harness and the raucous rolling wheel. And ask themselves if that's what he's really doing? What he seems to be doing? Watching the horse's hoof, its rise and fall, its reliable beat. Listening to it as intently as if it were speaking to him. And it makes them wonder at times, just what sort he is? With his juicy lucy shoes and his licence laws disdain. And no man refused the slate since he first took over. No matter who, no matter for how long.

Inside when the day is nearly over and the door is bolted at the top. There, amidst the bustle and the panic of the last few moments of buying time, they sit up at the counter to watch, in case he might stop. Suddenly – just stop. And for no other reason than to listen to the toc toc toc of stout corks popping against the clock.

And sometimes too, when releasing new porter from wood,

they'll see him stoop down to hear its purl and then not bother to mop up the spillage. Not that he was above it, they noted, in all fairness to the chap, brushing up the scobs seeming to be his favourite task. Him making little piles of blonde and ash and spit, in long lazy whispering sweeps that seemed to take all day. While a pink-faced curate stands by and frets. 'There's really no need sir, it is my job.'

Then he had to move to the factory, where the music took longer to find. At first he felt there must be none. Housed in an office where the silence was packed tight. Into an office where silence was the boss. And a man twenty years his senior kept rapping on his door, asking him for answers he simply hadn't got.

That was the time he got to thinking about them all: Daddy Jim Crow Rice, Master Juba; the ones that started it all. Their dances too. 'The Essence of Old Virginia', 'The Alabama Stomp' ...

By the time he discovered the inner office where the noise from the factory floor seeped up through its inside window, coming in with the draughts, in through the cracks. By that time he didn't have to recall them any more; by that time, they had come to live in his head.

Sometimes they look up at him, the girls with the pancakes tied to their heads, heads, heads. Sometimes they see him, standing there, his face serenely looking down through the punty-dented glass. Sometimes they nudge each other with their eyes. Look at him. Perched up there in his glass box. What does he want? What is he doing up there?

Up there? He is listening to the orchestra hint from the pit, he hears the music kick up and go.

He is waiting for the swish and gurgle of washing water to rummage and root into glass seams and hems. And further down then along the way, where others, already washed, tinkle smugly as they are carried away. Tittering together; oh me, oh my. And down in the bass lines, the machinery nags, chatters and nags, fully aware of its indispensability ...

Daddy Jim Crow Rice blackens his face with burnt cork and the minstrelsy begins. Master Juba carries it on. From opposite directions, they come, moving across the floor. Each one leading his own row of smiling faces around the periphery first, then in towards the centre where the two lines will eventually join formation. Gliding or short stepping then, turning or heeling, they will go again, each to his own. This time they climb right up onto the machinery to hoof it across the flat-capped girls. They shuffle sometimes, they toe-heel, sometimes they drag. Their eyes – shine white; their smiles – cut turnip clean. An endless line of cakewalkers, moving just for him. Each goes with his own beat, his own natural beat. Apart from the single file and its tacit direction, there are no rules. No two will move in the same way. For every trucker has his dance.

And looking down, he thinks he knows at last. What it's like from way up. Here, at the other side of the moonbeam. What it's like at the top of the house. How far.

On darker days when the lights come up early, he sees them moving beneath. And keeping his applause inside his head, still watching. Still looking out, long after the house lights have all gone down.